G000154446

The Wind Between Two Worlds

The Wind
Between
Two Worlds

Peter Crawley

Matador
9 Priory Business Park,
Wistow Road, Kibworth Beauchamp,
Leicestershire. LE8 0RX
Tel: 0116 279 2299
Email: books@troubador.co.uk
Web: www.troubador.co.uk/matador
Twitter: @matadorbooks

ISBN 978 1789014 471

British Library Cataloguing in Publication Data.
A catalogue record for this book is available from the British Library.

Printed and bound in the UK by TJ International, Padstow, Cornwall
Typeset in 12pt Centaur MT by Troubador Publishing Ltd, Leicester, UK

Matador is an imprint of Troubador Publishing Ltd

For Terrance Fear
and all those
who risk their future
to preserve ours

The first person:

The views and attitudes expressed in this novel are in no way to be confused with those of the author, even and especially when expressed in the first person. They are merely the voices and views of the fictional characters as featured in the novel.

Acknowledgements

As with every construction, however modest or ambitious and whether simple or complex, there are many people who contribute to the finished article. Some contributions are more profound than those of others and some people don't realise they are making a contribution even as they are doing so. However, it is only right and proper that the many are recognised, for without them *The Wind Between Two Worlds* would not have been written.

I must first thank those who have aided in the editing and copy-editing of this novel, particularly Mike Dodd, Gill Buckland, Jayne Steele, Pete Matthews and, of course, my wife Carol.

Then there proved to be a handful of main topics, or areas, where I found my knowledge inadequate and so sought the company of those who knew more and better. They are listed below but not, I hasten to add, in any order of significance.

Journalists Mike Dodd and Steve Anderson provided much assistance in both direction and information.

Mike Dodd generously donated a great deal of his time and permitted me access to his vast wealth of experience and knowledge of journalism. Also, he never appeared to tire of my often-naïve and occasionally impertinent questions. His copy of *The Universal Journalist* (Pluto Press) by David Randall told me much of what I needed to know about the process of reporting, and David Spark's book *Investigative Reporting, a study in technique* (Focal Press) added clothes to my central character's frame.

Steve Anderson also gave generously of his time, describing what it is like for a novice journalist to step into a newsroom and how the varying pressures and influences of the individual genres of journalism compete for the oxygen of exposure.

If I have strayed from the path, or plain got it wrong, the fault is mine and not theirs.

In matters military, I needed to draw on the experiences of those who had been in theatre. I needed to hear a first-hand account of the Royal Marines' actions in Basra in May 2003, and more recently those of the combined services in Afghanistan.

I was fortunate to be introduced to Lieutenant Colonel Rhys Hopkins, Royal Marines, by my cousin, Commander Kara Chadwick MBE. Rhys gave very freely and willingly of his time, and readily opened up for me the colourful sweet shop of his experiences. Without his invaluable input, and perhaps more particularly his extraordinary stories and descriptions of conditions on the ground in and around Basra, I would not have been able to recreate the atmosphere of life for the Naarda family during the liberation of their home city.

NJW 'Nick' Morgan, Captain - Retired, Royal Welch Fusiliers, was introduced to me by his father, Chris, an old school friend, and set me on the path regarding Richard Ross's personal notebook and how it was that troops came to notice the positive differences their presence made in Afghanistan.

Finally, Terrance Fear, Private - Retired, Princess of Wales Royal Regiment, spoke openly and honestly about the pressures faced by troops in the challenging terrains and temperatures of a country known to be the graveyard of armies. In many ways, Terrance started this ball rolling.

I may have played a touch 'fast and loose' in interpreting some of their information, so I hope they will forgive this author his manipulations.

In terms of reading, I must mention Jake Olafsen's biography

Wearing The Green Beret (McClelland & Stewart), *Honourable Warriors* (Pen and Sword Military) by Major Richard Streatfield, *In Foreign Fields: Heroes of Iraq and Afghanistan in their own words* (Amazon Media) by Dan Collins, *Seven Pillars of Wisdom* (Wordsworth Editions) by TE Lawrence, and *Going Commando* (Amazon Media) by Mark Time. The recollections of these gallant and determined men provided me with a much-needed insight into the minds of serving marines and soldiers.

On the technical side, Gary Dawson of Phoenix Corporate Communications welcomed me into his office and proceeded to keep me honest regarding phone-tapping.

As for gnostic religions, it is difficult to comprehend the personal challenges Lady ES Drower (1879-1972) must have faced in collecting and collating the depth and detail of the information contained in her indispensable, enlightening and educational tome, *The Mandaeans of Iraq and Iran* (Oxford University Press). Most of us have never heard of Mandaeism, I certainly hadn't, and many believe the gnostic religion to be extinct. It is not, and whilst it may in some respects be a lost religion, there are many who still adhere faithfully. Gerard Russel's book *Heirs to Forgotten Kingdoms* (Simon & Schuster) casts further light on the Mandaeans and reviews their faith in a modern context: it is a fascinating read in its own right, as are *Medieval Gnostics* (Pacific Rim Press) by Judith Mann, and *Christianity in Iraq* (Gracewing) by Suha Rassam. I have also received ready and generous assistance from Robert Ewan, the Catholic Chaldean mission's secretary in the UK.

Researching the city of Basra proved a completely alternative hoop to jump through. Reidar Visser's *Basra, The Failed Gulf State* (Lit Verlag) provided food for thought as did much that is readily available on the internet. However, I needed not only to understand the city as a geographic and historical entity, but also as an ethnically diverse crucible of cultures and religions. So it was, that I found myself door-stepping the Iraqi Association in Shepherd's Bush, West London. Faris Nuaimi and Thekra Omran welcomed me into their fold and drew back the curtains on the window to their former world. And they managed this not simply in terms of geography and history, but in terms of what life had been like in Basra and Iraq under the tyrant Saddam Hussein. Just as importantly perhaps, they helped me understand what life is like living as a refugee far away from one's homeland. Both Faris and Thekra impressed upon me the need for a refugee, or similarly displaced person, to be a 'citizen' and not merely a 'civilian'; to fit in, to integrate and to be a part of society rather than the exile, permanently longing from a close distance. Their input was fundamental to my research, and Faris's gem regarding *ghysayib*, 'pigtails', lodged in my mind and solved a considerable problem I had encountered in the narrative.

When it came to homelessness and rough sleeping, I knew the subject was going to prove not only challenging but also that it needed to be handled sensitively; for only those who have experienced the despair and hardship of homelessness and rough sleeping truly know exactly how wretched is their plight. I have, in researching this novel, spent much time in the company of and have worked with rough sleepers. I have also learned much about the presumptions and prejudices of people who, like me, are fortunate enough to have a home to go to. With those demons of presumption and prejudice in mind, if I offend anyone with my portrayal of rough sleeping, I apologise for my shortcomings.

At Troubador Publishing, I must thank Jeremy Thompson and Heidi Hurst for their faith, fair efforts and attention to detail. And at Blue Mushroom, I am grateful to Neil Haylett and Anabel Vazquez for their invaluable help with the cover image.

Preface

Just as there is no way one can truly understand what it is like to be homeless without actually being or having been homeless, there is no way one can properly understand what it is like to be, or have been, a refugee.

Ingrid Fear, the mother of Terrance, to whom *The Wind Between Two Worlds* is in greater part dedicated, introduced me to a young woman who had escaped persecution and torture in her homeland. For reasons of security, I will refer to her as Barika, which roughly translates from the Arabic as Blossom. Her pseudonym is appropriate, for that is how she struck me; as a woman who had blossomed to become a mother like a rare and beautiful flower. In my emotionally-charged interview with her, Barika patiently explained how and why she is now separated from her family and then went on to recount her harrowing journey across Europe to the United Kingdom — to safety. She, also, imbued me with a sense of how refugees feel, their sense of displacement and their sadness and longing, and how they come to terms with the seismic shift in their circumstances.

In the mid-seventies, I slept rough for a few weeks in mainland France and Corsica. Was it a hardship? At the time, I didn't see it as such because I was young and had a home to return to if I wanted or needed to. For much of the time I slept rough on the rocks of the old port of Cannes and picked up day work, varnishing and painting on the yachts berthed a stone's throw beyond the harbour wall. It was summer: the weather gods were kind and only now and again did one get soaked through. It was, though, a far from secure existence and I lived on one *pan-bagnat* a day and slept with my worldly possessions stashed in the bottom of my slug – my sleeping bag. Being robbed was unpleasant, though not unusual, and I recall all too readily being assaulted by what we have now come to define as a pair of paedophiles. Fortunately, I was physically competent and managed to defend myself, though I grew to understand what it is like to sleep the half-sleep of the vulnerable – of those who are not safe.

I had been writing and researching *The Wind between Two Worlds* for much of the year when, while working with Crisis at Christmas, I was asked to attend to a certain rough sleeper. Before I approached him, and wondering why I in particular had been singled out for the task, I asked my team-leader if there was anything I ought to know about this man.

"He's a big guy," I was told. "He's an ex-Royal Marine and he has a prosthetic leg. You need to get him up and into the hall so as he can get some breakfast before he has to go back out on the streets."

My mother comes from a military family – for many years she worked with the Armed Forces and Merchant Navy charity the Lest We Forget Association – and my father served in the RAF during the Second World War. So, meeting and attending to a man who had lost a limb in order to keep those at home safe, and who was now sleeping rough on the streets of London, left its mark on me.

The Wind Between Two Worlds is in many ways about the plight of others like Barika and that ex-Royal Marine, for both refugees and rough sleepers share that unhappy bond of needing to be safe. For those of us who are and have always been safe, it is difficult to comprehend being otherwise; but for those who are not, to be safe is everything.

I

"Simon?"

"Yes. Simon Peckham."

"Please come in. No need to take your shoes off."

"Oh, that's okay, quite used to it."

"Please. Sit."

"Thank you, Mr Naarda."

"Joseph."

"Of course, Joseph, thank you. Nice place."

"It is small, but it is home and we are very grateful. Tea or coffee? Or perhaps orange juice. The oranges are from my shop. Very fresh."

"Tea would be good, thank you. No milk, no sugar. Just plain will do fine."

"Ah, like we take it. That is good. Have you eaten? Please, there is flat bread, fruit, dried fish, lamb; and in this bowl, there is salt. I can bring you something sweeter, if you would prefer. How was your journey?"

"My journey was fine, thank you for inviting me. I left in good time, so I took the 205. It's more relaxing on the bus, and besides, Old Street, Shoreditch, Bishopsgate, the Royal London Hospital… Reminded me of so much, even if I don't care to remember all of it."

"I am pleased you have come. Last time we met… it was difficult."

"All a bit of a rush. All a bit difficult. Joseph, that last night when everything went so… so wrong, you said there were things, things I ought to know. What sort of things did you mean?"

"Things. Yes. What I meant was, things about my daughter. About her world and how it formed her. About how the experiences of her youth were responsible for her thinking. These things, I thought they would help you to understand her. However, Simon, I think we both have stories to tell. Perhaps you would do me the kindness of telling me where you first met her; where she began for you. Why don't you tell me what I don't know and I will tell you what you don't know; then we will both know more than we do now. That would be a fair exchange, would it not?"

"It would. And I'm quite happy with that. First though, I would like to ask you if you are happy for me to record our conversation and if I have your permission to use whatever you tell me. And by that, I mean, to publish what you tell me, to put your words in my story?"

"Of course, Simon. I'm quite happy. You may record our conversation and you may use my words. People should know how it was for us. They imagine and therefore they think they know, but they do not."

"And please, Joseph, if I tread too heavily on your toes, then do me the kindness of saying so. It is absolutely not my intention to ask you to recall events which might upset you. As I know all too well, the demons of one's past are sometimes best left to sleep."

"The demons of one's past… left to sleep. Yes, Simon, I think I know what you mean by this."

2

Three months before

"I wish they'd hurry up," Candy moans.

He glances down the line: twenty, maybe more before they make the doors. "Here." He slips off his black dinner jacket and drapes it over her shoulders.

"You don't half make it awkward," she says.

"Awkward? How?"

"Well, I can't have people thinking I'm some kind of wuss."

"Perish the thought."

"Well, a girl has her reputation to consider."

"Candy," Simon chuckles, "you couldn't perform a striptease in that dress; your act'd be over before it began."

"Si!" She kicks his ankle.

"Okay, you can thank me for the jacket later."

"Look," she fixes him with an uncompromising stare, "we're only here because you said you didn't have anywhere better to be."

"As if that isn't a two-way street."

Right now, anywhere appeals more than standing, freezing, in a queue outside a nightclub. And yet if there is any consolation, it is that Candy is easy on the eye and curiously at home on his arm. She may be a couple or three years older and occasionally brash, but she doesn't look a day over his twenty-five. In fact, she–

"Simon, you did remember to bring a mask, didn't you?"

"In the pocket."

She reaches and pulls it out. "Not exactly what you'd call flamboyant, is it?"

He'd tried to get something more adventurous, but… And the dinner jacket and dress-shirt are borrowed, and the plain black masquerade mask rather amateur in construction.

"Why don't you put it on?"

"When we're inside, Candy."

"Everyone else is wearing them."

"Not that slaphead with the bloke who's wearing the weird plague-doctor mask." Simon nods his head to where a bald man is trying to tie the cord back on his Tony Blair mask. "Didn't realise it was Hallowe'en."

The queue for the club makes for a colourful train. Young men, shirts loose, chat loudly, unaffected by the evening's chill; and young women giggle, totter and shiver as they swig from half-bottles they keep hidden in their handbags.

A man wearing a shabby black puffer over a grey hooded sweatshirt is working the line. He is trying his best to establish eye contact with his prey, but most either ignore him or pretend to look straight through him as though he is little more than a trick of the light.

Down the way, three men swap crude jokes and laugh too loudly, their bald heads poking out of their dinner jackets like undercooked pigs poking out of overcooked blankets.

As the hoodie approaches, he decides the men are not for asking and makes to pass them by.

One of the men, the shorter of the group, steps forward

4

to intercept him. "It's New Year's Eve for Christ's sake," his red plague-doctor's mask waggles. "We're all trying to get in the party mood here. Why don't you piss off and rain on somebody else's parade, you bloody sponger?"

The rough sleeper hesitates. He twitches and tenses, then thinks better of objecting and moves on.

Immediately in front of Simon stand two couples. One of the girls wears a silver-sequined harlequin mask, and a small pendant, round and dark like a tarnished coin, hangs from a choker at her neck. The tall, capable young man beside her sports a filigree metal mask which lends him a faintly androgynous look. He puts his hand over hers as she fishes in her purse.

"Could you spare any loose change for my mate?" the rough sleeper asks. "Only he's not well and I need to get him some medication."

The girl shrugs her partner's hand aside and draws out a note. "Here," she says. "For your friend. I hope he will feel better soon."

The hooded man stares first at the note, then at the girl.

He reaches out to take the note, but doesn't immediately let go of her hand. They pause for a moment, connected both by the paper of the note and the bridge between their eyes.

The girl, though, is uneasy beneath his gaze and slowly lets go of the note, removing her sequined mask as she does so. Her swept-back hair is black, jet-black, and she has a notable widow's peak and full eyebrows, which accentuate her long, broad nose.

Her tall partner tugs at her arm. "Soraya," he mutters.

The moment is over; the eye contact, the communication between the girl and the rough sleeper, whatever it was, is lost.

The rough sleeper takes another couple of paces up the line.

"Sorry my friend," Simon lies, "Haven't got any cash and my credit card won't help." He might as well not have bothered; the man has already moved on.

5

"Who the hell has cash anymore?" Candy mumbles. "Poor bloke."

The girl, the one her tall partner called Soraya, still hasn't replaced her mask and she watches the rough sleeper as he trudges away down the queue.

"That wasn't very bright," her partner says, loud enough for those around them to hear. "He'll only go and squander it on booze or drugs."

She glowers at him: "Sohail, doesn't your prophet teach you to be regular in your charity?"

Overhearing her reply, the man wearing the red plague-doctor mask sneers, "Your charity? You sand-niggers are all the same. If you didn't give them the money, they wouldn't be out here dossing on our streets."

The girl's partner draws himself up to his full height and steps forward.

The girl, though, takes his arm and pulls him back out of her way.

"For your information," she says to the man in the red mask, "I'm not a sand nigger, a sweat monkey, or even a porki or a bungy, I'm British and proud to be so. And if you can't handle that, then I'm not the one with the problem."

Simon eases gently in front of Candy and his movement attracts the attention of the man adjusting his Blair mask.

The man glares at him, daring him to get involved.

The shorter man briefly lifts up his red mask and spits on the pavement at the couple's feet. "Yeah, you're right, I am the one with the problem. And I'm the one who's going to have to sort it out, you gobby bitch."

Simon can see the CCTV camera up on the wall above the doors to the club and prays someone is watching.

The girl's partner, the tall now furious Sohail, moves in front of her. "What did you just call her?"

A mountain of a man, black suit, ID card hanging from a lanyard around his neck, appears out of nowhere. "We all good here, people?"

3

They present tickets, ID cards and smiles for the camera, and their evening eases into a gradual, if noisy, ascent.

Candy's gold swan-shaped mask matches both the blonde of her hair and the gold of the dress, and her dancing, at first languid and elegant, grows more energetic and provocative with each Moscow Mule she consumes.

Simon tries his best to relax and being able to hide behind the mask helps a little. But every now and then he has to muscle out a form of cordon sanitaire around Candy as other men crowd in to watch her perform.

If that's the worst of it, he'll put up with it. However, the greater problem is that his mind is strangely cluttered. For as attractive as Candy undoubtedly is, and as hard as he tries to pay her the attention she rather obviously craves, Simon cannot seem to banish the image of another girl from his thoughts. She is the girl from the queue, Soraya, who wore the silver-sequined harlequin mask and who gave the rough sleeper her money.

And if it is simply a vision of her which now distracts Simon, that wouldn't bother him, for there are many attractive girls in the club who catch his eye. What bothers him is the way the girl had shown her face to the rough sleeper. She had seemed to reveal herself to him solely for his benefit, not so that those watching might recognise her and appreciate her for her charity. On the contrary, her gesture had been curiously intimate; a show of regard to a man who had not a moment before been so very callously disregarded, a shadow of a man who—

Candy grabs Simon by his arm and leads him to the bar. "Another Moscow Mule for me and a Grey Goose and a beer chaser for C-3PO here."

"Just the beer, please."

"Call that dancing, Si? You could do with getting a little loose. You're all radar. Looking everywhere else, not where you're supposed to."

"Sorry. It's this mask. Now I know how a race horse feels as it's being led into the starting stall."

"Talking of being led," she says. Candy eases her mask up onto her forehead, reaches for him and pulls him towards her. "I know it's not quite midnight, but I could do with a little of your attention."

She leans towards Simon and kisses him. Not hard and not for long, but hard enough and for long enough to let the other women at the bar know that he is her property. "I'll be right back," she says, readjusting her mask.

It isn't the first time he's kissed a girl in public, yet Simon is surprised Candy has decided to nail her colours to his mast quite so early in the evening; surprised, affirmed and yet slightly nervous, and he can't think why.

He picks up his beer and as he drinks, feels as though he is being watched.

The girl from the queue is looking his way. She is draining her cocktail and every time her partner tries to talk to her, she turns away and ignores him.

Simon smiles and acknowledges her attention with a slight nod of his head. However, he then realises that she isn't looking at him so much as gazing into the space between them.

He colours with embarrassment, again grateful for the screen of his mask, and looks over towards the toilets: Candy is laughing in the queue. He looks back to the girl: she has started a fresh cocktail.

Soraya, he recalls her name, looks along the bar straight to where he is standing and after a while, he realises she is now staring at him.

He expects her to turn away. She doesn't. He expects her to approve him with a smile or perhaps even frown in disapproval. She doesn't. She simply stands, sipping her cocktail, and watches him, her look casually accepting.

Candy is on her way back from the restroom.

Not wanting to be caught gazing the wrong way, Simon turns.

As she approaches him, someone moves off the dance floor to intercept her. It is the man from the queue, the belligerent racist wearing the red plague-doctor mask.

She doesn't see him coming. Candy is too wrapped in smiling at Simon: a wish, an offer, a promise for later.

He smiles back.

The masked man times his interception so that he passes close behind Candy and, as he does so, he slips his hand under her skirt.

Candy is startled and spins round.

Whatever she screams at him is lost to the thumping music. But the aggression in her stance, in the way she points accusingly at the man, leaves no one in any doubt that she is properly upset.

The plague doctor stands, unfazed, absorbing her anger, perhaps even basking in its heat.

Simon fights his way through the throng. "You alright, Candy?"

"This bloke just touched me up."

"I know, I saw it. Ignore him. He's not worth the fuss." Simon puts his arm round Candy and shepherds her back towards the bar.

"Who are you saying isn't worth the fuss?" the man shouts at his back.

Simon knows the smart move is to ignore him.

"I'm talking to you, sonny. Did I hear you say I wasn't worth the fuss?"

Around them, people are gathering like spectators round a fight cage.

Candy stops and starts to turn.

"Don't look," he says. "Leave it."

"Si?"

He looks into her eyes and sees exactly what he fears. "Oh, surely you can't want me to—"

A hand lands on his shoulder and spins him round.

"Didn't your mother teach you it's bad manners not to speak when you're spoken to?"

"Look, my friend," Simon begins, summoning his anger, hoping it will feed his limbs with the necessary strength, "do yourself a favour and if you can't resist the urge, go play with your own arse."

The man slips his mask off, drops it on the floor and squares up, clenching his fists. Though he is shorter, he steps right into Simon's face so that he can look nowhere else other than straight at the man.

What he sees, Simon does not like. Instantly, he registers the lack of compromise in the man's expression; a look that tells Simon there is now no turning back and that his journey is likely to be short, severe and painful, and without promise of rescue or grant of mercy. It is the first time he has ever witnessed such spite and light tendrils of anticipation feather through his limbs.

"Go do *what?*" the man shouts.

Once more, Simon pushes Candy behind him. He can't look away from the man: he has to stand his ground. "You heard."

The light between then dims. "Is there a problem here?" a deep baritone voice drawls.

Simon glances up to his right.

A mammoth of Polynesian descent towers beside him: "Are you guys cool?"

Neither wants to deny the spat; to do so would be to climb down, to choose compromise, to lose face.

"Okay, gentlemen." The man mountain speaks slowly. Whether he does so because he wants his audience to understand him or whether it is because he is so enormous he is incapable of stringing words together quickly, no one is sure. "Why don't we step back and get on with enjoying our New Year celebration, huh?"

To Simon's complete surprise the man opposite looks skywards and snarls, "Just because you're big, doesn't mean I can't take you."

Simon exhales. In taking on the bouncer, the man has let him off the hook.

"That may be so." The bouncer pauses, thinking. "With respect though, sir," he reaches into his pocket and pulls out a small black buzzer, "if this was any other time and any other place, you'd be welcome to try. But right now, a few of the other security staff are on their way over and a couple of them are not as patient as me. So why not do like I say and get on with enjoying your evening? These people don't want no fuss."

The man waits. He isn't intimidated by the bouncer and wants him to know it. But, after a couple of seconds and much to Simon's relief, his expression then softens and he smiles. His smile, though, is not attractive: it is the leer of the fanatic, the smirk of the sadist, the look of a man used to feasting on the pain of others.

"Okay. All right. Why not? Another time," he says, relaxing, easing up. "That's a proper offer. Maybe we'll get to it sometime.

Anyway, boy, I like your style." And with that he picks up his mask, turns about and melts back into the crowd.

Simon is ready to collapse and hopes Candy cannot see his hands shaking.

The man mountain is still standing next to him.

"Thank you," Simon says. "That was perfect timing."

The Polynesian grins. "Good jokes and good cooling," he grins, pleasantly, "they're all about timing. Enjoy the rest of your night."

When they get back to the bar, Simon doesn't refuse Candy's offer of a vodka shot.

"You'd have taken him, Si," she says, confidently.

Simon shoots. "Yeah, of course I would." Only he wouldn't, the man was not for taking. He'd seen it and recognised it.

The rest of the evening shunts, like cooling lava, and during one of his many trips to the bar, a guy sporting a full-face silver joker mask eases in beside him.

"That girl you're with," the joker says, "she's... well, she's..."

"Yes," Simon agrees, not keen to hear the man's assessment, "she certainly is."

"Doesn't look like you two are hitting it off? I mean, she's all going for it and you..."

"That obvious, huh?" He is piqued to think someone has noticed. "Can't seem to get in the mood." It is the residue of adrenalin; the alcohol hasn't yet dispersed it. "These," he holds up a shot glass, "don't seem to be doing it for me."

"Not doing it for you, huh? It happens." The mask falls silent for a few seconds before saying, "You see the really big guy over there?"

"You mean the cooler? The Hawaiian or Tongan guy?"

"Yeah. His name's Tamati. If you don't mind a little medicinal stimulant, he's your man. Tell him Dom sent you. He'll sort you out. Got some great gear."

13

"Well, that's very considerate of you, Dom, and don't think I'm not grateful. Thing is, I don't blow or flip or chase or do any of that stuff." Simon chuckles. "So, you're probably wondering what the hell I'm doing here."

"Nope, buddy. Makes perfect sense. If I had a girl like that, I'd take her anywhere she wanted to go; drunk, sober, stoned or clean. Look, if you've had enough for the evening, I'd be happy to—"

"Your night for the good deed, is it Dom? New Year's resolution and all that?"

The mask laughs, just as it has been laughing all evening.

"Well, thanks Dom. I haven't had enough yet and it won't happen. Enjoy your evening. I hope you remember it in the morning." As Simon works his way back to where Candy is dancing, he can't resist looking over at the big bouncer.

For the rest of the night, Simon tries to behave as though little or nothing has happened to change his mood. But no matter how many shots he drinks, he can't seem to wash the sour taste from his mouth. He looks out for the girl from the queue and spots her deep in conversation with a scrawny-looking doll near the toilets. Soraya looks unsteady on her feet and her eyes seem slow and glassy. To Simon's surprise, they both disappear through the door to the kitchen. Soraya's partner, the tall lad she'd called Sohail, hasn't noticed; he is rooted at the bar, his expression rabid one minute, hangdog the next.

Come the bewitching hour, Candy delivers him a kiss so wildly enthusiastic it bruises his lips. Perhaps it is the heat in the club, the crescendo of music, the alcohol and the drug-taking; or perhaps it is the ersatz euphoria that grants both men and women the liberty of grabbing at complete strangers; Simon isn't sure which, but an oppressive claustrophobia overtakes him and, leaving Candy at the bar, he slips away.

A sign informs those leaving the club that post-midnight

they will not be allowed back in. He walks straight past, his eyes blinkered.

Outside, the air is cool and refreshing, and the broad avenue of Bishopsgate calm but for the flashing lights of an ambulance parked beside the alley which leads round the back of the club. Two paramedics wheel a stretcher-trolley towards it.

Simon removes his mask and wanders over.

A white-haired man lies prone on the gurney, a heat-reflective blanket pulled up to his waist, an oxygen mask covering his face.

"What's up?"

The young, female paramedic is busy checking the man over. "Oh, rough sleeper. Looks like he's fallen or worse." Her tone is pure and clean, her accent vaguely Scottish.

He notices flecks of red in the old man's oxygen mask. "Will he be okay?"

"Hope so. Excuse us, you're in the way."

Simon stands back as they load the trolley into the ambulance. "New Year's Eve, eh?"

"That's about the truth of it." The paramedic closes the doors.

Rough sleeping: it is one of the ideas he'd noted in his book of suggestions for articles. However, when he'd mooted it at one of the weekly team meetings, others had sniggered. One, an Australian by the name of Bobby Smith, had even gone so far as to dismiss it out of hand. 'Aw mate,' he'd griped, 'that's plain bloody tedious. It might be thought-provoking, but it's been done to death and it's just another social ill without cure. People won't read it: it makes them too uncomfortable.' The man's put-down had stung, but he'd let it go.

"What's his name?" Simon asks.

"Old Tom. Tommy Atkins some call him. We've seen him before."

"Where're you taking him?"

"What are you, a reporter or something?"

"Yes, strangely enough I am."

"Oh," she hesitates, now giving him the once over, "the Royal London, Whitechapel."

"Look, here's my card. Let me know how he gets on, will you?"

The paramedic stops in her tracks. She is slight and pretty. "Sure. Right. New Year's Eve. That'll be when I've got fuck all else to do, pal."

4

Simon makes a vague attempt to reign in his skittish thoughts while he identifies a persistent buzz. He blinks awake, fumbles for his phone, and presses it repeatedly until it shuts up.

The phone lays idle for a few seconds before chirping again.

Slowly, he realises that the irritating tone is not that of the alarm on his phone.

"Peckham."

"Simon?"

"Mr Barnes, sorry, Barnesy?"

"Who else? You with it or do you need a minute to collect your thoughts?"

"No, I'm all ears. What's up?"

"Thought you might be the only bloke in London without a muddled head this morning."

Simon remembers: the club: they wouldn't let him back in after he'd gone outside. Candy. He glances to his right. She is sleeping and just as attractive now as she was when telling him he was a bloody idiot for not reading the sign.

"Sure," he says, trying to prioritise. "What can I do for you?"

"Not me: you. It's what I can do for you. Anything on this morning?"

They'd got in at one and Candy had polished off the better part of a bottle of vodka before he'd had to put her to bed. He recalls standing, watching, wondering how much clothing he should wear when sleeping next to a girl who'd needed his bed more than she'd needed him.

"Would it matter if I had?"

The editor is evidently shuffling papers on his desk, searching. "Right, here we are. Got a job for you. Last night, a rough sleeper, mugged, in Bishopsgate."

"I know."

"Happened out the back of a nightclub— What do you mean you know?"

"I was there in the club. I went out and spoke to the paramedic, gave her my card. Said she'd ring and let me know how the old boy got on. Hasn't, of course. They took him to the Royal London."

"Then why aren't you down there? You know where it is, I assume?"

Simon looks back at Candy and notices the rhythmic rise and fall of the sheet at her breasts. "Yes, Whitechapel Road."

"Police don't seem to be taking much of an interest."

"Not certain that he was. Mugged I mean." Simon dredges the details from his obfuscated recollections of the evening. "Paramedics thought he may have fallen."

"Well, you'll be pleased to hear I've been thinking about your idea for a piece on rough sleepers: you know, Crisis, SCT, Mungos, the volunteers, what it means to those less fortunate over the festive season. Might help to have some real-time hum-int mixed in. Go check him out and get back to me, eh."

Real-time human-interest? Bobby Smith had loudly proclaimed

that stories about rough sleeping didn't sell and yet now his editor has decided to run with one.

The line dies, leaving Simon to stare at Candy as he wonders whether he can get dressed and leave without waking her. If he's honest with himself, the call from his editor is not wholly unwelcome.

Barnes: behind his desk when the rest of the world is focussed on getting over the night before.

Simon shakes his head in disbelief.

His sponsor: Barry Barnes, editor of the London Evening Star. A man he'd met only a couple of months before Christmas; a short, balding, fifty-something dipsomaniac, with a lived-in face and the pallid complexion of a creature who rarely sees the sun: a closet misogynist whose *joie* had been excised from his *vivre* and a *vie* that refused to believe in a *raison d'être* beyond supplying commuters with a bone to chew on on their journey home.

Still, the man had been good enough to employ Simon. That counted and counted for a lot; for no one he'd approached, not the nationals, the freesheets, the regionals or locals, had shown any interest in his CV. Sure, he could get work putting code on stories other journalists had written, who couldn't? But he was well aware that finding links and copying content for an online newspaper is, strictly speaking, a cul-de-sac.

At the interview, the editor had run through his CV: "Attended a minor public school. Left in the Sixth Form for a local state college where you completed your A-levels. Moved on to a red brick university; graduated with a 2:1 in Modern Languages. You passed your third year in the office of a Paris Glossy and you've got Teeline shorthand and a Level 3 Diploma Course in journalism."

As far as the other papers were concerned, though, Simon didn't have enough or the right experience and Paris didn't apply. Barnes had been the only editor who'd looked beyond his CV.

"You're fresh," he'd stated, "and you don't have any contacts, which is what this game is all about. Doesn't explain here why you left private school halfway through, which intrigues me, but you seem to be an easy guy to like. If you hadn't been, I'd have shown you the door before you sat down.

"But, what I am fed up to the back teeth with is data journos, the kind of guys who sit on their arses trawling the web for some graduate's dissertation out of which they hope to conjure some public interest. You know, how ten per cent of the population have consorted with either aliens or animals, or how many postmen dream of biting dogs. That stuff I can live without.

"So, what I do want from you, Simon, are stories; stories that possess merit, relevance and resonance; the kind of stories that'll make people pick up a newspaper and read it, not wrap their china in it.

"Outside of that, I like a punt."

Barnes had leant his head back, winced and stared questioningly up at the ceiling. "Yeah, alright, I know that's a little clichéd even for me, but I hope you get where I'm coming from though. Good investigative journalism, that's what I'm looking for. Give me that and maybe, just maybe, we'll keep you on. Get me?"

"Yes, Mr Barnes. I get you absolutely. You want Pulitzer Prizes not lies and damned lies."

The editor had paused and smiled. "Good! You've got it. And I don't want churnalism either. Rewrites of old press releases I can do without. I'll pass you some diary stuff: court reporting, upcoming events, socials, the odd royal and political meeting, stuff you'll know about in advance. Make of them what you can and if they're worth more than just a News-in-brief, I'll consider it. I'll also hand you some off-diary work: not necessarily the truck that's parked itself in the Knightsbridge store window or the footballer snapped sniffing petunias in Brompton Park, but stuff I'll need you to cover at short notice.

"I'll start you on £2,000 a month. But because I've no idea

what your work's like, I can't guarantee to include what you submit. Oh, and we'll retain all the copyright of your submissions. That's non-negotiable. Any questions?"

Simon had been busy keeping the lid on his jubilation and Barnes hadn't attempted to conceal his amazement. "Jesus, Simon, don't you want to know how long your contract is, what sort of expenses you're entitled to, anything?"

"Of course," Simon had replied, more humbled than embarrassed, "I'm sorry. How long *have* I got? Who *do* I apply to, to sign off on my expenses?"

"Six months and a girl goes by the name of Candace in accounts. Candace by name and eye-candy she is too. Don't tell her I said that. Good. We're straight for now. I'll get HR to give you a call, set things up. What about a beer in an hour or so? Small celebration?"

"Sounds perfect to me," Simon had replied. "Only, one thing, Mr Barnes—"

"Barnesy. Everyone calls me Barnesy."

"Okay, yes, thanks. Well, Barnesy, the thing is, I'm not much of a drinker."

"What d'you mean, you're not much of a drinker?"

Simon had shuffled, nervously. "Just thought you ought to know."

Barry Barnes had appeared completely flummoxed for a moment. It was as though Simon had just told the editor he was one of the ten per cent who consorted with aliens or had actually bitten a dog. But, realising he'd just offered his new charge a position and that it was by then too late to retract his offer, the editor had just coughed and wiped his hands over his thinning grey hair.

"Guess you don't have to put that on your CV, eh? Well, you won't find that helps in this business: getting people to talk is everything and booze is an easy key. Carry a packet of cigarettes on you, too. I don't know, perhaps it's something you'll pick up as you go along; we all have."

So, the London Evening Star had given him six months when no one else would give him the time of day, and all he had to do to make his position permanent was to get out and about and find a few stories.

Simon reaches for the door handle and twists it slowly. The door squeaks. Candy mumbles in her sleep.

5

The Royal London towers behind a Georgian infirmary, which sits gaunt and vacant, like an old uncle dozing in an armchair. And on the north side of the main road, back from the tented market stalls, cafés separated by red, gold and turquoise sarees and jilbabs, advertise kebab rolls, biryani, falooda and chat. An Air Ambulance thumps and whines as it circles to land.

Simon tucks his scarf tighter around his neck as he strides down the alley to the entrance. Motorcycles and scooters give way to a fleet of ambulances parked up beneath a terracotta-clad façade which in turn gives way to a rectangular cobalt-blue high-rise.

A black man in a blue parka is handing out leaflets as he proclaims the virtues of a religion most are only too happy to ignore. The choice is simple: left for A&E or right for the main entrance.

The receptionist, her full face framed by a grey hijab, stares back at him dully from behind the safety glass.

"Excuse me," he asks, adopting the most forlorn expression he can summon, "a friend of mine was brought in last night and I'd like to find out how he's getting on."

The woman's ebony eyes register no surprise. "What's his name, please?"

"Tom. He was admitted during the night, just after midnight." Simon looks away, dreading her next question.

She consults a list. "Name?"

He looks back and smiles, broadly. "Tom."

The woman consults the list once more and then looks back up, a wry smile infecting her lips: "That good a friend that you don't know his whole name?"

"Yes, I know it sounds strange. I've only ever known him as Tom."

"At school together, were you?"

"Funny you should say that," he counters hurriedly.

She blanks him for a second before leading him on, "Then you'd be about the same age, would you?"

"Of course not." Simon recalls the weather-beaten face, the white hair, the blood-spattered oxygen mask and the pretty paramedic who hadn't yet rung him. "Thomas Atkins. No, he's much older than me. He'd be in his seventies." He leans closer, trying to sneak a look at her list.

She snatches it from his prying eyes and turns it over. "Nobody with the name Atkins was admitted last night. Why don't you come back when you can remember his real surname?" She looks away as if to punctuate the end of their conversation.

"What about Atkinson?"

She blanks him.

"Oh, come on," he pleads.

A silver-haired old crone shrouded in a moth-eaten coat, her arms clutching at her more than ample girth, is waiting behind him. "Would you mind getting out of the way, sonny? Only if I don't get to see a doctor soon, I'm not going to be held responsible for the mess I'll be making all over this floor."

24

Simon surrenders.

His stomach complains loudly at the lack of breakfast, so he heads for the vending machines, which stand like sentries beside swing doors decorated with handprints. And while he is pondering crinkle-cut crisps, chocolate, and Lucozade, he notices beyond the glass a couple of paramedics smoking at the foot of a white wall smeared with graffiti.

He shuns breakfast and wanders over to them.

The two young women turn in to each other as he approaches.

"Sorry to bother you, ladies, could either of you spare a light?"

Relieved that he is not about to bother them regarding his in-growing toenail, they turn back to him and hand him a small yellow lighter.

Simon drags lightly on his cigarette. "Cheers. Needed that. Beats breakfast, eh?" As he hands the lighter back, he makes a play of being distracted by the man loudly proclaiming his divine rights and drops the lighter. "Sorry," he mutters, bending down to retrieve it. "Been a long night."

"Tell me about it," says the one who'd lent him the lighter.

"Oh, yeah, sorry." He hands it back. "That was bloody rude of me. Stupid, too. I sometimes forget us journalists are not the only people who have to stay up all night. Busy was it, your night? Or is that another stupid question? Half of London seems to be camped inside waiting to have their unidentified drinking injuries attended to."

The woman warms to him. She drops her cigarette and treads on it. "You a reporter then?"

"For my sins."

"Thought you'd be in the office listening to some celebrity's phone messages, not hanging about out here with those of us who've actually got better places to be." Her tone is laced with irony rather than the more expected resentment of one who works while others play.

"No. Not me. Drew the short straw, didn't I? New Year's Eve with Girls Aloud or 500 words on how you green-suited angels are out rescuing deserters from the Salvation Army. Which would you choose?"

Their confidence gained, the women are happy to smoke his cigarettes and shoot the breeze for a while. And when they are sufficiently relaxed, he steers them onto their night's labours.

One of them rolls her eyes and says, "You're kidding, right? Surely a guy like you wasn't really working last night? Even journalists get New Year's Eve off, don't they? I mean there's more to read on a piece of bog paper than there is in a rag on New Year's Day?"

"Sorry to disillusion you," Simon grins, sheepishly, "as it happens I wasn't working last night."

"Yeah, I bet," she moans, rolling her eyes. "So come on then, mate, spill the beans. You were all loved up with your Page 3 model, weren't you?"

"No, strangely enough I wasn't." He thinks of Candy, of her curves undulating and gyrating, of how other men had seemed to appreciate her more than... "I was at a club, Slick in the City. It's in Shoreditch. Do you know it?"

Her thin eyebrows arch in surprise. "Oh my god, you wasn't? Seriously? One of our lot was just around the corner from you about the time you was pulling your party poppers. Picked up some old rough sleeper round the back of the club. Tom, I think 'is name was."

"Was?"

"Yeah, poor sod. Someone said he'd been beat up. The crew reckoned he'd pretty much just fallen over pissed. Bit smashed up though. Last I heard he was up in ICU."

———

Visitor Lift 5 and Simon stifles his surprise.

Waiting for the same lift is the girl from the club.

Clearly, Soraya hasn't been home; she's still wearing the same black chain-hem bralet top, cigarette trousers and draped black jacket she was wearing when he saw her disappear through the kitchen door.

She doesn't notice him. Why would she? His face is no longer concealed behind his mask and he's wearing jeans and a leather jacket. Pale, hesitant and a little shaky, Soraya looks pathetically abandoned, as though her evening has only recently finished and not as well as she would have liked.

He stands back to allow her to enter the lift first. "Which floor?"

"Four, please."

He presses just the one button. "A relative? In Intensive Care?"

"What makes you think I don't work here?"

He smiles, vaguely amused. "Well, if I was a patient in ICU and my doctor appeared dressed like that, I might be inclined to forget my poor health and rise up like Lazarus."

Soraya pulls her jacket tight across her front and scowls back at him. "Not a relative," she says, focusing her attention on the doors. "A friend."

"Well, I hope whoever it is you're on your way to see recovers soon. I didn't mean to be rude."

"Oh, that's okay," she sighs, wearily, "I didn't mean to be rude either. It's been a long night, that's all." Her lips have surrendered their lustre, her hair its rich sheen. She tries to smile and comes up short.

"Good party?"

She frowns. "No. Horrible. Perhaps the worst night of my life."

"That bad, huh?"

"Yes, somebody spiked my drink."

"Spiked as in alcohol?"

"No, the doctor thinks it was probably Gamma-hydroxy-something."

"Gamma-hydroxybutyrate," he corrects. "Smells like brush cleaner; that's if you're lucky enough to notice it."

"Yes, that's what the doctor said. Bit late for that. Stupid of me."

The lift halts and the doors separate. Simon stands back again.

They wait patiently at the reception. Nurses come and go, keeping their heads down, avoiding eye contact, pretending the two of them don't exist. He stands immediately behind Soraya, his arms folded across his chest.

After a few minutes, a nurse in royal blue uniform appears and sits down behind the counter. "I'm sorry to keep you waiting. As you can see, we're a bit busy. Who is it you've come to see?"

"Yes, of course, I..." Soraya begins. The words won't come to her. An unpleasant thought, a horror story, the recollection of a nightmare flashes in her expression. She turns to Simon, "After you."

"Thank you, I couldn't." He extends a hand in the same way as he had when insisting she enter the lift before him.

They wait in silence for a couple of seconds, before the nurse says in a tone loaded with gentle concern, "Now let's not let good manners get in the way of why we're all here, eh. Who is it you've come to see?"

Soraya colours. "Sorry. Yes. Tom. He was brought in to A&E last night."

The nurse glances round at a squared and numbered whiteboard on which names are written in variously coloured pen. She turns back to her desk, clearly puzzled.

"Well, we have a gentleman with us. We don't know his name because he's been unconscious since he was brought in and we haven't been able to get any information from him." She looks back at Soraya, very obviously expecting her to produce some clue as to their patient's identity.

"He'd be in his sixties," she says, "grey straggly hair. Tom's homeless."

"And where was he brought in from?"

She turns and glances nervously at Simon. "Shoreditch. Somewhere near the nightclub, Slick in the City; near where Bishopsgate meets the Commercial Road."

The nurse is studying her: "Are you a relative?"

"No," she pauses, thinking. "I mean, I've seen him about and I talk to him occasionally. I just wanted to know how he is, that's all."

"Well, Ms..."

Soraya doesn't answer: she just stands her ground, waiting.

The nurse waits too, and when the silence has endured long enough for the nurse to realise that her visitor is not going to offer more than she already has, she says, "Wait here; I'll see if one of the doctors can see you," and before she leaves the reception, she leans to look past Soraya at Simon.

"No hurry," he says. "I'll hang on. Please, see to this lady first."

The girl, Soraya, tries her best to muster a smile in appreciation, but her anxiety seems to get the better of her.

A doctor appears from the passageway. He carries a folder, which he consults as he ushers her to a small waiting area.

Simon is content to linger, busying himself with reading the dos and don'ts of visiting ICU.

The doctor looks Soraya up and down, a wry smile of amusement, or perhaps scepticism, creeps across his face. "I understand you want to know how our unknown rough sleeper is getting on. I gather you think his name might be Tom, is that right?"

"Yes, as far as I know. It's not that I know him personally; it's just that I've seen him about and I've heard other people call him by that name. I completely understand if you'd rather not tell me how he is: patient confidentiality is important, I know."

"Well, young lady…"

"Soraya."

"Well, Soraya, seeing as we haven't got the first clue as to who he is, other than that according to our paramedics his name is Tom; and seeing as you are the first person to provide us with any real information about him, I don't suppose there's any danger of me abusing my Hippocratic Oath by telling you our patient is currently comatose. He requires a hemiarthroplasty; that's a replacement partial joint for his broken right hip. He also has a pneumothorax. a collapsed lung caused by one of his ribs piercing his right lung, and several nasty abrasions to his face."

The list of injuries hangs in the air, a harbinger of doom or perhaps the grim reaper patiently circling.

"Oh," he adds, "and I forgot to mention pneumonia."

Such an extensive list is shocking and Simon cannot resist wincing.

"I'm sorry, doctor," she says.

"Well, I'm sure none of these issues are your fault. You couldn't have given him his pneumonia and I can't imagine you causing the broken hip and punctured lung. We think he may have fallen."

"Seriously? He's been the victim of an assault?"

The doctor lowers his head, the way a judge might before deciding whether to allow evidence. "It's possible; quite possible."

"What about the police?" she asks.

"What about them?"

"They must know he's been assaulted."

The doctor sighs and flaps shut his folder. "As I said, it's quite possible he's been the victim of an assault, though they don't seem to be so sure of that. With bones as brittle as his it's as I said, he may have fallen badly. His blood alcohol count is very high, which again is fairly symptomatic."

"What will you do with him?"

"Do with him? In terms of what?"

"In the short term, I mean."

He sighs again and checks his watch. "In the short term, all we can do is stabilise him. The lung? We'll wait and see how bad the damage is. For the moment, we have inserted a catheter to remove the air in his chest cavity and he's on a respirator. The hemiarthroplasty will have to wait until we're happier with his general state."

The nurse reappears at reception. She looks towards Simon in expectation and he shakes his head subtly to suggest he's with the young lady who is deep in conversation with the doctor.

"Will he get through it?"

The doctor smiles a wan, slightly resigned smile. "We don't like to lose them, you know. We take it very personally when we do. Rest assured we'll be doing all we can."

Soraya waits, more than a little frightened to ask. "Long term?"

"Long term?" He checks a page in his file. "At the moment, his condition is serious enough that we're not considering the long term. Now if you'll excuse me, I must be getting on." He walks away, sweeping left around the reception. As he gets to the passageway he halts, turns back and asks, "Look, if his name really is Tom, you might like to try and find out if anyone's missing a husband or father with the same name.

"While he's here, *we* can only patch him up; that's the best *we* can do. The best *you* could do for him is to try and find out who he belongs to. If you can get him off the streets, then there is an even better chance of saving him permanently." He pauses and fixes the girl with a pained expression. "It's the streets that are killing him, you know; nothing else. Have a good New Year."

Simon watches as Soraya sits silently, examining her hands. He hears her sniff and turns to see her wipe her eyes.

She gets up and leaves.

He can't risk waiting while she takes the lift down in case he loses her, and so he delays until the moment before the lift doors close and ends up getting caught in them.

The doors stutter, and then open wide again before closing.

"Sorry," he says.

Soraya is staring at the floor, deep in thought.

He tries again. "I'm sorry. I'm always doing that."

She looks up, "Doing what? No, sorry, I wasn't listening."

"Going to be alright is he, your friend?"

"Oh, don't know. I hope so. He's a bit knocked about though." She turns her attention back to the floor.

"I don't mean to be rude, but did I hear you say he was homeless and that someone had assaulted him?"

"Mm? What? Oh, yes."

"How do you know? Did you see it happen?"

She has her arms wrapped firmly around her, as though she is cold and is distracted to work out how she could be when it is so warm in the hospital. "Yes, sort of," she answers dreamily.

"Probably fighting over some patch of pavement," he suggests. "I hear they can get very territorial about their own turf. Mind you, can't really call it turf, can you?"

She looks up at him, accusingly; hot coals of anger suddenly replacing the chill of her introspection. "It wasn't like that. It wasn't like that at all. I was there. I saw it. The man tried to pull that ape off me: now look where he's ended up." Her eyes begin to water and she wipes the cuff of her jacket across her face.

Simon, chastened, is unsure how to react.

Soraya is in her early twenties, he guesses, and her skin is a curious blend of tawny and fair, possibly middle-eastern, perhaps Iraqi or Iranian in origin. She is strikingly attractive, but what captures him are her eyes. Upstairs in the ICU, he had been concentrating on listening and had intentionally avoided eye contact with her; now though, stuck in the lift with her, he cannot escape her stare.

32

The lift stops. The doors open.

She throws him one final, damning look and marches out through the tall atrium of the main reception, pausing only to allow the glass doors at the entrance to part.

He catches up with her as she is striding across the concourse. "Hang on, please. Look, I'm sorry. And it does seem to be that since we've met I've done nothing but apologise to you, so—"

Soraya stops abruptly and placing her hands on her hips, fronts up to him a shade aggressively. "Listen, I don't know who you are and, frankly, I don't know that I care. And unless I'm mistaken we haven't met; all we've done is share a lift. So do me a kindness, leave me alone."

It is her eyes. They are a colour he has not seen before. They are almost gold at the centre, fading to light brown and dark blue around the rim; and they contain some fabulous radiance as though they are polished or glazed. For a moment, he is lost for words.

By not responding to her aggression, he confuses her and she too stands and wonders, although not perhaps in the same way.

"Yeah, I know all that." He scratches at the back of his head; an affectation many have told him he adopts whenever he is nervous. "However, I'd really value two minutes of your time. I'm not about to abduct you or assault you, or anything like that."

"No," she interrupts, "you're not going to do that. Twice in twelve hours and I might think the New Year has got it in for me." She pauses.

Simon, though, is still swimming in the ocean of her eyes.

"Well, get on with it," she orders. "It's cold out here and as I'm sure you've noticed, I'm not dressed for standing around making small talk. So, who are you?"

He drags himself from his stupor. "My name's Simon, Simon Peckham. I'm a journalist. I—"

"And what do you want, Mr Peckham?"

"I want to know what happened to the man Tom that put him in hospital."

"Why?"

"That's my job. It's how I pay my bills."

"Anything else?"

"I'd like to know what happened to you, too."

She shies away from him. "To me? Nothing happened to me. It all happened to Tom and that... that other guy. And if it hadn't been for him..." She pauses to catch her breath, and while she does she begins to shake and rub her arms. Her eyes dart about the hospital concourse and fill with tears. "That's all. That's all there is. It was my bloody fault and now look what's happened."

Simon steps towards her, but she throws up her hands to ward him off.

A hospital security warden wearing a black cap and high-viz jacket walks over and loiters a few paces away.

Simon, too, raises his hands, but in surrender. "Look, I'm sorry. Oh, again I'm sorry. Christ, this is becoming a habit." The young woman is deaf to his attempt at humour. "I shouldn't have bothered you. Can I get you a cab; phone someone for you."

She calms a little and looks about anxiously. "No, I'm all right. I'm... I'm sorry. I don't mean to be so unpleasant; it's just that it's not been a great night."

"Sure, I can only imagine. You're Soraya, aren't you?"

She shoots him a look that leaves him in no doubt she doesn't trust him.

"I only know your name because I heard you tell the doctor. Look here's my card. It's got my mobile phone number, and the address of my office. If you want to have a chat about all this, give me a call. No pressure. I won't hassle you. Just call me if you want to talk it over. Here," he says, noticing her reluctance to accept it. "Go on. You might as well have it. Throw it in the bin when I'm out of sight, if you want."

Soraya takes his card and slips it into her jacket pocket.

"Now, have you got enough money to get home?"

His simple question stuns her.

While she is thinking, Simon searches for the twenty-pound note in his pocket and hands it to her. It is the same twenty-pound note he could have given the rough sleeper.

Soraya shakes her head slowly. "I didn't think. I can't think why I didn't. I haven't got a penny on me."

"No matter. Take this. I'm not expecting anything in return. Absolutely not, no, nothing."

She glances up again: that same doubting look.

"Nothing!" he repeats a shade more forcefully. "Send me the money when you get yourself straight. Or, if not, put it down to experience. I'll claim it on expenses anyway."

Soraya hesitates, not understanding why a complete stranger should want to give up twenty quid so casually. "You sure?"

"Yes, I'm sure. Now go on, go home before you catch your death."

She takes the note and stands, staring back at him until she shivers, whereupon she drags the cuff of her jacket across her face, sniffs rather inelegantly and turns away and walks off down East Mount Street towards the Mile End Road.

Simon chides himself gently for not trying harder.

It is New Year, he reminds himself, and he recalls telling himself as he'd watched Candy empty his bottle of vodka that this year he is going to draw a measure of respect from his peers. And, if he wants to earn that respect, perhaps it's about time he started showing a little of the same to others. Besides, the young woman had looked as though she'd had about as much as anyone could take and he had only been going to rub her up the wrong way by pestering her.

"You see, Peckham," he mutters, "you can be nice if you try."

Someone is standing next to him.

"Good looking kid," the man offers.

"She is that." Simon turns. The man is coarse-looking. He wears a black puffer-jacket over a hoodie and dirty jeans. His stare is curiously penetrating.

"All right, was she?" the stranger asks.

Simon is taken aback by the man's question. And if he wasn't standing on the concourse of a hospital, with people coming and going, some loitering, others smoking, he might feel threatened, but for some reason he doesn't. "Seemed so. Why, do you know her?"

"No." The man turns about and walks away towards the glassed main entrance.

Simon watches him go, thinking it odd that a complete stranger should approach him like that. What was more unusual, though, was that the man's uncompromising stare seemed at odds with the way he denied knowing the girl. That, and that his tone, rather than being loaded with any salacious or prurient desire, was quite clearly laced with regret.

As he retrieves his phone from his jacket pocket, Simon looks back towards the alley out to the main road. The girl, Soraya, has gone.

6

"Barnes."

"It's Simon."

"Yes? What've you got?"

"Not much. Old guy. Homeless. Name is possibly Atkins, Thomas Atkins, though the medics are not one hundred per cent sure. May have been beaten up dossing out the back of the club. Police don't seem to be interested. Could be that he was knocked about by one of his mates. Could be that he was out of his tree and fell."

The girl, Soraya. He opens his mouth to mention her, then reconsiders.

"Doesn't look like much to me," he decides. If Barnes reckons there's a trail to be followed, he'll only want him to spend the rest of the day following it and Candy will want, if not deserve, some of his time.

"Right," says Barnes. The subsequent silence suggests he is either reading something or weighing up what more can be done. "Look, Simon, get down to that club and have a nose about, will you?"

"But—"

"Yes, yes, I know it will be closed and there won't be anyone around. Get down there all the same. Never know what you might turn up."

Simon sighs. "No peace for the wicked, eh?"

"No peace for anyone, son. What did you say his name was?"

"Tom. Might be Thomas Atkins. Why?"

Cogs and wheels are grinding somewhere up in the analytical engine of the editor's mind. "Heard the name before somewhere, that's all. Go and have a shufti and if it comes to nothing, then go and do what most other people do on New Year's Day."

"Which is?"

"I don't know," the editor barks, exasperated, "go for a cycle, take the dog for a walk, watch Spartacus, anything. Only don't do what I do, which is sit here watching the phone, hoping one of my journos is going to call with some juicy snippet that'll fill tomorrow's front page."

"I haven't got a bike, or a dog," Simon growls. "And I don't watch TV, much." He is talking to himself; Barnes has rung off. "I wonder if the Blind Beggar is open," he mutters. "Get about as much cheer out of a dead Henry de Montfort as I will out of a live Barry Barnes."

Sadly, the pub isn't, and Ronnie and Reggie Kray have gone to Chingford and George Cornell, the gangster Ronnie shot, has moved south of the river to Camberwell. Underworld to underworld. Like last year, they are all dead and buried.

The night club is locked and dark, the nearby pavements fouled with tokens of the previous night's excess. As Simon walks by, a street-sweeper stoops and stares: a straggler from a forgotten army.

He expects to see police tape across the entrance to the

alley behind the club, but there is none. And neither is there an information board appealing for witnesses to what the girl, Soraya, had claimed was the old rough sleeper's assault.

A rough sleeper: perhaps if the girl had told the police she too had been assaulted, the tape and the board would be in place.

It begins to rain. Wet rain. The kind that mixes and mists in the air: the kind that'll soak a man without him noticing.

Simon again hitches the collar of his jacket up around his neck and steps into the alley.

There is not much to report: cigarette butts, discarded cloth, vomit and two large dumpsters filled to over-flowing with multi-coloured bottles.

Opposite the back door of the club is an even narrower alley that seems to lead nowhere.

Simon wanders over.

At the entrance lies a brown paper bag. He bends to it, opens it and checks the contents: a small box of... He studies it: amoxicillin.

The further down the narrow alley Simon treads, the heavier hangs the air. And whereas over the way, empty bottles of Belvedere vodka and Monkey gin fill the dumpster; here he finds a weather-beaten sleeping bag, yesteryear's newspapers, a couple of soiled sheets of foam, further plastic bags stuffed with odd items of clothing, and a collection of food wrappers.

The odour is damp, musty and overpowering, and he toes a few of the items over in case anything interesting should be lurking underneath. A rat scuttles out and darts away into the dark corner.

Back outside in the lighter alley, Simon stretches his arms out, taking a moment to expel the stale air from his chest. "Nothing for you here," he mutters. "Nothing except pneumonia." The fresh air dizzies him; he turns left instead of right and trips over.

"Shape up, Simon." He looks down to see what it is that has made him trip.

A small black leather notebook lies on the ground; the size and kind he remembers his father keeping for addresses and telephone numbers.

He opens it and flicks through it. A single first name is written at the top of each page, beside it a second name and below it a legend of some kind.

The rain falls faster and harder, and his night is rapidly catching up with his day. He shivers, slips the notebook into his jacket pocket and heads back out in the lighter gloom of Bishopsgate.

EXCERPT I FROM TRANSCRIPT OF CONVERSATION WITH JOSEPH NAARDA

SP: Please, Joseph, tell me about your family. Where were they from?

JN: My father came from Dohuk, from the north of Iraq, and my mother from Basra, in the south. In the years before I was born, my father taught in a boy's college, in Baghdad. But when the Ba'athists came to power in 1969, they expelled all the Jesuits, my father included, so he moved south to Basra, to my mother's family home.

SP: Your father was a Jesuit?

JN: No, not a Jesuit, a Catholic. A Chaldean Catholic, not necessarily a Jesuit.

SP: What was Basra like in those days? I've heard people refer to it as the Venice of the East.

JN: Basra was a very beautiful city: canals lined with forests of date-palm and mulberry; melon orchards and vineyards. There was, of course, no architecture to compare with Venice, some places in the old town and in Az Zubayr very beautiful, but Basra was cosmopolitan. You see, Simon, all the spices and fabrics, the precious metals, sulphur, tea, all that trade from the Far East, it used to come through the Persian Gulf into the city. Basra was a gateway and as a result it was a busy place.

SP: You used the word cosmopolitan?

JN: Yes, cosmopolitan. I think that is the right word. I know a woman, she left Basra late in the 1970s. She told me that the first time she saw a camel was in London Zoo. She told me that in Basra, she had never seen a woman wear a niqab; a head scarf against the sun, yes, but not a niqab as such and certainly nothing like a burka. Most of the time, women wore abayas, a sort of robe, a cloak that was also a dress; it kept them cool. Yes, it was traditional, and it was suitable and functional, but women did not wear them because of religious custom.

But Basra was cosmopolitan not simply in terms of its ethnicity: Arab, Ottoman, European, Asian, African. I mean more in terms of religions. There would be Muslims trading with Jews, Jews trading with Christians, and Christians trading with both. Then there were Mandaeans, Zoroastrians, Shabaks, Samaritans and Druze. And every one of those religions would have had its own sects. Groups within groups, if you like. Particularly the Christians, where one had Chaldeans, Syriacs, Pentecostalists, Evangelists, Russian Orthodox and so on.

SP: You're suggesting this mix of people worked because of commerce, because of the trade through the city?

JN: Yes, that is what I believe. Trade, out of necessity, breeds tolerance. In the market, in the winter, one would trade grain, maize, millet, barley; and in the autumn goats, wool, horses and most of all dates. You know there are more than two hundred varieties of palm in Basra? And I'm telling you, Simon, the *Barhi* is the most succulent of all dates.

My grandfather, my mother's father, was a market trader. He

would sell dates to one man and buy coffee, sugar and the finest Indian silk from another. This is how he made his living. It was commerce. This was how and why everybody got on. After all, who would insult a man's religion if one's livelihood depended on doing business with him?

SP: And when they began to develop the Rumaila oil field, did Basra change then?

JN: In some ways, yes. You know what oil does, Simon? It makes everything grow; like water, only not so. The rich grow even more rich and the eyes of the poor grow even more green. However, in the heart of Basra everyone continued to talk and trade as if the world would always be so.

SP: And that was how it was? Even late into the 70s?

JN: Yes, that was how it was until Saddam came.

7

Simon tosses his front door key on the kitchen worktop. The nearly empty vodka bottle stands tall and Candy is still sound asleep.

His feet ache and his head thumps from the excesses of dance mix and the alcohol he is unused to drinking. A New Year's resolution: time to sign off on the social and sign up to a gym. The slaphead in the red beaky mask would have made mincemeat of him if that enormous bouncer hadn't shown up and Simon knows he wouldn't have lived it down, especially once Candy had whispered it round the office.

He makes her coffee, takes it into his bedroom and leaves it, steaming, by his bed.

The big bouncer, the outsize Polynesian, the go-to man for happy pills: the guy at the bar had said his name was Tamati.

"Simon?" she calls from the bedroom.

"Candy!"

"Thank God for that."

"Thank God for what?"

"For being there. I got up a while ago, the place was empty and I couldn't remember where the bloody hell I was."

"Take your time. No hurry," he calls back.

"Simon?"

"Candy?"

"You took my dress off?"

"Yes, Candy."

"Simon, did we…"

"Oh, absolutely, Candy. You were fabulous." Simon grins, certain she will pick up on his irony. He is, though, not grinning at any particular memory; more he's grinning at the fact that she will be lying in his bed trying her best to recall an event that never happened.

"Simon?"

"Don't get your knickers in a twist, Candy, I'm just teasing."

Half an hour later, Candy leaves. She is wearing an odd assortment of his clothes and although she doesn't give him the cold shoulder, she doesn't present him with a warm one either. "Thanks, Simon."

"For what?"

"For taking me out, for putting me to bed and for not taking advantage of me."

"Perish the thought, Candy."

She smiles. "Not for too long, I hope. By the way, your coffee is *so* not good." The door closes.

The kindling of any nascent euphoria regarding his prospects for the coming year are extinguished by a deluge of rain beyond the windows, so Simon resorts to the kind of behaviour so recently endorsed by his editor: he fixes something to eat and loses the afternoon to Spartacus.

He dozes through most of the movie and wakes towards the end, right at the part where Senator Crassus threatens to crucify the slaves to a man if they don't identify their leader.

45

Encouraged by Antoninus, the slaves and gladiators slowly rise to their feet, each and every one of them claiming to be Spartacus.

A light switches on in his brain. Simon hauls himself off the sofa and retrieves the small notebook he'd found amid the detritus in the alley.

No larger than the palm of his hand, the black leather of the exterior is gnarled at the edges and heavily creased in the grain. Every page is written in neat black Biro, the ink of the initial pages having faded with age. And aside from the date on the inside of the cover, 2003, there is no clue as to what the contents refer. Some odd pages, Simon notices, are crossed out with one single stroke.

The old boy, Tom, must have been in his sixties, if not his seventies. Why would an old rough sleeper start keeping a record of other rough sleepers he'd met since 2003?

Simon reads on. The notebook contains a list of at least sixty names, and it was the names of the characters all pretending to be Spartacus that jogged his memory. Each page is headed with a name, most probably a first name. That much is easy. And nearly all of the entries then contain second names, possibly surnames or, he realises as he examines each page, more likely nicknames. Below these is noted a city or town, then what looks like the name of a pub or club, more first names, some bracketed with the letter *d*, and finally, a reference of some kind: a professional qualification, a speciality, a talent or field of study.

Alphabetically, the references range from *AS* to *VM*, some of them being more complex. HW(ATK), HW(MOR), PW(MG) and PW(S). The notes in each page are obviously coded and although the names at the top clearly refer to the information recorded beneath, there is no definitive detail as far as addresses are concerned. What is more puzzling, though, is why the notebook should be set out in such a fashion that if it fell into the wrong hands, the new owner wouldn't at first sight find it easy to decipher. Clearly, the keeper of the notebook has wanted to keep the identities of those listed a secret.

"Well, he got that right, didn't he."

8

"Barnesy?"

"Yes, Simon. Take a seat. Anything?" The editor's face is as worn as his shoes.

"You been here all night, boss?"

"Nope. Just feel as if I have." Barnes groans as he lifts his feet back to the floor. "Sorry to have to ask you to get out and about on New Year's Day. Hope your date didn't mind."

"Would it matter if she—"

"Nope. What'd you dig up?"

"Not much, I'm afraid."

"Run it all by me again, if you wouldn't mind?"

"Went to the Royal London: spoke to a couple of ambulance crews. The man is homeless, a rough sleeper. Name of Thomas, possibly Atkins, they weren't sure. Paramedic thought she knew him. Picked up from out the back of that club off Bishopsgate, Slick in the City. Currently in Intensive Care. Didn't sound as though they thought they'd lose him, but then neither was the prognosis that positive. Police don't seem bothered."

Barnes interrupts, "Our man at the Bishopsgate nick tells me the police can't seem to make up their minds. No witnesses, they've had no reports of anyone missing and this Atkins doesn't fit any descriptions. Result? They've no interest."

"Hardly surprising if he's been living rough for a long time."

Barnes rocks back in his chair, clasps his hands behind his head and stares at the ceiling. "Was it assault or self-inflicted?"

"There was no police presence at the time and there is now no cordon tape or any sign appealing for witnesses." Simon shuts up.

There was, of course, the girl, Soraya. She'd said it was assault. She'd said it was her fault, too. And she'd said something about someone who had tried to pull the ape off her; something about it all happening to Tom and that other guy. What other guy? Was she referring to the man who'd assaulted the rough sleeper?

Simon could, if he chooses, tell Barnes about his encounter with the girl: it is material to the story, such as the story is. But a voice of caution holds him back. For even though Simon understands he owes the editor a certain depth of trust in return for taking him on when no one else would, he isn't sufficiently sure he knows his editor well enough to trust him with the story. If Barnes perceives it to be of value, he might be tempted to pass the story over to a more experienced journalist, which would leave Simon with nothing to show for his efforts.

"Have the police checked the local CCTV yet?"

"Didn't ask. Don't suppose they'll bother," Barnes says to the ceiling. "If no one moans, they'll probably let it go. Still, shame, could've done with something a bit more relevant, bit more *now* for the news desk. Think there's anything in it?"

"I can give you a few lines about how the police are under-resourced and therefore don't have the time to give a toss about every bum who gets busted up on their patch."

"Might be an idea. Oh well, can't do much for the poor bloke for the moment. Still, have a dig around a bit. See if we can do something with it. Never know, bloke might turn out to have an unusual back-story. You know, ex-Thatcher cabinet minister, spymaster, rocket scientist, decorated war hero, something like that."

Simon frowns, trying hard to resist relaxing into a similar bath of indifference. "Is that the right way to look at it?"

"Doubt it," Barnes muses. "but it wouldn't hurt to see if you can dig up a bit more about him." The editor pauses and returns to casting his thoughts about the ceiling. "Funny thing! War veteran. Just thought of it as I said it. The bell tinkled when you mentioned his name yesterday. Didn't they used to call soldiers from the Great War Tommys? I'm sure I remember reading it somewhere: The Last Tommy. No, hang on: The Last Fighting Tommy. Wasn't that Harry Patch? The last surviving Tommy who fought in the trenches in the Great War? I remember now. Made the Nelson, didn't he? III when he died. Was it last year or the year before?"

"Summer, year before last," Simon confirms.

"That's right," Barnes says, as though he is about to witness a revelation. "Tommy Atkins, that rings a bell, too." He stares harder at the ceiling for a moment. "Wellington or was it Kipling? Let's see. Ah, yes. Kipling wrote a poem, didn't he? *Tommy*. Something about a soldier going into a pub for a pint and getting lousy treatment instead. Got it: *O it's Tommy this, an' Tommy that, an' "Tommy go away", but it's "Thank you Mister Atkins," when the band begins to play.* The origin is a bit older, if I remember correctly. Flanders Campaign, middle of the nineteenth century. Wellington. Yes, Wellington asked a badly wounded private how he was. The soldier replied something about it being 'all in day's work' and promptly snuffed it. Private Thomas Atkins, that was supposed to have been his name." He sits back, taking in imaginary applause from the gallery.

"You know you're wasted at this job. Should be hosting University Challenge," Simon adds, oozing sarcasm. "Soon as Paxman retires, I'm going to put your name forward."

Barnes rides right across the slightly oblique compliment. "Might be something in that. Perhaps his name wasn't Atkins after all. Perhaps he is worth a nose."

"And perhaps," Simon is under no illusion as to which direction his editor is now travelling in, "nobody really gives a toss."

Barnes sits up straight, widens his eyes and opens his mouth to speak.

"I've got it," Simon cuts in as he stands, "I'll let you know what I can find, check missing persons, all that. Just one thing?"

Barnes smiles, almost affectionately were it not for the part cynical, part mischievous glint in his eye. "Ask away, son."

"The club, Slick in the City, have we got any *in* with it? Know anyone who works there?"

"Bobby Smith might. He knows most of the dives in and around town."

"Bobby Smith? The Australian?"

"Yes."

"Doubt he'd give me the froth off his beer. When I tried to introduce myself to him, he said something about my not being here long enough to warm the seat and wandered off."

"Mm, can be a bit prickly, Bobby. You'll get used to it."

Excerpt 2 from transcript of conversation with Joseph Naarda

SP: You mentioned your father had taught in Baghdad and that he was expelled from the college. In my experience, teachers tend to have strong political views, was that a factor in your father being expelled?

JN: Yes, it was why he was expelled. You see, Simon, to begin with my father had advocated the socialist principles and the pan-Arab ideology of the Ba'ath Party. He liked the idea that Sunni and Shi'a would be brought together to form one great Arab Nation. But as soon as Saddam came to power, the monster that was Saddam appointed his family and friends to the top positions, executed those they could not trust and murdered anyone who was brave, or foolish enough, to protest.

After he was expelled from the college in Baghdad, my father moved back to Basra to teach at the boy's school. Yet he felt betrayed by Saddam and could not let go of his anger. He must have spoken out of turn, because one day some men from the *mukhabarat* appeared at the school—"

SP: The mukhabarat?

TK: Yes, the *mukhabarat,* the secret police. They ordered my father to join the Ba'ath Party and when he refused, they threatened to have him dismissed.

SP: I understand Saddam distrusted the people of Basra?

JN: Distrusted? Despised? Yes, it was true, though Saddam did not look kindly on anywhere that wasn't Baghdad. He could not bear the thought that people in the fish market were talking about him behind his back. You know, Simon, it is difficult to believe but Saddam possessed a paranoia even larger than his ego.

SP: So, your father was dismissed for a second time?

JN: No, not exactly dismissed. One fine morning in January and I remember it so, so clearly... We had been blessed with rain the day before and the sky was blue and the air very fresh. My father left to walk to the school and as I watched him walk away down the road, I thought how lucky I was to have such a man of conviction for my father.

Sadly, it was the last time I saw him. It was the last time I saw him and the first time I began to understand that our world had changed.

9

They are standing at the bar of the nightclub, drinking cocktails.

"Never figured you to try this place again after what happened last time," she says, leaning against him and raising her voice just enough to make herself heard above a Cicada Remix.

"Yeah, I know, Candy. Just thought you might like another evening out; thought I might try harder. You know, if at first you don't succeed?"

"You thought, huh? Well, that's a first. Never figured journos for thinking. Conspiring, colluding and conniving, perhaps. Thinking? Blimey, whatever next? Mind you, Slick in the City isn't exactly the Front Line Club, is it," she quips, referring to one of the more favoured of journalist's watering holes. "Not that I'm not grateful, Si," she leans in again and winks conspiratorially, "but if I didn't know better, I'd think you were trying to bribe me into signing off your expenses; imaginative as some of them are."

"Candy?" he mocks, with a wry smile. "Even us hacks like a bit of downtime. You know: all work and no play-"

"Yes, Simon," she interrupts. "Yes, I'm sure it does. And there

I was thinking that all you prima donnas did when you got home was the crossword, read the dictionary or engaged in some other equally trivial pursuit. Fancy a dance?"

Candy is like Simon, in as much as she is tall and blonde, although Simon is fair-haired rather than blond. There, though, the resemblance ceases, as she is the one wearing a white sleeveless, open-knit T-shirt dress.

"No hurry. Let's have a couple more looseners," he says, desperate to swerve on the dancing.

He orders Candy her Moscow Mule, makes small talk and watches the bar staff, the waiters, the bouncers and the floor managers as they go about their business.

The tall, broad-shouldered and hair-braided Polynesian comes and goes. He looks unimpressed by all the flesh on display and, what with his vaguely morose expression complementing his lumbering gait, he seems casually disinterested in his work. Simon also notices that every time the hulking man passes through the entrance, he has to swipe his card in the same way that all the clubbers have to swipe theirs.

After a couple more cocktails, he asks Candy to dance. She, just as she had danced on New Year's Eve, moves as though her every sinew is pre-programmed to interpret the rythm into some form of sexual provocation. Simon just moves, uncomfortably, awkwardly, as though rhythm is a stranger he's only recently been introduced to. She laughs, though not unkindly, and when other men sidle into her space, this time she simply turns her back.

A squat youth, wearing a floral shirt and an excess of perspiration, steps in and attempts to make eye contact with her. When his attentions begin to wear thin, Candace stills, fixes on Simon, raises her eyebrows and nods towards the bar.

"Why is there always one?" she remarks, as she sips another Mule.

"Can't knock him for taste. That string vest you're wearing is..."

55

"Simon? You said you'd liked me in something sexy. What did you want me to wear, a burqa?"

As she says it, the squat individual who'd continually invaded her space on the dance floor repeats his mistake and pushes in next to her.

"Now that I'd like to see," he says, turning to face her.

"What?" she asks, irritated.

"You in a burqa." He leers rudely. "I've always wondered if taking all that disguise off adds a little spice to sex. What's your name, love? I'm Kenny, pleased to meet you." He holds out his hand.

Candy scowls, ignores his hand and inches away from him.

"Haven't seen you here before," he continues, edging round her.

Candy rolls her eyes at Simon, sighs and then turns her attention back to the young man. "I'm doing fine thank you, Kenny. Now piss off and find someone your own age to play with, there's a good boy."

Simon stifles a chuckle.

Their intruder, though, isn't fazed. "Don't be like that, love. I was just saying to my mates that any girl who can dance like you should be on the stage."

Candy bridles and sips her Mule.

"You don't by any chance work at Spearmint Rhino, do you? It's just that last time I saw an arse as good as yours, it was wrapped round a pole in Uxbridge."

Simon steps between them: "Listen, friend. The lady and I would rather you left us alone, know what I mean?"

The man who has introduced himself as Kenny, rounds on Simon. "Yeah," he says, "I do know what you mean. What I don't know is, what's a bird like 'er doing with a librarian like you? Don't you lot need regular chapters of beauty sleep?"

"Apparently not, no. Now look," Simon stands as tall as his humour will permit and steels his tone, "like the lady said, piss off and find someone your own size to play with before your mum shows up to take you home."

People around them at the bar shrink back expectantly. The barman disappears.

"Oh, not again," Candy moans.

Kenny steps forward so that his face is only inches from Simon's and glares at him, threateningly: "You sure you're up for this? You librarians ain't noted for your ability to mix it with the real stuff. Eh? Eh?"

"Now, we haven't got any trouble here, have we?" booms a deep-yet-gentle voice.

Kenny, like the Jack Russell he is undoubtedly bred from, bares his teeth. "Trouble?" he snarls and glances sideways up at the Goliath beside him. "No, no trouble. This idiot thinks he's hard. Well, let me educate you, you dozy tub of Hawaiian lard: you ain't hard enough neither. You might be big, but that means you'll only hurt yourself even more when you go down, same as all the others."

"Well, sir," the bouncer replies, calmly. "My name, just so that you remember it, is Tamati. Or to you, right now, it is *sir*. And I'm not from Hawaii. Close, but no cigar. And it's my job to make sure all you good people have a nice evening. So, is everything cool here?"

Simon smiles, apologetically: "Fine by me."

"Well it ain't fine by me," Kenny snipes, turning back and pointing rudely at Simon. "This tosser insulted me."

"Is that right, sir? Did you insult this man?"

Simon sighs. "Yes, I'm afraid I did. Stupid of me. Look," he holds out his hand, "I'm sorry. I apologise. It's just that this guy was bothering my girlfriend."

Candy beams at his declaration.

"Only," Simon continues, "I thought the policy was not to let minors in here, so I was surprised to find—"

The little man yelps, "Why you—" and leaps.

The bouncer reaches out as the smaller man passes him, fastens on to his collar and lifts Kenny far enough off the floor that his feet won't reach it.

"You're making this extremely hard for me to like you, sir," Tamati states. "Perhaps it's time you left."

"Hang on," he squeals, his shoulders hunched as though he is hung up on a peg, "I'm not the one who's in the wrong, I—"

Two other similarly black-suited heavies appear and the wheedling Kenny is frog-marched towards the door. As he leaves, the sea of clubbers parts and closes behind him.

Candy sniggers, "Wasted a good set of teeth when they gave him an arsehole, didn't they?"

Simon flinches. "Guess you must be used to that sort of thing. We've only been out twice and..."

"Mm," she grins, "in fact, so bloody often the compliment is beginning to wear a little thin." She links her arm in his and steers him back to the bar. "Now, where were we before we were so rudely interrupted?"

"Another Mule, Candy?" He slaps a couple of notes on the bar.

"Why not?" Candy watches him, slightly doe-eyed. "You know, she says, "if I didn't know you better, I might be inclined to think you'd have gone the distance with that guy just to preserve my honour."

"Why, Candy!"

Their evening wanders easily and loudly along, but Simon is distracted. Past midnight, he catches sight of the Polynesian bouncer deep in conversation with a stern-faced man at the bar.

Simon suggests it will soon be time for them to leave and without waiting for her response, herds Candy off the floor for a final cocktail. As he orders, he hovers behind the mountainous wall of the man's shoulders, waiting for him to conclude his conversation.

"Tamati?" he calls, as the man makes towards a door at the back. Simon notices the blue Security Industry Licence identification card hanging from the lanyard round the Polynesian's wide neck. He introduces Candy and while they chat, Simon makes a mental note of the name, the licence expiry date and the sequence of numbers as stamped above the silver chip on the ID card. As soon as he's got the details clear in his mind, he excuses himself and slips into the restroom to jot them down.

When he gets back, he slips his arm round Candy's waist and says to Tamati, "I wanted to thank you properly for cooling that guy. He was being a real pain. Left me no way out."

The vast Polynesian stares back at him. His blank expression does not suggest he is uncomprehending; rather it suggests he is more accepting of his lot, as though his having to eject people from the club is not unusual and therefore not worth remarking. "Sad guy. No bother, huh."

"Guess you must have to work out to keep yourself in shape," Simon says. "Some bro-science, eh?"

His face cracks into a smile; though it is far more fearsome than any smile Simon has met before. "Heaps."

"My name's Simon, Simon Peckham. Like London's favourite borough."

Candy rolls her eyes.

"Where do you work out, Tamati, local place?"

"Yeah nah bro, good place over in Bethnal Green. Back of the King's Head, know it?"

"Sure. Nice place." Simon takes one last glance at the Kiwi's licence card. "Thanks anyway, Tamati. See you around."

"Not if I see you first, Cuz." He grins, turns and lumbers away.

Candy is wide-eyed. "Man, he must be one of the biggest guys I've ever met. Nice though, eh?"

"Yes," Simon says, still watching the braided tower as he bends to get through the kitchen door, "he is that. Time to go. Why don't you get your coat and I'll meet you by the exit?"

"Do we have to, Si?" she mopes, draping her arm over his shoulder and subtly pulling him closer? "I was just getting used to being around you."

"Yes, we do. Now go and get your coat, there's a good girl."

Candy frowns like a child who's just had her teddy taken away, then sashays extravagantly away to the cloakroom, turning once to check he is watching.

Simon turns about and follows in the footsteps of the giant Tamati. When he reaches the same door, he opens it and is greeted by a fanfare of clanging pots and clashing dishes. A host of Asian and Eastern European faces look up at him, questioning. He waves an apology and leaves.

Fortunately, Candy is waiting for him by the time he has fought his way to the exit. They leave, and once outside she shivers and nestles close against him.

As they wait for the cab, a figure strides smartly up to them.

"Simon!" Candy shrieks, pulling him back away from the pavement.

But he isn't to be moved. He stands his ground and she shrinks behind him.

It is the diminutive Kenny. He doesn't look happy. "'Ere, guv, you didn't tell me you was gonna be in there 'alf the bloody night. I'm gonna charge you waiting time."

"Sorry, Kenny, mate," Simon says, casually. "Wouldn't have looked right if I'd come straight out. Get anything?"

"Sure, boss. That bouncer, the big bloke you was talking to. Boots, they call 'im. Regular pharmacy: Mandy, Special K, Honey Oil, usual disco funsters. Not sure about Boomers or Roofies; couple of blokes got a bit leery when I asked about the darker stuff, know-what-I-mean. Apparently, he don't do Crystal or Charlie. 'Suppose that means he's not a frontline trooper, eh?"

"Yes, Kenny. I suppose it does."

The smaller man digs in his pocket and hands over a couple of blue pills. "'ad to give a bit extra for the tabs."

"Librarian?"

Kenny sniggers, "Well, you being good with words 'n all. Thought it was appropriate."

Simon shakes his head in dismay and pays up.

"Cheers, guv," Kenny says. "Thanks for the job: I'm about if you need me. See you, eh?" And with that he is off up the road.

Candy swings Simon around. "Oh, Si," she mumbles in a pleasingly seductive tone, as she nuzzles his neck, "Thanks for a wonderful evening, you absolute shit."

EXCERPT 3 FROM TRANSCRIPT OF CONVERSATION WITH JOSEPH NAARDA

SP: Joseph, did you attend the school where your father had taught?

JN: Yes, I studied languages and mathematics. Unusual subjects to put together perhaps, but for me they share a certain construction.

SP: And after school?

JN: After I finished school and because my English was good, I worked for my grandfather. He was a merchant, a trader; dates mostly. You know there used to be twelve million date palms in the groves around Basra. Imagine, one million tons of dates. It was good work. I enjoyed it.

Then, five years into the war with Iran, I was conscripted into the army. Conscripted, you understand, not my choice.

We were sent to recapture the peninsula, at Al-Faw, which we did, eventually. It was a terrible battle. Barbaric. Brutal. And after we had captured it, the Iranians tried to take it back. Did you know that the Iranian troops herded children before them so their vehicles would not be damaged by the mines? They convinced these children that if they gave their lives for their God, they would become martyrs, that they would live in heaven and enjoy all they were not permitted to enjoy on earth. It is strange to think that now it is grown men who believe this. Children perhaps, yes, but grown men?

SP: You were fortunate to survive.

JN: Yes, I was very fortunate.

SP: And after the war, you returned to Basra?

JN: Yes.

SP: And your grandfather was still trading?

JN: No. My grandfather was killed in an artillery bombardment during the time the Iranians tried to capture Basra. Life is strange, don't you think? There I was, fighting only twenty miles from our city. I lived, he died, and that was the end of the family business. I returned to nothing. We had nothing.

SP: Your father had gone missing some years before and now your grandfather was dead, too. That made you head of the household?

JN: Yes, when I returned to the family home, all the women were widows.

SP: When did you meet your wife?

JN: I had met Salwa just before I was conscripted. Her grandfather was a silversmith. Many of the Subba, the Mandaeans, are silversmiths. They are truly gifted. They possess great ability with metals and their work is very beautiful, very fine. The old man had a shop in the Suk esh-Sheikh, in Basra. That was where I first saw her. I had gone there to buy a bracelet for my mother. That first time I saw Salwa, and from that moment, I knew we would be together.

During the long nights in those trenches, especially when I was certain I would be killed, the only thoughts that kept me from going mad were my thoughts of Salwa. Eyes gold and green like the sand beneath the sea; skin the colour of a burnished shield; and tall, so tall, so elegant. You have heard the expression 'as handsome as a Subbi'? Well, they are not all so. The Subba of the marshes around Basra are dark-eyed, dark-skinned and most of them short; they are not beautiful in the Western sense. Salwa, though, is of a higher caste. Her father was a *ganzibra*, a high priest?

SP: Yes, I know, Soraya told me. So, you returned from the war to find Salwa?

JN: Yes. I went back to Basra and, as you would say, every cloud has a silver lining, for that was when I met Salwa again. I saw her in the market; just like that. She was in the Hannah Sheikh buying green silk for a wedding veil, for a relation. It was as though all the troubles of the previous years had been lifted from my shoulders. It was as if they had never taken place. We were married soon after. A wonderful day. Her family came to our wedding even though they did not look kindly on her marrying outside their own. You know, sons-in-law are not permitted to take their faith. Not that I would have done, for by the time the war finished I had begun to question my faith. Like innocence and truth, faith also is a casualty of war.

10

Simon wakes up on the sofa, his neck sore, his head a shade tender and his ego more than a shade bruised.

Candy stumbles out of his bedroom. He is relieved to see she is dressed if, he decides, wearing one of his city-stripe shirts qualifies her as dressed. The shirt is sleep-creased and too short for her long torso.

"I suppose a cup of coffee would be too much to ask?" she moans. "And have you got any Omez and a paracetamol? My head and my stomach are a bit spiteful this morning."

"Omez?"

"Yes, Omez. Omeprazole."

"You didn't tell me you've got an ulcer, Candy."

"Well, I haven't, you muppet. It just feels like I have." She studies him, self-consciously pulling the hem of his shirt down.

"No, Candy, I don't have any Omez. You might find a paracetamol in the bathroom drawer. I know I didn't ask last time, but how'd you like your coffee?"

"Oh, you know," she giggles seductively, "like my men: strong and— Christ! Is that the time?"

Simon busies himself with the kettle and a cup. "Yes, that's the time. Will you be wearing that shirt all day or—"

"Don't be daft. I always keep stuff for the next day in the office in case the evening gets a little out of hand. Not like last night, if you know what *I* mean?" she adds, sarcastically.

"Look, Candy, I know it was a bit of a setup and I know I probably should've told you. Me and clubs? Chalk and cheese. I think that's only the fourth or fifth club I've ever been into since I left uni and I needed you to be kind of natural. If we'd have rehearsed it, the security would've sussed us."

Candy pouts, her blonde locks cascading around her face. "Yeah, well, thing is, if I don't get down the office before the others arrive, they'll think we... you know."

Simon smiles, warmly, putting his arm round her shoulders and kissing her on her forehead.

"Steady on, Si," she growls.

"Well, Angel, we didn't. Tell them that."

Candy is insulted. She pulls away. "No, thanks very much. I don't know what's worse, being hung for a sheep or a lamb."

His bedroom door slams.

When Candy has gone, Simon picks up the phone and taps in the number of the local Health Trust.

"Press office."

"Yes, hi, good morning, Miriam, it's Simon Peckham from the London Evening Star. Did you have a nice Christmas break?"

"Hello Simon, super, thank you. Haven't heard from you in a while, thought you must've been let go."

"Very droll, thank you Miriam." He recalls the last time he'd phoned the media office.

"What can I do for you, Simon?"

"New Year's night, or may have been just after, a man was brought into A&E by ambulance from down near Bishopsgate. I need to get an update on how he's doing."

"Now you know very well, Simon," Miriam's humour shrivels, "that I can't release any information regarding a patient's condition or progress without the consent of a relative. Is the gentleman in question a relative of yours?"

"No, Miriam. Not that I know of."

"Then—"

"On the other hand," he talks quickly, "I don't think he has any relatives; he's a rough sleeper." He allows a couple of seconds for the information to sink in and when she goes to reply, he interrupts her again. "And the reasons for my call are A, to find out how he is and B, to find out if anyone has found or has tried to find any of his relatives." His veiled accusation is a gamble. She might tell him to go to hell or she might not like the idea of his writing a piece about how homeless patients are chucked back out onto the street, or worse dumped in a pauper's grave.

"I must say, Simon, it's a better line than telling me if I don't give you the information you'll get the sack. What's his name; I'll see what I can do."

"Thomas Atkins."

"Which hospital?"

"The Royal London."

"Admitted when, you say?"

"New Year's Day, early morning."

"You want me to call you back when I've found him?"

"If you don't mind, Miriam, I'd like to hang on."

"You realise I can't give you much more than a very general idea, no details? Wouldn't want you to go printing something that would offend the relatives of, or prove detrimental to the recovery, of our patient." Her flat tone tells him she is doing something else while talking. "Atkins, Thomas," she repeats, "Royal London, December 31st." Miriam pauses. "Sorry, no can do."

"Oh, come on, I know he's there I spoke to the paramedics on New Year's morning and went up to the ICU."

"Unless he's been transferred?" she supposes. "In which case, I'd have thought I'd have a record of his discharge, which I don't. Are you absolutely sure his name is Atkins? Absolutely one hundred per cent really sure?"

Something about her tone alerts him. She's not being dismissive, which is how he expects her to be; rather she's...

"No, if I'm honest, I'm not. Look Miriam, this fellow is a rough sleeper and it's quite possible that whoever he belongs to doesn't know he's in hospital. If he hasn't got anyone to care for him, then there's not much I can do for him. But and it's a big but, if he has, don't you think he deserves a little luck. You know as well as I do that keeping him in hospital for the moment, only to patch him up and send him back out onto the streets, isn't going to help you keep him out of hospital in the long term. If you give me his surname, perhaps I can trace his family. That at least might give him a future and help lighten the load on your under-resourced and over-stretched NHS."

"Mm, nice line," she scoffs, amused. "You know, Simon, I don't get paid to do your job for you." Miriam pauses, as though waiting to see whether the coin she's tossed lands heads up or tails down. "However, all I can tell you is that one *Thomas Williams* is no longer with us."

Williams not Atkins. "Can you tell me where he's been transferred to then?"

Miriam chortles, "If I knew that Simon, I'd be one up on my rabbi and knowing him as I do, I don't think he'd take very kindly to that."

"I'm not with you."

"Oh, Simon." She waits, hoping. However, when she realises he is doing the same, she gives up. "Williams, Thomas, admitted as you suggest in the early hours of New Year's Day and sadly deceased later the same. And although he has a lengthy list of attendances, and not unusually many of them through the winter, so far no one has come forward to claim him. All of which means, I have no problem releasing this information to you so that you may enjoy greater success in locating them. Now, anything else I can help you with?"

Williams. Thomas Williams not Thomas Atkins. Barnes was right. Tommy Atkins was simply a moniker the other rough sleepers had pinned on the old soldier.

The fact that there is no one to care about the old man's passing saddens him and he makes a note to look out for the inquest. Simon puts down the phone and notices the small black notebook lying beside it.

He stares at it without seeing it. Then, when the ghost of Thomas Williams has risen and wandered away, he picks up the notebook and begins to go through it again.

11

There is little point in contacting the four national tracing services he would normally use, or accessing the two heritage sites and National Archive at Kew: the notebook doesn't present him with either full surnames or dates of birth. The only hard information lies in the first names and the list of towns and pubs.

After a good deal of head-scratching, he falls back on the logic that the details must run in the order of first name and nickname. And that tenuous supposition is why he is on the train rattling and swaying through the Sussex countryside.

The last entry, one of the few with a line across the page, reads *Enfield* and *Royal Oak*, the preceding name *Jo*, nickname *Cruds*. A couple of days before, Simon had taken the tube out to Enfield to search out the Royal Oak and ask if anyone at the bar knew of a Jo whose nickname might be Cruds.

After losing himself in the warren of streets that twisted and turned through the grey housing estates, he'd arrived at the Royal Oak only to find that some developer had levelled it and was busy carting the rubble away. He'd asked the digger driver but the fellow hadn't spoken any form of shared English, so he'd knocked on a few doors. Most of the residents hadn't lived in Enfield long enough to remember what the pub had been like in its heyday. If, they'd supposed, it had ever enjoyed one.

He was met with a similar welcome at the Highwayman in Epping, the pub named in the second last entry. The good news: the pub was still standing. The bad news: the pub was derelict, its windows boarded over with cold silver mesh.

The third from last entry notes the *Jolly Sailor* in Portslade, the names before being *Derek* and, perhaps unsurprisingly, *Del Boy*. And this time at least, he knows the place is up and running because he's phoned ahead to check.

The pub turns out to be a short walk down a breezy Boundary Road and by the time he arrives Simon can taste the wind-born salt from the sea. The Jolly Sailor is red brick and tile, and flyers at the windows advertise quiz nights, darts matches and discounted meals for pensioners.

Simon asks for a mineral water and perches at the bar. The porthole clock suggests he has made it in good time for the lunchtime crowd, sparse as it is.

Once he has allowed the stool to warm beneath him, he catches the barman's eye.

"You'd like to order something?"

"Oh, sure," Simon, though, hasn't thought to consult the menu. "Fish and chips, please."

"Certainly." He scribbles on a notepad. "That'll be eight pounds." The barman, though not tall, has to lean down beneath the rack of glasses hanging over the bar.

"Good value," Simon remarks.

"Well, it's not Brighton prices and we're twice the quality." He disappears to the kitchen.

When he comes back and has served a drift of pensioners, Simon beckons him over.

"Have you got a moment?"

The barman nods.

"It's nothing strange and I'm not the law or anything... Do you know a guy by the name of Derek?"

He rolls up his sleeves, as if winding up his memory. "No, don't believe I do. Derek, you say." He taps his lip and searches the textured ceiling paper. "Used to be a Derek, come in now and again; that was a few years back. Why? What's he done?"

"Nothing as far as I'm aware." Simon had expected a measure of reticence. "It's a family thing."

"You family, then?" he asks, his tone ladled with suspicion.

"No. It's just that someone may have left him some money and I'm trying to locate him."

"One of those heir hunters, are you?"

"Something like that," Simon offers.

"Derek?" He scratches his unruly mop of curls. "Nope. Sorry."

"Might be known by the name of Del Boy, something like that?"

"Del Boy, as in Trotter?" The barman raises his eyebrow and the corners of his mouth slope down, suggesting he may know the name and is considering whether he should admit to it.

"As I said, there might be a bit of money in it for him," Simon says, adding quickly, "That's if I can locate him."

"Used to be a lad come in here, wild lad. Hang on a minute, I'll ask out the back. The chef, she's been here longer than me."

He is gone a while and Simon strains to hear the discussion taking place around the corner. All he can make out, though, are the words 'not another bloody reporter'.

When the barman returns, his dour expression betrays whatever instruction the chef has supplied him. "Thought so. Used to be a fellow came in here called him Del Boy. Name wasn't Trotter, though, it was Roarke. Would only be natural if it was."

"How so?"

As the barman pulls back the tap handle, he explains: "Well, Del Boy as in Derek and Trotter. Only Fools and Horses, get it?"

"Of course, didn't see the connection." Except that he did or rather had. The puzzled look on his face is due to the chef's remark about the possibility of his being another bloody reporter. "So the bloke I'm looking for might go by the name of Roarke."

"Could do," the barman decides. "Must be hundreds of Dereks nicknamed Del Boy if their surname's Trotter."

"Yes, I bet there are." Simon pauses, studying the floor. "Well, you've been most helpful, thank you. Can I get you a drink for your trouble?"

The barman starts to accept, then changes his mind. He inclines his head very briefly towards the passageway through to the kitchen. "Best not, bit early to start. Leave you to it. Your fish and chips will be along in a minute."

When Simon has eaten, he makes to leave. But before he gets to the door, a short, round woman with piggy eyes, a button nose and chef's apron appears behind the bar. She scrutinises him as though he is some rare form of plankton.

"Great fish and chips," Simon acknowledges, and at the risk of overdoing it adds, "Much better than the stuff you get in Brighton."

The woman is unmoved by his compliment.

He walks back up Boundary Road, a freshening wind troubling the hair at his neck.

The screen of condensation on the window of a café draws him and he orders a cup of tea, hoping it will settle his indigestion.

Simon checks an online directory on his phone. There is an O'Roark in Shoreham, a couple of miles along the coast, and one Mrs Victoria Roarke in Portslade. He jots down the addresses, settles up and leaves.

The station taxi reeks of freshly applied bleach but, he is

relieved to find, the house lies only a few minutes the other side of the coast road.

Up past the Recreation Ground, the front gardens of the white bungalows are paved over for parking; their red-tiled roofs home to a spray of television aerials pointing skyward like swordfish bills. The taxi pulls up outside number 53.

Simon waits patiently at the door, studying the view: the Channel is washed battleship grey and a couple of miles offshore a coaster ploughs a lonely furrow. Seagulls wheel and squabble on the wind.

A middle-to-late aged woman answers the door. She watches and waits.

After an awkward silence, during which Simon decides she is either mute or suspicious of him, he introduces himself: "Sorry to bother you, Mrs Roarke, is Derek in?"

She looks him up and down. "Who wants him?"

"A friend. Actually, I'm a friend of Jo, Cruds."

The woman examines his shoes before asking: "Cruds, eh? You sure you're not from the bank? I don't want you going upsetting him now." She nods towards the side of the house. "He's round the back, working on his car."

"Thank you, Mrs Roarke." Simon steps back.

"You sure you're not from the bank; you're awfully polite," she calls after him.

Round the side, a narrow drive leads to a garden shed which doubles as a garage. The bonnet of an ageing red Mini protrudes from between the double doors, its front raised on axle stands, its grill faded, its headlights, like its front wheels, absent.

A thirty-something year old man is inching awkwardly out through the gap between the door and the car. He has close cropped dark hair, piercing grey eyes and a stubbled jaw. A vivid tattoo of a dagger runs down his right forearm and in spite of the cold, he is wearing shorts. His right leg is prosthetic.

At first, he ignores Simon. Then he reconsiders and turns to him. "Yes, mate. What can I do for you?"

"I'm not sure, really. Maybe nothing. Are you Derek?"

"To some." Sharp blades of aggression trim his response.

"My name's Simon; Simon Peckham. I'm a journalist." He holds out his hand.

"Well, if you're from the press, you can piss off right now. I'm done with you lot. To you bastards, we're bloody heroes one minute and common criminals the next. I wouldn't eat my fish and chips out of your copy. Go on, shove off." He walks towards Simon, all the while wiping his hands on an oily rag.

"I had a feeling you were going to say that." Simon thins his lips in apology. "But whoever you've been bothered by from the press, I'm not with them. And," he adds hurriedly, "I've no idea why they would be bothering you. I just need some information about you and Cruds and the others."

"Course you do, mate." Derek 'Del Boy' Roarke walks stiltedly towards him, the dagger tattooed on his right forearm all too prominent. "That's all you lot ever want. Like I've already said, I haven't got anything to add. So do me a favour and get off my drive before I throw you off it." He pauses, before shouting in a voice so loud it makes Simon's hair curl, "Go on, fuck off."

Simon holds up his hands in surrender. "Sure. Okay. I'll go. Just one question. Please?" He takes a step back, wanting Roarke to know he is on the move.

"It's always the same with you guys," Roarke mutters. "Just ten seconds, just one minute, just a couple of questions. Alright, go on, then. What do you want to know?"

"It's about Jo."

The man looks back, his expression flat, unpromising.

Simon is swimming in the dark. "Jo? Cruds?"

"Well, mate." He draws a large spanner from his back pocket and begins to clean it with the same rag he has just wiped his hands on. "If you're asking about Cruds, you mean Jo Crudup. What do you want to know about him?"

"Where can I find him?"

"Cruds? Where can you find him?" His tone suggests Simon is being as thick as his expression lets on. "In London, of course."

"Exactly where in London?"

Roarke scoffs. "Could be anywhere, really."

"How so?"

"Well, right about now and depending on the wind and the tide, he could be anywhere between the Isle of Dogs and Richmond. Though recalling how good the little bugger was at getting in and out of confined spaces, he might have got past Richmond Lock and be all the way up to Kemble which, if my memory serves me correctly, is where the source of the Thames is located. Mind you, having chucked what was left of him off Tower Bridge a couple of months back, he'll be doing well to have made it that far." He pauses, waiting to see if his information has sunk in. "You got that, mate? Reading from the same page, are we? Or is your existence that cushy you don't understand what they get up to at a crematorium?"

Simon looks round for a significant hole in which to hide. "Yes, I've got it. His ashes. I'm sorry. Sorry for your loss, I mean."

"Not my loss, mate. Bloke was a first-rate arsehole. Bloody good arsehole, though; one of the best men I've ever seen behind a GPMG. Now clear off before I do something with this spanner it wasn't rightly designed for."

———

The train lurches to a halt at Haywards Heath. A dowdy woman with a smell under her nose sits down opposite him.

Simon accesses the announce.jpress website using his phone and searches the family notices. He enters *Jo Crudup, Enfield,* then a date range for the last two months and a notice type as *acknowledgement*. His phone signal is interrupted continuously, but eventually the details come up.

Jo Crudup: Acknowledgement

Jonathan James Crudup, 24, 32 Roland Crescent, Enfield, passed away at Chase Farm Hospital on 1ˢᵗ November 2010, as a result of wounds sustained whilst in the service of his country. Only son of Brian and Agnes and partner to Josephine, the family would like to thank the doctors and staff of Selly Oak Hospital for all their attention and care, and to thank his many service colleagues for their support. He will never be forgotten.

A photograph of wild flowers accompanies the acknowledgement and the publication credit notes the *Enfield Herald* for *14ᵗʰ December 2010*.

Simon thinks back to meeting Derek Roarke. He shudders when remembering the violence of Roarke's voice, the vivid tattoo of the dagger on his forearm and the bare stump of his thigh fastened to his prothesis.

He scrolls through an expansive montage of garish military tattoos. Nothing similar appears and he stares dreamily out the window at the sodden pastures of the Weald racing by.

As they approach Gatwick, he watches the jet airliners queuing to land from the east. Simon googles *Parachute Regiment tattoos*. Most feature winged parachutes or death heads and dragons. *Royal Navy tattoos* feature mostly roped anchors, hearts and crowns. And after a lengthy process of recollection and deduction, he recalls a recent documentary of the Royal Marines on active service in Afghanistan.

Images of a double-edged Fairbairn-Sykes fighting knife jump straight out of his phone screen. Some are patched *Royal Marines Commando* below the haft; others are tattooed straight and simple from elbow to wrist.

"So that makes sense. Roarke and Crudup were in the Royal Marines together, both of them serving in Afghanistan."

The lady opposite sits up and looks down her nose at him.

He checks the information from the acknowledgements and obits against the entry marking Jo Crudup in the notebook: Brian and Agnes, his parents and Josephine, his partner, are all mentioned.

What had Derek Roarke said? "Best man I've ever seen behind a GPMG."

Simon glances up, then back to his phone. The code is the key to unlocking the qualifications or specialisations listed in the notebook. He googles *Royal Navy* and accesses the dedicated website. He scrolls along to *Marines* and down to *Specialisms*.

The letters at the bottom of each page aren't codes, they are abbreviations and each one corresponds to a listed career or specialism. *AS* equates to Armoured Support. *VM* to Vehicle Mechanic. *HW(ATK)* to Heavy Weapons (Anti-Tank). *HW(MOR)* to Heavy Weapons (Mortars). And the last one *PW(S)* to Platoon Weapons (Sniper). GPMG, which Simon googles and learns is the abbreviation for general-purpose machine gun, isn't among them; rather a Platoon Weapons (Machine Gunner) is listed as *PW(MG)*.

By the time the train pulls into Victoria, Simon has deciphered most of the abbreviations in the notebook and written the full version beside each name.

The old snoot sitting opposite is intrigued by his note-making and glowers back when she sees he has noticed her watching.

Simon sits back and congratulates himself on solving the riddle of curious abbreviations. Now that he knows Jo Crudup died on active service, it is logical to assume that the names on the pages lined through belong to those who have gone the same way. There are too many and the knowledge of their intimate details— their nicknames, the names of their nearest and dearest, and their favoured watering holes and specialisms—has brought these characters starkly to life. The loss of them generates a curious ache within him.

And though it is pleasing that he now understands what the notebook contains, there are two more fundamental questions that need to be answered: who does the book belong to and who among the characters whose first names he now knows will be willing to give up that information?

The train clacks and lurches into Victoria Station. Simon tucks the notebook in his jacket pocket and stands back for the lady opposite to exit first. She doesn't acknowledge his manners.

Excerpt 4 from transcript of conversation with Joseph Naarda

SP: With your grandfather dead and the business finished, how did you support your new wife?

JN: I found work in the Rumaila oil field, near the Kuwaiti border. They told me my English would help with talking to foreign engineers, even though most of the time I found myself doing manual work. It was hard work and hot and the money was not good, so to make enough for us to get by I used to make and sell alcohol, in the evenings at home. I made it from dates and raisins and, when I could buy it, from sugar cane. It was like Arak, only better and very popular. Soon I was doing well enough to open a small shop.

SP: Wasn't the Rumaila field tied up with why Saddam invaded Kuwait?

JN: Yes. Correct. Much later, it was. Saddam accused the Kuwaitis of drilling from beyond the border at an angle. He said they were stealing his oil.

SP: *Was it true?*

JN: At the time, I did not think so. None of us did. You must remember, Saddam did what he wanted. He was capricious. A true tyrant. And he possessed a green eye for the black money of Kuwait. Perhaps for the prestige of conquering it, too. As I said before, he liked to be worshipped as the valiant warrior. Valiant with the lives of others? Certainly. Vain? Absolutely.

SP: *And the First Gulf War began soon after Soraya was born?*

JN: Yes. First, Saddam invaded Kuwait and second, the Coalition Forces threw him out and separated Saddam from his oil fields, though he set fire to many. In the daytime, the smoke struck out the sun and, at night, the flames lent the sky a deathly glow. Imagine hell and you will know the colour.

SP: *And afterwards?*

JN: And afterwards, the Shi'a rebelled, thinking they would keep Saddam out of our city. Many Shi'a came in from Iran and many soldiers who had been in the army defected to join the rebels. Saddam, though, was ruthless. He drained the marshes so that we could not grow food, he put chemicals in the rivers so that we could not fish and he used poisoned gas to kill entire villages. Many of Salwa's people were relocated or worse, were murdered and buried in mass graves.

SP: *What about the years after that first invasion? Was life made hard for you?*

JN: From that time, life became hard, very hard. We had very little food and what there was, was incredibly expensive. Also, very little clean water. Many generations had laboured to create our Garden of Eden and in only a few weeks, Saddam had turned our Garden back into the desert it had once been. No, I am wrong, there was worse than desert; there was desolation.

SP: *Desolation?*

JN: Yes, desolation. You see, Simon, after Saddam had poisoned the land and the water, we had to deal with all the pollution the war had left behind. The air was toxic, contaminated with both the smoke from the burning oil wells and the radiation from the munitions of the war. Depleted Uranium, I think I'm right in calling it. Children began to die before they had the chance to grow and babies were born with the most dreadful disabilities: stomach and kidney tumours, leukaemia, encephalitis, skin complaints, paralysis. Many were born with such terrible conditions that their families killed them and buried them secretly. After all, there were no medicines to treat them, no hospital facilities, no vaccines and even no doctors.

It was like a bad dream. Except it wasn't a dream. We know this: our family still bears the scars.

You know, Simon, when I tell people this, they think I must be talking about something that happened in another world, in another lifetime. But this did not: it happened only a few years ago and it happened in a world that was supposed to have learned the lessons from the war to end all wars.

12

"Hey, Tamati?"

The gargantuan Polynesian hesitates, his braids swinging as he lurches to a halt.

"It's me, Simon Peckham. You helped me out of a fix in the club the other night, remember?" Simon has dressed down just enough to give the impression he doesn't conform to any particular social group.

Tamati trawls his memory, his face eventually cracking into a smile. "Oh, yeah. Peckham. Like London's favourite borough. Sure, I remember."

They are standing outside a kebab café, a few doors down from the money transfer shop Tamati has just vacated and just around the corner from the gym behind the King's Head, where he had told Simon he works out.

"Got time for a fruit tea or power-juice or whatever you 'crowd supervisors'," Simon punctuates with his fingers, "drink when you're off duty?"

"Na, man. Got places to be. Thanks all the same."

"Come on big guy. I owe you one from the other night. Got me and my girl out of a hole. What about a spot of lunch? Bet you've worked out down the King's Head already, eh?" Simon glances down at the man's feet. "Can't be cheap to fill those size fifteens of yours."

Tamati looks down at his feet, as if to check they are still where they should be. When he looks back up—or rather halfway up—he grins.

"Doesn't have to be Turkish. We can do Thai, Chinese or sushi?"

"Nah, bro, kebab's good."

They take a table at the back and Simon encourages Tamati to squeeze into the seat furthest from the door. A stack of lamb, dripping with fat, rotates. A heavy-faced Ottoman slices.

"Lamb or Chicken?" Simon asks. "Shish or Doner? Pitta or chips? Guess you have to keep a pretty strict diet to stay in your kind of shape."

"You got it. Chicken. Meat only and a salad, please. Too much salt and grease with the lamb."

Simon orders and while they wait they debate the benefits of protein over carbohydrates. Their meal arrives quickly.

"Club open most nights?" Simon mumbles as he tucks into his Doner.

"Not Sundays."

"Pay good?"

"Na, man. Wages don't take into account how much it costs to live round here and there's no point in living too far out when you don't quit work until four in the morning." The knife and fork disappear beneath his expansive hands. "Mind you, the whole Uber thing has made it a lot easier on the wallet and those guys seem to work all hours."

"Still," Simon licks his thumb, "once you've taken the costs out, there can't be a much left to send home."

"Make no mistake, bro. Hardly seems worth it."

They chew the fat for a while.

Tamati cleans his plate and Simon, too, closes his plate and sits back, watching.

The silence stews until it is thick enough to stand their cutlery in.

"What's on your mind, Cuz?" Tamati asks.

"Couple or three things bothering me, my friend." Simon leans forward, though not so far forward that he is within easy reach. "Or make that more than a couple or three. And before I mention them, don't go all cocoa-bananas on me. Just listen to what I have to say." He waits.

Tamati nods.

"First thing: your SIA Licence." Simon states.

"What about it?"

"It's not out of date; that would be too obvious."

"So, what's the problem?"

"The problem is the licence isn't yours. Yours has been revoked and what you're hanging is someone else's. Or to be more accurate, the sixteen-digit licence number on your SIA refers to someone other than you. The photo on the card is you, no doubt about that. It's the numbers on the database that don't match."

Tamati grows about a foot and his eyes darken. "What are you, man? SIA inspector or what? You don't dress like one of them types."

"No. Keep your braids on, my friend. I'm not from the Security Industry Authority."

"How the hell do you know the licence isn't mine?" The big man rests his trunk-like forearms on the table and flexes his hands.

Simon sits back. "Bear with me on this, Tamati. Like I said, keep your hair on for a minute and just listen. I know the licence number isn't right because I've checked it. That's the easy part. But wearing an invalid licence is enough to get you and your employers

85

into a bucket-load of trouble. They get fined and get a slap on the wrists for not checking you out properly. You, my friend, get blacklisted, laid off and don't get to send your monthlies home. The injustice is that your employers can afford to hang you out to dry. That's a given. But, can you afford to hang your family out in the same fashion?"

"No such thing as a free lunch, huh?"

Simon bridles his smile. "No. Never has been and never will be. So at least we've worked out a couple of things. One: I'm not the law. Two: either they haven't checked your licence or they know your licence isn't straight. Same difference. They'll claim incompetence and you'll then end up on the wrong side of both them and the law."

Tamati sighs and relaxes briefly. "You said there were three things?"

"Yes, my friend, and this is the tricky bit." Simon summons his most uncompromising expression. "Friend of mine came across a couple of these in the club the other night." He fishes the blue pills from his pocket and flashes them quickly before putting them away. "Not so strange, really. Probably lots of *E* floating about every nightclub in town. And I'm sure loads of them get passed around or even dropped on the floor by people too hopped to remember where they put them. What bothers me, Tamati, is where my friend found them."

The big man's expression is as abstracted as those found on the faces of the monumental Moai on Easter Island: the kind of face on which a well-swung crowbar wouldn't leave a dent.

But Simon doesn't have a crowbar stuffed down his trousers; all he has is a pinch of knowledge to go with a good measure of braggadocio.

"My guess is, Tamati, that your employers don't pay you enough for you to split your wages between living in London and sending your dues home, and that to supplement your income you spread a little happiness around your tribe at the club. Now either they know what you're up to or they're incompetent. And knowing that your employers exist in what one might call the shadier margins of our society, I doubt it's the latter. Either way you find yourself stuck firmly between a rock and a hard place, and I'm the only one who can help you out."

Finally, the big man's head flops forward. His braids beat at his ears. "What are you man? You work for some other gang? What do you want? You said you're not the law?"

Simon hides his triumph. "No. It's as I said, I'm not the law. I'm a journalist and it's not in my interest to hang you out to dry. Believe it or not, I do my best to protect my sources, particularly when it comes to dealing with the kind of people you work for.

"What I want from you is a copy of the CCTV footage from the street and the foyer, and a printout of the entry register for New Year's Eve."

Tamati looks up. His eyes widen. "What? How the hell do you expect me to be able to get those, man?"

"Shouldn't be hard, my friend. Leastways not to a man as resourceful as you have shown yourself to be. I've even brought you a nice couple of 128 gig USBs to load the info onto."

"And what do you want this information for, bro?"

"Just looking for someone who may have been in the club that night, that's all."

The bouncer is chary of him.

"Look," Simon says, softening, "there's a girl I bumped into. Met her through work. She said she was in the club on New Year's Eve. We had a bit of fling and I, stupidly, didn't get her number. Thought it'd be nice to track her down. See if she wanted to... you know."

"You expect me to believe that?" Tamati moans.

Simon's stony expression betrays nothing of his white lie.

"You believe what you like, my friend. Just get me the list and the recording."

"You know what they'll do if they catch me trying to download this kind of data?"

"You know what I'll do if you don't. Look Tamati, if you get me the list, this all goes away." Simon turns to the counter and asks for the bill. When he turns back, the big man is still imagining. "Come on, my friend, you're quite capable of looking after yourself. Isn't that what you do for a living?"

"And what if I don't get you this stuff?"

"Then you and your employers can look forward to seeing your dubious enterprises plastered all over the front pages of the weekend tabloids. That's what I do for a living." Simon turns and glances at the Ottoman by the till. "I'll need a receipt, please?"

13

Simon rings the doorbell and waits.

He'd got lucky. One of the early entries in the notebook had read *Billy*, no second or nickname, *Liverpool, Mossley Hill* and *The Halfpenny*. He'd phoned the pub and asked to speak to Billy.

"Billy 'oo?" the answer had come back.

"Billy in the Royal Marines," he'd said, "I was having a chat with him the other night and—"

"Dunno 'oo yer on abou' mate. If you mean Billy Martin, 'e 'asn't been in since 'e was barred. And that were a good while ago."

The online telephone directory had done the rest.

Through the stained-glass panels of the door he sees a shadow darken the hallway. Locks snap. A bolt is drawn down and the door is pulled back.

"Do you have some kind of identification?" She is a good foot shorter than him, mid-thirties and her hair is jelled and spiky in a punkish manner.

"Sure." Simon hands over his blue press card.

She examines it briefly and then hands it back. "Well, even

though I wouldn't recognise you from the photograph I guess you must be who you say you are. Come in." She walks away down the hall, leaving him to close the door.

"Thank you for agreeing to see me, Ms Martin. I hope this isn't too much of an inconvenience."

"No bother, but I have a Pilates class in an hour so you'd better have a list of questions ready. This way." She ushers him into the front room.

The room is small. The parquet floor uncluttered apart from two green-leather Parker Knoll chairs sitting either side of a polished brown-tile fireplace. And judging by the clean and blacked grate, the hearth hasn't met with any warmth in a good while. The walls are decorated with Liverpool Football Club paraphernalia; the standout being a signed shirt pinned behind a glass frame, the liver bird emblazoned in gold on the chest. A photograph of Steven Gerrard holding aloft the Champions League Cup beside a slightly younger version of the woman who has just answered the door holds pride of place on the mantelpiece.

"Nice place you have here, Ms Martin," he says.

"Know Mossley Hill, do you?"

"No, not really. Isn't Penny Lane somewhere round here? You know, the Beatles song?"

"Yes, love, it is. As I said I haven't got a lot of time. Would you like a quick cuppa? Can't offer you anything stronger, don't keep it in the 'ouse."

"Tea would be nice, thank you, Ms Martin. That stuff they serve on the train is..."

"Look, love, you'd better call me Loretta." The word *look* comes across as a long *luke* and *love* more as a short *lov*, and he recalls that when he'd first spoken to her on the phone he'd formed the impression that she might turn out to be a waspish individual. She isn't. Loretta Martin is square of build and a double string of pearls brightens her matching black skirt and blouse. "How do you take it?"

"No sugar, no milk, Loretta. Thank you."

"Sounds a bit fancy." She raises an eyebrow over her thick-rimmed glasses. "Be all right in a mug?"

While she is in the kitchen, Simon studies the photos on the mantelpiece in closer detail. Among the pantheon of Kop heroes stands a silver-framed photograph of a Royal Marine. He stands stiffly at attention in his blue tunic and white cap banded red. A stern and constipated-yet-unembarrassed expression is chiselled into a broad face.

"Yes, that's Billy." Loretta hands him the mug.

"Good looking fellow."

"He is that. Regular babe magnet is my Billy. More bloody trouble than he's worth, that I will say. Please, sit down. What can I do for you? You said you wanted to see me about Billy, though why you needed to come all the way up here instead of plain asking me over the phone I've no idea."

The pitch of her voice rises towards the end of each sentence as if each assembly of words is arranged solely to represent some form of aggressive plea.

"If you'd prefer to give me his contact details, I'll be happy to ask Billy directly."

Loretta Martin's brow furrows and she turns her head slightly away from him to look at the photograph. "It's like I said on the phone, Simon... Peckham, that's in London isn't it? Is that Peckham you're from or is that really your surname?"

"Simon, please."

"All right, Simon. Look, Simon, it's like I said on the phone: my Billy's not the sort to talk to the papers and it'd be more than my life's worth to give you his telephone number. 'Sides he's away just now." She hesitates, watching him for his reaction to her obfuscation.

"In fact, it'd be best if I asked you what you want to talk to him about. I wouldn't want to be quoted as saying anything bad about him in your paper and I know how you people get to twist words. This conversation is off the record. Isn't that what you said?"

"I did, Loretta. And I mean it. But—and if you don't mind my asking—why is your Billy so set against the press?"

"Well, that's easy." She sits forward and fixes him with a beady stare. "When you lot broke the news about Prince Harry being in theatre, in Afghan, my Billy went berserk. And properly berserk, too. Said you lot had endangered every man on the ground; said the Taliban would be targeting every uniform in theatre, hoping they would be lucky enough to get a shot at young Harry. He said it would put all his mates in more danger, not to mention HRH. Poor bloke was only trying to do his duty like the rest of them. 'A potentially fatal irresponsibility', my Billy said it was." She sits back and waits.

Simon feels the colour rise in his cheeks. "Unfortunate. Though we can't really take the blame for that. That was an Australian magazine that broke the story, not the British Press."

"You'll excuse me for saying, Simon, but once the news was broken you people didn't mind bellowing it from the rooftops. Could've denied it, couldn't you? Could've said it was a load of bollocks: some loud-mouthed Aussie who didn't know 'is arse from 'is elbow. But no, eh? Bloody good excuse to sell a bit more copy. That's all it was to you wankers."

Her assault silences him for a moment as he imagines her leaping from her seat in the Kop to hurl a stream of abuse at the referee.

Simon changes tack: "If you don't mind my asking, Loretta, you're an accountant, aren't you?"

She fixes him with a glacial stare. "Yes, as a matter of fact I am. How d'you know that?" She studies Simon. "Look, Mr Peckham, just why are you looking for my brother?"

"Billy's not married, is he? Not got a partner, I mean?"

"No. Always said he hasn't got time for that. Says only a fool would marry a man who passed so much time in harm's way. Not that he doesn't get plenty of offers, mind."

Drawing the black moleskin notebook from his pocket, he flicks through it and hands it to her, holding it open at the page which refers to her brother. "It's not so much Billy I'm looking for as whoever it is," Simon hesitates, as a thought occurs, "or was, who wrote this about him."

She frowns as she reads.

"I'm assuming," he carries on, "Billy used to live here. You'll see the entry notes Mossley Hill and the Halfpenny pub. I got your telephone number through the phone book on the internet."

"Says 'ere," she looks over at him, her eyes welling up, "*Billy, Liverpool, Mossley Hill, The Halfpenny, Douglas(d) and Annie(d), Loretta(FCA)*. Yes. Well. Mum and dad. They've both been gone a while now? Probably just as well really."

"I'm sorry for your loss, Loretta."

"Thank you, Simon. Nice of you to say."

"What do you mean by *just as well?*"

She thinks for a moment. "Well, just as well because they never got to see Billy the way he was when he came back from Afghanistan. All that bloody anger and nowhere to put it. Suppose we should count ourselves lucky really. Be thankful for small mercies when you get them."

"How so?"

"Well...," she begins. Then she thinks better of whatever it was she was going to say and bends her head back to the book. "This book mentions me and what I do. 'Ere, that's 'ow you know I'm an accountant. I was wondering 'ow you knew that."

Simon nods. "Yes, it's how I knew or thought I knew."

"Not just a gawky looking prat, are you?"

In spite of the backhanded compliment, his face reddens.

Loretta flicks through the pages, pausing at the occasional entry. She stops and returns her attention to Simon. "I know some of these blokes. Some of them served with Billy in Iraq and then in Afghan. These pages that are crossed out, they're the ones who've died, aren't they?"

"I'm afraid so. I wasn't sure what the notebook meant until I got in touch with Derek Roarke. He told me Jo Crudup was dead and I figured out the rest."

"Johnnie Bell, Mike Owens, Jed Thomas and Jo," she confirms in a solemn sing-song tone. "Tough time for too many of them. Oh, and their families. You spoke to Del Boy, eh? How was he managing?"

"Honestly?"

"Of course honestly. Man loses a leg; it doesn't get more honest than that. How was he doing?"

"Bit grouchy to tell the truth." Simon holds up his hand to stifle her objection. "I'm sure I'd be the same; probably more so. Wasn't all washed up with nowhere to go, though. Still seemed to have a bit of fight left in him."

Loretta chuckles; a small, sad, dismissive reaction to her conjuring a vision of the man they called Del Boy.

"Always was a moaner, was Derek. Leastways that's what Billy was always saying. Said he was a man to get the job done, though not without having to moan like buggery about it first. 'Size of the task never equal to the earache the anticipation caused' or something like that."

"I can believe it," Simon adds, remembering the sight of Derek Roarke wielding his spanner. "It's who the book belongs to that interests me."

"Well, Simon, it belongs to you now, doesn't it?" she says, as though he is as stupid as she thinks he is gawky. "You've got it. Where'd you find it?"

He watches her for a moment, unsure as to whether or not he

should tell her the truth about where he found the notebook. Then he remembers that Loretta Martin is a season ticket Liverpool supporter, and therefore likely to spot a fraud the moment he trots out onto the pitch.

"I found it in London on New Year's Day. It was lying on the pavement near where a homeless man died. The police think the man may have fallen and injured himself; the injury resulting, ultimately, in his death."

Loretta examines the notebook, fingering the frayed edges and studying the margins. "And you think this may have belonged to someone who knew Billy? He wasn't in London over the New Year, you know. In fact, he wasn't even in the country."

"No." Simon shakes his head. "I don't think what happened was anything to do with Billy. And I don't think the notebook was much to do with the old man who died. What I do think is that the notebook belonged to a man who was somewhere nearby at the time and that he may know how the old man was hurt. And if I think that, then the police may eventually draw a similar conclusion and start looking for this man."

She sits up straighter and looks over at Simon a shade belligerently. "You're not listening to me, Mr Peckham. I've just told you Billy wasn't in the country over New Year. He's been gone since November. Abroad. Libya, if you must know. Security on some oilfield. Never tells me much. Just leaves a few contact numbers. Anyway, that's not his handwriting and though he was pretty good with words, he wouldn't have kept a notebook like that. Never likes people knowing what he's thinking, does Billy. Always quotes that line from Godfather whenever I ask him what he's thinking."

"Please, Loretta, I don't think for one minute your Billy has anything to do with the old man passing away like that. All I need to know from Billy is who the notebook belongs to. Nothing else. Just that. Who it belongs to."

Loretta Martin sighs with relief and allows herself time to cast him a more questioning glance.

"You'll find, Simon, that the notebook belongs to Billy's ex-boss, Richard Ross, Captain Richard Ross. He's the only bloke who would never call my Billy by a nickname."

"Richard Ross," Simon repeats. "He was Billy's boss in the Marines?"

Loretta frowns at him as though he is the only individual on the planet who doesn't know. "Yes. His boss. Billy was a Lance Corporal with Ross when he was a Second Lieutenant fresh into Iraq and later, about the same time Ross was promoted Lieutenant, my Billy got his third stripe. Then they were together in Afghan, although Ross was a Captain and Billy a Warrant Officer by then."

"Do you know if Ross is still in the Marines?"

She glances up at the ceiling a little to his left and shifts in her seat. "I'm afraid you'd have to ask Billy that."

Her sidestep of his question is not lost on him.

"What was he like, Billy's Captain? Did you ever meet him?"

"A couple of times. Was up here a couple or three years ago. Hauled Billy out of the Sedgley Park nick one night after he'd overdone it at a stag night. Seemed like a nice enough fella. Proper gentleman."

"Billy think he was good at his job?"

Loretta now searches the floor for her answer. "All right, I guess. Bit green around the gills the first time in Iraq, I think that was what Billy said. Though he never complained about Ross the way he did some of the others."

Simon pitches his tone somewhere between casual and sympathetic, "You said Billy came back with a lot of anger. Was that at the end of his tour or when he left the service?"

"Both. He came out of the Royal Marines after his last tour. And yes, more anger than a man has a right to."

"How did that manifest itself? What was he? Violent? Morose? Uncommunicative?"

"All of those and more." She pauses, remembering. "Seemed all right on the outside; a few lumps, bumps and scrapes, nothing that wouldn't mend. Wouldn't let me fuss over him, mind. The more attention I tried to pay him; the more he'd withdraw. Pretty standard stuff, if you know what I mean."

"No, I'm sorry, I don't. One reads about it, but I've never witnessed it up close and personal like you must have. Please, go on."

Loretta studies Simon. Her expression suggests she is wondering whether he absolutely really wants to hear what her brother's homecoming was like and whether he has the breadth of mind necessary to understand it's effect upon those close to him.

"You remember," she begins, "when you were at school and you'd come home and your mum would ask you how you were and how you'd got on at school today?"

"As if it was yesterday."

"Well, mum and dad left the house to the both of us; only Billy wasn't ever here of course. So, when he came back I'd be like mum used to be. I'd ask him how he was and he'd say he was 'fine'. I'd ask him how his tour went and he'd say 'fine', and how his leaving-do went and he'd say the same. And as soon as you asked, he'd scowl at you as though you had no bloody right to. It was like your mum asking how an exam had gone when you knew bloody well the results weren't going to be out for a good while so what was the point in asking.

"We'd go down the pub and his old mates would come up and ask him how he was and he'd say 'fine'. Only you could feel he wasn't. It was like he was next to you in body, but his mind was somewhere else. And the more they asked, the more he seemed to resent them asking. Then his fuse got shorter and shorter, and every time a bulb broke or a tap dripped he'd blow his stack and blame the world, or worse, me. Came home one evening to find me enjoying a little company and lost it completely. Threw my friend out and threatened to do for her if she ever came back. It was enough to drive a woman to drink. Made me a nervous wreck. And those of our friends what would still talk to us gave up on him. Once he was barred from the Halfpenny he'd go down town every night looking for someone to upset him just so's he could give 'em a good hiding. And I'd sit 'ere wondering what time Frankenstein was going to get home and how many heads he'd be wearing. Got so as I couldn't wait for him to be gone."

"And now he's in Libya?" Simon prompts.

"Yes. One of his mates works for a security firm: risk management, he calls it. Thank bloody God he did too! How he didn't end up in prison is anybody's guess."

"Did you try to get in touch with any of his old buddies? What about Captain Ross?" Simon asks.

"No, not Captain Ross. I didn't feel right writing to him. I wrote to Paddy Jennings; he was in Billy's mob. Liked Paddy, did Billy. Didn't hear back from him. Didn't really expect to."

"They got on okay, Billy and Captain Ross?"

She looks up to his left again, hesitating. "Yes. Okay as far as I know."

Her first sidestep had pricked his curiosity: her second intrigues him. "Guess they must have been through some tough times in Iraq and Afghanistan?"

"Well, Mr Peckham, we're not conditioned to take lives, are we? Not normal for people to have to do what our lads do. We wander about the neighbourhood without so much as a care while they, men like Johnny, Mike, Jed and Jo pay for our privilege with their lives. Oh aye, and Del Boy with his leg. Not bloody right, is it?"

"No, Loretta, right it isn't. Absolutely it isn't," Simon agrees, "but... No, but nothing." He clears his throat, remembering

Roarke's oddly futuristic prosthetic and how he wore it as though it had always been that way and never anything else. "What can you tell me about Captain Ross? Would you still have his address?"

For the third time in as many minutes, Loretta Martin pauses as she glances up and to her left. "Er, no. I didn't keep it. Billy would probably have it somewhere. When next I speak to him I'll be sure to ask and, if he still has it, I'll send it you." She looks down now and picking her phone from the table beside her, she checks it. "God, is that the time? Look, I didn't realise we'd been talking so long and I'm due at the gym in ten minutes. Would you mind if I saw you out?"

"No, not at all." Simon takes a card from his wallet and hands it to her. "I've taken up far too much of your time already. Before I go, you said Billy and Captain Ross got on well together, don't you think it's strange they've not stayed in touch?"

The young accountant gets up, straightens her skirt and takes his card. When she faces Simon, she avoids looking him directly in the eye, "No, Mr Peckham, I don't. It's just the way men are, isn't it? Best of friends one minute; best of enemies the next."

14

When Simon returns from convincing his editor that he is-really is-working on a whole raft of stories, a padded manila envelope lies jammed halfway through his letter box. The postmark is City and the envelope bears no sender's details.

He grabs a bottle of water from his fridge, takes a relieving swig from it and opens the envelope. Two CDs. There is no accompanying note and the handwritten address on the front is barely legible.

Simon grins. He'd only half expected the bouncer to cough up. If he hadn't heard back from him, he was going to have to revert to Plan B; whatever that was going to be.

He fires up his laptop and loads the first cd.

After granting a few permissions and accepting several warnings that the contents may not be sufficiently secure to open, he locates a program capable of converting the enclosed material into the correct format. A file opens and an Excel spreadsheet loads up onto the screen.

The column to the left of the page records an index of times and names. In the centre, against each entry, runs a list of details: date of birth, type of identity card and registration details. Most of the cards recorded are either photo-card driving licences, official 18+ Passes or NUS cards. The odd entry denotes a UK or foreign passport and a few relate to foreign identity cards.

Simon glances down the long list and realises that he will have to marry the names and times against the CCTV footage which, he hopes, will be recorded on the second cd.

He saves and closes the file and loads the remaining cd. After yet another string of permissions and warnings, black and white CCTV images with the time displayed in the corner, appear on a split screen. One half shows the queue stretching away down the pavement outside the club; the other covers the turnstile in the foyer where the entrants scan their ID. The camera is linked to a database recording the photograph of the card holder's face to prove they match that on their ID card. As the club opened at eight in the evening and last entry was just before midnight, Simon pauses the footage, throws together a plate of food and then settles down to trawl through four long hours of the five hundred or so faces.

Around ten, the buzz of his phone startles him.

"Simon Peckham."

"It's me. What're you up to, Si?"

Me who? He wracks his brain. The previous few hours of cross-checking names to faces whilst simultaneously watching two screens has dulled his senses.

"It's me, Candy."

"Oh, hi Angel. What can I do for you?"

She pauses. "Si? Don't give me all that polite office protocol bullshit. I was just wondering if you fancied a drink. You know, to make up for dragging me out to that bloody awful club last week."

He returns his attention to the screen. "No, can't. Sorry, I've got too much on just at the minute."

"Mm, I was just wondering what you might have on." She giggles. And when he doesn't reply, Candy carries on: "Seriously, Si, you're working? Pull the other one, it's got bells on."

"No, really, Angel. I'm working on a story and need to concentrate. Another time."

She purrs down the phone at him, "Wouldn't you like me to come by and help you with your spelling. I could bring some food... a bottle of wine. We could put on some music. Have a little dance."

"Thanks, but no thanks." He can hear several female voices in the background. Someone offers a loud and marginally lewd encouragement; others snigger. "Angel?"

"Yes, Si?"

"Have you been out on the lash straight from work?"

She laughs. "Sure, I have. What else is there to do on a Friday night? Don't you remember what we said about all work and no play makes Simon a—"

"Yeah, of course I remember. However, in my case, all play and no work makes what the Americans would call Jack. And if I don't get this article up for Barnes soon, I won't be earning enough money to go out and play with anyone. It's a nice idea, but no thanks. Why don't you tuck yourself up in bed with a nice bit of chick lit and I'll see you on Monday."

He doesn't want to let her down too heavily... Then her stinging rebuke comes to mind. "Angel, last Saturday you said you thought I was, to quote you, an absolute shit: why the sudden change of heart?"

Candy growls in frustration. "Si? Can you imagine how much of my own humble pie I'm having to eat just to make this call?"

Simon watches the screen. So far, he has seen nothing unusual in either the crowd queuing for the club or the clubbers clocking themselves in at the door. A few drinks and a swift immersion in

Candy's charms are beginning to seem a warm and very welcome distraction.

"Angel?"

"Yes, Si."

"What time we did we get to the club on New Year's Eve?"

"What time? Ooh, well, we did a bit of pre-lash at yours and must have got down the club about ten. No self-respecting young lady would dream of starting any earlier. One simply wouldn't have lasted the pace," she says in a faux-regal accent. "Except that we didn't need to, what with you getting locked out just after midnight"

Those egging her on spout a geyser of hot giggles.

"Brilliant, Candy. Well done. Now be a good girl: go do as I suggested and I'll see you on Monday."

"Si?"

"Monday, Angel. I'll bring you a box of chocolates."

"Si?"

"Yes, Angel?"

"I meant it, you know." Her tone hardens. "You're—"

"Yes, I know: an absolute shit. Goodnight, Candy."

He drops the phone on the sofa beside him and fast forwards the video to ten o'clock.

As he slows the film, a sudden movement down the queue in the left screen catches his eye. He plays the recording back.

A figure appears from the right and walks slowly down the line. He falters every other step and engages those queuing in brief conversations.

Simon plays the video back and forth, frame by frame. He can just make out the group of men including the guy in the plague doctor's mask, and the four including the girl Soraya, who were immediately in front of him.

The lean individual who appears from the right has his hood up over his head and faces away from the camera. He solicits the queuing clubbers. But, as Candy had pointed out, no one carries cash any more, and even though the party goers are as benevolent a crowd as any beggar could hope for, only occasionally does anyone gift him the odd coin.

As the rough sleeper gets a dozen or so people down the queue, he lingers. The man in the plague doctor's mask steps forward and speaks. Both he and Candy had witnessed that. Then the rough sleeper exchanges a brief conversation with the girl and he gets lucky; she does give him money. Finally, he asks Simon, who doesn't, and the guy trudges away down the line.

The broad-shouldered Tamati heaves into view, lumbers down towards the group, no doubt wanting to know what the fuss is about, and the beggar turns tail and crosses the street.

Simon forwards the recording, watching the group shuffle towards the entrance. He realises his heart is thumping as though he knows what he is about to see will be important. Over the previous couple of hours, he has felt a curious detachment in his viewing, a voyeur waiting for... he's not sure what to happen. And his prying leaves him feeling slightly ashamed: a spectator at a motor race anticipating the excitement of a crash or a witness at a trial waiting for the jurors to present their verdict.

"Calm down, you idiot." He takes a swig of his water.

Simon watches as the two couples who had been in front of them in the queue walk through the outer door. He then switches his attention to the recording at the turnstile.

The girl is wearing a sequined ball mask. She has long dark hair and wears a draped jacket over a bralet top and slim trousers. It is Soraya. Because of the stiffness of her gait and the way she seems nervously uncomfortable in her surroundings, she is clearly no seasoned clubber. She is with three others: a second girl and two young men, one of them tall.

When the group gets to the turnstile, Soraya tries to hand her identity card over to the supervisor at the door. He waves her offer away and instructs her to swipe it through the card reader. She laughs, embarrassed, swipes her card and starts to move through the turnstile, expecting it to yield to her progress.

It doesn't and she bangs against it, awkwardly.

The supervisor speaks to her and directs her to remove her mask and show her face to the camera.

Again, she laughs. Again embarrassed. She takes off her mask and offers her face. Her smile is both coy and self-effacing.

He plays the video back and watches a half-dozen times as she removes her mask and smiles up at the camera. It is Soraya. There is no doubt she is the same girl he saw in the club and at the hospital; the same girl who was asking after the old man in intensive care. She is the girl with the incredible topaz eyes; the girl he lent the money to and who posted it back to him in an envelope without enclosing either her name or any other contact detail.

Simon cross checks her entry against the information on the other stick. The time displayed on the image reads 21.52. The details logged at the same time read an out of town university, her name - *Parisa Khasani*, her DOB - *22/10/1988* and the validity - *09/2009 through 12/2012*, *followed by* a sixteen-digit reference code.

Parisa Khasani. Her name? Parisa?

Simon is certain she had introduced herself to the doctor as Soraya. He dredges his memory for the film of that New Year's morning: intensive care, the doctor, he had called her 'young lady' and she had corrected him with her name 'Soraya'. That was the name she had given the doctor. And the deeper he dredges, the clearer comes the recording in his mind that she didn't give her name as Parisa.

15

"Good morning," Simon offers in his brighter-than-bright, Monday-morning spirit, "I'm sorry to bother you, is that the Student Services Helpdesk?"

"Yes, how can I help?" Her accent is all neatly pruned privet hedge.

"Oh, that's good. My name's Davis, I'm the manager of The Coffee House in Bishopsgate, the City of London. I wonder if you can be of assistance. When we cleared up yesterday, we came across a wallet containing some cash and a National Student's Union identity card. We'd like to return it to the holder. Perhaps you would be kind enough to give me the student's address so we can pop it in the post."

The phone quiets for a second. "I'm afraid we can't give out personal details." Her tone, though pleasantly modulated, is now more barberry than privet. "That would contravene our data protection policy. Why don't you post it directly to us and we'll forward it? I can give you the address. Got a pen?"

Simon takes down the address, even though it is staring back at him from the university website displayed on his laptop. "The thing is, and I wonder if you would bear with me for a minute, the wallet contains an amount of cash and if we can't forward it straight on, we'd prefer it if the holder presented herself here to collect it. If the holder doesn't come and claim it I'm going to have to hand it in to the police. You can probably understand how complicated that's going to make it for her and I'd rather hoped to keep this simple."

The penny slowly drops. "Oh, okay. I see where you're coming from." She thinks for a minute. "Why don't you give me the holders details as written on the card and I'll see if I can get a message to her."

Simon sighs, relieved that he is at last getting where he wants to go. "The card reads that her name is Parisa Khasani, her date of birth is 22nd October 1988, and the sixteen digits at the bottom of the card read-"

"Hold on for a moment, would you, I'm just accessing the right screen for her details." She taps away at her keyboard. "Right, here we are. Read away."

Simon recites the sixteen-digit reference.

"Sorry, could you read that out again more slowly? I think I must have taken it down wrong."

He reads the numbers through once more, being careful to enunciate the numbers with a brief gap between each one.

"No, sorry again," she says, uncertainly. "Those numbers don't seem to be matching up. I'll check our register of students. What did you say the name was?"

"Khasani," Simon spells it out and then repeats it: "Khasani. Parisa Khasani."

"Mm, sorry, we don't have a Parisa Khasani registered in our list of admissions at the moment. I've got the full list up in front of me and there's no Khasani on it. Are you certain that's the name?"

"Yes, certain." He spells it out again, even more slowly, but the seeds of his doubt are already beginning to germinate.

"No, sorry, can't help." Her tone is now prison brick wall. "What I think you have there Mr... sorry, what is your name?"

"Davis."

"What you most likely have there, Mr Davis is a fake identity card. There are a considerable number of them in circulation. We'd very much appreciate it if you would either hand it in to the police or send it to us. Where did you say you are from, Mr Davis?"

He rings off. "Damn. Right again, Simon. Her name wasn't Parisa Khasani." He checks the card details against those of the other three people with the girl: all of them are registered to the same university.

Excerpt 5 from transcript of conversation with Joseph Naarda

SP: When your daughter was born, that must have been a special day for you, the day you became a father?

JN: Oh, yes. Becoming a father? How could a man forget that?

SP: Tell me about that day, how did it begin? Were you present at her birth?

JN: No, not present. Not exactly. The *jiddah*, the midwife, she sent me out.

SP: What time was that? Was it night or day?

JN: Early. Very early. The sun was not up and yet it was unusually hot. And I remember I was feeling nervous; nervous and lonely, and yet not at all alone. The eyes of the heavens, they were smiling down on me; watching and waiting as if they, like me, knew something truly extraordinary was about to happen. My wife, you know she is Mandaean?

SP: A Mandaean? One of the Subba. *Yes.*

JN: Well, Salwa was hoping that our child would come later,

in July, during her New Year. She was hoping our child would be born on one of her White Days. You know what I mean by this, White Days?

SP: Yes. The celebration days. The five days during which the Mandaeans believe their world was created. Yes, please go on.

JN: Well, it would have been auspicious, or so Salwa believed. But our child was impatient to come and the *jiddah* brought a cotton blanket for Salwa and the sheaf of *gasbah*, the reeds, for her to hold onto during her pain. The *jiddah* then sent me out to collect butter and salt for cleaning the baby. And I had to find more water; enough water for my wife to be baptised immediately after the birth. I remember I was walking down the road. Well, I think of it now as a road; it wasn't much more than a dusty alley, not like the roads here. And by then our home was very small, very basic, some water, some electricity, not all the time. It is strange how one remembers a place as being better than it really was. Do you know what I mean by this?

SP: Yes, I do. You said you felt lonely. The midwife sent you out, that would have made you feel excluded. And nervous? Surely, any man feels the same before the birth of his child?

JN: Of course, you are right, these were natural feelings. However, Salwa had seen blood on the last moon and she believed there would soon be war. It is one of her superstitions that when one solitary cloud obscures the moon, war will follow.

SP: Salwa predicted the coming invasion of Kuwait?

JN: Yes, the invasion of Kuwait, it began five weeks later. Perhaps that is why I was so apprehensive. Perhaps it wasn't only the nervousness of becoming a father. Perhaps it was fear; a fear that my child would be born into a world of chaos; a world in which she would, like me, never really find her place.

SP: Is that how you feel now? Stateless? Still without a sense of belonging?

JN: Sometimes, yes. Without a sense of belonging? Yes. I still find it hard to be a citizen as opposed to a civilian. But I have long believed that simply because we are born in one place, it doesn't mean we have the right to call that place our own.

SP: So, that night, the night you became a father?

JN: Yes. Of course. Well, it had been hot, the hottest June for many years, and one did not know where best to be: outside in the flames of the sun or inside in the furnace of one's home. But I remember it not only because of the extreme temperature, though; I remember it because of other things.

SP: Other things?

JN: Yes. Salwa's omen, which I have already told you about, the *jiddah* who sent me out and the sense that something extraordinary was about to happen.

But more important than these things was that I remember searching the sky for the Dawn Star; it appears at that time of the summer. And at the very moment I saw it there, sailing close by the eastern horizon, I felt a breath of cool wind and heard the first cry of our new-born child.

All in that very same moment, I saw and felt and heard these things: the star, the wind and the voice. And it was as if time was standing still. As if God was being patient with me, while he waited for me to understand that I was in that moment suspended between the heavens and the earth, between his two worlds.

Now, one must take into account that Salwa wanted to give her child a name that would live well with the stars. In the Mandaean culture, the time and date of the birth and the name one gives the child all possess significant numerical values. You know, the signs of the Zodiac and the order in which they come, that kind of thing. And this star, the Dawn Star, it gave me an idea. You see, Simon, most people would know this star as the Seven Sisters: the Greek name is Pleiades. But to us, the Dawn Star has always been *Thorayya* and when it appears, it brings with it the cool wind from the north. This wind, we also call *Thorayya*, the *Barih Thorayya*.

So, I gazed at the star, embraced the wind, and I listened to our daughter proclaim her arrival into the two worlds. This, my friend, is how we came to give her the name Soraya.

16

The atmosphere in the waiting area by the lifts is thick with the stale air of people confined. A balding, corpulent man, sober suit and dark tie, stands as one used to standing for long periods. Around his neck hangs a lanyard attached to which is an identification card: he is a City of London policeman.

The lift doors open and a cackle of students emerge.

Simon ignores them and leans against the wall by the door to the courtroom. He studies his phone.

The students chatter and make fun of each other.

"Woman," one of them pipes up from beneath her hijab, "what are you bothering with that for? You know our exams are still a long way off."

Whoever her barb is aimed at does not rise to the bait.

"God," the girl tries again, "you're so together. Always givin' it the righteous student, ya?"

The girl sitting beside Simon, raises her face from her text book, "Exams in a couple of months, Sabina. Not that far away."

"You're such a teacher's pet, Soraya."

Simon looks down, slowly. He cannot see her face because she wears a headscarf. Not a hijab like the girl called Sabina who sits across from them, nor a more concealing chador which another of the girls is wearing. The girl Sabina has just addressed as Soraya has her head covered by a shemagh, a casual headscarf.

The material is a deep yet vivid blue, patterned with exotic fruits and angels and birds, and fringed at both ends with small tassels.

He cannot see her face because of her scarf and cannot bend down to look for himself as he stands right next to her and to do so would be obvious and awkward, especially if she isn't who he thinks, or perhaps even hopes, she might be.

A woman wearing a white blouse, neat black jacket and skirt comes in from the door to her left. She carries a clipboard and pen, and hovers until the group of eight have noticed her and silenced respectfully.

"Good morning, my name is Catherine. I am the Coroner's Officer for this case. Would you all please follow me?"

The students stand. The girl, too. She turns towards the door. Simon is in her way.

It is the same Soraya he'd met three months before on New Year's Eve and again at the hospital the next morning.

She hesitates, looks at him, looks away and back again, and then frowns.

Simon is met with a curious inward-gazing yet confused expression.

Soraya moves to step round him.

He holds the door open for her.

She smiles and mumbles her thanks.

They file through a short corridor and into a light, airy office. Signs leave the students in no doubt that their mobile phones are to be switched off. A raised platform hosts a desk with a microphone, and behind it sits a crafted wooden chair. A table to the side supports recording equipment, and college writing chairs line the room beneath the windows.

Beside the students and their tutor, the only others present are the officer of the court, the policeman, and a pinch-faced, primly-dressed lady who chews the end of her pen.

Just when they have gotten themselves comfortable, the Coroner's Officer asks them to stand and a grey-suited man strides in and sits down behind the main desk. He settles and organises and opens several files.

"Good morning. Please be seated," he begins, his tone business-like. "My name is Graham, David Graham, and this is the inquest touching on the death of one Thomas Iestyn Williams, date of birth 14.04.1950: date of death 01.01.2011."

Thomas Williams, a rough sleeper who looked eighty and yet died aged sixty on New Year's Day. Simon notes the details and studies the coroner. Mr Graham, a seemingly innocuous official, is so powerful that he could, if he decides it is in the interests of the court, halt the wheels of industry grinding noisily beyond the window.

"Now," he says, looking up to satisfy himself that everyone is awake and prepared, "we have some students present. From the University of East London, I believe. So, what I will do is lead you through the process as methodically and logically as I can. There will be time for questions later."

Mr Graham smiles briefly. "The reasons why we hold an inquest are several. We hold an inquest if no death certificate was issued because a doctor was neither present at nor before the death; if no medical attention was given for an illness that occurred before death; if no medical examination was made by the doctor issuing the death certificate during a period of 14 days before death; if the death occurred…"

His style reminds Simon of a man taking a brisk walk.

The coroner turns a page.

"What we are here to establish is who the deceased was. In this case where he died; when he died; how he died-as in what was the cause of his death—and finally, what were his last movements in the hours leading up to his death?" he pauses to satisfy himself all are keeping up.

"What we do *not* do at an inquest is apportion blame or, if it is the case, put anyone on trial for the death. That," he pauses again, "is for others to do and…"

Simon struggles and decides to listen rather than write. As he looks back up, he catches the girl Soraya watching him. He turns his attention back to the Coroner.

"Under certain circumstances, for instance if matters of national security are involved, we will hold an inquest in private, though in Mr Williams' case this would appear not to apply.

"First of all, it is our duty to establish who Thomas Iestyn Williams was." He addresses his officer: "Catherine, I believe you have that information, perhaps you would be good enough to…"

The Coroner's Officer stands, smooths down her skirt, picks up a bible and swears herself in.

"Sir, Thomas Iestyn Williams was not registered at any current address. His last known address was that of his parents, John and Anwen Williams of Port Talbot in Wales. They passed away in 1992 and 1993 respectively. We therefore could not acquire any photographs for the purposes of identification. On speaking to neighbours, we believe their son, Thomas, had not been to visit for some years prior to their death and was, apparently, not present at either funeral. It is believed he has a brother who departed the United Kingdom for Australia in the 70s. Taking this into account, there would appear to be no interested parties present here today."

"So how," the Coroner asks her, "do we know the deceased is beyond reasonable doubt Mr Williams?"

"From fingerprint records, sir. The deceased was fingerprinted at St Pancras Mortuary and on checking these we found Mr

Williams was known to police. He was convicted of common assault in 1994 and again in 1997. On the first occasion, he was fined. On the second he was also fined. Unable to pay either fines, he was ordered to undertake community service. Over the last twenty years he has been picked up several times, the last time being in May of last year when he was moved on from sleeping rough in the grounds of St Leonard's Church, High Street, Shoreditch. Hospital records also show that in the last two years Mr Williams attended A&E departments at Bart's and the Royal London for what were minor injuries more usually associated with falling. Suspicions were that on both occasions these injuries were self-inflicted and used as an excuse to occupy a bed for the night owing to the fact that outside temperatures were extremely low. Before that. . .''

The Coroner's Officer recites a long list of minor public order offences committed by the deceased, most of which involved alcohol, verbal abuse and trespass.

Simon is unsettled, not so much by the sad litany of Thomas Williams' misdemeanours; rather by the way the girl Soraya keeps staring at him. In doing so she makes it difficult for him to stare at her, something he finds he cannot resist doing.

"We have also ascertained that Mr Williams was prone to giving his mother's maiden name when questioned and we therefore believe he was stopped on more occasions than those on record. Our investigation also led us to ascertain that Mr Williams served twelve years in 2nd Battalion the Parachute Regiment; being discharged on medical grounds in 1989. He was awarded the Military Medal for bravery at the Battle of Goose Green, Falklands War, 28th May 1982. Upon his discharge, it appears he took a number of part-time employments in the Port Talbot area then, some years later, moved to London where he took similar work before becoming a rough sleeper.''

Old Tom. A war hero.

Barnes had told Simon to dig about a bit in case the deceased turned out to an ex-Thatcher cabinet minister, spymaster, rocket scientist or decorated war hero. Well, Simon had dug about, which is why he's at the inquest, and old Tom is or was a decorated war hero. It is a welcome reward for Simon's efforts, though a reward layered with melancholy that someone who risked his life for the security of others should end up so unloved.

He looks across at the students. As they sit taking notes, do they perceive the deceased as nothing more than an irrelevance to be examined and reported? Is he a simple statistic to be measured alongside the vast array of other statistics concerning how people pass away? Is that where rough sleepers, homeless or vagrants lose their identity? Is that where they become part of a separate narrative and where they make the transition from *a person who* to *a number which*?

"Thank you, Catherine," the Coroner says. "So, we have established who the deceased was by matching his fingerprints against records. Now we come to where and when." He turns another page and reads on: "Shortly after midnight on January 1st this year, an ambulance was summoned to Parker's Walk, Bishopsgate, East I." He looks up over his glasses briefly: "For those of you who don't know where this is, the alley provides pedestrian access to the rear of commercial properties on the east side of where Norton Folgate—a road that extends up from Bishopsgate—becomes Shoreditch High Street, a road perhaps better known as the A10."

The Coroner reads on: "The report here states that Mr Williams was found unconscious with abrasions to his face and difficulty breathing. While the paramedics were treating Mr Williams, he suffered a cardiac arrest and was treated at the scene in the ambulance." He taps his desk. "We have a report here. He was then taken to the Royal London Hospital, where he was treated in A&E and later in the Intensive Care Unit. Sadly, he did not recover from his cardiac arrest and was pronounced dead at 14.00 hrs that same day."

Simon had seen Soraya at the hospital at eight: the old man had lasted six more hours.

"I see," he continues, "that the death certificate was issued by the doctor at the Royal London Hospital. However, because Mr Williams was picked up inside the boundaries of the Square Mile, in the City of London Ward of Bishopsgate, the Coroner's Office at Poplar has passed this inquest over to us." He grimaces a shade sarcastically, suggesting the Coroner at Poplar has done so in order to reduce his work load.

One of the students raises her hand.

He pauses, smiles warmly and looks up to address the students. "Yes, I know; confusing, isn't it. As I made plain earlier, we'll have time for a few questions later." He returns to studying his file. "So, we know who the deceased was, where he died and when. Now, to how he died."

Simon wrests his gaze from Soraya.

"The doctor's report from the Royal London states that Mr Williams was suffering from, amongst other ailments, a collapsed lung or pneumothorax, a broken hip and pneumonia. He also, it was noted, presented with several abrasions to his face. The post mortem carried out at..."

Simon picks up his notes again and realises that his last entry is underlined twice: 2 Para, MM, Goose Green, the details of which shouldn't be too difficult to trace. His day is made. Barnes will lap it up. From Hero to Homeless. All he'll need is a photograph. The Parachute Regiment should be able to supply that.

"...shows that Mr Williams also suffered from hepatic cirrhosis, a parasitic infestation, varicose veins, was malnourished and suffered from periodontal disease; all of which are, very sadly, well documented maladies of many rough sleepers. His blood alcohol is noted at 0.2 per cent. This is a significant percentage and means Mr Williams may have been suffering considerable motor impairment and even possibly that he was in a state where he might have been, and again I stress *might have been*, prone to blackout. However, as to the actual cause of death, outside of heart failure no specific cause can be attributed. It is the opinion of the pathologist," the Coroner looks up once again, "and it is only an *opinion*, though one formed from years of experience, that Mr Williams injuries may, I repeat *may*, have occurred as the result of a fall rather than from violence at the hands of another."

At the mention of violence, all of the students sit up and take notice. Simon watches Soraya. She is staring hard at the floor.

Mr Graham turns a page and addresses the sober suited man sitting adjacent to the Coroner's Officer. "I believe the City of London Police have something to add to this. DS Chalmers?"

Detective Sergeant Chalmers rises and introduces himself: CID, City of London Police, Bishopsgate. The Coroner's Officer swears him in.

DS Chalmers briefly consults his notes. "Sir we were called to Parker's Walk, off Norton Folgate, on New Year's morning by paramedics attending Mr Williams. They were concerned that Mr Williams had been the subject of an assault. When we arrived, Mr Williams was the only person present and apart from the paramedics, there was no other person attending or who appeared to be involved with the deceased. The ambulance was called anonymously from a payphone in the foyer of the nightclub, Slick in the City, the back doors and emergency exit doors of which open onto Parker's Walk. We later interviewed several members of staff, but no one supplied us with any information regarding the deceased or information that might have led us to believe an assault had taken place."

Simon recalls Soraya telling the doctor, upstairs in A&E, that Thomas had been the victim of an assault. And later, he'd asked her if she'd seen it happen and she'd said 'Yes, sort of.' It was such an odd reply, because she'd either seen it or she hadn't. Later, though, she did admit that she had seen it and that the deceased had been trying to help her.

"In the course of our investigations," the policeman checks his notes once more, "we viewed CCTV coverage of the area and we have Mr Williams in the company of a second, unidentified man recorded in the area at 19.30hrs the evening before. We also have the second unidentified man alone some three hours later in Shoreditch High Street."

The Coroner sits up, "DS Chalmers, do you mean to say that with all the CCTV available we have no other record of Mr Williams' movements? I thought there were cameras at the top of Norton Folgate."

"There are, sir. However, the actual entrance to Parker's Walk is adjacent to a CCTV unit and this unit is one used only for recording traffic offences. As a result, we have been able to gain no further information through this medium. It is also interesting to note that when the emergency call was made, it was only an ambulance that was called for and not, initially, the police."

Simon is watching Soraya out of the corner of his eye. She grows agitated, rubbing her forehead and fidgeting in her seat.

"Your conclusion is, therefore?" Mr Graham asks the detective.

DS Chalmers lays his notebook on the table beside him, "Sir, our conclusion, and given the additional evidence from the deceased's medical record, is that it is highly likely that Mr Williams sustained his injuries from a fall and that no other person was involved. Therefore, it is the considered opinion of the City of London Police that no crime has been committed and that Mr Williams' death is not considered suspicious."

Simon half-hopes and half-wills Soraya to do it. She has to. Simply has to. And like a spring coiled so tight it cannot possibly remain intact, Soraya raises her hand.

Her friends all look round.

"Woman," the one called Sabina pipes up, "the man said questions are for lai'er."

Soraya keeps her hand raised.

The Coroner sighs, glances at the student's tutor and raises his eyebrow.

The tutor leans over and tries to push Soraya's hand back down.

But every time her hand is batted down, Soraya raises it again. Her face is pale and strained; her eyes glassy, as though she is in a trance.

"Sir," she says, "I know only interested parties are supposed to talk. And I know interested parties are supposed to register their interest with your Officer if they want to. However, I have something to say that I believe you need to hear."

Though the Coroner is irked, he carves a smile through his frustrations. "Certainly, young lady, if you must? What is it that you have to offer that bears relation to the death of the Mr Williams?"

Simon is urged to leap up and cheer her on. Tell her and her friends that what she is doing must be done. That it is right and that it is courageous.

Soraya's bottom lip trembles. She glances nervously either side at her course mates and slowly turns back to the Coroner.

"It's about Mr Williams, sir. I know he didn't sustain his injuries in a fall. He was assaulted."

The Coroner leans forward, his elbows on his desk, his curiosity piqued. "And pray, do tell us young lady, what is your name?"

"Soraya Naarda, sir."

"And how exactly *do* you know Mr Williams was the victim of an assault?"

The weight of expectation hangs in the air. Soraya looks around once more, still deciding, still unsure. And yet... And yet now that she has stepped up to the end of the diving board, it becomes obvious to those around her that she cannot turn away and climb back down. They are all watching, all waiting, all wondering if she has any other option than to jump.

"Because, sir, I saw it happen."

17

The Coroner adjourns the inquest to allow the police time to make further enquiries and Soraya's course-mates file out, honking and cackling, each one of them revelling in the opportunity to throw their classmate looks both curious and strangely envious.

Simon perches on a desk close by and pretends to tap out a text on his phone.

Even though DS Chalmers has already been officially introduced by the Coroner, he insists on flashing Soraya his shiny badge, its city shield enamelled in red and white and graced by two Tudor dragons.

"First off, would you be kind enough to give me your name and address, young lady?"

"Soraya?" interrupts her waspish tutor. "Perhaps we should have a talk. Don't you think—"

"No, I don't." She turns back to face the policeman. "Yes, of course, Detective Sergeant Chalmers. As I said, my name is Soraya, Soraya Naarda. I live with my parents in Bow." She waits patiently while he scribbles her details down in his notebook.

"So, what can you tell me about this assault to the deceased? Let's start with when and where."

"New Year's Eve, I was in the club, Slick in the City, with three friends. I had a row with my..." she glances sideways at Simon, then nervously at her tutor, "my boyfriend and I needed some space and this girl offered me a drink and a cigarette so we went out the back through the kitchen. I think she... well, I don't know because when I went to the hospital the next morning and the tests were inconclusive. The doctor said it was most likely that..." Soraya blinks away the beads of humiliation rising in her eyes.

"Is this lady your tutor?" Chalmers asks, pointing with his pen.

Soraya nods.

He peers at the tutor. "Excuse me, I think it might be better if you attended to your flock."

The tutor cavils, briefly, and leaves.

Simon tries to blend in with the wall colour.

Soraya's eyes are now glassy with tears.

"Look, Miss," Chalmers soothes, "I know this isn't easy for you. No one wants to admit to being a bit stupid and we all like a drink when we're out celebrating. What's more important is that you give me all the details you can recall from that evening." He waits while she dabs a tissue at the corners of her eyes. "And it doesn't matter, for the moment, whether you had consumed a little too much alcohol than was good for you, because what is important is that if poor Mr Williams was subjected to an assault then it is our duty to find whoever it was that assaulted him. We need to bring them to book so they don't go about assaulting other rough sleepers. Are you with me on this, Miss Naarda?"

"Yes, officer, I know. And that's why I'm telling you. I'm just so sorry I didn't say anything earlier."

"No matter, miss. You're doing the right thing now." He pauses, readying with his pen. "You went outside with this girl and you were sharing a smoke..."

She waits, looking down, marshalling or perhaps censoring her thoughts. "Yes, and I don't smoke. How stupid was that?"

"Miss Naarda?" the policeman is saying. He bends into her line of sight. "You went outside with another girl and..."

"Oh, yes. Sorry. I was just trying to remember what happened. It wasn't very nice. This man, he appeared out of nowhere. He grabbed me round my shoulders and tried to kiss me—"

Chalmers' curiosity isn't so much pricked as stabbed. "He assaulted *you* as well as Mr Williams?"

"Yes, he put his mouth against mine and tried to kiss me. I tried to push him away. You must believe me. I tried. But he was much stronger than me and I couldn't get away from him."

"Would you like a cup of water, Miss Naarda?"

"Yes, thank you. I'm sorry. That would be nice."

The Coroner's Officer emerges and hands her a plastic cup.

She drinks too quickly and splutters.

"We can do this another time, if you would like?" DS Chalmers offers.

"No, it's okay. I'm sorry. What was I saying?"

"You said this man appeared and grabbed you and tried to kiss you."

"Oh, yes. That's right. He was trying to kiss me and I was trying to struggle, and that's when Mr Williams appeared. He said something to the man and then he tried to pull him off me. The man pushed Mr Williams away and then I think he hit Mr Williams in his face."

"You *think*, Miss Naarda, or he *did* hit Mr Williams?"

"No, definitely he did. He let go of me and hit Mr Williams and then threw him into the wall. Threw him really hard. God, it was awful. It was as though Mr Williams was a doll. He just bounced off the wall and fell down. The man, he bent down and punched him in the side of his head, and then kicked poor Tom really hard in his side. I guess that was what broke his ribs, that last kick. I've never seen anything so violent before. Well, at least I don't think I have. I'm sure I would've remembered seeing something like that if I had. And the worst part was I couldn't help Tom. I really couldn't. I couldn't move. I wish I knew why."

"Shock, probably," Chalmers explains. "Where was this other girl while all this was happening? This girl," he adds, his tone a little sceptical, "you'd only just met and who you were sharing a cigarette with when everyone else was inside celebrating."

His scepticism doesn't impress Soraya. From appearing desolate a second before, suddenly she is rejuvenated by her anger. "I don't know where the other girl went, officer. How could I know? I was lying on the ground watching Mr Williams, scared I was about to be raped. Can you imagine what that felt like?"

Soraya doesn't wait. "No, I don't suppose you can. Big man like you. Tell me, Detective Sergeant Chalmers, what were you doing on New Year's Eve? Were you down the pub with all your mates, wondering who was up for a snog?"

Simon watches, spellbound, perhaps even a shade sorry for the policeman.

Chalmers reddens, chews his lip and makes to react. Then, very swiftly the policeman suffocates whichever demon has crept into his mind and takes a step back to wait for her to calm down.

Her rage, now out from within, diffuses and dissipates in the space between them.

Tears wet her eyes again and Soraya is "Sorry, so very sorry."

"That's alright, Miss Naarda. I'm sure this isn't easy. Please, go on. Then what happened?"

"I don't really know after that. After that, I suppose, the man went away. As I said, he let go of me when Mr Williams came. Perhaps Mr Williams frightened the man off. I remember going to try to help Mr Williams and he said he was okay, so I went back inside."

"Was it you who called the paramedics?"

"I don't think so. I had no credit on my phone, so I couldn't have done."

"Maybe you asked your boyfriend; that's if he was still speaking to you?"

"No, my friend," she confirms, emphasising the word *friend*, "didn't make the call. I didn't tell him what had happened. In fact, I haven't told anyone what happened until just now, so there would be no point in you interviewing him."

"You don't want to give me his name, then."

"Not unless I have to, no."

The policeman smiles, this time confidently. No longer is he quite so empathetic, quite so compassionate.

"Well, Miss Naarda, maybe you won't have to. I'm sure the club will provide us with the details of whoever was there on New Year's Eve." He doesn't wait or watch for her reaction. "One further question: did you see the man who assaulted you in the club that evening?"

She hesitates, evidently trying to remember. "No, I didn't see him in the club. I couldn't have seen him, everyone was wearing masks."

"But you did *see* him, so you would remember him if you saw him again."

Soraya dries her eyes. "Let me put it this way, detective, I remember he was wearing this horrid red mask. He took it off: he couldn't have put his mouth against mine otherwise. Apart from that I don't recall much about him at all other than that he was a loathsome, smelly, ugly slaphead who was much, much stronger than me. Oh, yeah, that and his saliva. I won't forget that. You know why, detective? Because it tasted like glue; the kind of glue we used to use when pasting bits of paper onto a collage at school. And no matter how often or how hard I brush my teeth, I can't seem to get the taste of it out of my mouth. Then again, how would I know? Maybe that's how all men taste? Now, will that do or would you like me to make something up? You know, something more graphic so it seems more authentic."

DS Chalmers winces and frowns as he takes another step back. "Is that all you can remember? Really all?"

Simon sidles out of the room. As he gets to the door he hears Soraya say, "What? Oh, yes, detective, really all. Really, really all. But if you give me your contact details, I'll be sure to get in touch when or if I do remember any more."

18

Simon waits in plain view directly across the busy Upper Thames Street from the high rise that houses the Coroner's Court.

Soraya hauls the heavy glass door shut behind her and hesitates until she sees him.

She looks so different from New Year's Eve. Then, she had worn that black bralet top with the chain hem, her hair swept back from her face and her face concealed behind the silver sequined mask. And later the next morning, standing freezing outside the Royal London, she was all too visibly suffering from an unhealthy dose of the morning afters. Simon could not wrest his gaze from her then. He cannot now.

Soraya is wrapped in a heavy coat, her hair covered by her blue scarf, her face pale and pellucid. She looks to her right as the traffic slows at the lights and picks her way through the melee of cars and lorries.

"I was hoping you would wait," she says. "It's Simon, isn't it, Simon Peckham? You lent me the money to get home. I did send it. I hope you got it."

"I did, yes, thank you."

They stand, looking at each other, unsure of how to progress.

"You-"

"I-" he interrupts.

A gust of wind funnels through the arch beneath Cannon Street Station and they close their eyes to the cloud of dust driven before it.

When Simon opens his eyes, he finds he is looking up at the fourth floor of Thames Wharf, the room in which he has just witnessed Soraya leap from the ivory tower of her anonymity.

DS Chalmers is standing at the tall windows, his gaze fixed upon them.

"Have you got time for a cup of coffee, Soraya? A drink or something? I mean, I think it's going to rain."

"That would be nice. Yes. Thank you. I definitely need something after that."

He leads her up the slope and along from the station to where Corinthian pillars grace the entrance of a coffee shop. Simon stands aside for her to enter.

Soraya hesitates again, either surprised and amused by his old-school manners or simply feeling awkward about going into a place, any place, with him. He isn't sure which.

They order and take seats at the long counter.

"I-" she begins. But whatever it is she was going to say, her words fail her again.

"That was perfectly brave of you, Soraya. I was hoping you were going to say something. And before you go thinking I may be some kind of stalker..." And Simon, too, stumbles; his concentration hijacked by the many questions her eyes are asking. "What I mean is, I had no idea you were going to be here. It's a coincidence, nothing more. I found out Tom's surname; the hospital supplied me with it. I cover a few of these and I'm researching for a piece I'm writing, which is why I decided to attend."

"What piece?" she asks, nervously.

"A story. A piece I'm putting together, about rough sleeping."

"Look, Mr Peckham—"

"Simon, please."

Soraya studies him for a moment, weighing him. "Look, Simon, I've probably just landed myself in a whole heap of trouble by telling the Coroner what I saw. And my parents are going to be upset enough when the police turn up at our flat wanting to know what I was doing out at a nightclub, when I'd told them I was playing perfect daughter at a girlfriend's house." She winces. "Never mind the fake ID, having my drink spiked, getting assaulted and going to the hospital. So, the last thing I need is for you to—"

"Go making things worse. Yes, I can imagine."

Her expression suggests he can't.

"Okay," he adds, "I can only try to imagine. How did it go with the detective, Chalmers?"

"I'm not blind, Simon. And I don't think you're deaf. You know very well how it went." Annoyance flickers in her eyes and her expression is wonderfully defiant. And yet... And yet the anxiety lurking within her eyes suggests she is swimming both out of her depth and too far from shore.

Simon is at odds with himself, too. To lie, to box round the houses and to wheedle from her the information she may give up, would be easy, but... "Okay, so now I've told you what I was doing at Tom Williams' inquest. What were you doing there?"

"It's part of my course, I'm reading forensic psychology at the UEL." She glances at him and then lowers her head to stare at her coffee cup. "I want to work with youth offending teams. I want to stop kids from ending up on the streets. I think young people deserve a second chance, don't you?" Soraya bends her head to sip her coffee, then raises her eyes back to his, watching for his reaction.

Simon is self-consciously aware of her scrutiny, "Yes, of course. We all need second chances."

"Need?" she repeats, considering, frowning in question. "Need or deserve? Everyone needs something, Simon; it's just that some are more deserving."

"That's a tough number, working with young offenders. One could say thankless."

"Just because it is thankless, doesn't mean it isn't worthwhile, Mr Peckham."

Her reverting to his surname squares him up a little. "Sure, Soraya. And don't get me wrong, I admire your sense of altruism. But haven't you got enough of your own battles to fight?"

Now, she raises her head and stares deep into his eyes.

Such bare attention completely unnerves him.

"We all have our battles to fight," she states. "And not all of us are adequately equipped to fight them. Doesn't your newspaper fight for the rights of those less fortunate; those less capable of fighting for themselves?"

"Sure, we-"

"Isn't that how you persuade the public to hand over their cash for your copy? 'How we pay our bills', wasn't that what you said when you introduced yourself?"

He recalls their conversation. "Yes, it was. Exactly that: how we pay our bills."

"*And* how you line the coffers of your bosses' bank vaults and subsidise their pensions, by championing the oppressed or representing the downtrodden or raging against the inequalities of life. Isn't that how you sell your newspapers, by selling the story of someone else's poor bloody misery?"

Simon reels. "Yes, if you want to look at it that way. However, we do a lot of good, too, like bringing other people's misfortunes to the attention of the world. We initiate campaigns, raise funds and make it impossible for the establishment to sweep the misfortunes of others under the carpet. Tell me, Soraya, what does your family do?"

"Do?" She is startled by his change of direction.

"Yes, do, for a living. Does your father work in the City?"

She shakes her head, dismissively. "Oh, I get it. Because the first time you met me I was wearing those clothes and I'd been out at the night club, you think I'm some poor little rich girl who passes the time partying and living it up. Some *it girl* with a passion for lost causes."

"No, that wasn't what I meant at all. Poor little rich girls don't need to borrow money off strangers to get home: they usually take a limo."

He pauses.

"No, what I meant was where does your sense of altruism come from? If you didn't possess it in spades, you wouldn't have stood up in front of the coroner just now. You'd have been more likely to think *hey, poor Tom, he's dead, so what's the point.* But you didn't, did you? Or rather you couldn't or wouldn't let yourself, even if your actions are going to make your life uncomfortable. That sets you apart and I'm interested to know why. What does your father do?"

Now, it is Soraya's turn to pause. "And you won't go putting whatever I tell you in your paper?"

"Not in so many words, no. If you don't want me to, I'll find a way round it. You seem to be under the impression all of us hacks are cynical enough to manipulate the truth for our own advantage—"

Soraya begins to interrupt him.

Simon raises his hand to silence her. "And I won't say we don't. Well, not all of us. Not all of the time. There's no need for me to go quoting you directly. I can find a way round that, if you'd prefer."

He knows he should feel insulted by her denigration of his

chosen profession, but he isn't. Or, rather, he doesn't want to. Is it her childish honesty? Her apparent naivety? Or is it her spirit that touches him? And then he realises what it is about her that fascinates or perhaps even beguiles him. All the others, Barnes, the other journos, even Candy and even perhaps the faceless readership, they all expect something from him: they all expect him to deliver the words, the copy, the bright fruits of his daily labours. Whereas Soraya, a girl he's met once and only briefly outside a hospital on a cold New Year's morning, seems to want nothing more than his company. That she expects nothing more from him, frees Simon from the yolk of his adopted obligations and the pressures they bring to bear.

"Your father..." he begins for her.

"My father has a corner store in the Mile End Road and my mother works in a laundrette. I'm studying for my degree at the University and I've no idea how I'm ever going to pay off my student loans working with youth offenders. I look at it this way, the world gave me, us, a second chance and I feel obliged to repay the favour."

"You want to tell me about your second chance?" he fishes, casually.

"No." Soraya pauses. "Leastways not right now."

"You said *us*; was the second chance granted to you or your family?"

"To us. To my family and me. Although I was very young at the time; too young to really understand what was going on or what that second chance would mean."

"Isn't it up to your father to repay that debt, not you?"

"My father runs a soup kitchen every Thursday, near Old Street. He attends to the hunger of many homeless people. I help him, as does my mother. It's his way, our way, of making up for the opportunity we've been handed."

"To be a Believer, one must be grateful?" he offers.

135

She stares at him, a little aggressively at first. Then her expression softens into a quizzical, slightly amused frown. "I look to you like a Muslim, huh?" Soraya circles her index finger, indicating her headscarf.

He doesn't reply.

"Truly?"

"Okay," he surrenders, "it's not strictly speaking a hijab. What is it, a shemagh or a shayla?"

"It's a headscarf, Simon. And just because I wear it, it doesn't mean I am a Muslim or want to be. You are quite right though: Muslims say that the first step to becoming a Believer is to be grateful. Whereas Christians say first you must believe in God and then and only then will you be rewarded for your belief. I am neither. If I'm anything, I'm Mandaean. Lapsed perhaps, though probably more Mandaean than not."

"Mandaean?"

"Yes, Mandaean. And that's for some other time, too," she says. "You do know there are fundamental differences between Muslims and Christians in the way they see gratitude?"

Simon nods, careful not to nod so enthusiastically that she might think him patronising. "I understand the difference between the concepts."

Soraya grins, mischievously. And even though the downlights in the coffee shop shine white and bright, and the glass before them permits a stream of late winter sun to reflect in from the windows of the building opposite, the world pales beside her.

"A concept, Simon. Is that what you think gratitude is: a concept? Because for Muslims, *Shukr* isn't simply a concept; it is perhaps the greatest virtue."

Her subtle rebuke embarrasses him.

"Soraya, when I met you on New Year's morning at the hospital you said there was another man present when you and

Tom Williams were assaulted: 'that other guy' was what you said to me. Something tells me you didn't tell DS Chalmers."

She waits, staring at him; weighing him up again and again fidgeting nervously in her seat.

When she doesn't answer, he says, "I think I know why."

"You do, huh. Well what makes you think that? I might have meant the man who tried to... to..." As she remembers, so her eyes tear and her words escape; a flight she was unable to take on New Year's night.

Simon is drawn to lay his hand on her shoulder, to reassure her. He wants to. *So* wants to. But, he doesn't. He holds back, not wanting to spook her.

"You might have but you didn't, did you, Soraya? And it's why you didn't that intrigues me. Is it because you think he might get the blame for Tom getting beaten up, or maybe even for his murder?"

Her eyes are glazed over with the sheen of trying to remember. And though Soraya is looking straight at him, her concentration lies elsewhere.

Slowly, he tries to reel her in. "Old Tom, God bless him, might have been an ex-paratrooper, but after listening to his litany of medical ailments, it doesn't sound to me as though he was up for dragging some thug off you."

"He tried," she says, dreamily. "He really did try. He was so brave."

"Look, Soraya, given the circumstances anyone would have been petrified."

The focus returns to her gaze and her brow furrows. "Petrified? Yes, I was. Completely and utterly petrified. I've never felt so helpless. As I said, the worst part was *not being able* to help Tom. I wanted to and if I could have, I would have."

"Probably just as well you didn't. You might have been hurt like Tom, perhaps worse. You can't know."

Soraya quiets and glances down at her hands, as if they had been responsible for her inaction. "No, Simon, I couldn't. Physically I couldn't. That girl had put something in my drink."

"You think the girl and the bloke were together?"

"No, I don't think so." Soraya widens her eyes as she frowns. "I don't remember seeing them together."

"You saw the guy who assaulted you in the queue, but you told Chalmers you didn't remember seeing him in the club."

"Oh yes, I did, didn't I?" she says, and screwing up her face in concentration she holds the palm of her right hand up to her forehead. "I've only just remembered. We exchanged a bit of, I don't know what, banter? I suppose you'd call it that. In the queue to get in. That's why he called me a gobby bitch. I put him down in front of his mates. That's why he thought I owed him. I'd forgotten that. How come you remember it?"

"I was there, in the queue behind you. I was watching you."

"Yes, of course. You were. I saw you. You didn't have your mask on. That was when I noticed you." Soraya is staring at her hands again, this time as though the riddle of that evening is written in the lines of her palms. "And that guy, he was there with his mates. There were two of them. Big guys. The third one, the nasty guy, the one who had a go at me, the one who beat poor old Tom up, was smaller. He was about my height and he wore that dreadful mask..."

"The plague doctor mask," he prompts, "the mask with the curved red beak."

"Yes, that mask. The plague doctor. The other two had strange faces on theirs."

"Blair and Bush?"

"Yes. They all had their masks on; all except one, the one with the Tony Blair mask, and I didn't get a proper look at him. The only time I saw their faces was later outside the back—"

"All three of them were outside?" he interrupts, surprised. "All

138

three, later, when Tom got assaulted? You didn't mention the other two to Chalmers, why?"

"Oh God!" Soraya moans, still staring at her hands. "The whole thing was my fault, wasn't it? If I hadn't put him down, he..."

Now Simon does reach out and he lays his hand on hers.

The lunchtime crowd is building and time-pressed office workers push past to queue up for soups, sandwiches and salads. A burly construction worker, sand-encrusted yellow jacket and hardhat, nudges against Soraya.

"Sorry, love," he offers.

Soraya doesn't so much as flinch; she is lost in what she perceives to be her part in the rough sleeper's passing.

Simon squeezes her hand softly. "Don't go there, Soraya. There's no point and you didn't tell the guy to beat up old Tom: the guy did that all on his own."

"Yes, but if I—"

"No, Soraya, don't," he instructs, gently. "There's nothing to be gained by giving yourself a hard time."

She is not listening to him and she is oblivious of the crowds in the coffee shop. All she can hear is the harpy of her guilt whispering in her ear.

Simon watches and waits. "If ifs and ands were pots and pans, there'd be no work for tinkers'..." he murmurs.

Soraya comes to, "What was that?" She grips his hand, squeezing it so hard it hurts.

"Nothing, just a poem I read." The pressure on his hands slackens and keen to keep her talking, he asks, "So what did this *other guy*, the guy who was with Tom; what did he do? Did he try to help you?"

She lets go of his hand, drains her coffee and takes her phone out of her bag. Soraya examines it, reads what he assumes must be a text and, while she responds to it with a speedy shuffle of her fingers, asks, "What guy?"

139

"The other guy who was there with you and Tom?"

Soraya continues to text. "I'm not sure who you mean, Simon. There was only me and Tom and the guy who assaulted me."

"And the girl whose name you can't remember."

"Oh, yeah. And her."

"And the other two guys who were with the guy who assaulted you; the guys you forgot to tell Chalmers about."

"Yes, them too." She continues to concentrate on spelling out her message.

"And the *other guy*," Simon states.

"Mm, what guy?"

Simon studies her. She is without doubt the most beautiful woman he has ever set eyes on. Woman or girl, he isn't sure.

For now, though, she is hiding by pretending she is not really present. It's what most people do when they realise they have been talking to him for too long and their conversation is heading into unwelcome territory. It comes as a subtle change in atmosphere, a slight shift in body language or as a curtain hauled across the window to their minds. It is how Soraya is behaving now, as though she has already left his company even though she is still sitting next to him. And she delivers Simon a look so deadpan, he cannot make up his mind as to whether it is the lie or the obvious truth she is hiding behind.

"I guess I must have meant the man who assaulted me."

"Okay, I get it," he doesn't bother to reign in his sarcasm, "there was just you and Tom and the bad guy, his two mates and the girl. I guess old Tom must have put the wind up the lot of them. Good thing he happened to be dossing out the back of the club or you'd have been in big trouble."

"Yes," she says, "big trouble. That's why I feel so wretchedly guilty about what happened to Tom. That's why I had to speak out at the inquest. And that's why I'm going to find myself in deep shit if I don't get home before DS Chalmers comes asking the kind of questions I don't want to be answering in front of my parents." Soraya draws the policeman's card from her bag and rolls her eyes at it as though it is an invitation to a flogging.

"So," she looks up at him, "if you don't mind... Oh, and by the way I really appreciate the coffee, thanks." She pauses, thinking. "It seems to be the way of things when we meet, doesn't it? I end up thanking you for... well, for helping me out." She delivers Simon a vaguely sad smile, turning the corners of her mouth down just sufficiently so that he will properly appreciate that she's not leaving because she wants to, it's just that... she must.

Soraya hitches her bag over her shoulder. "Thank you. Really, thank you."

"The pleasure was all mine. Here, please, my card." He writes his address on the back.

She chuckles as she reads it. "Just in case your phone number's not enough, huh?"

He colours. "You forget, you returned the last one I gave you..." Simon hesitates, "...in the envelope with the money. Keep this one in case you remember something else about New Year's Eve and need to talk." To deflect her from picking up on his blushing, he adds, "You don't happen to need money for the bus, do you?"

She laughs, embarrassed, and slips his card into her pocket. "No." Soraya turns and walks away, and when she reaches the doorway she turns to look back. Framed by the pillars, she smiles and waves her Oyster card at him.

19

One of the entries listed in the notebook is *Patrick*, nickname *Paddy*, and Loretta Martin had said she'd written to a Paddy Jennings.

The name comes nearer the back, suggesting he has seen service more recently. The entry reads *Bracknell* and *The Goose*. Also, the *King's Badge* which Simon learns is not a pub; rather it is an award given to the best all round recruit in training. The entry records Paddy's interests, too. They include the *Royals*, Reading Football Club, *Iron Maiden* and *Valentino Rossi(God)*. The entry contains no details of family and lists Paddy Jennings specialities as *PW(S)* and *ML*, which Simon now knows stands for platoon weapons sniper and mountain leader. A footnote tells Simon that Jennings *can fix anything*.

Fortunately, Paddy Jennings is listed in the online phone directory and when Simon calls the number a quietly-spoken woman answers to tell him he is "very fortunate to catch Paddy. He's on leave. I'm just here cleaning."

Simon thinks quickly and delivers a spiel about how he is writing a piece for the newspaper on whether servicemen believe the forces prepare them adequately for life on the outside. After Afghanistan, that is?

"It's not like being in prison," the woman responds, put out. "I'll pass on the message, though he's very busy. He's to report back the day after tomorrow."

Jennings rings back that very afternoon and they arrange to meet the next lunchtime at The Goose, a pub close by Bracknell station.

Chobham Common rattles by, sun light flashing through the pines like the blank frames of an old movie reel.

Simon closes his eyes and projects the CCTV recording from New Year's Eve on to the screen of his mind. He has run through the incident so many times it is as though he has copied the recording directly into his consciousness.

The first part that springs to mind is the disturbance in the queue, so he rewinds and begins again.

The rough sleeper trails down the line, tapping people for spare change. He pauses at the group before Soraya's. There is a brief exchange between the rough sleeper and the man wearing the red plague doctor mask, possibly the thug who Soraya says assaulted her and old Tom, definitely the same guy who mauled Candy. Next, he approaches Soraya. She is with two young men and another girl. The rough sleeper stops and speaks to her. She responds and hands him the note. They stand, both holding the note, both staring at each other.

They hold each other's look for three, nearly four seconds. Why? Is his look an appreciation of her charity, an acknowledgement of her generosity or an expression of his gratitude? Is hers a recognition of his existence, his circumstance or his right not to be blanked, snubbed or ignored simply because he is less fortunate than others?

Or is it something stronger?

Her father runs a soup kitchen, that would surely be enough to dispel anyone's prejudices towards rough sleepers; that would surely imbue her with a purer empathy.

As the train slows at the level crossing at Sunningdale, Simon is minded to think that in handing over a twenty-pound note Soraya *was* being overgenerous, especially when considering she is a student whose father makes his living from a corner store. But then her selfless benevolence, her completely natural almost naïve altruism, is just one of the reasons he finds her attractive.

By comparison, Candy's animal magnetism is designed to draw the bull in men. She needs them to want her. They feed her ego in the same way as handfuls of silage are fed to a cow, and Candy must have her daily intake or she will deflate. It is, Simon has decided, not her looks that he finds unattractive, rather it is her ego and its constant need of feeding.

Soraya's draw, on the other hand, is not that of the magnet; it is the glow of the light in the distance, it is the promise of a destination which one has for so long been searching. Men, other men, might walk the same path and not notice her glow because they are not looking for it, their eyes are drawn elsewhere. Or perhaps it is that other men have no hope of seeing her light because she will not permit them to. Soraya permits only those who she thinks will appreciate her light to see it, and it is that subtle arrogance, so alternative to Candy's raw prurience, that Simon finds so very attractive.

The recording runs on: the plague doctor snipes at Soraya. Soraya snipes back. Her boyfriend, partner, whatever he is, takes exception. The enormous Tamati arrives and cools the situation.

Simon replays the recording back and forth.

With him and Candy behind them, Soraya and her friends file slowly down to the entrance; the closer they get to the doors, the clearer their image. It is, however, the group of three men who interest him now.

They are shaven-headed: two tall and one short, and they joke with the security staff as they swipe their ID cards and gurn at the camera.

Earlier in the morning, Simon had flicked up on his laptop the list of those entering the club, synchronised the times and noted down the names of the men and the types of ID cards they used. All three had used photo-card driving licences noting their addresses.

Simon closes his eyes and forwards his mental film to the part where Soraya had realised she needed to swipe her ID card and look into the camera before the turnstile would ease open. He freezes the film at that point and sits for a few minutes staring intently, at her image. She is embarrassed and coy and unpretentious and—

The train rattles into Bracknell station and he leaves his seat to stand by the sliding doors.

Soraya has not told him the truth about what happened out the back of the club; that much is obvious. The day before at the coffee shop, she had packed up and left the moment he'd asked her about *that other guy*. There is little doubt that she is protecting whoever it was that came to her rescue and, as much as she would have him believe it, it wasn't Tom Williams. Decorated service veteran he might have been, but he had very obviously come off worst in whatever had gone down.

So why would she want to protect someone who had come to her rescue?

The train lurches to a halt and eventually the doors slide back. Simon steps down onto the platform and heads over the footbridge to the station concourse. The pub, The Goose, is right across the road.

———

He orders a mineral water and settles at a round table by the window. Seconds later a blue and white striped Yamaha sweeps noisily round the side of the pub.

Patrick Jennings, garbed in black and white motorcycle leathers, the name FIAT emblazoned across his chest in red lettering, carries in his left hand a garishly bright orange and yellow helmet. He is slender of build and his gait is robotic, as though his limbs are attached to his torso by metal pins articulated by wires.

"You must be Simon Peckham, then."

"I am." Simon rises and offers his hand. "Good of you to meet me, Patrick."

"Paddy."

"Get you a drink, Paddy."

"Sure. Lime and soda. Off back down the West Country when I leave here. Bit of a schlep. Better a soft drink."

By the time Simon has returned with Jennings's drink, the Royal Marine has removed his fluorescent yellow gloves and shrugged his upper torso out of his leathers. His black hair is flat, short and curled, and his face keen and lean, like that of an eager marathon runner.

"Good health, Paddy, and thank you again for agreeing to meet me."

"No problem. Lucky to catch me. Now," he says, as though he is convening a meeting of the local round table, "I haven't got long and you want to know how guys like me think we'll deal with the more mundane aspects of ordinary life after all the excitement of Afghan, eh?"

"That's about the strength of it. I know a lot of the troops who come back find it difficult to adjust to Civvy Street."

"Civvy Street?" Jennings scoffs. "You've been watching too much soap on TV, my friend. Not so much like that these days. Sure, it'll take a bit of getting used to, why wouldn't it? Guys tell me that first off, your sleep pattern's all messed up; you watch where you put your feet like a buzzard on steroids; you strain to listen out for the slightest footfall; and you think it's all going to kick off every time you hear a car backfire.

Jennings leans forward and fixes Simon with a maddened stare. "But that's all to be expected, isn't it?"

"I wouldn't know, Paddy. That's why I'm here."

Unexpectedly, Jennings's face breaks into a cheeky grin. "That's all part of the game, isn't it, eh? Just another day in the life of a bloke who was once serving in theatre. Listen, a kid buys a ticket to a rock concert. It's no good him complaining to his mum when he gets home that he's gone deaf because the music was too loud."

"It's that simple?" Simon asks, infecting his tone with sufficient surprise.

"It is for some." Paddy sits back, sips his lime and soda. "It isn't for others, for sure." He pauses, glancing across the bar as though the answer to *why some* and *not others* is written on the blackboard of specials. "But it *is* about buying the ticket. Remember, nobody forces you to sign up. When you volunteer, you should have, no, you must have, a fair idea of what's going to happen when you have to pull the trigger or when your mate steps on an IED. Nobody can tell you exactly what it's like and everyone reacts differently to it when it happens. As my old man used to say, 'Don't pick up the gun unless you've got the balls to use it, because the bloke you're pointing yours at won't be thinking twice before using his'. Same goes for having to live with it all afterwards."

"What does make it easier for some to adjust and not others, Paddy?"

Jennings raises his eyes and, pushing his chin forwards and tensing the muscles of his neck, bridles his lips. "We're all different, mate: no two blokes are the same. The same goes for the women and, let me tell you, there's just as many brave women been out there as men. Braver sometimes." Jennings' pitch is concise and pithy, like a well-rehearsed lecture.

147

"And while some of us are better equipped to deal with the horrors of it, others may have to suffer a greater dose; and we all have no choice but to deal with it. Usually, we do that by putting it aside so it doesn't get in our way."

"You make it sound rather elementary, is it?"

"Listen Simon, I've seen men I'd always thought of as mentally bullet proof break down in tears purely because they've reached their capacity. And, like computers, once your mind has no more capacity, no more random-access memory available, overflow is inevitable. But remember also that the computer in your head has already stored all those terrible images and all that appalling information, so it never gets permanently deleted. You never get to wipe it from your mainframe. You're never allowed to forget it."

A lecture in amateur psychology, Simon hadn't expected. Perhaps he is being treated to Paddy Jennings' exclusive method of dealing with all that has been, and may yet be, thrown at him. He is, after all, on his way back from leave.

"Coming back, was that tough? The first few weeks, I mean?" Simon asks.

"Sure. Absolutely it was. Though by the time you'd sat on your arse at Bastion waiting for your transfer, you were a bit bewildered. You know, feeling a bit spare after feeling so indispensable."

He sits back again, stretching his long, slender arms above his head.

"Guys have told me that it's not until a few weeks later that you notice the buzzards start to circle the carrion in your thought. No one can train you for that. They don't issue equipment or send you on courses for dealing with that."

"So how do you deal with it, Paddy?"

"Yeah, how do I deal with it?" He examines the round table top for a second. "Don't know, really. In theatre, you get to talk to the Field Mental Health Team. They make a difference, a good difference. Me, I read a lot; I find it helps."

The entry in the moleskin notebook reads that Paddy Jennings *can fix anything*. Is that how Jennings will deal with life after Afghanistan? By breaking his inner-self down into component parts so that he can understand what makes him function and then reconstruct himself into one better, healthier and more efficient whole?

"Funny thing," Jennings continues, "I read this book the other day. Found it in a box of books in a car boot sale. It's about the Mau Mau uprising in Kenya, in the fifties. It's written by an American; forget his name, Robert something. In the book he quotes an old Basuto proverb which says, roughly, if you take away a man's traditions, then you had better have something of value to replace it with, otherwise you'll have trouble on your hands.

"I've been wondering, lately, whether life's like that. The service is full of traditions: it's your way of life. And being out in Afghan you get a heightened sense of that: living for your mates, wanting to get the job done, wanting to perform well for your team. Christ, never mind all that 24 hours, wide-eyed awareness that gets to be such a huge part of your routine.

"And when you get back, other than an enormous sense of pride in a job well done, you're not left with much. Especially when you lot spend half your time telling us how the situation is just as bad now as it was before we stuck our necks in. How you've lost your limbs and your mates their lives for nothing."

"Do you feel you made a difference?" Simon asks, expecting a broadside in reply.

Paddy Jennings stares at him for a few long and very unsettling seconds. But he doesn't go to his guns. Instead, he exhales long and hard; a sigh laden with frustration rather than insult and injury.

"Look, Simon, it's difficult for you guys to understand. You don't see it first-hand like we do. People will tell you Afghan is medieval. It isn't. It's way more backward than that." He throws his arms wide, palms out. "We're talking year zero in attitude here. An eye for an eye, love thy neighbour and hate thine enemy. Christ," he glances up at the ceiling as if beseeching Valentino Rossi, "it's bloody biblical. The Crusades were almost sophisticated by comparison. Imagine getting stuck in the middle of the Crusades with a shit load of technology, high explosive ordnance and only a rough idea of what success translates as. Getting the locals to talk to us was only one part of it. Oh yeah, and the bloody Taliban did their level best to stop that. Even when we could gain the local's trust, they knew it was at the risk of bringing a whole load of shit down upon themselves and their family." He sips his drink.

"As to making a difference? It's what the Army call *The Tomato Factor.*"

Simon is none the wiser and doesn't try to hide his ignorance.

"Look," Paddy says, "when you first arrive in a village, there's not much on offer in the market. Most of the produce has been either requisitioned by the Taliban or the locals are too shit-scared to bring it out and flog it to you. By the end of your tour, six or eight months depending, you notice the tomatoes are back on the stalls. That means things are beginning to return to normal. That's the difference. Sounds small, I know, but that's one way of judging your reward against the effort you've put in."

"I see." Simon nods, thoughtfully. "So, what are you going to do when you leave, Paddy? For a living, I mean."

"Oh, not sure yet. Might stay in for a while. I'm down at Lympstone for the moment, part of the training team. I've got half a plan to run an MOT shop with a pal of mine; do a bit of welding, mechanics, that kind of thing. Could be quite handy; get to take a bit of time off now and again." Jennings pulls back the cuff of his shirt and glances at his wristwatch. "And talking of time, I'm due in the West Country in a couple of hours so, if you don't mind, is that about what you wanted to hear."

"Yes. Thank you, Paddy. It's pretty much exactly what I wanted to hear and I'm very grateful for you taking the trouble of affording me your time. By the way, are you married?"

"Was."

"Sorry."

"Don't be."

"Casualty of war?" Simon probes, gently.

"Nope. Didn't need a Warrant Officer to teach me that lesson."

"Didn't mean to be rude, sorry," Simon offers. "Just wondered."

"No problem, mate." Jennings grins. "I know where you're coming from. Just plain shouldn't have gone there in the first place. Nothing to do with the uniform.

"Now, I'd best be off or there's a pretty young hairdresser who'll think I prefer your company to hers. And although it's been good to have a chat…" Jennings smiles, warmly, until a cloud blows up and shades the light in his smile, "By the way, where did you get my name and contact details from? Only we usually get asked first if…"

"No, I didn't seek anyone's permission, I took a chance. You see, I came across this." He draws the moleskin notebook from his pocket. "Your name's in here; some of your contact details, too. The rest I got off the internet."

Paddy Jennings looks down at the small black book and cannot seem to drag his eyes away from it. Eventually, he looks back up at Simon, his eyes wide with disbelief. He glances back down briefly, clearly unsure of whether he should touch what Simon is offering.

"Go on, take it. It's no longer live." His attempt at humour cuts no ice with the Royal Marine. "I see you know what it is."

"Yeah, the boss's bible. How the hell did you get hold of that?"

20

Jennings, not for a second taking his eyes off the notebook, takes it and sits back down.

"Get you another drink?" Simon asks, heading off to the bar.

"Sure thing. Make it a pint... a bitter. Don't suppose one will hurt."

When he returns, Simon realises Jennings has neither moved nor opened the book. He is simply sitting, holding it in his palm and staring at it in wonder as though it is made from the most delicate porcelain.

"The boss's bible?" Simon murmurs, to draw Jennings from his stupor.

"Yes. His bible. You know the boss then?" he says, finally looking up.

"Captain Ross? No, never had the pleasure."

"Then where did you..."

"Found it on the pavement, on a street in the City."

"Found it? In the City? In London?"

"Yes. That's about the long and the short of it. How it got

there I don't know, but there it was, lying on the pavement amongst some old newspapers."

"You've read through it then," Jennings says and falls silent again.

"Shock and awe?"

"You what?"

"I said," Simon drags Jennings eyes back to his, "shock and awe. Isn't that what they called it when they let loose all those cruise missiles on Iraq in 2003? Overwhelming power. A spectacular show of force designed to paralyze the enemy. It's what you look like you've just been hit with, Paddy."

Jennings rapidly thumbs through the notebook until he gets to the entry written about him.

Simon shifts a little awkwardly in his seat. "Took me a while to work out exactly what it was."

"I see Billy Martin is in here. He and the boss were inseparable. Together in Iraq right through to Afghan."

"Mm, I spoke to Loretta Martin, Billy's sister."

"You did? Meant to be bright, that one," Jennings remarks. "Billy was always going on about how uber-intelligent she was. Accountant, isn't she? What did she have to say about Billy? What's he up to?"

"Bit cagey on that. Probably in Libya, probably working in security or something like that."

"Oh, yes. That'll be Billy. Always had a nose for the money. Didn't mind the risky stuff. Said that's what he'd end up doing. Private work, I guess."

"She wasn't sure."

Jennings reads odd pages before getting to the back once more. "Cruds is here. Page crossed out. Poor old Cruds. Mind you, he wasn't the easiest of blokes to get on with. Good tunnel rat though."

"Yes, that's what Derek Roarke said, though his language was a shade more colourful."

Jennings chuckles, remembering. "Yep, best of friends; best of enemies, those two."

A bell rings in Simon's head. "That's what Loretta Martin said about Captain Ross and Billy."

"What, best of friends, best of enemies?"

"Exactly that."

Jennings looks up, frowning. "I guess she would do. Bit of history with those two."

"In what way?"

"So, where is the boss? Does he know you've got his bible? Is that why you've come to see me? Trying to track him down, are you?"

In as much as Jennings has just blanked Simon's question, now it is his turn to sidestep. "In a manner of speaking."

The Royal Marine puts the notebook down on the table and leans towards Simon, his body angles all hard and aggressive, his voice harder. "Listen Mr Peckham, if the Boss has gone on the missing list or is in any kind of trouble, you'd better come clean sooner rather than later. There's more than a few of us would still get out of bed for him, especially after that business with Del Boy. There's plenty of us owe him. Where is he?"

Simon considers a second sidestep. However, Jennings' version of shock and awe is infinitely more intimidating. "That's the problem, Paddy. I don't know. Believe me, I wish I did. The names in the notebook have led me to a few of the guys, like you, who've served with him. Derek Roarke wasn't up to providing me with any useful information and Loretta Martin only gave me a few pointers. As there are no details about Captain Ross in his notebook, I've no idea where to start. I don't even know where he lives or if he's still wearing the uniform."

"No, not the boss. Got out right after coming back. He'd had a bellyful by then. Have you tried asking down at Portsmouth? If he's in trouble, they'd be your best bet."

"Yes, I figured that. And no, I haven't asked them."

"Why not?"

"Because..." Simon begins. What Jennings has pointed out is true. Why hasn't he gone down the more direct and obvious route? He has kept the notebook for longer than he has a right to. But, it is the key to a bigger story, his story and not one he is inclined to give up without a fight.

He looks back at Paddy Jennings, understanding how simple it would be for the Royal Marine to simply reach over and throttle him. Then he remembers Soraya and old Tom Williams and the three obnoxious slapheads from the nightclub. They are also a good part of the reason why he has kept all the information to himself.

"Because, Paddy, I'm not sure if Captain Ross isn't in some kind of fix. I don't know whether he's gone missing or what. And until I've found out a bit more about him, I'm not inclined to go ringing any official alarm bells, if you know what I mean?"

Jennings glowers back, then softens. "Yes, Simon. I think I do. Captain Ross was the best boss I ever served with; best by far. Thought of his men first. Not like some others I could mention." He frowns hard, the faces of those *some others* very obviously coming to mind.

"Well, Paddy, mustn't hold you up any longer. Specially if you've got a long ride." He reaches for the black moleskin notebook.

Jennings, though delivers Simon a second dark look and flaps the notebook in his face. "Give me a good reason why I should give this back to you when it clearly belongs to Captain Ross. Way I see it, I've more right to this than you have; at least my name's in it."

"Because, Paddy, I found this in a dosser's corner in the City of London. And it doesn't take a genius to work out that wherever it is you're off to lies in completely the opposite direction. And, if that isn't sufficient, you might like to recall that it was me who

155

managed to work out what this notebook is about. All of that plus the fact that I tracked you down might tell you I've got a better chance of finding Richard Ross than you have. So, stop waving it about and hand it over."

Jennings ceases flapping the notebook in his face and watches and waits.

The man sitting opposite Simon is no stranger to fronting up to somewhat more lethal adversaries than a tabloid hack armed only with a promising intellect, as Barnes has very generously suggested. And there is little to be gained by making an enemy of a man he might need later. So Simon, too, waits and watches, and grows aware that he will gain more by allowing Jennings to steal the moment.

"Look, Paddy, the most important issue here is that I find your old boss. It's not about what's in it for me. Sure, I'm chasing a story, that's what I do. And for what it's worth, and if I'm right, it's Richard Ross who needs my help most right now." Simon splays his hands in mock supplication, though careful not to overplay it. "What do you say?"

Jennings extends his moment in the sun. "Okay, Simon, you keep the book on one condition: if you do track Captain Ross down, I want to be the first person to know about it. Got that?"

"Got it. Thank you, Paddy." Inwardly, Simon sighs with relief. He pockets the notebook. "What I need are a few details about Ross. Where he lived, would be a start. Apart from asking the powers-that-be, who will only quote data-protection anyway, I've no way of gaining any more information about him. So where does Richard Ross come from? Where did he live and where can I find his family?"

Jennings frowns and searches the table. "Ross was from Wales; born down that way too: The Black Mountains, near where the SAS train."

"Brecon?" Simon interrupts again.

156

"No, not Brecon. Aber..." Jennings trawls his memory.

"Abergavenny?"

"Yes, that's the place. There was always a bit of banter as to whether or not he really was Welsh. I believe it's quite close to the border."

"Go on, Paddy. What else?"

"I think his parents might have passed on; his dad anyway. The boss's father was in the army: Welsh Guards, a Major. Billy Martin once told me his father expected the boss to follow the same route. For some reason, he chose us over his father's old regiment. Billy would probably know why, you'd best ask him. They were tight, as I mentioned. Came from different backgrounds, but no less tight. Billy was with the boss first time out in Iraq."

"As I said, Loretta Martin told me," Simon interrupts. "And in Afghanistan, later."

"Yes." Jennings hesitates. "Yes, and the boss was married, wasn't he?"

"Was?"

"Yes, was. It's as I say, you'd best ask Billy Martin. He'd know the bones of it." The Royal Marine pauses.

"Something happened between the two of them?" Simon presses. "Loretta Martin said they were the best of friends and the best of enemies. And you said there is a bit of history between them. What did you mean exactly?"

Paddy Jennings has said enough, or possibly too much, and Simon watches as he unfolds himself from his seat and stands to stretch. "Yes," he says, "and I also said you'd best ask Billy when you get hold of him. Right. I must be off or I'll be out of a warm bed for the night. Thanks for the beer and remember to keep me up to date."

"Yes, Paddy," Simon agrees, getting to his feet, "I promise. If I find him, even if he's back home in Welsh Wales I'll let you know. For all I know he probably will be by the time I catch up with him."

The tall, slender man with the keen features collects his gaudy helmet and offers his hands. "I'll wait to hear from you, then. By the way, have you got a card with your contacts so I can send you my mobile?"

Simon slips one out of his wallet and hands it over. Jennings already has his number, yet the request for his card is a flag to let Simon know that the Royal Marine has all of his details and is likely to come looking for him if he doesn't get back in touch.

"I'm sure we'll have good cause to speak soon, Paddy."

"Hope so, mate. I bloody hope so."

"It would, though," Simon continues, "help me a great deal if you could let me have a photograph of Captain Ross. If you don't have one, a regimental photo would do. Just something for me to refer to. I haven't the first clue what your Captain Ross looks like."

"Yes, I can manage that. I'll email it through to you at the weekend. Cheers."

A minute or so later, the rotation of the planet is suspended by the roar of a Yamaha.

21

He steps up to the porch, pulls the knocker back and lets it drop.

The clump of iron on hard wood amplifies the sepulchral hush fostered by the cold air.

When the noise draws no response, Simon counts slowly to ten, tries again and waits.

Decorative lions guard the steps up to the door and the grey Pennant sandstone walls are capped and crenelated, affording the house a medieval, almost castle-like facade.

Inquiring eyes observe him nervously from across the empty flowerbed. "Can I help you?"

"My name's Peckham, Simon Peckham. I have an appointment. Are you Mrs Ross?"

"Noooo," she hoots with very open disdain, pulling her shawl tighter about her shoulders, "I most certainly am not. Wait there." She vanishes.

Simon stands and waits. He isn't cold. Not yet.

The lady reappears. Her hair is now tied back; her shawl arranged just so. "Would you come this way? I'm sorry I didn't hear you; it must have been the washing machine." She talks hurriedly in a lilting Welsh brogue, snipping the ends off her words the way a gardener might dead-head a rose. "We haven't used the front door for a while. People come to the back door, you see; deliveries really. Mrs Ross doesn't have many visitors these days."

Simon follows her in through the backdoor; it squeaks loudly as she closes it behind him.

"Long journey?" she inquires. "Would you like to wash your hands before I take you in? I'll bring coffee through in a while. That is unless you prefer tea. Mrs Ross only drinks coffee. The cloakroom's through there." She points towards a door at the back of the kitchen. "There's no lock. No one will bother you. Here, let me take your bag."

"Thank you." He passes her his shoulder bag containing his laptop, and even though he has no call to, he goes to the bathroom and exactly as the woman has suggested, washes his hands. The small cloakroom is stone-cold and basic; the basin Victorian, deep and round and rimmed with a blue border and delicate floral detail. The best that can be said of the taps is that they function, for they are plain and stiff, like the toilet, from the high cistern of which hangs a heavy-linked chain.

The woman is percolating coffee in an individual pot on the Aga. Next to it a heavy iron kettle shoots steam from its spout. The lady smiles as though now that he has washed his hands he is more acceptable. "I'm Mrs Phillips."

Simon notices how firm and rough her grip is; firm like she has spent her years lifting heavy kettles and rough, perhaps from fetching and carrying firewood.

"Pleased to meet you, Mrs Phillips. Tea would be good if it's not too much trouble."

"Builders, Earl Grey, Chai, herbal?"

"Earl Grey, please. No milk, no sugar, thank you."

"Very good, Mr Peckham. You like it the way it should be

160

taken. People have confused tea with some kind of soup. After all it is supposed to be an infusion. I'll take you through now. You've spoken with Mrs Ross on the phone?" She smooths her apron down, removes the clip from her hair and regathering the strands, pins them back again. She bends forwards as she does so and he realises it is the only time she had taken her eyes off him, apart from when he was in the washroom. There is an organisation and efficiency about Mrs Phillips, as though she is the manager of a royal court.

"Yes."

"I see," she says, looking back up at him. "In that case I must mention that Mrs Ross is not a well lady and talking tires her. I will bring the tea and coffee in and then leave you both to it. I will return in half an hour to check on her and if I think she is weary, I will make it plain to you that you should call a halt to your conversation. Is that clear?"

"Very naturally," his tone is solicitous, that of a mourner approaching a coffin. But, as there is no coffin: "I'd just like to ask her a few questions. I hope not to take up too much of her time.

"As long as that's understood Mr Peckham." Mrs Phillips fixes him with her large owl-like eyes, wondering whether or not he can be trusted to do as she asks. When she finishes her wondering she adds, "I must say, I expected someone older," and turns on her heels, assuming he will follow.

She leads him through the dining room. The oak panels and table are so dark they appear to suck the light from the leaded windows; the room smells of beeswax and he can feel the chill of the flagstone floor through the soles of his shoes. The only relief to the gloom is supplied by the candelabras, pepper shakers and blue glass and filigree salt boats gracing the table. However even they look cold, as silver so often does.

When they reach the door at the far end, the housekeeper halts abruptly and repeats the same pantomime as before, smoothing her starched white apron and re-pinning her hair. Her rigmarole encourages Simon to check his shirt is not hanging out of his trousers.

Mrs Phillips knocks twice on the door, pauses as if counting to three and then, without waiting for a reply, turns the handle and pushes. "Mr Peckham, mam," she announces.

Mrs Cynthia Ross sits by the fireplace in a claret-toned wingback, leather armchair. Her skin, what little of it that isn't concealed beneath her red lipstick and black tea-gown, is paler than white and shows an almost transparent and leukemic sheen, as if she is fashioned from candle wax. The veins on the back of her delicate hands stand out as though yet more blue wax has melted and dribbled out from her cuffs.

Mrs Phillips waves Simon to a chair opposite; a chair occupied by a bundle of fur that could easily be mistaken for a cushion. The dog sniffs and flops lazily to the floor.

"You must excuse him, Mr Peckham," Cynthia Ross says. "Unfortunately, the last visitor sat on him and he has not yet seen fit to forgive the world for the insult." Her voice is stronger than her slender neck has a right to suggest.

Once Simon is seated, Mrs Ross waves her housekeeper away and waits for the door to close before speaking. "I expected someone older."

"That's perfectly natural," he says, "most people think we're all worn-shoed windbags."

"Meaning?" Her tone lies halfway between accusation and casual disinterest.

"Meaning, Mrs Ross, that I haven't got round to fitting the stereotype. Well, not yet anyway. I'm fairly new to the job, so if I ask the wrong questions or appear too intrusive, I'll be relying on you to say so."

"Oh, don't worry, young man. I will."

"Good. Thank you."

"Would you like a drink?" She sits forward.

The train journey had lasted two and a half hours, though it had seemed longer, and the taxi up from the station can't have taken more than fifteen minutes. Simon is minded to suggest it's too early, but decides it will be in his better interest not to risk causing the woman offence.

"No, thank you, Mrs Ross. Mrs Phillips said she is about to bring in tea. Sorry to disappoint."

"And there I was thinking all journalists were on day release from Alcoholics Anonymous."

"Haven't yet graduated to that yet either." He is reminded of what Barnes had told him at his interview. "Apparently that comes later."

And at that, he hears another swift double knock at the door and Mrs Phillips strides purposefully in and sets a tray down on the ottoman.

"Thank you, Mrs Phillips, that'll be all for now. Would you be kind enough to do the honours, Mr Peckham? Black, please."

He pours her coffee and passes it to her. From between the cushion and the side of her chair, Cynthia Ross extracts a half bottle of what looks like brandy and decants a good measure into her coffee. Simon looks away quickly, pours his tea and sits back.

When she has sipped and sighed, Mrs Ross puts down her cup and fixes him with an uncompromising stare. "So, Mr Peckham, or Simon, if I may?"

"Yes, please do."

"So, Simon, you said on the phone that you wanted to ask me about Richard; said you might have news of him?"

"That's right, yes, though I'll get to the news a little later, if you don't mind?"

"Well, you being a journalist," she says, her nose raised just so, "I understand you must have your questions first, so fire away. What would you like to know?"

"Firstly, do you have other children?"

"No. Richard is an only child."

"And your husband, Major Ross?"

"No, Major Ross passed away just over a year ago. Heart attack. Probably all that booze he'd consumed in the mess. Drink and a hard existence: a bad recipe for longevity."

"I'm sorry for your loss. He was in the forces, too?"

"Welsh Guards, like his father before him." She pauses. "Would I be right in thinking you know Richard was in the forces, though not the army of course. How?"

"I'll come to that, if you can bear with me. What is or was he like, Richard? As a lad, I mean?"

Mrs Ross smiles, wistfully. "Oh, he was in many ways an unusual and yet ordinary boy. A bit of a loner, happier in his own company than in the company of others and therefore pretty adept at finding ways to occupy himself. He was an average student; not bad at the academic stuff, very competitive at sports, especially rugby. But apart from books and cinema, Richard was more at home in the outdoors than in the classroom. He'd spend most of his weekends and holidays up in the woods." She points over her shoulder.

"One night he didn't come home; he must have been only thirteen. His father was in Canada, training or something, and I searched all over for him. Had to call the police out in the end. One of the game keepers eventually found him up in the oak-wood; middle of the night, calm as you like, roasting a pigeon over a fire."

"Age thirteen?" Simon asks.

"Yes. Surprised us too. His father had bought him an air rifle, hadn't told me, of course, and Richard was snaring rabbits and foraging for mushrooms and berries. He'd find all sorts of stuff I never knew you could eat." Mrs Ross sucks on her lip for a moment. "He was pretty good at having stuff out the kitchen, too.

And there I was thinking Mrs Phillips had been filching potatoes. She must have known what he was up to; thick as thieves those two."

"So, Captain Ross taught himself to be self-sufficient."

She smiles. "Self-sufficient. Yes, that's a good way of putting it. When he was here, his father was forever taking him rough shooting or salmon fishing on the Usk; that or to Cardiff for the rugby. They got on well enough, even if there was no great warmth between them. The Major wasn't that kind of man. More's the pity," she adds, not bothering to conceal a regret laced subtly with contempt.

"Richard must be, what, thirty?" he suggests.

"Yes. But in a strange way, he was old before he was young."

"You came to motherhood quite late."

Mrs Ross smiles. "That's a neat way of putting it. Gosh, Simon, aren't you good with words; you make it all sound so charming, so easy. You're right, though. You see, I didn't want children, not in the beginning. I think it was something to do with my husband being absent much of the time: The Middle East, West Germany, Northern Ireland, Cyprus. So not unnaturally, the distinct possibility that I might have to bring up a child or children as a single parent didn't appeal. My husband didn't feel the same way, but he was one for respect so he didn't take issue with me over it. Then, later on, I realised that life had already taken my husband away, what with the Major being committed as much, if not more, to the Army than he was to me. I hope you understand what I mean by that?" She searches his face, hoping.

"Yes, I can, Mrs Ross. Even though I don't have any experience of it, I'm beginning to recognise there's more to it than meets the eye."

"You see, Simon, a force's wife has duties; duties not dissimilar to those of her husband. The forces adopt him and that leaves you no alternative but to adopt the forces. You get used to your husband missing birthdays and anniversaries, Christmas and holidays. And you get used to playing second fiddle; being despatched from one grubby pillar to the next godforsaken outpost every time you think you've just made your house a home." She pauses to draw breath, contemplating. "Wales Forever," she mutters.

"Sorry?"

"Wales Forever, the motto of the Welsh Guards. I often wonder if Wales For-Never wouldn't have been more apposite. And it's even harder on children. They have to grow up in the same uncertain environment, so they learn how to grow up pretty fast and learn to survive without the security and comfort of a more conventional life style. That isn't easy. It comes at a price."

"Part of that price being," he adds, keen to encourage her loquacity, "that as a wife you didn't feel it was right to introduce a child into an already over-crowded marriage?"

Mrs Ross sips her coffee, which must now be cold. She grimaces. "Correct, Simon. Correct. It took me a long time to realise that I had lost my husband to his life and that I was going to be left with nothing to show for my second place. No silver medal, nothing. It sounds rather selfish when put like that, doesn't it?"

Simon hesitates before answering, "It does, Mrs Ross, yes. However, I'm not sure many people understand what it means when one talks of the cost of their safe-keeping. Most people consider the ultimate sacrifice to be the laying down of one's life in defence of... of one's country, one's beliefs, one's way of life or one's freedoms. Few people consider the bigger picture; by which I mean the collateral effects of serving one's country."

She blushes. But rather than embarrassment, her colour, the way her hands clamp over the arms of her wingback chair and the earnestness with which she sits forward, suggests she has taken offence to his definition of her loyalty to her husband. Her husband and, perhaps a few yards further up the line, her Queen and Country.

"Collateral damage, is that what you think army wives suffer, Simon? Collateral damage?"

"No, I apologise, I didn't mean to imply—"

"You did and don't." Her colour fades as quickly as summoned. "You've no need to apologise for an opinion many harbour but few have the courage to put into words. Curiously enough, I agree with you. But the term is depersonalising; it's meant to apply to incidentals, to the unintended, to non-combatants, to by-standers. Forces wives may not be classed as combatants, but we are more than simply by-standers. We also serve who only stand and wait."

"Milton," he says, to let her know he recognises the quote.

"Yes, though I've adapted it to suit my purpose." She smiles in appreciation, perhaps not of him so much as at the convenience of her adaptation. "Not much of a one for sonnets, really, though that one struck a chord. Somehow, it encapsulated the loneliness of it all. Blindness, wasn't that Milton's curse? Well, that's how a forces wife can feel at times: a witness blinded by her husband's sense of duty."

Cynthia Ross closes her eyes and frowns.

Simon waits, patient and polite, and while he waits he takes in the dim room in which she has sought to hide. There are no photographs either on the sideboard or hanging on the walls. Paintings? Yes. But no mementos, no keepsakes and no tokens of the parts her husband and son have played in her life.

She opens her eyes and catches him in his appraisal. "No, Simon, there are no photographs, and I'll tell you why. It was after Bloody Friday, July 1972, when the regiment lost that sergeant in the bombing of the bus depot in Belfast. I've no idea what the Major had been up to over there; he would never discuss any of it with me; said I would be better off not knowing.

"Somehow, the IRA learned his name, got hold of this address, it was the Major's father's house originally, and I received a number of threatening letters through the post. They, the IRA, had already murdered seven people with a bomb at Aldershot Barracks. Ridiculous, when you think about it. Five of them were women who worked in the kitchens and one of the others was a catholic chaplain.

"So, there we were beginning to understand that none of us were safe; not even here in what some people would think of as the back end of beyond. As a precaution, though, I had to put up with a succession of Special Branch officers living with me for the next six months. Nice fellows though they were and even though I knew it was for my own good, I found the whole business very invasive. It was like they had gained entry to my inner sanctum without my permission. I took it very personally.

"Then, at dinner one evening, I noticed the detective looking at my photographs just like you were expecting to look at them a moment ago. And when I saw him studying them, I felt as though each photograph was baring a part of my soul to him; as though through each image he was being permitted access to my innermost thoughts. After that, I felt strangely naked under his gaze. It was as if I no longer had a life of my own.

"You see, Simon, what happened to my husband and his men happened over there, in Northern Ireland. It was their war. Their private war, if that makes sense. It was not happening to me, here. But, suddenly, shockingly, it *was* happening to me, and it was happening *here*. The Troubles had found me and there seemed nowhere to hide.

"The next day, I packed up all the photographs and, for some reason, never got around to putting them out again." Her eyes glaze over as she recalls the images still wrapped, still packed in boxes in the attic, still hidden from view.

"That was some time before you had Richard," Simon points out.

"Oh yes," she comes to once more. "It was before Richard; before I'd grown brave enough, or maybe selfish enough, to have a child."

"And Richard?" Simon asks, aware that Cynthia Ross is growing paler, if that is possible considering how pallid was her complexion when he first walked in.

"I mean, when you'd had Richard, didn't you want to have photos of him around the place. Without suggesting any disrespect Mrs Ross, that would be perfect natural. Wouldn't it?"

"Yes, it would. It would be perfectly natural, Simon. Now though, you're beginning to step on my toes a little," She pauses to gauge his reaction. "I told you I'd tell you when you asked the wrong questions and I think you've had more than your money's worth."

He thinks to ask her for a photograph of Captain Ross, then remembers that Paddy Jennings said he would email one through at the weekend. Jennings hadn't, yet. Simon makes a mental note to gee him up when he gets back.

Eager to change the subject as swiftly as possible without getting too much off track, he asks, "With regard to Richard: he went into the Royal Marines rather than follow his father into the Guards. Do you mind my asking why?"

"No, not at all, Simon. It's the right question." She considers how best to reply. "Richard had his heart set on going to Sandhurst and then, with a bit of luck, following both his grandfather and father into the Welsh Guards. That was the way it was going to be. That was his plan. Then, just after he left school, Richard and his father fell out in the biggest possible fashion."

"Over?" Simon prompts.

"Oh, the usual stuff fathers and sons fall out over. They were too much alike, both strong characters, both rather too ready to recognise the failings in each other, that sort of thing. It happens. Afterwards, later, Richard decided he wanted to prove to his father that he was the tougher of the two, and the training of a Royal Marine officer is, supposedly, a fair bit harder than it is for Foot Guards officers. That's why young Richard opted for the

Royal Marines. Sons made in their father's mould," she scoffs. "Men!"

Simon studies her, also growing aware that whatever her illness, the hour glass of her energy is beginning to run down. "Do you think your son's time spent learning to be self-sufficient up in the woods stood him in good stead for the training? He must have been a step or two ahead of some of the others of his intake."

"Undoubtedly. Though through that last couple of years before he went in, he rarely frequented his camp."

"Something turned him away from it?"

"Couple of things, yes. I prefer to remember it as a healthy distraction: the fairer sex. A perfectly normal hobby for a seventeen-year-old and I wasn't displeased to see it. There was something else, though." She hesitates, remembering.

"Please, Mrs Ross, do go on."

"It was one night, deep into mid-winter, the snow had come. I was lying in bed, awake, staring at the ceiling, praying he wouldn't freeze to death up there in the woods. I was thinking of taking him a thermos flask. He probably would have growled at me for it: he never let you know it if he found the cold hard to bear. I was lying there trying to stop myself from weakening when I heard the backdoor slam. Imagining that he might have come back suffering from frostbite or food-poisoning or worse, I went downstairs and found him sitting in the kitchen."

She glances nervously at Simon. "Well, he was stark naked and his hands and face were smeared with blood. He was a ghastly sight; really, quite ghastly. I covered him up and cleaned him as best I could, and quickly worked out that it wasn't his own blood and hoped to God he hadn't killed someone. Next thing, I found myself making all those usual noises a mother tries to make when scared witless by her son. After a while, I realised he wasn't listening to me. In fact, he couldn't even hear me, he was in some kind of trance. He just sat there staring at the floor.

"At first, I thought he must be suffering from hyperthermia, so I kept him warm and called the doctor. He came up soon after, examined Richard and said it wasn't the cold, it was a form of hypnotic or ecstatic state, possibly a fit of some nature. The doctor gave him an injection, to relax him. Poor boy didn't even flinch when the needle went in. The medicine didn't seem to produce any noticeable effect, so we just sat there, helpless, watching and waiting.

"After an hour or so, he woke up. Just like that, he woke up, asked us what we were doing sitting in the kitchen in the middle of the night and went upstairs to bed. The doctor and I were absolutely staggered."

"Did he remember it in the morning?" Simon asks.

"No, not a bit of it. When I mentioned it, he had no recollection of the incident." She is as bewildered now as she very obviously was then. "It was all very strange, but it saw the end of his staying up there overnight. And if all it took was a sudden dose of sleepwalking or the shock of butchering some animal, then I decided he would be the better off for it."

Cynthia Ross yawns, not bothering to raise her hand to cover her mouth, and, as if on cue, there is a knock at the door and Mrs Phillips strides in.

"Now, Mr Peckham, I'm afraid I can't have you tiring Mrs Ross out; she's tired enough without all this talking."

"Yes, of course, I wouldn't want to outstay my welcome." He rises to his feet. "I—"

"Simon," Cynthia Ross says, clearly, irritated by her housekeeper's interruption, "you still haven't told me what news you have of Richard or why you have come."

Mrs Phillips backs away, reverently, saying, "Well then, perhaps you would conclude your interview or arrange to come back some other time." Rather than leave the room, she hovers by the door.

"Please, Simon," Cynthia Ross gathers herself as if for one

171

final assault, "do you have news of my son? You see, I've not had much news of him since his..." She glances self-consciously at her housekeeper. "Since his... Well, since he was in Afghanistan. Have you seen him recently?"

Seen him? Only on a grainy CCTV recording of him begging down a line of masked revellers.

On the train down, he had tried to balance what news he would be best supplying in return for what further information he might obtain. Also, all the information he had assembled pointed towards Captain Richard Ross, late of the Royal Marines, tours of Iraq and Afghanistan, now living rough on the streets of London. Of course, the streets of the capital are a far cry from the verdant pastures of the gateway to Wales. And yet if one swapped brick alleys for oak woods, then Richard Ross is probably as well equipped to survive as anyone schooled in the arts of living off the land.

So Simon had decided to tell her the truth: the undeniable truth that though her son had risked his neck for his country, he had now been tossed out, like waste material onto the slagheap of life. And he, Simon, was making it his business to find out why. And why was he making it his business? Not through any great altruistic thirst or hunger for salvation, but because if he doesn't come up with some good investigative journalism within a couple of weeks, he too will be waste material and therefore likely to end up alongside Richard Ross on the very same slagheap.

Honesty has, so far, proved to be his best asset.

Now though, he recognises that Cynthia Ross is unwell: bruised by her emotions, depleted by whatever physical illness affects her and so very desperate for some form of reconciliation with her only son. Informing her of her son's... what? Fall from grace? His descent into purgatory? His...

"No, Mrs Ross, I'm afraid I haven't seen him. I believe he's living in London; exactly where I'm not sure. Someone I spoke to told me they'd seen him and thought I should talk to him. As you probably know, the government has commissioned an inquiry into the Iraq War and I'd like to get Captain Ross's take on it."

She stares intently at him as he watches for her reaction to his sophism.

The cold, watery light of her eyes gradually withdraws, her red lips surrender their colour and her cheeks appear to collapse inwards, lending her a cadaverous countenance.

"Oh, Simon, I had so hoped you would have more news than that. I feel you have cheated me. You promised to give and I see now that you have only come to take. What a shame! I suppose I should have expected nothing less from a journalist."

Simon does not approach her to shake hands, for she has turned her head away and closed her eyes.

"Thank you, Mrs Ross," he says, politely and with measured respect, "I'll be only too pleased to let you know when I do locate your son. And thank you for granting me this time with you."

She ignores him.

22

Mrs Phillips collects a woollen rug from a side table and drapes it carefully over Mrs Ross's legs.

"I'll show you out, Mr Peckham," she says, holding the door for him.

Simon follows her out through the dining room and into the kitchen.

"Don't take her ire too personally, Mr Peckham," she says, once the door is closed behind her, "it's as I said, Mrs Ross is not a well woman."

It is not what he was expecting her to say; rather, he expected her to admonish him for his perceived subterfuge of not bringing any real news of Richard Ross. That she thinks no ill of him, rescues his conscience. "Thank you for that. I had not intended to disappoint her, it's just... She's not at all well then?"

The housekeeper unties her apron, checks her face in a small compact and sets about readjusting her hair again. "No, Mr Peckham, Mrs Ross has Multiple Sclerosis. As it turns out, she's been suffering with it for God knows how long. Definitely long before The Major passed away. He, being how he was, you know, not being one to suffer the complaints of others gladly, thought she was malingering. Yes, malingering! Even used that exact word once. Wretched man. Terrible migraines she had; so bad some days it was all she could do to get out of bed. Still, I suppose he had no way of knowing that when you go down with it in your late fifties you are likely to have the more progressive type. Medical he was not, and the milk of human kindness he had not supped for a good while."

She is happy with her hair. "Mind you," she adds, smoothing down her skirt and turning to face him, a sharp twinkle to her eyes, "wouldn't want to get too close to paying that man a compliment, now would I?"

"I see," is all Simon can reply.

"Good. It's important for you to know what he was like. Not that I want to speak ill of the dead, but..."

She is perhaps not as old as he had at first thought. Her face is well lined and when she smiles it becomes obvious to him that that is how her lines have been earned. Mrs Phillips' demeanour suggests warmth and reason, not the owlish inquisitor he'd met when standing outside in the morning frost.

"It's important for you to know the man in order to understand the woman, that's what I always say."

"And right you would be to, Mrs Phillips."

She clears some cutlery from the kitchen table. "Never mind the Mrs, my name's Elen. The only people ever to call me Mrs Phillips were The Major and Mrs Ross; them and the last English Class I taught at the village school. And that was twenty-five years ago. Would you like a lift back into town, Mr Peckham?"

"Simon, please, the same applies or nearly applies. The last person to call me Mr Peckham was my English tutor, who informed me I didn't know the difference between tortuous and torturous. I had only been trying to introduce some levity into a rather dull discussion group. Apparently, my humour was extrinsic."

"Not in the anatomical sense, I hope," she chuckles.

"What about Mrs Ross?"

"Oh, she'll doze now, probably until I get back. I've some shopping to take care of, so you're not taking me out of my way."

Elen's small, elderly-but-tidy blue Renault is parked just beyond the gates.

"So, Simon," she begins as she pulls out into the narrow, potholed lane, "you *are* looking for young Richard, though not simply to find out whether he thought he was right to be fighting in Iraq?"

He doesn't reply.

"I thought not," she mutters. "You don't need to speak to many of them to know what they thought of it. That man Blair. Should be shot. Him and a few others."

Again, he doesn't reply.

"I appreciate you decided not to upset Mrs Ross. That was good of you. Is young Richard in some kind of trouble? You can tell me straight, I've known the boy since he was in nappies. All the while he was away he was asking me about his mum: letters, emails when he could. She thought he didn't care. He thought she didn't."

Young Richard. Elen Phillips still thinks of him in terms of being young Richard. The Winslow Boy. The Four Feathers. Captain Richard in harm's way. Young Richard at heart.

"The answer to that is, I think so. And I think he's living rough on the streets in London. There are far too many people living rough, let alone too many ex-servicemen, and I'm trying to find out why. I believe Captain Ross has been involved in an assault; an assault in which a man died, in London, over New Year. If that is true and what happened is what I think happened, then it means he went to the aid of the young woman who was one victim of the assault. However, and for various reasons, the police might not see it that way and I wouldn't want him to get into trouble for something he hadn't done. That's why I'm trying to find him."

"Oh, you won't find young Richard, not if he doesn't want to be found. You remember Mrs Ross telling you about him roasting a pigeon up in the woods?"

"You were listening?"

"Of course." Mrs Phillips pauses, waiting for him to appreciate that it is she who is the organ grinder and Mrs Ross the monkey. "Well, anyway, he built a camp up in the woods to get away from his mother and father's quarrelling. They never had any idea where he was most of the time and the police wouldn't ever have found him. They'd already been up in the woods once and had walked straight past his camp without noticing it."

He turns to look at the housekeeper and cannot tell whether she is smiling or simply concentrating on the windy lane. "You told them."

"Yes, I did. In the interests of his mother's sanity I did, though I never let young Richard know. I'd been letting him have the odd bit of food, even though he caught most of it himself. Smart boy, young Richard. Determined. Clever. Resourceful. Could be a bit sneaky, but on the whole very level-headed. If he doesn't want you to find him, Simon, you won't and this time even I've absolutely no idea where he's got to."

"You've not heard from him?"

"Only once since, not long after... after he returned from Afghanistan, after... And it wasn't a telephone call I care to remember."

"Because?"

"Because," she pauses and wipes at her eyes as though to clear away a wayward eyelash. "Because he was beyond drunk and dreadfully distressed, and no matter how hard I tried or how patient I was with him, I couldn't get him to listen to anything I said. It was very unpleasant. No, it was worse than that, it was beyond painful. A grown man dissolved in tears is bad enough. When you've seen the boy grow into that man, it tears your heart out."

"Can you remember much, if anything, of what he said? Did he tell you where he was? Did you call him back?"

She wrestles a handkerchief from her pocket and blows her nose. "He was pretty much incoherent, tell the truth. And when I tried calling him back, his phone was switched off. I've tried a few times since then. No luck, I'm afraid. I've no idea where he was calling from; sounded like a pub. Not home, I don't think."

"Does Mrs Ross know you speak to him?"

"Spoke to him, Simon, spoke to him. And yes, I think so. One thing she's not is stupid and she knows full well she's responsible for breaking her own heart as much as anyone else is."

Simon sits quietly. They are almost back in town and the station is only a couple of minutes away.

"When you said he wasn't calling from home... 'not home' you said. Do you mean not here in Abergavenny?"

"No, not here. At his home, near Tiverton."

"I see," Simon says, stifling his surprise. Paddy Jennings told him Ross was *from* Abergavenny; he hadn't said Ross lived there. "His home? You mean, he didn't live here in Abergavenny?"

"No, why would he be living with his parents, the man's thirty years old?" This time, though, they are sat at a junction, briefly, and Elen Phillips wrests her attention from the road and glances at him in disbelief. "Young Richard has a cottage just outside Tiverton, not far from Taunton, Norton Manor, where his unit 40 Commando are based; bought it when he got married."

"Paddy Jennings told me Captain Ross was married."

"Yes, Simon, *was married*. Poor girl."

"Was, yes, of course. His wife. I had meant to ask Mrs Ross. Why *poor girl*?"

"Because she died, while he was away this last time. While he was on his tour, in Afghanistan."

Until Paddy Jennings had mentioned it, Simon had not entertained the idea that Richard Ross might be married. And when he did, Jennings had used the past tense and Simon had not picked up on it.

Richard Ross was a Captain in the Royal Marines. He was married. He was someone and Simon realises the reason for his presumption lies rooted in his perceptions of a rough sleeper as being someone cast out onto the street; someone who has walked or run away from their responsibilities and their obligations; someone who has forfeited their right to be regarded as someone other than someone who was.

Richard Ross *was* a Captain in the Royal Marines. He *was* married. That is simply his past. That is his history. And just like everyone else, he is entitled to his past and his history. He does not have to surrender it solely because he is rough sleeping.

Richard Ross *is* now a rough sleeper. Richard Ross *is still* someone.

Simon's presumption is naïve and narrow. He recognises it and is disgusted by his arrogance, his ignorance and perhaps worst of all his conceit.

"Mrs Phillips, sorry, Elen. How long have you got before you have to be back with Mrs Ross?"

She purses her lips as she looks both ways at a junction. "Long enough for a cup of tea. What time's your train?"

They sweep into Station Road, pass the white-walled, slate-roofed Great Western Hotel, and park up in a line of cars. A red telephone box stands sentry opposite the pink-bricked Italianate façade of the station and the Whistle Stop cafeteria is, like the tea being served, warm.

"Please," he begins, as they sit down, "imagine I know nothing about Richard, something I'm starting to understand is all too obviously true. He was married?"

"Yes. He was. And married to a lovely young girl. Sarah. Sarah Loveridge as she was."

"When did they meet and where?"

"Oh, down in the West Country. He was on a school cadet weekend, orienteering on Exmoor. He told me he and the other cadets were camping in this field when this big farmer came up to them and told them they should have asked permission before pitching their tents. He was like to ask them to leave until young Richard managed to charm the man into allowing them to stay. That was when he first met Sarah, the farmer's daughter. They were married just before young Richard went off to Iraq, that first time."

"Excuse me, Elen, why do you and Mrs Ross refer to him as young Richard? I should have thought he'd earned the right to be known by his first name; it's not as though, as you yourself pointed out, he's that young anymore."

She studies Simon for a moment and then scratches her cheek, thoughtfully. "I suppose we know him as young Richard because his father, the Major, was a Richard, too. When they fell out, young Richard decided he wanted to be known as Ric from then on, didn't want to be thought of as his father's son."

"And why did they fall out?"

"In a word, Sarah. The Major was happy to meet her at first; happy to have her about the place. Then, when he realised how keen they were on each other, he started behaving poorly towards her. Well, not to her face exactly, more rude about her to young Richard; finding fault with her, comparing her to Mrs Ross and not in a very complimentary way. It all got rather nasty and believe you me, when that man got it into his head he didn't like someone, then that person usually ended up coming off second best to him. Egregious: do you know what that means, Simon?"

"Sure. It means insufferable, atrocious, intolerable. Monstrous? Was that what Ric's father was, monstrous?"

"All of that and more," she sighs. "I wouldn't have followed him into the jaws of hell; I'd have shot him before we got there."

Simon is a little unsettled by the portrait she paints. "But why the change in heart? You said he liked her one minute, then not the next. What changed?"

"I believe it was something to do with the Major knowing long before most people knew that his son was going to be going to Iraq and later to Afghanistan. He had this idea, this notion or whatever it was, that young Richard wasn't going to be coming back. He said Iraq was an illegal war that nobody wanted and that Afghanistan was the graveyard of armies. His argument was that if Alexander the Great, the British and the Russians couldn't tame the place, then no one ever would. He believed it. Couldn't tell Mrs Ross for fear of frightening her rigid. And because he believed it, he said young Richard didn't have any right to be marrying a girl only to make a widow out of her." She sucks her teeth, loudly. "I suppose there was some sense in it, the Major having made a widow of his wife even though he'd lived."

"Instead of which," Simon suggests, "the reverse happened. Captain Ross went to Iraq and Afghanistan and survived both, only to have his wife taken from him."

"Yes, it was a poor state of affairs." Elen's eyes water and she takes a noisy slurp from her teacup by way of distraction. "Worse part of it was, he loved her so very much. I often wonder if he poured all the love he didn't get from his parents into Sarah. Didn't ask his parents to the wedding, though it hurt him not to. Sarah tried to get him to change his mind, but he was no little like his father in that regard; a bit stiff, you know, once he decided on something. I went, of course. The wedding was marvellous; honour guard, all that ceremony, all the boys in uniform."

"What was she like, Sarah?" he hesitates, watching her. "Look, I'm sorry if talking about this is painful, Elen. You can go, if you'd prefer? The train must be along soon."

"No, that's all right." She blows her nose, dabs at the corners of her eyes and glances around.

A spectacled man opposite has his nose buried in a broadsheet.

"Sarah was a bright Devonian lass; an English rose, you might say. One of those girls for whom the sun is always out: straw blonde hair, fresh cheeks, blue eyes, always smiling, always looking forward, nothing ever too much trouble; bit of a tomboy in an adventurous sort of way, which was pretty handy considering how wild young Richard was. Mrs Ross doted on her; The Major, well I've said my piece."

"And where did they live? Near Taunton, you said."

"Yes, a cottage on the Loveridge family farm, the one young Richard had camped in with the cadets. The wedding was in a church, near a pub. Oh, The London Inn. Yes, that's right, the pub was called The London Inn. I only remember it because it seemed a strange name for a pub right out in the middle of nowhere. And the church, it had this plaque on the wall; told this story of a family who'd all died in a shipwreck... Isn't it odd how one remembers the strangest things?

"The reception was in a marquee in the Loveridge's garden. Mid-summer it was. It rained. Just like that, it rained. It wasn't forecast and all these cars got stuck in the field. Young Richard spent half his wedding night towing them out. Sarah thought the whole thing terribly funny; she was that kind of girl. That's what made her so wonderful, that way she had of turning bad into better."

Simon steels himself. "Do you mind my asking how... how she died?"

She wrests her eyes from the table top and fixes him with a cruelly damning look. "Yes, Simon, I do. All you need to know is that it was very tragic; a car accident, see, and only a couple of days before young Richard was supposed to be coming home on leave.

"Simon, I heard you say to Mrs Ross that she was to tell you when you'd overstepped the mark. Well, now you have. You've made me think of things I try to avoid and," she looks up, pretending to read some writing on the opposite wall, "by my reckoning your train is due any minute."

"Yes, you're right, Elen. And I shouldn't have asked; I should've thought to look up the information rather than rekindle the more wretched of your memories, I apologise."

The housekeeper is now looking her years, as though the flames of her recalling have all too quickly aged her.

"Oh, that's alright, Simon. Mrs Ross was right; you do have a way with words. I suppose that's why I'm sat here with you, waiting for your train." She reaches into her jacket, fishes out a piece of paper and a pen, and scribbles. "Here is my number. Please promise me that if you catch up with young Richard, you will do me the kindness of calling. Whatever you find and however you find him, please let him know that there are those who still care very deeply about him. And Mrs Ross may be the architect of her sorrows, but she doesn't deserve to suffer alone. Please tell him she is sorry; I know she is."

"I will, Elen. Surely, I will. Look, just one quick question before I go?"

Her eyes plead that he be gentle with her. "Yes, of course, go on."

"That episode the Captain had when he was in his teens; the trance or fit, when Mrs Ross had to call out the doctor?"

"Yes, what about it?"

"Well, it's just that I'm surprised he passed his medical with that incident on his record. I should have thought any kind of adolescent fit or seizure would have precluded him from service?"

The mischief briefly returns to her expression, only to be replaced by a mournful longing. "Not necessarily. I used to stay up at the house when the Major and Mrs Ross were away on engagements. Poor young Richard suffered terrible night terrors; wake up he would, screaming about people dying and him standing there helpless, watching. Simple night terrors, I suppose, and not particularly unusual when a child grows as fast as he did. Some of them even terrified me. Mrs Ross probably persuaded the doctor to leave all that stuff off his record; she can be a very persuasive woman when it suits her."

Simon, though, is still unsure. "Wouldn't that have provided her with exactly the excuse she was looking for to stop him being passed fit? Wasn't that what she really wanted, to stop him following his father into the armed forces?"

"Oh yes, Simon. That was precisely what she wanted. And yet as selfish as she could be, young Richard's mother was never one to stand in the way of her son. I know it may sound strange, but that is both the dichotomy and the duplicity of motherhood. That is a mother's war and it never ceases."

Excerpt 6 from transcript of conversation with Joseph Naarda

SP: What was it like for Soraya to grow up in Basra?

JN: After the war there was no primary school for her to attend. There were schools, yes, but girls were not encouraged to attend. Saddam wanted girls to grow up to be domestic servants; to be handmaids and to bear little Ba'athists, not to be able to think for themselves and certainly not to be intellectual. So I educated Soraya at home. Remember, my father had been a school teacher. From him I had learned much history and English and as a result I was perhaps well placed to teach. Also, Soraya attended Sunday school at St Ephrem's, the Chaldean church; it is by Al-Istiklal, in the Ashar quarter. And Salwa insisted on teaching her daughter the ways of the marsh people, the Mandaean ways.

She was a good pupil, keen to learn. Like the sand that soaks up the rain, Soraya would absorb information very quickly. And she was always the first to talk to people, too; though this was not always the best way to be.

SP: When you say she was always the first to talk to people, was that dangerous? I can imagine that after the war you had to be careful who you spoke to.

JN: Yes, it is true. One had to be careful. I remember, on the street where we lived there was a man, an old Shi'a, a widower. Before the war, he would come to celebrate Ashura with us, it is a festival for both Arabs and *Subba*, and Salwa would prepare *lofani*, a communion.

When his son did not return from the war, the old man assumed he was dead. This, quite naturally, affected him very badly. He stopped going out. He rarely spoke to anyone. We worried about him. Then, seven years, yes, Simon, seven years later, we heard he had received a letter from Kuwait, from a man telling him he had met his son in a hospital and that his son would soon be coming home.

The *mukhabarat* found out about this letter. They said his son was a deserter and would be punished. However, the boy did not reappear and they suspected the old man of hiding him. They searched and when they could not find the son, they arrested the father and took him to the *White Lion*, the jail. They interrogated him, hanging him upside down and beating him for many days. If he knew where his son was, he did not tell them and by the time he was released, he was not much more than a shadow.

During this period, Salwa noticed that some of our food was going missing. We did not have much, so it was not difficult to notice, and because of all the sanctions, food was expensive and not always available.

One day, Salwa put out some dates on a plate on the kitchen table, counting them so she would remember exactly how many there were. In the afternoon, she went to the market, leaving

Soraya alone in our home. When Salwa returned, there were not so many dates as she had counted and she asked our daughter who might have taken them. Soraya explained that a reed bird, a warbler you would call it, had flown into the kitchen and stolen them away. Of course, Salwa and I knew that this bird only eats insects and that it is not large enough to fly carrying even a single date. Yet, Soraya described the bird in such detail, it's white underneath and its long, slender bill, that even we began to believe this bird might be the thief in our kitchen.

Salwa decided on a plan. She added a little Baharat to the dates. Baharat is a mixture of spices not dissimilar in colour to the dates. She counted them, left them out and went to the market. This time again, when she returned, some of the dates were missing. Salwa put Soraya's fingers to her lips and tasted immediately the flavours of pepper, cumin, chilli and cinnamon, and knew for certain that it was Soraya who was taking the dates. After much denial and argument, our young daughter confessed that she had been taking the food and eventually she admitted that she was giving it to our neighbour's son. For two months the young man had been living in a derelict property, two streets away, and he had been relying on Soraya and her friends to bring him sustenance.

SP: *She risked her life and yours in doing so.*

JN: Yes. It was a very dangerous charity and we pleaded with her to stop. Soraya would not. She refused, staring at us without fear and accusing us of the most terrible cowardice. I remember it as if it was yesterday: her eyes burning with a golden flame, her countenance very aggressive. She told us that this young man had done nothing to us or anybody else, so we should be ashamed of ourselves. What right, she asked, did we have to refuse him help?

SP: *You're saying her altruism, her compassion, her concern for those less fortunate, was evident from a very young age.*

JN: It is true, Simon. And even at eight years old she possessed the extraordinary ability of being able to make you ashamed of ignoring your better instincts. From then on, Salwa prepared food for our neighbour's son and Soraya delivered it; though I must tell you, Simon, it frightened me to death. Where such courage came from, from which side of the family, I have no idea.

23

Leaving the Black Mountains behind, the train rattles and winds south past Sebastopol and Cwmbran towards Newport.

Simon reflects on his day and notes his conversations with Cynthia Ross and Elen Phillips, arranging the many fragments into an order of significance, aware that he now possesses some of the pieces to the jigsaw that will provide him with a more complete picture of Richard Ross. But, as yet, there is still much to learn if he is to understand exactly why the former Royal Marine has surrendered to the streets of the capital.

That Elen Phillips enjoys a much closer relationship with Richard, or young Richard as she is wont to refer to him, is obvious. Obvious and not surprising given his father's more oppressive proclivities and his mother's burning self-interest.

The Major: a second-generation career officer from one of Wales' most prestigious regiments. A man who, according to Elen Phillips, had never supped the milk of human kindness; his character forged in the fires of conflict and tempered to the beat of boots upon a parade ground. A man used to giving orders and getting his own way.

And yet nothing about the Major strikes Simon as either unnatural or uncommon. He was a twentieth-century soldier; the product of an army fashioned for the period by an often-flawed system; an army without which chaos would undoubtedly have reigned.

"Isn't that what soldiers do?" he mutters, absentmindedly. "Fight like men; die when called upon to?" Clearly, Richard Ross was, in that curious way of many sons, driven to emulate his father.

Emulate or compete with? Compete with or live up to?

Is that what motivates Simon to make it as a journalist? Is he in some way in competition with his father? Is that why he finds himself sitting alone on a draughty train on a wintry day in Wales?

He catches the thought and unwraps it. Does one really have a choice?

The bright white waters of the Afon Lwyd seem to lend his focus a gentle clarity; a clarity and a certainty, as though such things have always been so and he doesn't need any Freudian science to explain why they should be otherwise.

Unlike the Major, his father had been the editor of a tabloid: a paper not so committed to the virtues of sincere or sophisticated reportage, more a newspaper devoted to the dubious sensationalism of headlines. Headlines concocted and generated with one single aim: to persuade the masses to part with their money. The advocacy of such a rationale in itself, Simon had, or has, no truck with. He'd long ago come to terms with the truism that even the most wanton of headlines can cause people to stop and think.

For as long as he could remember, Simon had thought of his father as a newspaperman and that thought, that concept, had encouraged him to want to be the same. Then, suddenly and quite shockingly, because Simon was offered no explanation or reason for the shift, his father had been a newspaperman no longer. He had sold his soul to the highest bidder who would have him as their head of public relations and that, to Simon, had been a betrayal. That was the moment his father had ceased to be the person Simon had grown up believing in.

Hindsight, though, had taught him not to be so holy; or at least not so holier than thou. And life, as old Tom Williams had surely figured out, is nothing if not a concatenation of betrayals. At the least, and quite possibly at the same time at the best, his father had never tried to force his will upon Simon, not like the Major had upon young Richard.

So that's what the Major and his son had fallen out over: a girl. That's what Mrs Ross had been going to say when she said she'd not had much news of him since... That was why she beat about the bush when he asked what father and son had fallen out over. She had both generalised and prevaricated, and then dismissed the subject in much the same manner as one waves away a bothersome fly.

Mrs Cynthia Ross: a woman who has suffered through a life striated and criss-crossed by flaws and fractures not of her own making. A woman married to a man already hopelessly committed to another woman who goes by the name of Service. A Service far more demanding than any flesh and blood woman. A mistress who will never let go. And all those years of infidelity have taken their toll on Cynthia Ross, both psychologically and physically, and now she holds the world responsible for the price she has paid in precisely the same way the mother of a casualty of war holds the world responsible for the loss of her infant.

A line of Binyon's *Ode of Remembrance* comes to him: *Age shall not weary them, nor the years condemn.* And how appropriately it applies to Cynthia Ross, for even though she has never raised a rifle, she is both wearied and condemned by the legacy of an incomplete marriage and a cruel disease; a disease by which her autoimmune system lays siege to her very own fibre; a self-destruction of sorts, an irony without humour.

And what of the housekeeper? With the father passed on and the mother rendered incapable by her mordant remorse, Elen Phillips is, next to Paddy Jennings, Simon's best and most competent ally. However, even she has made the point that if Richard Ross doesn't want to be found, he won't be. In which case, his only hope is to tempt Richard Ross into finding him, and for that he will need a considerable draw.

He snaps shut his laptop and turns his mind to the girl, Soraya.

Two and a half hours, a change of trains and a synthetic sandwich later Simon alights at Paddington Station. It is dark, and heavy rain is herding early commuters in off Praed Street. But rather than take the tube, which he knows will get him home in half the time, Simon decides he has had enough of the train and opts for the bus.

The 205 crawls eastward along the Marylebone Road and he is content to sit upstairs, warm and dry, as Sherlock Holmes' statue, the bald dome of Madame Tussauds and the colonnaded portico of Holy Trinity Church inch by.

After a journey that seems to have taken far longer than his train return from Abergavenny to Paddington, Simon alights at Old Street.

He nips smartly between the passing cars to cross the East Road and as he steps onto the pavement a rough sleeper he has noticed about the neighbourhood shuffles out of the shadows.

"Spare us a bit of change?"

His hoodie sodden black with rain, the man is dwarfish and faltering. Much else Simon cannot make out as the fellow wears several layers of clothing and it is only when he turns his head to look up, questioningly, that Simon is lent full view of his face.

Dark hair splays from under the brim of his hoodie framing his craggy features. However, it isn't his appearance that fixes and then upsets Simon; it is his stare, the distant emptiness of which reminds Simon of the hopelessness of Cormac McCarthy's The

Road. A look that implies the man has suffered some form of emotional Armageddon: a desolation from which he may never return or recover.

Simon fishes in his pocket and guesses by their weight and milled circumference that he has located two-pound coins. "What's your name, friend?" he asks.

"Eddie," the man utters, confused that Simon should ask.

"Well, Eddie, here's a couple of quid. Please do me a favour, try not to spend it on grog or spice or whatever the flavour of the month is, eh?"

"Yeah, right'o guv, will do." The rough sleeper taps his forehead in some form of salute and is gone, dissolving back into the shadows, a spectre from a séance.

Simon hesitates. Will Richard Ross be grateful to be reclaimed from the streets?

He had expected to receive something more in return for his subbing the rough sleeper a couple of quid. More of what though, he doesn't know. But something. Anything. Not gratitude from Eddie, that would be unrealistic and Eddie probably isn't Eddie anyway. But something other than gratitude. An affirming inner glow perhaps, a warming residue of well-being afforded him by his sudden charity? Or even an exhilarating rush such as one might expect to get from a recreational drug? But, instead... instead of benefitting from any reward, he feels peculiarly guilty, realising it is the first time he has put his hand in his pocket in such a manner. It is the first and only time. And for the second time in the day he is disgusted by his arrogance.

Yes, he has raised money for charitable causes before: striding through the Peak District, cycling the Pennines or running 10kms around town. Yet that money was raised through internet donation sites, a form of hand-out by sterile proxy, and his efforts seem to count for little right now. For not until a moment ago has he handed money directly to someone who needs it more than he

193

and the raw novelty of his action leaves him feeling exposed, as though an all-seeing eye has now and for the first time fastened its gaze on him.

He turns away and strolls off north up East Street

But then again, it hadn't been his money, had it? It was change from the expenses Candy had approved for his day trip to Abergavenny.

"You must have something for a bit of lunch," she'd told him. "Can't have you getting all skinny on me."

———————

Haberdasher Street, and the days of the button, bead and ribbon makers are recalled only in name. Now, bared plane trees, their slender fingers stretching upward in vain appeal, line a terrace of apartment buildings for which city workers cough up the exorbitant rents commanded by a convenient and newly fashionable postcode. Cars and vans thump and bounce over the sleeping policemen, and a dark, damp flannel of yellow-bellied cloud hangs low over the city.

A figure wearing a black coat is loitering by the iron railings outside the entrance to his block.

Simon slows his step.

"Soraya?"

She turns, startled, "Oh, Simon." Her scarf is soaked through and hangs limp around her face, shrouding her expression. She has a newspaper under her arm and, judging by her angular awkwardness, something on her mind.

"Good to see you. Just passing by?" he asks, pitching a liberal dose of irony into his tone to try to convince her he is not being patronising. His measure falls short.

"No."

"Sure. Well, I was… Well, never mind." He had been going to

tell her that he'd hoped she might call. "You seem upset, Soraya. What's the matter?"

She glances nervously up and back down the road, then at him. "Look, Simon. I... Could we go inside, I need to talk to you."

He pauses by the door and bathes in the glow of her extraordinary eyes. As he lingers he realises she is fighting back tears.

"Yes, of course. Come in. You look freezing. How long have you been waiting?"

"Too long. I tried to call you a while ago. Your phone was off."

Simon had turned his phone off before meeting Mrs Ross and had forgotten to turn it back on. "I've been on the train, in to Paddington, then in on the bus. Probably no signal. Sorry." He unlocks the door and stands back for her to take the stairs. "First floor. On the left."

The flat is warm, though not sufficiently warm that she is prompted to remove her coat.

They stand and face each other.

"Simon, I—"

"Soraya," he interrupts, "why don't you give me your scarf and coat? You must be soaked. Use the towel in the bathroom, there. I'll get us both something to drink, then we can talk." His need to comfort her grows strong. "It really is good to see you. I've been hoping you would call. No, that's not true. I would have called you, only I didn't get your number. Stupid of me."

But she does take her scarf and coat off, and she hands them to him, though keeping a firm grip on her newspaper.

"Something stronger, then," he decides. "When you're dry, the living room's through there. I think I have some vodka left. Not sure about tonic. Might have Coke or Pepsi."

"Tea, please. No milk. Lemon, if you have it?" She glares at him and turns about, into the bathroom.

Though Simon is vaguely amused by her pique: her manner

195

suggests he has committed some faux-pas. He locates a lemon, washes a mug and makes them both tea. Tea, which he serves on a tray.

When he gets to the living room, Soraya is sitting upright on the sofa. She sits back as he places the tray on the low table.

He thinks to sit beside her, but her mood seems a touch prickly, so he chooses the small armchair opposite her.

"I hope that's okay."

"Nice flat," she observes. Her face is tight. Her expression deadpan.

"Yes, it is. It's not mine. It belongs to the father of a friend. A friend from university. He—"

"Nice to have friends, huh? Friends with places like this, I mean."

"Yes, I'm lucky. I—"

"Simon? You work for a newspaper, right?"

"Sure, the London Evening Star. I'm on a sort of probation, a six-month trial, though if I don't come up with—"

"A good story? Is that what you need, Simon? A good story?" Her tone is captious, if not disparaging.

"Sure, it's what all journos want. Generally, I cover diary stuff: courts, engagements, official visits. I get to cover some off-diary stuff, too, if I'm lucky enough to be in the right place at the right time. You know, accidents, emergencies, things that come out of the blue."

Soraya studies him, waiting.

When her silence grows too onerous, he asks, "Why?"

"Look..." she begins. Then she steps back from whatever it was she was going to say and reconsiders for a moment. "Simon, when we met after the inquest last week, you said you were researching a piece for the paper. Was that true or were you hoping to find out more about me?"

He shakes his head and frowns. "No, it was nothing to do

with you per se. And I had no idea you were going to be there. That was simply a coincidence. One I'm grateful for though." His smile, his warmth is not reciprocated. "Why?"

"A coincidence, huh? Just like you being at the Royal London on New Year's Day? Just like you following me up to the Intensive Care Unit and hanging about to overhear what the doctor told me about poor Tom Williams?"

"Hang on, Soraya. I'm not sure where you're going with this. I happened to be at the hospital because my editor asked me to check out some rough sleeper who'd been admitted. He knows I'm working on a piece about rough sleepers and the charities that support them, and he called me because he knows this place isn't so far away from the hospital. So again, why?"

Her tea grows cold. "You don't read the papers much, do you, Simon?"

"No, not much."

"And what about your copy? Does that get syndicated, if that's the right term. You know, sold out to other papers?"

He chuckles, self-effacingly. "Might do, if I wrote something my editor deemed worthy of printing."

"So, you didn't write this?" Soraya pushes her copy of the London Evening Star across the table towards him.

Simon reaches and notices the paper is open at an inside page. He skim-reads the page, searching for an article that might stand out or mean something to him.

"Towards the bottom, on the right," she says, without taking her eyes off him.

MURDER PROBE DELAYS INQUEST

Police have launched a murder investigation into the death of rough sleeper and Falklands veteran Thomas Williams, City of London Coroner David Graham was told. He adjourned the inquest into Mr Williams's death after hearing from University of East London forensic

science student Soraya Naarda that she saw a man assault Mr Williams
outside Slick in the City nightclub on New Year's Eve. Police originally
believed that Mr Williams, 48, died of natural causes.

"One of the girls on my course found it."

Simon exhales, slowly, reads through the News-in-brief once more and places the paper back on the table. He looks over at Soraya. He is embarrassed, uncomfortable. "You think I wrote this?"

"Didn't you?"

"I was there at the court and I passed my record of the inquest to my editor."

"Meaning?"

"What I mean is I didn't write that directly. There must have been someone else present. Whoever it was probably put the information out; could have got it from one of your course-mates outside." He had, of course, included her name and status in his detailed report of the inquest.

Soraya searches the ceiling and starts to count on her fingers. "Apart from my class and my tutor, there was the Coroner, the Coroner's Officer and the policeman, Chalmers, and you, Simon."

"No, there was someone else there, wasn't there? A woman, late forties maybe older, sat a couple of chairs down from me, chewed her pen when she wasn't taking notes."

Soraya's face lights up, briefly. "I figured she was the court recorder or someone."

"No. She wasn't associated with the court and besides, the proceedings are recorded on tape and transcribed later. My bet is she was a freelance."

"A freelance what? Court reporter?"

"No, freelance court reporters are licensed. They cover court proceedings and depositions, admin hearings, that sort of thing. No, she must have been a freelance journalist, though not the knocking on doors variety. They hang around inquests and trials, take notes, then try to sell what they've covered to whoever will pay them for it. Either that or she was covering the inquest for a daily."

The possibility that someone else might be on the trail of Richard Ross gnaws at him.

Soraya looks sceptical. "So what you're saying is, this isn't your work?"

"No, not directly."

"How do I know that, Simon?"

"You don't. There's no way I can convince you of that and I don't really understand why I should have to. Either you'll believe me or you won't, and I'm not going to say I couldn't give a toss because that *wouldn't* be true. What I'm after is a different story. Maybe bigger, I don't know. Maybe not so big. Definitely more relevant socially and one that is worth more than a few lines on an inside page. That might involve you, but it's not the reason I... Look, Soraya..."

Soraya, though, is still suspicious of him. She waits and watches and when he doesn't continue she prompts him, "So, what is the reason?"

To tell her the truth would be easier, if only the truth was plain. And if the notebook and Richard Ross are not related to her assault, then he's going to look pretty foolish, both to Soraya right now and to Barnes in a couple of weeks' time, when he will need to hand in his story or whistle for his job. The fear of failure rises in his throat.

Simon takes a sip of his tea. "I'm not sure how I can convince you, Soraya. All I know is that if I don't come up with a decent story for my editor, I'm sunk and my landlord's charity extends only so far. If I can't pay him the rent arrears I've promised to pay him when I get a permanent post, then I'll be out on the street with the rest of Tom Williams' mates." He is talking too fast and his tone is strained.

"Okay, Soraya, I'm being straight with you. But are you being straight with me? When we met outside the court and went and had coffee, I didn't get the impression you were telling me everything that happened on New Year's Eve."

"What makes you think that?"

"Well, I remember at the hospital when I asked you what had happened you said, 'it all happened to Tom and that other guy.' Who did you mean by *that other guy?*" He has been here with her once before, at the coffee shop after the inquest. That time, she'd packed up and left rather than answer him directly.

She looks away, quickly, her eyes searching the wall for an explanation. "What I meant was that other guy; the one who assaulted me. I thought I told you all this."

"There wasn't just one other guy, was there? There were three of them. That's what you told me. And I was there when you told DS Chalmers what happened. I don't remember you mentioning the other men. And when I spoke to you outside the hospital, you didn't mean the ape who assaulted you, did you? You meant someone else: *that other guy.*"

Soraya sits bolt upright on the sofa and fumes. "What the hell do you mean, giving me the third degree? I'm the one who doesn't trust you. I'm the one who came here looking for answers. It's what you journalists do, huh? Turn the tables on your victim, then bleed them for what you want out of them?"

"No, I don't want you to bleed. Unless I'm very much mistaken, Soraya, you've done enough of that lately. What I want is the truth. Because if you don't tell me, I doubt there's much chance of you telling the same to the police and that will only get you into a barrow load of trouble.

"Look at it this way, Soraya. Poor Tom Williams might have been an ex-paratrooper and he might have been tough enough to survive on the streets for much of his life but, and you heard the doctor's appraisal of his health, I don't believe he was either fit enough or strong enough to drag some ape off you and then deal with his two mates. You heard the medical evidence in the court, poor Tom had broken ribs, a bust hip and a punctured lung. He wasn't exactly X-man. So who was the knight in shining armour who came to your rescue?"

She opens her mouth to speak: no words come. Instead, her beautiful, topaz eyes begin to glimmer and she raises her arm and wipes at them with her sleeve.

"Soraya," he says, though this time more softly and with more than a teaspoon of sympathy, "there's got to be a reason why you don't want to talk about this other guy and, strange though it may seem, I don't care what that reason is. Perhaps your assault was worse than you've said or perhaps you still feel in some way responsible for what happened to old Tom, I don't know. What I do care about is not thinking the wrong thing about you or getting on the wrong end of the stick about what happened. And it's not just the story I'm after; it's you, Soraya. I like you too much to want to risk thinking it all wrong."

"No," she moans, "I can't. I will only make it all so much worse. He—"

"He," Simon repeats. "He."

He should tell her about Richard Ross; tell her he thinks it only fair. And he is prepared to until he sees Soraya is in tears.

She hides her face behind her hands.

Simon gets up and moves over to sit next to her. It is an involuntary reaction and once he is beside her, he isn't sure what to do next.

Soraya decides for him. She leans her head against his chest and soon enough her crying turns to sobbing and her shoulders heave as she tries to catch her breath. Her emotion, whatever store of dark thoughts she has locked deep inside her since her assault, now bursts through the seal of its confinement and haemorrhages in hot tears against his shirt.

He sits and waits, wanting to soothe her torment with some words of comfort, trying to think of the right thing to say. But nothing either appropriate or adequately reassuring comes to mind, so he simply sits and holds her and comforts her, hoping she can feel the warmth in his heart.

After a few minutes, her sobbing subsides and Soraya breaks the bond of his security to sit back.

He offers her his handkerchief, an act of such gentlemanly kindness that it embarrasses them both.

Soraya laughs through her tears, dabs at her eyes and then almost as a counterpoint to his charm, blows her nose. When she has finished, she doesn't know what to do with the handkerchief and, glancing about nervously, ends up putting it in her pocket.

"I'm sorry," she says, blinking away the residue of her distress. "I—"

"For what?" he asks. Simon puts his hand on her arm, a casually friendly and conciliatory gesture. "For thinking I'm something I'm not. For thinking you've made a fool of yourself by coming here. Which you haven't. You're not being fair with yourself, Soraya. It's as I said, you're not responsible for what happened to old Tom."

She smiles apologetically. "Yes, you're right. Life's not fair, is it? Tom Williams knew that. That's what he was trying to get away from: the unfairness of it all. Trouble is, I feel like I'm being chased by a ghost. Every time I think that what happened has settled down or gone away, it jumps right out of the cupboard and reminds me it's still there, bigger and even more threatening than before.

"Have the police been to interview you about the assault?"

"No. They rang me and asked if they could send someone. I volunteered to go to the Bishopsgate Police Station instead. At least they didn't just turn up. Must be thankful for that, I guess."

"When have you got to go?"

"The sooner the better was what they said, so I'm going the day after tomorrow."

"Wednesday. What time?"

"Four o'clock." Soraya frowns.

"Want me to come with you?"

Her frown deepens. "What? Just so you can fleece me for more information for your story? What am I now, Simon, just another bullet point in your research?"

"Soraya?" His reserve of patience runs out. "If every time I try to help you with this mess you—"

"Simon?" She tries to smile. "You know you're far more attractive when you're embarrassed."

"Sorry, only I—"

Soraya, lifts her finger to his mouth to quieten him and glances towards the door. "I should go."

"No, don't. Really, it's—"

She grasps his hands, holding them together wrapped tight in hers.

"Yes, Simon," she says, "I must. I didn't come here for it to be like this. This morning, one of the girls on my course waved the paper in my face and, well, I thought you were responsible. My anger got the better of me, which is unlike me, and I wanted to take it out on you. I came here with the intention of giving you a hard time. The stupid thing is, I realised only a couple of minutes ago that I wasn't really angry with you, and even if you had written it I don't think I could be angry with you for long."

"So," Simon encourages, gently, "what's wrong with being angry? Everyone gets angry when things don't go their way. There's nothing unusual in that."

"Maybe for you." She smiles. "For me, though, it's what my parents would say is deeply out of character. I don't do anger. Never have. Well, not until recently."

"What's changed then?"

Soraya rolls her eyes. "Oh, I don't know. Full moon, stars out of alignment, seasonal affective disorder, the pressure of the coming exams, not having my *skandola*—"

"*Skandola*? Enlighten me, please. What's a *skandola*."

Now, she looks deep into his eyes. "It's a seal-ring. Simon, you remember me telling you my mother is Mandaean?"

"Yes, when we met after the inquest. You said it was for another time. Is that time now?"

"Maybe. Maybe not. Don't look at me like that, she's not a witch doctor. A gnostic or mystic, perhaps... It's an ancient religion from southern Iraq, from the marshes."

"Is that where you are from, originally?"

Soraya, still looking deep into Simon's eyes, ignores his question.

"My mother believes her people are descended from Noah. She believes in the teachings of the book, the Ginza Rba, and John the Baptist. She also believes in the hereafter, the realm of light, and that Jesus was a rebel who betrayed the book and popularised religion to suit his own ends. The *skandola* is a seal-ring, my seal ring. It is used at weddings, births, deaths and, curiously, at exorcisms. Because there was no priest present at my birth, the midwife, the *jiddah*, she sealed my belly with it."

"What is it made of?"

"Iron."

"And it's plain or holds a crest or family symbol?"

Soraya looks up. "No, not a heraldic or family crest; not in such terms. A serpent, devouring its tail, surrounds a lion, a scorpion and a wasp. For the Mandaeans, the serpent or dragon, represents water and life and the continuance of existence."

"What goes around comes around? The ouroboros? The circle of life?"

"Yes," she says, her eyes now a little dreamy, "what goes around comes around. I hadn't thought of it quite like that. The lion, the scorpion and the wasp gather up unclean souls and cast them into the mouth of the serpent, *Ur*. Then, later, when those souls have atoned for their sins, when they are clean again, the lion, scorpion and wasp take them back from *Ur* and deliver them to the realm of light where they exist forever in peace."

"And, the *skandola* is the ring you've lost?"

"Yes, I've worn it since I was a child. Always. Everywhere. Although I didn't wear it as a ring. I keep, no that's wrong, I've kept it on a chain round my neck."

"You were wearing it on New Year's Eve. I remember seeing it. Where did you lose it?"

Soraya sits up a little straighter. She looks at him, her eyes wide, seeing and yet not seeing. "That man, the man who assaulted me and old Tom, he took it from me. He snatched the chain off my neck. I felt the tug of the chain at the back of my neck and my *skandola* was gone, just like that. It was like losing a part of me, a limb, a chapter of my life, my innocence, something like that. Am I making sense, Simon?"

"Yes, of course. If you've had the *skandola* with you forever, losing it would change how you behave and feel. There's every reason why it would upset your balance and make you angry?"

"Wow, that's weird," she says. "Coming here and talking it out with you has made me understand what's been wrong these past three months."

Soraya thinks for a moment, then says, "All of which means I must have come here because I feel you're about the only person I know who would take my anger and not hate me for it. Quite why that should be, I don't understand."

They sit and gaze at each other until the intensity of the moment drives him to want to kiss her. "I—"

"Yes, I do too. But," she interrupts him, breathing in slowly, as if inhaling the intimate vapour drifting between them, "why don't we take this slowly?"

When he begins to answer, she holds her finger up to his lips once more.

"There's lots of reasons why this, we, won't work. So, don't say anything. I'd like to meet up again sometime. If you'd like to, that is."

Simon nods, "Sure, I would. You can bet your life on it."

"Well," she says, "let's hope I don't have to do that."

Her scarf and coat are almost dry, and he voices his concern that they aren't completely dry and either she should stay a while longer or he could lend her one of his scarves if she isn't to catch cold.

"To lose my *skandola* is bad enough," she says. "My scarf, now that would be..."

As they walk the stairs down to the front door, Simon checks the timeline of events that has brought them together to see if there occurred a point at which their meeting became inevitable. Without doubt, the News-in-brief served to steer her in his direction, but...

He opens the door for her. "Soraya? Why don't I come with you?"

She frowns. "Why would you want to?"

"Well, I... I would like to, that's all."

"Don't be daft, Simon. You've only just got off the bus. Much as I appreciate you being the perfect gentleman and all that, the 205 stops only a hundred metres from my place. Thanks all the same, but it's not necessary."

"We could get something to eat?"

"Simon, Enough. Leave it, please."

"Okay, but I'll walk you down to get the bus." He slips his arm through hers.

They stroll down Haberdasher Street, avoiding the puddles, and as they turn left into East Street, Simon keeps an eye out for the rough sleeper who had tapped him just an hour or so before.

The same bus that had brought him from Paddington will take her to Bow and it arrives with indecent haste. The middle doors swing open.

"Simon, are you sure you want to come with me to the interview?" she asks, hurriedly.

"Perfectly sure. I'll meet you at the police station. I'll call you."

"You don't have my number." Soraya hovers on the step. Behind her, people are waiting to get on.

"You've got mine. Message me. Better still, call me when you get home?"

"In an hour, then."

He checks the time. "About nine?"

"Yes, nine." She turns and is swept inside by a sea of raincoats.

24

"How was your journey?" the farmer asks.

Henry Loveridge is a bluff, ruddy faced and wild white-haired individual; a man fashioned for humping both straw bales and lame animals, or so the breadth of his hands and depth of his chest suggests. Neither is he a man to be cowed by the rain which hammers both the windscreen and the heather-cloaked moors rising up either side of his Land Rover.

"As it goes."

While he'd waited for Soraya's call to tell him she'd arrived home safely, Simon had located the address and number of the Loveridge house and called. A sharp-voiced woman had taken his contact details and said the farmer would be back as soon as he was in. And when, not long after, Loveridge did call back, instead of asking Simon what he wanted, Simon was agreeably surprised when the farmer asked what he could do for him.

"What you could do for me," he'd replied, slowly and carefully, "is give me a minute or two of your time to talk about Richard Ross which, I understand, may not be something you want to do."

"And just why wouldn't I want to talk about Ric?"

He'd anticipated the question and had thought long and hard about his response. Farmers: the rise of the sun, the fall of the rain; the birth, life and death of livestock; beginnings, middles and ends. Not that one would compare losing a child with any amount of rural pragmatism. "Because of your daughter, Sarah. I'm sorry for your loss, sir. Please accept my condolences."

"Thank you, Mr Peckham, your condolences are accepted and appreciated. If you don't mind my asking, how did you come to find out about Sarah?"

"Elen Phillips told me, Mrs Ross's—"

"Yes, I know who you mean. Fine lady, Mrs Phillips. More than one can say for either of Ric's parents. But that's by the by and thank God their son was not gifted their more disagreeable genes. Tell me, Mr Peckham, have you spoken to Ric?"

"No, sir, that's why I'd like a few minutes of your time."

"A few minutes is it now. A second ago it was one or two."

"Well, the time I'll need depends on how much you've got to say, Mr Loveridge."

"And you work for a newspaper?" The farmer had gone quiet for a while, thinking; probably remembering his daughter and wondering whether he needed to protect his memory of her. "Right. First thing, Mr Peckham, you'd better call me Henry. Second, I've got too much on my hands to come up to London just now, so you'd better come here. And third, get the train down tomorrow and let me know when you'll be arriving at Tiverton Station; I'll be there to pick you up."

It had been that simple, that straightforward.

They turn up a steep-sided, narrow lane. Water flushes down towards them and clouds hang heavy over the moor. Simon glances sideways at his chauffeur. His eyes are blue, light blue and a shade rheumy, as though they both survey the road and look elsewhere.

"I'll not take you to the house, if you don't mind. Jane, Sarah's mum, is still a bit raw for talk. We'll go to the cottage. It's not tidy, mind. Not much been done since Ric went off."

"Of course. Whatever suits."

A cut in the side of the road leads them up into a broad field. The Land Rover bounces and bucks.

Without taking his eyes from the track, Loveridge asks, "You want to talk about my son-in-law, but you've not met him?"

"No, Henry, I'm looking for him. The reason for my wanting to talk to you is that I hope you might be able to offer me some information that could help me find him."

"Looking for a story, are you?"

"You could say that, although that would only be half of it." Simon lurches in his seat and reaches out to hold onto the dashboard.

Up ahead stands a white-walled cottage, isolated but for a couple of outhouses and a barn stacked with hay.

"And the other half?"

"The other half, and I'm not really sure about too much of it, is that I think Richard might end up in a fair bit of trouble if I don't find him."

"Meaning?"

"Meaning, I think he may have been involved in an assault on New Year's Eve. Not an assault he was responsible for; one he might just get the blame for if I can't find out exactly what happened."

Henry slows the Land Rover and pulls up outside the back door of the cottage. He makes no move to get out; rather he sits, hands on the steering wheel and stares straight ahead through the rain-spattered windscreen. "Go on."

"As far as I can work out, Richard went to the aid of a rough sleeper, who had himself gone to the aid of a girl who was being assaulted by three men outside a nightclub in London. The girl got away pretty much unharmed, though naturally she is somewhat traumatised. The rough sleeper, the man who Richard had been dossing with, was injured and died soon afterwards. Again, as far as I can work out, Richard—"

"Let's refer to him as Ric, shall we? That's his chosen name, even if it isn't the name he was given."

"Yes, of course, Henry. As far as I have been able to work out, Ric must have seen off the three men involved—"

"That would be him," Henry says. "That fits. Had an almost psychotic hatred of that sort of thing, did Ric. Couldn't bear any form of cruelty; not to women and children, nor animals. Strong young man, quick, trained in the use of force."

"As you would expect of a Royal Marine Commando," Simon agrees. "The problem is that if the police fail to track down any of the three men, or if they do and their story goes against Ric, there is a distinct possibility that Ric might be held responsible for the man's death. That may sound like a good story, however it's not one I want either to write or read. If you don't mind my asking, how long has Ric been gone?"

Loveridge thinks for a moment. Then, taking his dinner-plate-sized hands off the wheel, he paws his unruly mop of white hair and rubs his face in the manner of a man recently woken from sleep. "Four maybe five months; maybe a shade over that."

"And you've not had any contact with him since?"

"Not a word."

"He was away when—"

"Yes. In Afghanistan, on tour. That was before... He came back two days after. Didn't come back here straight away, mind, he went directly to Selly Oak Hospital in Birmingham."

"He was wounded?"

"Yes."

"How bad?"

"Got caught up in one of those IEDs. Improvised Explosive Device, I think that stands for. Terrible things. Ric told me the

211

Taliban used to fill them with all sorts of bad stuff: nuts, bolts, needles, human excrement, anything they thought might maim or disable. If the blast don't kill you or blow your limbs off, the nuts and bolts will carve you up. And if that don't finish you, the infection will. Terrible bloody things."

"How long was he in the hospital?"

"Four weeks, give or take a day. We held off on Sarah's funeral for as long as we could; tried to give him time to recover. Had to go ahead in the end. Didn't want to, of course. They told Ric he wasn't fit enough to attend, so he discharged himself. Turned up that morning looking like death. Had to go back into hospital for another two weeks after.

"Come on, let's go inside," he says. "I don't know about you, Simon, but I could do with a cup of tea."

They climb out of the Land Rover and make to the back door. Once inside, Simon spends a couple of minutes cleaning the mud off his shoes while Henry fills and puts on the kettle.

"How do you take it?" the farmer asks.

"Black, no sugar, weak, please."

"Frightened hot water we call that." Henry throws him a look suggesting his taste is a shade boutique for the wilds of Exmoor.

The kitchen is cramped, the windows brindled with condensation. Muddy boot prints mark the stone-effect vinyl floor, and purple latex gloves, outsize syringes, drenchers, markers, taggers, castrators, teat-topped bottles and aerosols of antiseptic dye litter the work surfaces, all gathering dust.

The two of them sit down on powder-blue painted penny-seat chairs either side of a rustic pine table. Henry Loveridge passes Simon his mug of thin tea, before ladling several spoons of sugar into his own clay-hued brew.

"How certain can you be that it was Ric involved in the scrap?" he asks, stirring, lost in thought.

"I found a notebook. Here, have a look for yourself."

Loveridge handles the notebook gently, deftly, the way a farmer might cosset a premature lamb. "Yes, that's his writing. Sarah told me he kept a book like that: details of the men he served with, families, personal stuff. Thorough, that was Ric. Left nothing to chance." He drinks. "Where did you find it?"

"In the alley near where the assault took place. It was where I think Ric and the other man were sleeping."

"If you've not clapped eyes on him, how do you know he was there when the assault took place?"

"Henry. Do you have a photograph of Ric? I mean, a photograph I could have a look at, here?"

The big farmer doesn't move for a few seconds. He just sits and looks back at Simon. Eventually he wipes his hand over his face, same as he did in the car, and gets up, opens the door into the hall and leaves.

A minute later he is back, three silver photo frames in his right hand. He lays them on the table, face up.

A quick glance confirms to Simon that one of them is Ric and Sarah's wedding photo. He is suddenly and acutely aware that Loveridge had baulked at retrieving the photographs because his now deceased daughter is smiling back from one of them: the happiest girl on her happiest day; a scene that could only compound a father's misery.

Before handling them, Simon says. "I'm sorry, Henry. I cannot imagine how tough this must be for you."

"It's not easy, I'll grant you that, Simon. But it's how it is."

The newlyweds are posed together before church doors. Ric is wearing his Blues, white cap banded red, ceremonial sword at his side; Sarah a simple, strapless white dress, her blonde hair pinned back, a bouquet of yellow 'Molland Lilly' held at her waist. As completely remarkable as the photograph is, the vogue, the élan and the sophistication of their wedding attire run a steady second to the radiance of their smiles.

Simon looks up; Loveridge away.

In the second of the three frames, Richard Ross wears his green Lovat uniform and green beret. He stands at attention, his features apparently hewn from a similar stone as that of Loretta Martin's brother Billy, the Warrant Officer Paddy Jennings had told him was inseparable from Ross. Simon studies it for a few seconds before moving on to the last.

In this, Ric Ross lazes on a wooden bench, his right foot up, his right elbow resting upon his knee. He wears blue jeans and a white shirt, a dark sweater looped over his shoulders. The casual repose reminds Simon of those he has seen in any number of men's clothing catalogues, even if the young man in question doesn't look quite so professionally relaxed. His light-brown hair shorn short, his torso lean and his features sharp, the Royal Marine exudes an air of efficiency and fitness. But what interests Simon most is the mark, a coin-sized blood scar or graze just above Ross's right eye.

"This mark," Simon points to the photograph, "here on Ric's forehead."

"What of it?"

"Is it a scar, a wound?"

"Was there that first time I met him in our field. Was there last time I saw him. Not that unusual; people have them."

"Yes, Henry, people do have them. But, I'll bet, not many men who just happened to be dossing outside a nightclub on New Year's Eve in the City." Simon studies the photograph again and tries to equate the image of the clean-cut, casually dressed, carefree young man with that of the shambling shadow he saw briefly when in the queue to the club and has seen several times since on the CCTV recording.

"You've no doubt, then?"

"Not much, Henry. And if I'm right and this is Ric, then we need to find him. And quickly."

Soraya's forthcoming interview with the police comes to mind and he considers asking Henry for the photograph.

"It's how we find him, Henry, that's what bothers me. Tell me, if you don't mind, what's he like? What kind of a man is Ric?"

"How do you mean, what kind of man?"

"Well, you've told me he couldn't abide any kind of violence towards women or children or animals. Unless I'm mistaken, *psychotic hatred* were the words you used; strong words too. So, what else was there to him? Did you like him? Are you happy to have him as your son-in-law?"

The farmer raises his head and narrows his eyes. "Of course! What sort of a damn fool question is that?" He doesn't wait for an answer as he taps the pine table hard enough to dent it. "It wasn't his fault what happened to our Sarah. She knew what she was doing when she agreed to marry him; knew there was a chance he wouldn't come back and she'd be left to a life of mourning. Just didn't think it was going to turn out the other way round, is all. That first time, when he went to Iraq in January of 2003, she wasn't too unhappy about him. Couldn't be, could she?"

"I wouldn't know." Simon recalls what Cynthia Ross had said. "It takes someone special to deal with all that worry."

Henry slurps from his cup, then bangs it back down on the table. "Went away a boy; came back a man, didn't he. Had a bit of growing up to do, just like we all did when we was that age. No doubt he saw some stuff that would darken any man's sight."

"How do you mean?"

"I don't know. He came back a bit serious. Lost a little of the twinkle in his eye. He told Sarah about it, whatever it was; wouldn't tell us. And Sarah, God bless her cotton socks, was so loyal to him she wouldn't tell us neither. But he wasn't the same. Probably the experience of it all, I suppose."

The big farmer examines his own hands, as if he might read in the deep lines of his palms the story of what had happened to the young subaltern.

"When he went away that second time to Iraq, must have been a year later, it wasn't too bad. Except that Sarah got it into her head that if he went away she'd never see him again. She said he kept having these dreams, seeing the faces of the dead in his sleep. I suppose that's only natural after seeing some of the things those young lads saw."

Simon sits bolt upright. "The faces of the dead? In his sleep?"

"Yes. Wild dreams, he used to have. I remember one night he was so bad, Sarah had to call the doctor out. Give him some sort of sedative. Said it was something to do with Post Traumatic Stress Disorder. Sounds like a bloody good excuse for something a doctor doesn't understand, if you ask me."

Simon isn't listening; he is trying to recall the words of Elen Phillips when she referred to the young Richard's night terrors. She said he used to wake up screaming about people dying with him standing watching, helpless. Or if not exactly that, something like it.

Simon leans forward, resting his elbows on the table. "These dreams you say he had, did they persist? Were they worse when he came back or just before he went?"

"Bad when he came back from Iraq that first time. Worse in the weeks before he went off to Afghanistan. Middle of lambing, if I recall correctly. Put the wind up Sarah something rotten, it did. Ric said he believed something bad was going to happen; said he knew who it was going to happen to as well. I don't think he meant Sarah; that wasn't nothing to do with what went on out there."

"But, something bad did happen out there, didn't it, Henry? Paddy Jennings, one of Ric's men, told me I should ask Billy Martin. You must have met Billy Martin?"

"Warrant Officer 2nd Class Billy Martin. Hard as a dog's head, as we would say. Toughest and bravest, most handsome and most charming man you'll ever meet."

"Yes, most people would seem to be in awe of him," Simon adds.

"Also," Henry carries on, "the most self-centred, self-absorbed, vainglorious shit I've ever had the misfortune to come across. Now, I'm not one to speak ill of a person…"

"A narcissist."

Henry taps the table again. "In one."

"Not your cup of tea."

"No. Talking of which, would you like another. Something tells me you're going to take up more than the two or few minutes of my time."

"For sure." Simon passes his mug. "I can't remember who said it, but either Martin's sister or Jennings said there was a bit of history between the two of them, Ric and WO Martin. Best of friends, best of enemies, something like that. Do you know what that was about?"

The broad-shouldered farmer, keeping his back to the table, pauses from filling the kettle. "I do. Yes, Simon, I do. And I'm not much of a one for telling tales out of school either. However, seeing as you're looking for Ric and no one can hurt our Sarah now, you might as well know. When Billy Martin was home on his mid-tour break, he came to see Sarah, here, at the farm. Brought her a letter from Ric. They went out for the evening; went out for dinner. Next thing I know, I get a call from Sarah. She's locked herself in the bathroom and she's whispering that Martin's drunk and keeps trying it on with her. Says he's getting angry, thinks he might be getting a bit worked up." He pauses, continues filling the kettle from the basin tap and, placing it on its stand, switches it on at the wall plug.

"So," Simon prompts, "you came here and threw him out?"

"Yes, don't mind admitting I was a bit wary of him. However, he was a proper baked dinner by then and I was proper savage with him. All it took was a swift right hook and he lost his legs.

217

Squared him up and threw him in the barn is what I did. Took his car keys off him and took Sarah home."

"And the next morning?"

Henry turns to face Simon, his expression hard as the Devonian rock beneath the heather-cloaked moor. "Came back here, put the keys in his car and left him to it. I saw him skulking in the kitchen. Chances are I'd have lost my temper, so I left him to it. He was gone by the afternoon."

"And Sarah?"

"Well," his expression softens, "she said we weren't to worry about it. Asked us to forgive him. Said it was more about the pressure he was under than it was about the man himself; all that stress and strain. Said he was better than that. But that was how Sarah was: quick to forgive."

"And that was the end of it?"

Henry sighs. "Not to my thinking. I could see she was more than a bit shook up.

"That evening Sarah went to the cinema. The weather was pretty bad, worse than today, and when I suggested she didn't go, she said she wasn't going to let a little rain stop her from seeing her friends. A little rain," he scoffs. "I knew what she meant.

"Her friends called about ten, wanting to know where she was. The police come by here soon after. Seemed there was no one else involved. No alcohol, nothing. Doesn't make sense: she knew the road too well. I suppose she can't have been concentrating..."

Keen to save the farmer from having to recall too many painful memories, Simon suggests, "Not how one would expect a mate to behave though, is it?"

"No." The kettle boils. Henry pours. "Give the man his due, he telephoned next morning to apologise for his behaviour. I couldn't bring myself to speak to him, of course. Not after what he'd done. Not even if he was supposed to be one of Ric's closest friends. Couldn't do it, could I?"

"Did Ric have many friends? You know, old school friends, friends from Abergavenny, friends outside of the Marines?"

"A few came to the wedding; not one or more really close though. That's the daft part of it." Loveridge looks suitably baffled. "They was supposed to be best mates, Ric and Martin. Ric even pulled Martin out of the police station one night up in Liverpool. Not much of a way to atone for one's sins, is it?"

Once he's sat back down, they discuss the ever-lengthening list of Richard Ross's tough breaks. Starting with the break-up with his parents, the loss of his father, whether the two were close or otherwise, the stab in the back from the man Ric thought of as his best friend and, most recently, the loss of his wife: the slope is steep and unforgiving.

"That was one of the most wonderful things about Ric and Sarah's relationship," he adds. "They weren't only in love with each other, they were each other's best friends, too. Soul mates, if you like."

Rain smacks at the windows and water pools in the farmer's eyes. He scrapes his teaspoon around the base of his teacup in ever decreasing circles.

"I've heard it said," Loveridge mutters into his tea, "that there is no greater pain than is felt by a parent who loses their child. I tell you, Simon, I know this to be true. It's enough to destroy a man. And if Ric loved Sarah even half as much as I loved her, then the man must be in some terrible pain."

"We have to find him," Simon states. "We must."

"Of course, we must. How, is the problem. What are you going to do?"

"Damned if I know, Henry. When did you last see or hear from him? Elen Phillips told me Ric rang her from a pub, not long after he returned from his tour. She said he was drunk; *incoherent* was the word she used. She tried to talk sense into him, but the listening had gone out of him. I suppose that was some time after Sarah's funeral."

"That's likely. He looked incapable at the service and didn't touch a drop at the wake, such as it was. I think," Henry clangs his spoon onto the table, picks up his mug and takes a good pull, "the last time he was here was when he came back that second time, after his second trip to Selly Oak. One of the lads told me he'd seen a shiny new car outside the cottage. Probably a rental: Ric was more a motorbike man. Didn't have a car. Sarah used to drive him in hers.

"Well, I got down here as fast as I could, only to see the car driving off across the field. I came inside; place was tidy, nothing unusual, no note, nothing, clothes still in the wardrobe, milk in the fridge, post unopened."

"The post?"

"What about it, Simon?"

"What do you do with the post? Must be a good few letters piled up over the last months."

"Oh," Henry sighs, "I sort through it, chuck most of it out, keep what looks personal, you know, letters of condolence, bank, card companies, insurance, service correspondence. There's a fair stack in the hall."

Simon waits, leaning his head on his hands, watching.

After what seems an age, the penny drops and Loveridge's brow furrows like the turned lines of sod out beyond the windows. "No, I'll not do it. They're addressed to him. Not mine to open. Wouldn't be right."

"Henry, if Ric's using his bank card or credit card, which I know he isn't much of the time because I've seen him on the CCTV begging, we could—"

"Begging, you say?"

"Yes, begging."

"Jesus, Mary and Joseph! What's the man come to?"

Simon shares the man's dismay. "That's another reason why we've got to find him. The man is drowning out in the storm drain and we are the only ones who can offer him a rope. If he's been using his bank card or his credit card, the record on his statement will tell us which cashpoints he's accessed. We're all creatures of habit, Henry; we all get used to doing things a certain way. The records on his statement might give us an idea of where he's dossing, though I doubt he's anywhere near where the assault took place." Simon pauses. "Do you see, Henry, it's up to us. Ric has no one else."

The ruddy-faced farmer will not give up any of the letters. He cannot be persuaded, no matter what logical or reasonable pretext Simon puts to him, and soon enough they run out of conversation.

When he drops Simon back at Tiverton Parkway railway station, the rain is incessant and they wait in the Land Rover for a while, hoping it will abate long enough for Simon to make it inside without getting soaked.

"If," Loveridge says, "it comes to it and you cannot do without my help, in London I mean, all you have to do is call me. You have my phone number. We owe it to Ric and to Sarah to do what we can. Whatever you need, Simon, please call."

"Thank you, Henry, I appreciate that."

They shake hands and the farmer fixes him with a meaningful stare. "You know, you're not like I'd assumed you would be."

"You mean I'm younger than you thought?"

Henry smiles. "No, not that. Although, yes, I had expected someone older. It's just that we get used to reporters on the television and in the papers being a certain way. Though God knows I've given up reading them. They spoon feed us all this useless, irrelevant, bad news, so we come to think of journalists as being like flies. You know, brush the furze—the gorse—and the flies all jump. Not you though, Simon. You seem to me like a lad who's got a bit of heart and I'm grateful for what you're doing. I hope you find your story."

———————

Loveridge's endorsement buoys his spirits through the long train journey back to London. If he'd required any more confirmation that his decision not to document their conversation in shorthand had been the right one, he cannot imagine it. Though common and correct practice, any form of recording would have served only to tongue-tie the farmer and Simon's objective had been to get the man to relax, to talk openly, to give up some snippet of information that might help him find the missing commando. Earning his respect and the offer of his help is reward enough; being entrusted with the photograph of Richard Ross is an added bonus.

He phones Soraya, his call diverting immediately to her voicemail. As he leaves his message about meeting her at the police station the next day, she calls him back.

"How you doing?" he asks.

"Okay." Her tone is bright, perhaps too bright. "How is your day?"

"For my sins, I'm on the train. Outside, wet and windy; inside, crowded and steamy. All set for tomorrow?"

"Simon?"

"Yes."

"What's going to happen tomorrow, at the police station?" Soraya's brighter tone hasn't lasted.

"On a general level, you mean?"

"Yes. Will it be like a question and answer session or will I just be allowed to tell them what I remember?"

"It'll be simple. You shouldn't worry. One, they'll ask you if you understand why you're making the statement. Two, they'll ask you to set the scene: who were you with, who else was involved, where did it happen and so on. Three, what actually happened. Four, they'll want a description of anyone involved. And five, they'll probably use a plan they call ADVOKATE, which runs from A, the Amount of time you were at the scene through O, whether your view was Obscured, and on to E, ironing out any Errors or discrepancies in your statement."

"What if I can't remember?"

"Then you tell them you can't. You don't have to tell them why; all you have to say is that you can't."

Excerpt 7 from transcript of conversation with Joseph Naarda

SP: That courage you speak of, was it the naïve courage of a child, or was she precocious? Did Soraya properly understand the dangers of the time?

JN: With a child, who can know? I would not say she was naïve: she was never naïve. One might look into her eyes and believe so, but one would never know what she was thinking. Perhaps this silent courage, this calm, she had inherited from her mother's side, from the Subba.

SP: This courage in caring for the young deserter: surely, she must have known fear at some time? Isn't that how a child learns to be brave?

JN: With Soraya, I'm not so sure. If she was ever frightened, she never acted so. I'll give you an example. A year or so after the incident with my neighbour's son, we went to the river. It was a Sunday and, like my grandparents had so many years before, we took with us a picnic and sat by the cool waters to watch the reed boats come and go.

By that time, we had been blessed with a second child, so while Soraya wandered by the river bank, Salwa and I would sit with her little sister and eat our picnic.

After a while, Soraya came walking back up the path. She was picking up stones and skimming them across the water. I remember thinking she did not have a care in the world and that is exactly how it should be for a child of her age; how it should be before they learn the realities of our troubled world.

After a while, the flies began to bother me; sometimes when there was no breeze they were so thick they cast a shadow upon the water. I commented on this and suggested it was time for us to go home.

Soraya, without looking up, merely observed that the flies were much worse where she had been walking, because there was a dead man swimming at the bottom of the bank.

At first, I did not realise what she had said and I went about gathering our things. Then I stopped and looked at her, and my expression must have given away my surprise.

"Yes, papa," she repeated, "a dead man."

I left Salwa to clear our things and walked quickly down to where Soraya had been playing. I wanted to see for myself that she was not making this up.

Sure enough, there was a dead body, a naked man, rolling lazily in the tide as though he was doing some sort of strange breaststroke. He had clearly been stabbed many times and his corpse was bloated and blistered.

Even though the sun was high, I felt a sudden chill and began to sweat. My skin was cold, like that of a lizard, and I hurried back to where the girls were waiting.

Salwa frowned, wanting to know where I had been. I shook my head. Soraya, though, was curiously unaffected by my doubting her. She merely said, "Did you see the man, papa?"

"Yes, my child. It is terrible to witness such a sight. Try not to let it upset you."

"It won't," she replied. "He is dead now and the *tahma* will take his body out into the bitter waters of the sea. If he was a good man, his *nshimta* will pass into the realm of light. If he was a bad man, his spirit will go to *Ur*. There is nothing one can do except to say *masiqatha* for him. And besides, papa, we are all born of water, aren't we? At our end, we will all return to it."

Now the *tahma*, for the Subba, is the lifeless fluid of life, the *nshimta* is the soul and the *masiqatha* are the prayers they say to help the soul find its way to paradise. I tell you, Simon, this way she had of being able to look at life and death as though one is nothing more than a natural extension of the other, astounded me.

SP: Would you say Soraya was detached from emotion?

JN: No. I am not suggesting she did not know emotion, or that she did not appreciate the concept of loss. On the contrary, she cried as most children do: when they have hurt themselves, when they are unwell or when someone they know dies. Yet this composure I speak of, this serenity, was surely present in her at a very young age.

25

"Are you sure you want me to come in with you?"

"Yes." Soraya is wearing her headscarf and she is as beautiful as she had looked to him two nights previously. She does, though, look anxious.

The City Police Station, a pale 1930s Art Deco four-storey edifice, sits sandwiched between fast-food shops fronting the broad and constantly bustling Bishopsgate.

"They may not like me turning up like this."

She leans in towards him, closing her eyes. "Yes, but I do," she murmurs, kissing him on his cheek. When she steps back, she looks up at him, frowning. "Are *you* really, really sure you want to?"

"Certain." Simon bathes in her look. "Listen, you know why you're here. I'm only here to hold your hand, nothing else."

"What does that say?" she asks, looking up, nervously.

A coat of arms bids *Domine Dirige Nos* to all who enter.

"It says that it is for the people to direct the police and not the reverse."

"Is that what I'm supposed to do, then? Tell them what they should be asking me."

"In a way. Do you know what you're going to say?"

She nods. "Yeah, as if? Come on, let's go."

DS Chalmers, his suit similar in colour to the faded hue of the building's facade, thanks Soraya for coming and throws Simon a slightly off-hand glance, suggesting he is welcome but will remain so only as long as he doesn't get in the way.

In a stark almost unforgiving interview room, a stout, plainly dressed police woman waits. Chalmers introduces her. She smiles. They sit: Chalmers and the WPC opposite Simon and Soraya at a table on which stands a recording device. Chalmers turns the device on, states the time and place, notes the case number and those present, and then hesitates, turning to Simon to ask him to identify himself. "Purely for the record."

"Are you a legal adviser?" Chalmers asks. "We're here to take a personal statement. Miss Naarda is not under caution."

"No, I'm not a legal adviser. I'm here as a friend and at Miss Naarda's request."

Rather too obviously, the detective jots his name down on a slip of paper, which he then passes to the WPC. He halts the recording. The WPC leaves the interview room, only to return soon after.

"If you would kindly switch off your phones? Saves us being interrupted."

They do so.

DS Chalmers starts the recording. He tries his best to put Soraya at ease by smiling, thanking her for coming and stating that they are present simply to take a statement from her concerning an incident at Parker's Walk, Bishopsgate, on New Year's Eve 2009, at around a quarter to midnight. An incident which, itself, concerns an assault to her and a rough sleeper, a Mr Thomas Williams, "who has since died. Please, Miss Naarda, you understand why we have asked you to come in and make a statement?"

"Yes."

The interview then follows roughly the same five-point plan Simon had set out to her the evening before: She was at the club, Slick in the City, with three friends...

Soraya relays the events of that evening surprisingly calmly and without deviating too far from the report she initially supplied DS Chalmers at the inquest. She leaves nothing out and only grows agitated when she recalls the description of the thug who molested her, the repugnance of his assault and the violence of his attack on the old man.

The avuncular detective consults his notebook, makes odd side footnotes, and glances at Simon now and again. He presses Soraya gently for a more accurate description of her assailant and of the girl.

She reaches for Simon's hand at one point, squeezing it not so much in prompting him to speak, so much as needing to draw comfort from his presence.

The woman police officer smiles warmly.

"Miss Naarda," Chalmers asks, "a couple of questions, if you don't mind?"

"Of course. Could I have a drink of water, please?"

The WPC leaves the room and returns with polystyrene cups filled with tepid, limpid refreshment.

Soraya sips. "Please, what is it you want to ask?"

Chalmers face straightens as though what he has listened to so far is little more than a child-certificated trailer, undemanding of her consideration or attention. "Miss Naarda, because you were present at the inquest, where you volunteered the information regarding your assault and that of the assault on poor Mr Thomas, you should be aware that the City of London Police have launched a murder investigation." His tone is now less agreeable, less sympathetic.

Soraya nods. "Yes," she says, her tone matching his, "one of my course friends showed me a newspaper article. That made life extremely uncomfortable for me. You should have told me that you'd launched an investigation. Really, you should have."

"Yes, of course. You are quite correct. Once the decision had been taken, we should have informed you. Please accept our apologies for that oversight."

Simon is minded to suggest Chalmers is being a shade disingenuous, if not slyly dishonest. However, he can see no profit in antagonising the detective, so he decides to keep quiet.

"It's important you understand that the information you have supplied may well be used in evidence if a prosecution results from this investigation. With that in mind, I must stress how accurate and reliable your statement needs to be. If at any stage you should decide to retract or modify any of this statement, it will make it very difficult for us and the Crown Prosecution Service when, or if, it comes to charging your assailant. Do you understand that?"

Soraya thinks for a moment, before replying in a voice so cool and level that she might be delivering a talk in Sunday school, "Completely. Yes, I do understand. But do you understand, Detective Chalmers? Do you have any idea what it's like to have a man slobber all over you, while he violates you? No? Probably because it's never happened to you and I sincerely hope it never does. Because remember, once you've been violated, you've been violated. It's a knot you'll never untie, a stain you'll never remove and a fact you'll never allow yourself to forget." She leaves her come-back hanging in the air, staring first at the detective and then, very pointedly, at the WPC, who sits back and fidgets uncomfortably.

Chalmers is stunned and takes a few seconds to recover his composure. "Would you like to take a break, Miss Naarda? I'm sure this must be very traumatic for you."

"No, I'm good, thanks." Soraya keeps her gaze on the WPC.

"Right. Okay. Then, as I said, there are a few questions I need to ask you."

"Fire away."

"You say that this girl..." he consults his notebook, "she must have spiked your drink with some form of drug. What makes you think that?"

"Because one minute I was slightly, you might even say happily relaxed and the next I found it almost impossible to speak, my vision was blurred and I had little or no control over my limbs. I felt dizzy, nauseous and confused. In effect, I suddenly felt as though I'd drunk ten times the amount of alcohol I had drunk."

"You're used to alcohol?"

Soraya is subtly indignant, "Are you?"

He ignores her retort. "What I mean is, being a Mus—"

"Detective?" Simon cuts in, hoping to calm Soraya by reaching for her wrist and squeezing it firmly. "Miss Naarda's religious persuasion, whatever it is, is not relevant. And not only that, your assumption that Miss Naarda is a Muslim is way off the mark. You're out of order."

Chalmers acknowledges Simon's leap to his friend's defence with an appeasing glance. "Yes, of course. Let me put it this way, Miss Naarda, you tell us you went to the Royal London Hospital and asked for your bloods to be checked. You say the tests showed that there was no evidence of any such drug in your system. How do you explain that?"

"In the same way the doctor explained it to me: sufficient time had elapsed between ingesting the drug and having the tests. The length of time the drug remains evident in one's system depends on the amount of the drug, the concentration of it and my metabolism. The tests didn't give a positive result; they were inconclusive—"

"Forgive me for interrupting," Chalmers says, his tone dry, "you're a forensic science student, aren't you?"

"Yes. And yes, we have done some study of these types of drugs. Please, Detective Chalmers, indulge me for a moment, allow me to put this to you: you probably know how to drive a car, would that be true?"

The detective isn't amused. "Yes."

"Can you put your hand on your heart and tell me you've never had a car accident; one that wasn't your fault; one that you didn't see coming?"

Chalmers coughs, irritated. "Is it possible that this girl was not the only person who could have spiked your drink?"

"Yes, it's possible. My friend could have done it, or the barman, or a passer-by. The club was pretty crowded. However, I know my friend well enough to know that he's not that kind of guy. And as far as the barmen go; if they'd have spiked my drink, they probably would have spiked everyone else's and I can't see what good it would have done them. As far as someone else in the club doing it: we had our own roped-off area. Natasha, and I know that really was her name because I've just remembered overhearing one of the kitchen staff call her that as we were going out the back, was the only stranger I took a drink off all night, so it must have been her."

Soraya pauses, drawing breath. She isn't, though, quite finished. "Is that forensic enough for you, Detective Chalmers?"

"How old are you, Miss Naarda?"

"I'm not yet 21, if that's where you're going?"

"And Slick in the City only admits those over 21, am I correct in thinking that?"

"Yes. Absolutely. And that's why I used fake ID. And where did I get it? Down the market. It doesn't matter which one, Brick Lane or Brixton, because you can get fake ID in most of them as far as I know." Soraya gloats, pleased with herself for having stolen the policeman's thunder. "Ever dropped your iPhone down the toilet? No? Well if you do, let me know and I'll let you know where to get it fixed without sending it back to Apple."

DS Chalmers' careworn expression suggests he is beginning to rue getting out of bed. "Just one last point, Miss Naarda: we have studied the CCTV from New Year's Eve in and around the top end of Bishopsgate. We have images of Mr Williams coming and going at various times of the day and up until seven in the evening. There are a number of other individuals recorded in the vicinity. One of them is a man who we believe to be another rough sleeper; a man known to have frequented the area and who was often seen in the company of Mr Williams. Can you remember anyone else being with Mr Williams that evening?"

Soraya does not rush to reply. Instead she gazes down at the table, searching, as if deep in thought. "No, not that I recall."

"Are you sure about this, Miss Naarda?" Chalmers stares hard at her, watching, waiting. "Perfectly sure?"

"Mm, perfectly."

"Right," he decides. The compressed atmosphere of the room reduces as though a pressure-release valve has been opened. "We also have a group of three men, walking, no, to be fair one of them is hobbling while being supported by the other two, in the vicinity of the club at midnight. They may, of course, have been under the influence of alcohol; that wouldn't be out of the ordinary." This time he resists the temptation to throw Soraya a look. "What is unusual, though, is that they should be walking down the road right at or just after your assault occurred; a time when most of London was more concerned with welcoming in the New Year as opposed to hobbling away from it."

Soraya looks up, the relief in her expression palpable. She turns to look at Simon. He smiles.

"So, Miss Naarda," Chalmers continues, "we are inclined to think these three or four men may be something to do with the man who assaulted you and Mr Williams, and we are in the process of trying to identify them, which is, sadly, not proving easy. Do you have any idea who they might be?"

233

"No. If I did I'd have told you at the inquest. Can't the club tell you? Haven't they got CCTV? I remember having to stare into the camera when going through the ID check. They must have records."

Chalmers nods. "Indeed, they do. Or indeed they usually do. The owners of the club usually retain them for six months, or so they have told us. All of which means we should by now know the identity of these three men if, that is, they had been in the club."

Simon shifts in his seat.

"In that case," Soraya begins, hope rapidly replacing relief, "you must have an idea who they are. Wow, that's brilliant, Detective Chalmers. I—"

He breathes in, deeply, and holds up his hand as if to halt a stream of traffic. "Yes, Miss Naarda, brilliant it would be. Without doubt, brilliant is exactly what it would be. Sadly, though, it isn't. And it isn't because the CCTV recordings and the entry log for New Year's Eve have gone walkabout."

Soraya is astonished, likewise Simon, even if his astonishment is manufactured as opposed to natural.

"Don't they have to retain records by law?" she asks.

Chalmers looks briefly to the ceiling. "No. There is no legal requirement that demands they have to either keep them or produce them." He sits back, deflated.

"You said they've gone walkabout," Simon repeats.

The detective consults his notes. "Yes, Mr Peckham. That is correct, they cannot locate them. Now," he leans forward once more, a conspiratorial edge to his tone, "and here's the strange part of it, they have located the records for the nights they were open either side of New Year and it is only the records for New Year's Eve that have gone missing. All of which leads us to believe that someone has removed them, possibly a member of staff known to these three men or to the other individual, the rough sleeper, seen in the area that night."

They sit in silence for a full and empty minute, each of them looking at the other, all of them crestfallen.

"Is that the end of it?" Soraya asks.

"No, not the absolute end of it." Chalmers sighs. "It is only the end of it until we can either get our hands on that recording and the log, or until we have by some other route managed to identify the people we think are involved."

Simon thinks, quickly. "What about other CCTV?"

"We are looking at other closed-circuit information. Many of the businesses in the vicinity have their own security systems. But you must understand," he shifts his gaze to Soraya, "this provides us with an enormous case load of material to sift through and this is one reason why we need to be so sure of your statement. Beyond that, I would like to thank you for your time and apologise for asking you to recall the more unfortunate events of New Year's Eve."

DS Chalmers notes the end of the interview and turns off the recording device. "Please rest assured, Miss Naarda, we will explore every avenue in order to find the person or persons who assaulted you and Mr Williams." He closes his notebook, casts the WPC beside him a knowing, weary glance and stands.

As they file out of the room, Chalmers is met at the door and handed a note. He halts and turns to Simon. "Mr Peckham, might I have a word?"

Simon glances at Soraya. "Wait for me outside, please. I won't be a minute." Then, to the detective, "Of course."

Chalmers leaves him and disappears into another room. When he returns he is accompanied by a lean, dark-suited man.

"Mr Peckham, this way if you wouldn't mind?"

They step back into the interview room. Chalmers closes the door behind them.

"What can I do for you..." Simon asks.

"Carver, Detective Inspector Brian Carver." The newcomer's manner is abrupt, and though he stands tall, he is not quite tall enough to look Simon directly in the eye. "Simon, if I may, it is the practice that when a member of the press plants his feet in our garden, he makes himself known to us."

"Sure, I realise that—"

"A minute, please." His tone is insistent. "You're quite new to the job or so your editor, to whom one of our officers has just spoken, tells us, so there's no reason you would know the rules. And, talking of rules, there is no statute that a member of the press has to make him," he hesitates, "or herself known to us. It is, however, the form. How long have you known Miss Naarda?"

"A while. A few weeks. Can't remember exactly. Why?"

Carver is lean of build and his features sharp. "Do you have any interest in Miss Naarda; any interest other than an interest that is purely social? I mean, she's a strikingly attractive woman so that would only be natural."

Simon, though, isn't drawn. "Again, why?"

"Well, it could be that you just happen to be her friend, a friend who is a journalist; that could simply be a coincidence. However, it could also be that you have latched on to Miss Naarda in order to worm your way into our investigation; in order to get yourself an inside track; a story. How the police don't give a stuff about the death of a rough sleeper, how under resourced we are, though that would be fair to say, or how we don't have the time to investigate every death and perhaps how incompetent we can be and so on." He yawns, theatrically.

Simon makes to object.

The detective bats his objection away. "Let's not start mudslinging until we find ourselves in the mire, shall we?" Carver waits.

"Good. Your editor says you're a bright lad." He pauses again. "Your father was in the newspaper game, wasn't he? Thought I recognised the name. Not always the best friend to us, your father. However, I am not one to punish the son for the sins of the father, as the Bible would have it."

Simon goes to object again, but swallows his protest. As his feet are currently planted in the Detective Inspector's garden, and for the moment the police don't know how much information he holds, he reasons it might be in his better interest to humour Carver.

"Again, good," Carver repeats, pleased if not profoundly delighted. "Let me suggest to you how this works best. If you are in possession of any information that might have a bearing on this case, or for that matter any future case, you'll find it better in the long run to let us have it. As you know, there is no law that compels you to hand over to us whatever it is that you might know: however, it would be in your better interest to consider doing so. Am I making myself clear?"

"As mud, Brian, if I may."

"You may, Simon, and long I hope will you continue to do so. You see, it's a sort of give and take thing, a quid pro quo, you scratch my back and I'll scratch yours. It's worked this way for a long time and with good reason. It's one of the ways in which we all help our world go round. Now then—"

"There's more?" Simon asks, feigning surprise.

"Oh, yes, Simon: there's more. Do you know the club Slick in the City?"

"Sure."

"Ever been there?"

Simon is careful. Chalmers suggested the police had already approached the club for their records. And though the log and the CCTV from New Year's Eve is missing, it is likely in the course of their investigation that the police have studied the recent entry logs and CCTV. "Yes, a few weeks ago like, I suspect, hundreds of others."

"And that is where I realised I'd seen your name and your face before. That's what we're supposed to be good at, eh, us Bobbies? I must say, Simon, you do manage a good line in attractive women. Miss Naarda know about that blonde bimbo you go dancing with?"

"First, she's not all that bimbo and second, I'm not sure my private life is any concern of yours, Brian."

"Oh, come on lad. Don't go all soppy on me, you're better than that. Or at least you should be if you really are your father's son." Carver pauses, waiting for perhaps another objection. When none appears, he carries on, "Now, I will be talking to the employees at the club and my guess is one of them has got rid of the logs. Why? Well, that's what we need to find out, isn't it? So," the detective taps Simon hard on the chest, "if *you do* happen to trip across any information that has a bearing on this investigation, do yourself a favour and give me a bell first. Like the cuckold once said, don't let me be the last to know."

Simon looks down at the finger jabbing him in his chest. "You know that constitutes assault, don't you, Brian?"

Carver leers, his humour evaporated. "Oh yes, Simon, I know the law. And, in fact, I know how to prosecute the law, just like your dad knew how to abuse it. Now perhaps you'd best not keep Miss Naarda waiting too long, eh? Might catch her death."

"You were long enough," Soraya says, her nose crimson, her lips quivering.

"Yes, sorry about that."

Car exhausts fog the street like coal-fired chimneys. Pedestrians scuttle.

"What did he want, the policeman?"

Simon, taking her hands between his, rubs them. "Wanted me to meet another policeman. Turns out the other man knew my dad."

"Your dad? He a policeman too?"

"No. He's in PR."

Soraya looks up at him, gathering from his chopped reply that Simon is unlikely to elucidate. "Fancy a coffee?" she asks, her frown a shade pleading.

He pulls himself to, banishing for the moment Carver's menacing tone. "No. Sorry. Would love to, really, but—"

"You can't," she finishes for him, adding sarcastically, "Got to get back to the office. Drum up a, what was it, News-in-brief about my interview?"

If Carver's strangely enigmatic comments regarding his father haven't wound him up sufficiently, her distrust of him winds his spring one too many turns. "For Christ's sake, Soraya, I'm not sure what you want from me. You turn up at my door, accuse me of being a first-rate bastard and then ask me to come to a police interview with you. So, I come to the interview, hold your hand and keep my mouth shut... okay, until that detective suggests you can't handle your booze because he thinks you're a Muslim—when, apparently, you're not—and yet again you accuse me of being insincere." His exasperation reaching crescendo, Simon hunches his shoulder and splays his hands. "Is it me who's going in circles, or are you just pushing my merry-go-round for fun?"

Soraya steps back, both confused and riled by his sudden indignation. "Oh, I must have got that wrong then. I thought I was the one under pressure here. Listen, don't think I don't appreciate you putting yourself out for me, but anybody would think you're the one who was assaulted on New Year's Eve."

His phone chirps and his frustrations get the better of him. He turns away from her to read his message.

It's Barnes: *Had a call from B'gate nick. Office now would be good.*

When he turns back, Soraya is gone. Gone as though plucked by a wind and borne away.

26

"Sit down," Barnes mumbles, as he finishes reading an email.

The office is cool and yet sweat blooms at the editor's armpits and collar.

Simon does as he is bidden, nervous in anticipation, yet still irritated by his mishandling of... well, most of the afternoon.

"Right." Barnes studies his protégé for a few seconds, evidently unsure as to whether to bite him or simply scrutinise him until sleep deprives him of a better alternative.

"Simon, I suppose you're wondering why I've called you in?"

"Yes boss, I mean, Barnesy. As you mentioned in your text, you got a call from Bishopsgate Police Station. Seems I over-stepped the mark."

Barnes's wadded face creases into a cheeky grin. "Hole in one, young man. And like all holes in one, however unexpected they may be, and be they by scratch golfer or club pro, they deserve applause. Thought I'd hauled you in to bust your balls, if you'll excuse me mixing my sporting metaphors?"

Simon exhales heavily. "Yes."

"Ah, don't worry about the Old Bill. They don't like their shiny steel toecaps being trodden on. They're so wrapped up in their own petty rules, they haven't noticed we've thrown them out the window and they're littering the pavement." The editor grins. "No, Simon my boy, they think you're in here receiving a hundred lashes of willow branch."

Simon clears his throat. "Thank you. I thought that was going to be considerably more painful."

"No, sod the bloody Mushrooms. However, best not antagonise them too much or they might make life difficult for us next time we need them. Know why I call them Mushrooms?"

"Didn't know you did."

"Because I like to keep them in the dark and feed them on shit, that's why." He grins. "Best left that way, too. Now, what did I want you for. Oh yes. I thought we ought to have a little pow-wow about how you're getting on; not so much a half-time chat, more a moving towards extra-time exhortation. Some of the diary stuff you've been covering is okay... in fact, your submissions have been pretty good really. Haven't used all of them, though that's not because of the quality of your work. So no problem there you'll be pleased to hear."

He doesn't mention the News-in-brief following Tom Williams' inquest.

"Your expenses have been a little... shall we say progressive. Trips to Liverpool, Bracknell, Abergavenny, Tiverton, the odd taxi and erroneous don't-ask-me-why couple of quid here and there. Nice kid that Candy; good at her job. Absolute cracker, too." Barnes' eyes glaze over. "Nightclubs?"

"A nightclub," Simon points out.

"Yessss." The editor thrums his bottom lip. "Go on, what are you working on? Is it how gangster rap encourages drug taking? How nightclubs should be made to stump up for eardrum, liver and nasal septum reconstructions?"

"No, I'm working on a story."

"About what? And don't give me The Old Curiosity Shop on it; a brief synopsis will do."

How to precis all that he has learned since meeting Soraya on New Year's Eve? "You remember your call to me on New Year's morning? A rough sleeper was beaten up out the back of a nightclub. He was taken to the Royal London, didn't make it. You said there might be something in it. Sent me over there."

"Mm, go on."

"His name was Thomas Williams. Ex-Falklands para hero. Police didn't think it suspicious and were going to let it go that way.

"For me, though, something wasn't quite right. I didn't know what, couldn't put my finger on it, but something wasn't right. So, I went along to the inquest and it turned out Williams had gone to the aid of a girl who was being assaulted out the back of the club. He got seven bells kicked out of him and now the police *are* treating it as murder. You remember the Nib? The girl involved, Soraya Naarda, went to Bishopsgate Police Station to give a statement, this afternoon. I'd met her outside the Royal London on New Year's morning, and again at the inquest, and she asked me if I'd go along. And that," Simon states, in a tone which he hopes will discourage his editor from wanting to gate-crash his story, "is that. That's what Merseyside, Berkshire, Wales, Devon and a dull evening with Candy in a bear pit like Slick in the City is all about."

"Know where you're going with it?"

"I believe so."

"Think it's got enough weight?"

"Yes."

Barnes considers, still thrumming his bottom lip, still watching, still weighing. "Mm, something tells me you're not giving me the full story..."

Simon meets his editor's stare.

"And don't think I don't understand why. But what I need you to understand, Simon, is that the boys working the news desk need guys like you to supply them with material they can use to fill the front pages. And they, and I, would take considerable exception to being scooped by another paper on a story that was already known to one of our own journalists. Call it the tyranny of the desk, call it what you like, but like it or not we are all slaves to the news desk. Now then," he leans forward, "it's also important for you to understand that one of my roles in this great undertaking of ours is to reckon the value of each and every story that lands on my desk. And that makes me the man who decides how much your story is worth and when and where it should be told."

Whatever, or however much, Simon has left out, he is not inclined to reveal. As he keeps telling himself, if Ross is connected to the murder of old Tom Williams, then he has a story of value and it is his and his exclusively. He isn't about to cede control of his story by gifting Ross to Barnes only for the editor to offer the rough-sleeping former Royal Marine up to the news desk, like some tasty titbit. So, Simon waits and watches and keeps his own counsel.

"Okay," the editor eventually decides, "I'll give you some more rope, but try not to hang yourself. There's more than a few out there," he points towards the door, "who would like to see you fail just so they can deal me the I-told-you-so card." Barnes stands up and reaches for his jacket: the game talk is over.

"Now then, Simon," he says, "one last question."

"What are you, a detective?"

"Part of my job, eh. To know what's going on. Wish I did: wouldn't feel like I was trying to catch water half the bloody time. No, what I've been meaning to ask is why haven't we been out for a beer yet? Don't like a drink? Is it a medical thing? Habit you can't control? What? Your dad could put it away with the rest of them."

Simon is staggered to learn his father had been a drinker; he'd never in his life seen him touch a drop. His mention of *detective* suddenly reminds him of Carver's disparaging comments.

"No, it's quite simple really. I got horribly drunk when I was seventeen. And when I say horribly, I mean horribly. The worst you could imagine. One of the guys in my class... well, you know how knowledge is power. Anyway, this guy said he'd heard stuff about my dad. Not good stuff, either. Not knowing any different, I couldn't deny it, and seeing as he'd insulted my dad, I had to stand up. Broke his nose and skinned my knuckles. Ended up trying to drink the episode out of my mind. Had a girlfriend at the time: was quite keen on her. Actually, I was more than a bit keen on her. She bore the brunt of my frustrations. Wasn't me talking, of course, it was the booze. Not unreasonably, she told me to take a hike. Can't blame her, really. I lost her all the same. Swore I'd never put myself or anyone near me in the same situation again."

As he explains, he realises he hasn't told anyone the reason why he doesn't drink much: not the friends he made either in or after school, nor those he made later at university. Now, the telling of it seems curiously cathartic.

"Is that why you got thrown out of school?"

"More or less."

His editor, his hand on the door knob, is waiting. "Okay, okay. Now that you've got all that off your chest, I've got about an hour before the fun starts. Coming for a beer?"

The pub is crowded. Shirt-sleeved city traders dilute the residues of their disappointment; suited bankers loosen their ties; and paint and plaster-spattered craftsmen lay the dust of their labours.

Without asking Simon what he wants, Barnes orders two pints of warm, flat brown ale.

"Oh, nearly forgot," the editor takes a long hard pull at his pint, "got another call from the police today. You must be flavour of the month. Seems some bloke wrote himself off on his motorbike. Police chased him for twenty miles. Clocked him at three times the speed of sound. And when they scraped what was left of him off the road, they found your card in his pocket. They tried calling you; your phone was switched off."

"Paddy Jennings," Simon mutters at his beer. "Dead?"

"Comprehensively." Barnes finishes his pint and orders another.

"Bracknell," he says under his breath. There would be no photograph of Richard Ross from Jennings now. It is just as well Henry Loveridge had let him have one of those from the cottage. The thought occurs to him that by introducing Ross's bible so late into his conversation with Jennings, Simon had made him run late. Not only that but then he'd sat and watched the serving Marine drink a pint of beer. 'Don't suppose one will hurt', he'd said. And then there was the matter of whether he'd prompted Jennings to recall the horrors of a particular incident from his last tour.

"Go on, tell me."

"Royal Marine. Tour of Afghanistan. Tough. Polite. Intelligent. Well-read. Adrenalin junkie," Simon says, recalling what Jennings had told him about the burden of his experiences. "Wasted lives, I suppose?"

"They all are," Barnes agrees. He puts down his pint and reaches up to lay a paternal hand on his young charge's shoulder. "Look Simon, take it from me, you can't get too involved with these people. In the next few years you'll meet hundreds of people you'd wish a better life for and it won't benefit you one iota to wish it for them. Get used to it. It's part of the job. A shitty part, granted; but a part we can't get away from."

Simon picks up his glass and takes a long, slow sip from it, closing his eyes, savouring the taste, saluting Paddy Jenkins.

"God bless Mr Jenkins," Barnes mutters.

"'Ear! 'Ear!" interrupts someone standing behind them.

They turn.

"Another one of your awful history jokes, Bobby?" Barnes mumbles.

"Aw shit," the Australian moans, reaching into his pocket and pulling out a twenty-pound note. He hands it to the editor.

"Told you, Smithy," Barnes says, the joy of triumph evident in his tone.

The Australian grimaces. "You, you lightweight," he says to Simon, "you've just cost me a score and now I'm going to have to use my sissy card to buy a round."

"How's that?"

"Well, Barnesy here bet me he'd get a drink down you before you left."

"Left?" Simon repeats. "You mean left this evening?"

"No, you lean streak of piss," Smith snarls, "before you leave the job. Now all I've got to look forward to is winning the sweep on how long you'll last." Bobby Smith sucks his teeth and looks like he is about to spit. He doesn't, though, he just turns his back on Simon and carries on to join others further down the bar.

"He doesn't like me, does he?"

The editor looks a shade sheepish.

"Oh, I get it," Simon says, "they all think I'm not going to stay the distance."

"They don't," Barnes confirms. He sups from his glass, examines the contents and smiles ruefully. "But I do."

"How long have I got?"

"Well, it's like I said: we're getting near time added on, but I think we're good enough to take it into extra time. Specially if this story you're working on comes good. Your father was a class act, despite what you might hear, so there's no reason you shouldn't be. Just try not to get too close to the work, eh?"

Learning that the Sword of Damocles has, for the moment, been returned to its scabbard invigorates Simon. He drains his jug and, catching the barman's eye, orders another two pints.

His editor blinks. "Steady as you go, Simon."

"Talking of my father, Barnesy, why did he turn his back on journalism? What changed him?"

"You've never asked him?"

Their beer is placed before them and while Simon plumbs the depths of his pocket, his editor pays.

"Whenever I've asked, he's either stonewalled me or given me the run around. Only thing he ever said was 'had enough of poaching'. All a bit enigmatic, really."

Barnes hesitates. "Going from editor to public relations. I guess you could see that as going from poacher to gamekeeper."

Emboldened by the first alcohol he's drunk in a while and spurred on by DI Carver's disparaging comment, Simon charges across his Rubicon. "That's not an answer, Barnesy. You knew him; what prompted the change in him?"

The editor smiles to himself. "You don't let go, eh Simon? Like a dog with a bone, I like that. That'll serve you well." He drinks, rather obviously buying time. "Okay, if you must know, it was a Code of Practice issue. You've done the hard yards, what's the IPSO Code of Practice got to say on financial journalism? The first point; get it right and I'll pay your taxi home."

Simon shuts his eyes in concentration, clears the screen of his mind and opens a file. He reads it and when he's sufficiently confident, he opens his eyes and pretends to recite from the optics behind the bar: "Even where the law does not prohibit it, we must not use for our own profit financial information we receive in advance of general publication, nor should we pass such information to others."

"Cock on, Simon. I'm impressed."

He isn't finished. "Two: we must not write about shares or securities in whose performance we know that we or our families have a significant financial interest in without disclosing our interest to the editor or the financial editor."

"And the last?" Barnes suggests, pleasantly surprised.

Simon takes a sizeable pull from his jug; his turn to buy time. "We must not buy or sell—"

"That'll do, thank you."

"—either directly or through nominees or agents, shares or securities about which we have recently written or about which we intend to write in the near future." Simon suffocates the smirk welling from within.

"Good for you, Simon. I bet that no-good excuse for an Australian couldn't recite that, drunk or sober."

"So which part of the lexicon did my father abuse?"

Barnes is mid-way through another extended gulp when he stops, suddenly, and puts his jug down. "Listen, Leo Tolstoy wrote that a king couldn't fail if he knew the answer to three questions: the first is, what's the right time to begin; the second, who should you or shouldn't you listen to; and the third, what's the most important way to react?

"Now, you want to be a journo and journos live off information. And because I liked your father, I'll tell you what happened to him so that you don't go getting the wrong version from anyone who doesn't know the bones of it. Specially from someone who's got an axe to grind, like Bobby Smith. Now you might not like what I tell you but, like all journos know or should know, what counts is what you do with the information. Remember, causing others pain simply because you are in pain is no basis for a defence."

Simon is unsettled. "Sounds like the old doctor one-two: if they say it won't hurt, you know it's going to; if they say it will, then God help you."

"Right. In that case, this will very probably hurt." Barnes, who until now has been addressing both the bar as much as his protégé, shifts his feet to face Simon directly and lowers his voice.

"In a nutshell, an oil drilling company was floated on the stock market. It wasn't a big float, some interest if generally considered a bit chancy. Your father takes the risk and buys a sizeable tranche of shares. Over the following weeks the share value gradually increases. Then, a journo on the financial desk writes a very positive profile of the company; a piece your father clears for print. Rumours of a big strike in Nigeria begin to circulate, a couple more positive articles from the journo appear, again which your father approves, and the share price soars.

"Some time after, the whispers start. A rival financial paper prints a story about how the company has no real prospects, that the directors have lied about the strike in Nigeria and that the share price is fabulously inflated. Result, the bubble bursts spectacularly and a lot of people lose a lot of money."

"Including my father?"

"No. Turns out later that your father sold his shares a few days before the whole thing went pop; pocketed a pretty return, too."

"There was an investigation?" Simon asks.

"Yes. IPSO looked at it, as did the police. In the course of the investigation, the journo on the city desk said his original story had not cast the company in such a positive light and that he had been pressured by your father to modify it. Your father, of course, denied it; just as he denied pressuring the journo to put the subsequent stories together. The journo offered up his original drafts, which he had on file, and admitted to writing the exposé which, he said, your father also squashed. The journo then passed the exposé on to a rival paper, stating it was his moral obligation to do so."

Simon steels himself, fearing there's going to be more and worse. "Go on, please."

"The upshot was that the police went for your dad, but the Crown Prosecution Service wouldn't run with them. They said there wasn't enough in it, said that even in the face of all the evidence it was one man's word against another. You see, your father had been sharp enough not to commit any of his instructions to either paper or email."

"And IPSO?"

"Well, IPSO did their usual thing: chewed over this, recommended that and eventually took their false teeth out and put them back in the glass by the bed."

"How much money was it, Barnesy?"

"Bit shy of half a million."

"Half a mill? But my dad wasn't short of money. God knows, he paid for my private education."

Barnes winces. "At the time, your father was going through a bad patch."

"A bad patch?"

"You know, Simon, this is one hell of a hard business. Simply to keep our heads above the ever-rising tide of effluent, we can't avoid treading on a few heads or shaking hands with the odd devil. Doing that comes at a price. In order to pay that price, we all depend on our own devices: our mechanisms for getting through it, if you like. They're necessary evils; necessary and usually deleterious. The modern way is to rely on a daily injection of pheromones: get down the gym, get your bike out, run marathons, that kind of thing. With me," he mutters, holding up his half-empty glass of beer and gazing dreamily at it, "it's alcohol.

"But," Barnes raises his finger in the manner of a preacher admonishing his flock, "I'm fortunate enough to recognise the devil in the bottle. We face off against each other whenever I feel him getting the edge on me; dry out for a stretch, a week away in the hills or maybe a health spa. That's how I keep him at bay. For some, though, it's the Columbian marching powder, and once that's got a hold of you, you don't just recognise the devil, you become him.

"For the unfortunate few, it can be both. And that's the worst of all worlds. The drugs and alcohol will isolate you, trample all over you and make a poor man of you in pretty short order."

Simon doesn't need any further clarification, even though in a curious way he'd like to hear it so that later he'll be able to quote Barnes' exact words.

But, the editor's insinuation that his father had blown his career up his nose while pouring what was left of it down his throat is starkly damning and the ensuing silence weighs heavily. "So that was why he walked away? He got the blame?"

"Not directly. They let your father walk: he was too big a fish for their weight of line. The journo, on the other hand, wasn't. He wasn't so lucky. He got hung out to dry."

"The journo?" Simon wonders. "Who was he?"

"Bobby Smith."

He had been inclined to stay in the pub and drown the garish images of his rather depressing day: Carver, Soraya, Jennings, his father, Barnes, Bobby Smith and all those letters he'd never received answers to. However, Smith had nodded down the bar and his gaggle of acolytes had looked over at Simon as if he wasn't wearing any trousers.

The Australian's act had been carefully designed to provoke him, just as had that of his schoolmate so many years before. That someone should want to, had annoyed him almost as much as the act itself.

Barnes had cottoned to it, slapped a twenty quid note on the bar and told him to get lost.

Comfort or relief or charity, Simon wasn't sure which, had arrived from an unexpected quarter and he had been disinclined to abuse his editor's generosity. Besides, having just learned that his father had at one time been an alcoholic, a drug addict and a liar, he'd decided there was little profit to be had by staying just to get into a spat with Smith. The only tangible solace is the free cab-ride home, thanks to his memorising the Independent Press Standards Organization Editors' Code of Practice.

Bobby Smith, though, lurks beside him in spirit, if not in flesh; a rival, an adversary, a vexatious spectre. Hamlet's ghost, conjured from the gloom by his newfound Horatio, Barry Barnes.

Simon watches pedestrians march along the rain-swept pavements and recalls that in the middle ages, lepers had not been permitted inside the walls of the City of London. They'd had to content themselves with alms flung their way by healthier and wealthier commuters passing through the gates. Well, *his* father might as well have hung a board around *his* neck with the word *LEPER* scrawled on it in bright white chalk. Simon is tainted by paternal association, if not wholly toxic by relation, and he now knows that is the reason why none of the papers had taken his applications seriously. It is also the reason why the Australian has needled him from day one.

Smith, having been publicly hung out to dry, was never going to be taken seriously again. He'd been bumped from City Desk to Gossip Column, from financial metropolis to metaphoric gulag, from respectable stock to laughing stock, and it was therefore only natural that he should bear Simon more than a competitive measure of animosity.

His editor had said he would have to tread on heads and shake hands with the devil if he was to succeed and Candy had let slip that competition amongst the journalists was so intense that some of them had resorted to hacking celebrities' phones. She'd told him that Bobby Smith was the worst culprit and that in pursuit of headlines the management were turning a blind eye to his nefarious activities. Perhaps Smith is a devil he needs to shake hands with; a head he needs to tread on; an enemy to be kept closer.

Barnes had been right; Tolstoy's third question is surely the most germane. How is he to react?

As the taxi lurches and winds its mazy way toward Haberdasher

Street, his desire to succeed is doubled and redoubled again. He must prove Barnes right and Smith wrong. He must prove his father wrong and himself right. He must, above all, prove himself. He smiles: he needs no greater motivation than to prove others wrong.

The black cab pulls up outside the flat. Rain slants like a thousand tiny darts unleashed, glistening through the glow of the street lamps.

"How much, mate?" he asks, through the narrow gap in the glass division.

"Seventeen quid." The cabbie glances at the meter as if to tell him he shouldn't have needed to ask.

Simon hands over Barnes's twenty quid note. "Keep the change, my friend. Have one on me."

"Cor blimey, mate! When was the last time you bought a pint?"

27

The phone chirps. A text. A violent assault. Worship Street, Shoreditch.

Simon glances at the clock: 3.00 AM.

The cab drops him off on the corner, outside the Queen of Hoxton.

The City Café, like the Queen two doors down, is long closed and the dank darkness of the narrow side-street conjures a Dickensian claustrophobia.

Strobes of neon-blue draw him down to the junction with Clifton Street, where police tape prevents further progress. A small and disparate group of insomniacs stand gawping.

"What's going on?" Simon asks.

"Murder!" states a gaunt individual, not shifting his gaze from the melee of lights and policemen.

"Man or woman?"

"Some poor bloke." The man's breath corrupts the night air with a white fog of alcohol; his eyes are wide, round and fixed, his nose hooked and uneven.

"How do you know?"

"How do I know it was a bloke or how do I know it was murder?"

"Both, I suppose."

"Well," the man sighs, "because he looked like a bloke, he was covered in claret and he wasn't moving. Anyway, what are you: a copper or a reporter or something?"

Simon considers the man's question and rapidly comes to the conclusion that at the moment he is all of the above and yet officially none of them. "A something."

At this affirmation of association, the cadaverous night-owl perks up. "Oh."

"Were you here when the Old Bill pitched up?"

"Yes. Found him, didn't I?" he states, in a flat, casual tone.

"Sorry, found who?"

"Him," he nods towards the gaggle of police. "Like I said, covered in blood. Not normally out this late. Wouldn't have been, only I got the DCM."

"DCM?"

"Yeah, the Don't Come Monday."

Simon is none the wiser; his expression advertises it.

"You know, the sack, laid off, royally fucked. 'Bin round a mate's place, having a few drinks, commiserating. Well, commiserating and celebrating, if you know what I mean?"

"No, I don't. Well, maybe sort of. How long ago did you find him?"

"Oh, 'bout half an hour." The witness sniffs, loudly. "Funny, isn't it? You live all those years, then *wallop*, it's all over in a second. Mind you, you work your arse off for thirty years and all it takes is ten seconds to get told you're surplus to requirements. Good morning, good to see you, here's your P45, now fuck off. Funny old game, eh."

"Did you call the police?"

"No. Not me. The cabbie. He calls the police; I trips over the body." He bends and rubs at his right knee. "Got caught short. Needed a pee. Slipped into the doorway and trips right over him. Frightened the bloody life out of me." His knee continues to bother him. "I flags down the cabbie. He calls the Rozzers." He pauses. "It was the Americans, wasn't it?"

"Sorry?"

"The Americans. They bought the company. Surplus to requirements: that's what the bitch in HR told me. Fancy that, eh?" His chuckle is a mixture of irony, resignation, or rather termination, and insult. "Fancy that, eh? Me, surplus to requirements. Hope my missus don't see it that way."

"You said he was covered in blood?"

"Yeah. Covered in it, mate. The cabbie had a torch. We looked the bloke over. All black from the blood, he was: sick as a dog, I was. Terrible sight." He belches, remembering. "Beg pardon." He knocks at his chest. "Got some severance pay though. Not much. Keep my pension, of course. Not all bad news, I suppose. Who did you say you was?"

Simon ignores the question. "Definitely dead? Not breathing, nothing?"

"As a post, mate. Well, there's a hole in his chest 'n his throat's open like a piece of flexi-hose. In air-conditioning, I am." He quiets, thinking for a second, then adds, "or was. That's how I know what it looked like; just like a piece of PVC flexi-hose someone had run a Stanley blade over. Terrible. I suppose he could have breathed through it. Not for long, though. Not with that much blood. Should think he drowned in it. His head was at a weird angle. Eyes open, all glassy. Horrible."

"Someone cut his throat?"

"I should cocoa. Slit his throat right across from 'ere," he lifts his hand to the left of his own throat and drags it across to his right, "to 'ere. Must've stabbed 'im in the chest, too. Wasn't no coming back from that, mate." He sways like a wayward willow in a whispering wind. "And I mean black bloody, he was."

"Peckham?" a man calls.

Simon looks up. Carver, the detective from the Bishopsgate nick, is walking towards him.

"Concrete jungle keeping you up?" he asks. Carver wears a belted overcoat and a bored expression.

"Drums a bit loud for sleeping. What's the story?"

"Story? Well, that's your business. Me, I don't have much time for fiction."

"Okay, tell me the truth then. Who's been murdered this damp and chilly night?"

Carver hesitates, his eyes widening. "Who said it was murder?"

"This gentleman," Simon turns and points.

The night owl has suddenly and silently glided off into the dark.

"This guy I was talking to, a minute ago, said he found the body. Found it while he was relieving himself."

"So that's why the corpse is soaked in urine. Thought it was some kind of prejudice against rough sleepers. All too common, I'm afraid. What did he look like, this bloke?"

"Tall, drunk and unemployed. Nose like Fagin, eyes like that snake in the Jungle Book. If you hurry you should pick him up before he makes it as far as the Queen."

Carver turns around and hurries over to speak to a colleague, who immediately jogs off up Worship Street in the direction of Curtain Road.

"Doing your job for you now, am I?" Simon asks.

"I suppose I should thank you for that, Mr Peckham."

"Simon, DI Carver."

The detective straightens. "Okay. Alright. Thank you, Simon. Look, we may have gotten off on the wrong foot, so let's leave that out, shall we?"

Unsure as to whether he should touch the hand of a man who'd rather too freely disrespected his father, Simon studies it for a moment before shaking. Carver's hand is cold and slender; his grip vice-like.

"What else did he have to say?"

"Not much. A man he didn't know has had his throat cut and been stabbed in the chest. Said he stumbled, literally, on the corpse. Said it was pretty grisly." He pauses before asking, "So what do you know?"

"Not much more than that," Carver admits. "Whoever did this, did it properly. Good with a knife; first strike a slice from ear to ear which nearly took the victim's head off, the second straight through the heart. Grisly doesn't really do it justice." He winces in apology of his pun. "Some of the blood's dried; not all of it though, wouldn't do at this temperature. First impression is it must have happened sometime before midnight."

"No one heard anything?"

"No one we've spoken to so far. The victim also has a wound to the back of his head. It's possible he got it falling in a struggle or more likely he got whacked before being dragged in out of the light; fair amount of blood on the pavement. He would've been lying there until first light if that bloke hadn't come across him. Imagine opening up to find that on your doorstep: be enough to put a man off his muesli!"

Simon waits, turning the image over in his mind. "No, sorry, can't picture it. Contrary to what you might think, my imagination only stretches so far."

Carver glances at him. "Okay, it was a cheap shot." He lifts the cordon tape over his head, steps over and stands beside Simon; a gesture clearly designed to suggest both of them are, or should be, on the same side.

Two Scene Of Crime Officers, ghostlike in white coveralls and masks, are working the area around the doorway. Slowly, methodically and diligently, they study, kneel, swab, collect and photograph.

"No sign of the weapon?" Simon asks.

"No. Wound like that, it won't be a penknife, that's for sure. We'll have to do the drains and sewers."

"You?"

"Not me exactly, some poor SOCO will have to get down and dirty. Still, that's what they get paid for; that and having to look through all that gory mess. Can't say I've seen one as terminal as that in a good while. Brutal, efficient and perfectly final."

"Random attack?" Simon asks.

"Could be. Plenty of nutters about. If you asked me," Carver glances at the young reporter, "which of course you aren't, it's so brutal that the crim—sorry, the criminal, whoever did this—is either a surgeon, a serial nut or a trained assassin. It's too direct to be a random attack. Maybe he's the kind who wants to send a message."

"A message? What sort of message?"

"Buggered if I know. Homophobic, perhaps; drug deal gone wrong; turf war, racial motivation, paid-for hit. Who knows?"

"Mugging?"

"Not in my book. Too clean for that, no signs of a struggle and the victim wasn't the kind who would've gone quietly into the night."

"You've managed to ID him then?"

"Yes."

"And you know him?"

Carver eyes him, wondering whether he is worthy of a little trust. "Look, Simon, you know that little chat we had about the girl, Miss Naarda, and what happened to her at that club on New Year's Eve?"

"Yes, Brian. Your man went in a bit heavy with her."

"Mm, possibly. DS Chalmers got the feeling there was some

stuff she wasn't telling him. Got the feeling she's protecting someone, if you know what I mean?"

Simon hesitates. "Yes, I think I do. And," he holds up his hand to halt the detective's interruption, "before you ask, I certainly don't know why or who. Go on."

"Well, we've had the drains up at the club. Couple of guys working security didn't have the right accreditation and one of them has gone on the missing list: big Polynesian fellow, goes by the name of Tamati. Wouldn't know anything about him, would you?"

"No, Brian, I wouldn't." Simon pauses. "But if I did?"

"Well, if you did, it would be in your better interest to tell me. As I said, you know how it goes: you scratch my back, I'll scratch yours. And as I said, you're a bright lad and it wouldn't do you any harm… in the long term. If she told you some little detail about her assault, something she's conveniently forgotten to remember, you'd be sure to share it with me, wouldn't you, Simon."

"Okay, I get the message. If she does, I'll be sure to. It will be my pleasure. Now, what about the victim? Who is he?"

"Name's Grant, Charles Grant, 36 years old, hails from the fair town of Ilford and is known to us. Bit tasty. More talk than trousers, if you know what I mean? Handling stolen goods. Cautioned for possession on more than one occasion, though we've never managed to collar him when he's had enough on him to prove he's dealing. Got off an ABH charge a few years back. Said he was somewhere else at the time. One of his less than charming pals stood up for him and, we think, got to the victim's family. Paid 'em off. Wouldn't testify. Apart from that, a couple of minor offences, the odd pub brawl, football hooligan, affray at a British National Party rally; known associates in the English Defence League, neo-Nazi stuff, nothing that serious."

Simon recognises the fly Carver has cast his way. "Nothing that serious?" he repeats, as though Actual Bodily Harm and racially-aggravated Affray are, in the great assortment of crimes, not to be taken more seriously than traffic offences. "Long way from Ilford," he says. "Trains from Liverpool Street; could've been on his way to or from the station?"

Carver is staring at the pavement, as though he is trying to remember the owners of the many feet which have trodden it.

"You said *one of his less than charming pals?*"

Carver turns to gaze squarely at Simon. "Yes, I did, didn't I?"

"You also mentioned the EDL, the BNP and the neo-Nazis?"

"Seems that way, Simon."

"Mm, there's around 10,000 signed up to the BNP, though they're a bit busy shooting themselves in the foot these days. And there's somewhere between 20 and 30,000 of the EDF floating about, though they don't have a formal membership, so nobody really knows. Neo-Nazis?" Simon considers, then shakes his head, clearing the statistics from his thought. "I get the feeling you're not too bothered about what's become of poor old Charlie here. So we're talking known associate, aren't we? Someone you lot don't like. One of Charlie's *less than charming pals.* Who's holding back now, Brian?"

Carver chuckles in a manner that suggests he believes he is playing the same game as Simon and wants him to know it. "Hold off on using the information I've just given you until I let you know we've informed the family. Then, if all goes well, you should be able to get it into tomorrow evening's rag. I'll keep it quiet until later in the evening, that way you've got a head start on the dailies. Paint it whichever way you like; scum like Grant and his lot don't deserve any better."

"Sure," Simon assures him, "I'll keep it under my hat until I hear from you. And now, talking of hats, which you weren't, it's too late and too bloody cold for standing about out here without one. Thanks for the chat, I'll wait for your call."

"And you," Carver adds, "be sure to give me a bell if that bird of yours starts whistling a different tune."

"Talking of feathers."

The owl of a witness reappears, firmly tethered. He glowers at Simon.

"You might need a bio-mask for that one," Simon suggests.

"Urinating in the street," Carver says, grinning. "An offence under the Public Order Act, 1986, liable for a fine of up to £1,000. That should be enough to loosen his tongue."

"Strictly speaking, he wasn't though, was he, Brian? He was pissing on a corpse he didn't know was there. Not likely to cause harassment, alarm or distress to the living, now was he?"

Detective Inspector Carver, still grinning, offers his hand a second time. "Good point, Simon. Pissing on a corpse he didn't know was there. Not sure how to write that up."

"Hey, Brian, if all else fails, fall back on your imagination." This time, however, Simon dives his hand in to get a proper grip, looks Carver directly in the eye and meets his squeeze.

As he walks away, Worship Street echoes to a name: Charles Grant. Grant, Charles. He repeats the name over and again. And each time he repeats it, he grows more certain that Grant is one of the names on the entry sheet from Slick in the City.

28

By the time he gets back to Haberdasher Street, Simon's mind is too wired with possibilities to permit sleep. He runs through his notes of the list of entries from New Year's Eve.

Charles Grant's name is there, right alongside the names of the two others who argued with Soraya in the queue for the club. He turns on his laptop, inserts the cd containing the visual recording of those entering and forwards the video to the part where the three men enter in front of Soraya. They all wear face masks: one Tony Blair, another George Bush and the third, the hooked red beak of the plague doctor. One by one they remove their masks and present their faces for the camera. Their body language is boorish, bellicose and disruptive, just as their behaviour had been in the queue beforehand.

For the benefit of the record, all three gurn at the camera, as if auditioning for some dystopian counter-culture movie. The tallest of the three, the one sporting the George Bush face mask, is listed as Charles Grant.

Simon sits and again runs through the video of the queue outside the foyer.

He sees the three men. By the time they reach the foyer of the club, they have been queueing outside for almost half an hour and seem ignorant of or perhaps inured to the cold. They are brutish men or, perhaps, merely juveniles in adult bodies.

Simon recalls the detective Carver's words defining Grant as the *all talk and no trousers* sort. So, on balance, perhaps the world is better off without one more delinquent sociopath. Maybe the killer has done everyone a favour.

Carver said Grant had form, so it could be that he'd gone to score some drugs and a deal had gone sour. Carver had also implied that Grant was tasty, meaning he wasn't the sort to fall easy prey to a mugging. Whoever had done for him must therefore have been pretty competent at the physical stuff. But what was Grant doing so far from home? A night out on the town? Nothing unusual in that. And Worship Street is only a couple of hundred yards around the corner from Bishopsgate and the club, Slick in the City.

He checks the website: Thursday night, now last night, Ladies Night.

Thursday. For some reason, the day of the week is significant.

He glances at the time on his laptop, gets up and inches back the curtain. Though the streetlamps are still lit, dawn is not far around the corner and he has to get the Nib together so that as soon as Carver tells him Grant's family has been informed, he can send it through to Barnes.

Though he aches from too long out in the cold and damp, his night's work has furnished him with a sense of optimism. The added bonus is his burgeoning association with Carver: Barnes had told him contacts were crucial to his work and Carver is his first real contact in the City Police.

Of course, the detective is playing with him as much as he is with the detective and Simon recalls ironing the smirk out of his expression when Carver mentioned Tamati. The big Polynesian has gone on the missing list; that in itself was no surprise. However, the detective's mention of Soraya has knocked Simon slightly off his game.

He wanted, no needed, to keep her as far away from Carver as he could, otherwise it wouldn't be long before Richard Ross's name entered the equation and any chance of him finishing his story before it was blown wide open would be gone.

Soraya. He imagines her tucked up warmly in bed after an evening of study.

Thursday. No, Soraya wouldn't be studying on a Thursday evening. Thursday evenings she helps her father out in his soup kitchen near Old Street.

"Soraya," he murmurs, and so many theories fly past he cannot hope to catch them all; rather he snatches at a few and jots them down on a pad.

Soraya and Grant at the club. Richard Ross and old Tom out the back of the club. Soraya and old Tom assaulted out the back of the club. Worship Street, around the corner from the club and roughly on a walking route from Old Street to Liverpool Street Station and from where one would catch a train to Ilford. Carver and Soraya. What is Carver's interest in Soraya? Grant murdered. Soraya. Her father's food van. Thursday. Old Street, not far from Worship Street. And finally, and again: Richard Ross, not at the club, but nearby and very probably at the same time as the assault by Grant and, very probably, his two associates.

Simon recalls what Carver had said about the killing: it had been 'too clean' for a mugging; the killer must be 'a surgeon, a serial nut or a trained assassin'.

A trained assassin.

"Oh, Soraya. Grant came to threaten you and Ross was watching."

29

His bleary eyes resent both the light and the vapours of the hot tea, and it doesn't take him long to throw the News-in-brief together.

SHOREDITCH STABBING

Police appealed for information after 36-year-old Charles Grant, of Ilford, was found stabbed to death in a shop doorway in Worship Street, Shoreditch, early today. Anyone with information should call police on 101 or Crimestoppers on 0800 555111.

As far as a more in-depth biography of Grant goes, it takes him a couple more hours to cobble something together. The paper's archive and a Facebook page both yield photographs of Grant at a BNP rally and at various football matches, and a further internet search supplies enough colour for Simon to paint him in even more gritty detail. Grant's family and friends won't like the finished portrait, but he doubts whether it will do Grant's reputation any harm. Everyone knows the Libel Reform Campaign is in its infancy, and the provision for having to prove that an article causes a claimant's reputation *serious harm* is not yet included in any proposed legislation. Not that Simon's biography is capable of causing harm to a man who is dead, even though his friends and family may think otherwise. And Barnes will think better of the News-in-brief if Simon doesn't clutter it with DI Carver's damning assessment of Grant's contribution to society.

It's a game. A game of letters bought with information as currency; a game that opens in a dismal side road of the city and ends in a blacked-out undertaker's van.

What bothers him more, though, is whether he should tell Carver about the connection between Grant, Soraya and Ross.

The detective believes Simon has a name to trade: the name of the rough sleeper caught on CCTV. If he makes the trade, Carver is likely to take the easy option of fingering Ross for the murder of old Tom and just possibly Grant, too. If he doesn't, is he placing Soraya in too great a danger?

It *must* have been Ross who came to the aid of Soraya and old Tom on New Year's Eve. And the link between Soraya and Ross and Grant is too strong to ignore, which will make Ross the prime and probably only suspect.

Yet the portrait of Ross as murderer doesn't hang square on his wall. Either he has got the veteran of tours in Iraq and Afghanistan wrong or something, some trauma, perhaps that of losing his wife, has tipped Ross far over the edge.

Beyond the window, the metropolis stirs. Where once a boy delivered newspapers, a man with a horse and cart delivered milk, and the chorus of house sparrow, starling and wood pigeon competed with the sweet chimes of St John's and St Monica's to rouse folk from their slumbers; now the shrill sirens of the emergency services shriek that time is a fixed commodity and one must get on.

Simon yawns and stretches and checks his diary: AGMs, trading updates, conferences, publications, inquests, trials, tribunals, a controlled demolition, a protest and an unveiling. All in a day's work.

————

His phone rings.

"Simon?" The woman's voice, soft and lilting, is vaguely familiar. "It's Elen, Elen Phillips."

"Yes," a pause. "Oh, Mrs Phillips. How are you?"

"I'm fine, yes, thank you. Elen will do. Look, I hope I'm not calling too early..."

"No problem, Elen, I've been up for a while." He glances at his phone: 8:00 AM. "What can I do for you? Is Mrs Ross alright."

"Yes, yes, we're both fine thank you. It's just that when we met, you asked me to call if there was anything I thought you ought to know about young Richard, anything significant."

"Yes, I did. What's come to mind?"

"Well, you remember Mrs Ross telling you about that time young Richard came in, in the winter, in the middle of the night, all naked and covered in blood? That night she'd lain awake worrying he would freeze to death up in his camp."

"Yes, I remember. She called the doctor. He thought Ric might have had some kind of fit." He rifles through the litter of his desk, locates his notebook and flips through it. "She said the doctor diagnosed some kind of hypnotic or ecstatic state."

"Exactly, that's what he said, hypnotic or ecstatic. Well, I remembered something she told me the very next morning; something young Richard said while they were waiting for the doctor." Elen Phillips hesitates. "It sounds a bit odd, I know, but after she'd cleaned him up and worked out that none of the blood was his, she asked him where the blood could have come from. As you can imagine, she thought he must have been in some terrible fight or something."

"What was his response?"

"Well, apparently, he just sat there, staring at his hands and said 'I killed a deer'. Just like that. 'I killed a deer'."

"With his bare hands?" Simon asks, "Or he shot it and got all the blood on his hands when he skinned it?"

"No, wait. The next thing he said was, 'I beat it to death with a rock'. Of course, Mrs Ross asked him why and he said he didn't know. He said 'it just happened', as though he couldn't help himself."

"And that was it?"

"Yes. Sort of."

"Sort of? What you're saying is he suffered some kind of sudden bloodlust, some kind of adolescent killing frenzy. Like a dream, only a dream that took shape and became real."

"Yes, it does sound like it, doesn't it? Only that isn't what I mean by sort of."

"Then, what sort of *sort of* do you mean?"

"Well, the next day, I took young Richard up into the woods and asked him to show me the deer. Thought we should clear it up. And as if the rest of it wasn't strange enough, he showed me exactly where he'd killed the deer. There was no carcass, no blood and not even the smallest sign that something unpleasant had happened."

"Nothing at all?"

"No, Simon. Nothing. Well, I asked him how it could be; no dead deer and him being all covered in blood like that."

"And he said?"

"He just stood there and told me it must have been a dream. How could it, Simon? Where had all that blood come from?"

"Beats me, Mrs Phillips. Perhaps he couldn't remember where it happened."

"No, I even asked one of the local game keepers to have a ferret about. He found nothing either." She pauses.

Simon can hear her thinking. "Go on, Mrs Phillips. I get the feeling there's something you've yet to tell me."

"Look, I thought it best not to bring up the business about young Richard and his strange turn. You know, let it go, forget it and hope it wouldn't happen again. But then the other day I bumped into Mrs Sheers, and it was she who got me thinking. You see, her husband David used to deliver the post and not so long after that business, I was in the kitchen and Mr Sheers came to the door with a letter that needed signing for. I had my hands full, cleaning some trout that Ric had brought in. Usually he did that, but I wanted him to get on with his studying, so he answered the door.

"Well, nothing happened. Nothing. The place went quiet. I called; no one answered. I dried my hands and went to the front door. And there was young Richard, standing staring, shaking, looking back at Mr Sheers. Poor Mr Sheers. It was ever so awkward. He didn't know what to do. Young Richard was all pale and trembling. It was as though he was in the company of a ghost. Couldn't get a word out." Elen Phillips' voice fades as though she has been distracted by the same ghost.

After a brief pause, she recovers. "In the end, I had to pull him aside, sign for the letter and apologise to Mr Sheers. And once he'd gone, I took the boy back to the kitchen, sat him down and waited. We must have sat there for fully half an hour before I ran out of patience and told him to go back to his schoolwork."

Simon presses his phone against his ear. "Carry on, Elen. What was it about your postman that made Richard react so?"

"Well, I don't like to think of it. Don't like to tell anyone. It sounds so ridiculous, you see."

"Elen, I'm sure it won't sound ridiculous and I'm not likely to go around repeating whatever it is that you want to tell me." He can feel her confidence ebbing away, her motivation for ringing him deserting her. "Elen, there are now even more reasons why

I need to find Captain Ross as soon as possible. I will explain them if you would like me to, although it may be better for you to trust me with this. If you think this information will help me find Richard, please tell me now. We are fast running out of time. What went on between him and Mr Sheers?"

She exhales loudly down the phone. "Okay. Alright. Well, a week or so later, Mr Sheers was involved in an accident. His post van skidded off the Merthyr Road and he was killed."

"I'm sorry to hear that, but what has that got to do with Captain Ross, or young Richard as he was then?"

"Well, that was the strangeness of it all. You see, the day of Mr Sheers funeral I had to leave early. Young Richard asks me where I am going. I tell him and he looks at me all sheepish and says 'I'm sorry for Mr Sheers. I knew it was going to happen and I couldn't tell him'. Well, as you can imagine…"

"He knew Mr Sheers was going to die?" Simon asks, keen to erase the disbelief from his tone. "He had some kind of premonition?"

"I suppose he must have. Well, I didn't make the funeral, did I?" Elen Phillips says, rather too obviously put out. "I sat young Richard down and told him he'd better tell me what was going on."

"And he said?"

"When he'd been up at his camp and killed that deer, he'd gutted it; and as he was gutting it, a picture of Mr Sheers appeared before him right out of the all the blood and mess. Said the moon was up and he saw Mr Sheers' face outlined in the entrails of this deer. Small wonder he was so petrified."

For a few seconds, Simon is lost for how to respond. And not wanting the silence to extend to a point whereby Elen Phillips will think him as perplexed as he surely is, he grasps for something to say. Slowly, and ever so slowly, it comes to him. "But that wasn't the one and only time something like that happened, was it?"

"No, Simon. It happened once more, much later, when he was first home on leave from the Royal Marines."

Elen Phillips takes a while to gather herself before explaining that Richard Ross had walked into town, to the pub. There he'd got talking to a woman, a divorcee, one who was known to dilute the sorrows of her husband's departure with regular draughts of alcohol.

Something had happened between them: an argument, a difference of opinion, perhaps even an overt display of young Richard's sympathy that embarrassed her in front of her friends. Anyway, after young Richard had left, the woman had drunk herself into a near stupor, fallen out with her friends and staggered out, only to be recovered from the Usk the next morning. She had, sadly, drowned.

Elen had approached him about what he remembered of the evening, but he had been reluctant to tell her anything, saying 'it had all been a misunderstanding'. However, when she pressed him, he had eventually admitted that whilst out night-training on Woodbury Common he'd fallen asleep and dreamt that in much the same way as he'd killed the deer with a rock, he'd killed a rabbit and had seen the woman's face in the viscera of the animal. The new Marine had pleaded with her not to tell his mother or father and Elen had acquiesced, thinking him quite naturally overwhelmed with exhaustion after his weeks of arduous training.

She recognises, now, that she should have done something about it. Absolutely, she should have. At the time, though, she had not been able to think how best to help. Elen tells him that she felt guilty, wretchedly guilty, and wished if only... if only she'd done something back then, perhaps he wouldn't be in such a god-awful mess now.

Simon, for his part, is sympathetic, maybe as sympathetic as the recruit had been with the doomed woman, and he impresses on her that she shouldn't hold herself responsible for what happened:

so much dark water has passed under the bridge that it is now no longer sensible nor right that she should blame herself.

"If I can think of some way in which you can help," he says, "please believe me, I will call."

As he puts the phone down, Simon knows his platitudes are, as with all platitudes, wasted; but it is all the moral encouragement he can think to offer.

30

"When I grow rich, say the bells of Shoreditch," he says.

St Leonard's Church lies at the corner where the Hackney Road meets Shoreditch High Street, and a sign on the iron railings into the church garden decrees that the police will be called if loiterers are caught in the grounds after closing.

The pedimented Tuscan portico, with its four giant columns, stands proud and boastful, and the tall steeple reminds him of St Mary-le-Bow in Cheapside. "I do not know, says the great bell of Bow."

A pop-up coffee stall stands behind and to the left of a row of wooden benches, and a half-dozen lean, bedraggled individuals are gathered smoking on the church steps.

Armed with only a packet of cheap cigarettes, a lighter and Henry Loveridge's photo of Richard Ross, Simon orders a tea and sits watching the men. It is Friday and the Spitalfields Crypt Trust runs a film club as part of its Drop-in service.

He notices there are no women amongst the group huddled on the steps and reminds himself that only around ten percent of rough sleepers are female.

The statistics he has learned rush back to haunt him: most rough sleepers are white, nearly half between twenty-five and forty-five years old, and a larger percentage either alcohol or drug addicted or both. Some thirty percent have already seen the inside of a prison and ten per cent are most likely to be ex-forces. Nearly all of them, though, share some form of mental illness. The statistics he has pulled together for his story about rough sleeping make for depressing reading.

He steels himself, finishes his tea and hopes the men will be more approachable now that they have arrived at the safe haven in which they will pass their afternoon.

An older man loiters on the periphery of the group. He wears a faded denim jacket over greyed tracksuit pants. His thin face is unshaven, his shoes worn, the laces missing, and he sits on the cold flagstones patiently stripping the contents from old dog-ends, diligently storing each morsel of tobacco in a plastic pouch.

"Hi there, how you doing? Cold today, isn't it?"

"It's always cold," he mumbles, without looking up.

"Yes, you're right, it is. Fancy a smoke?"

"Oh," the rough sleeper says, startled. "Sorry, I didn't mean to be…"

"No matter. Here, have another one for later."

The man stuffs the second cigarette behind his ear and bends to the lighter, studying Simon's face as he inhales. "I've seen you before somewhere."

"Have you now. Might have been down the Church Path at St Martin-in-the-Field, I've been down there looking out for a friend. I'm Simon." He doesn't offer his hand.

"Don, Donald."

"Yes, of course. How are you doing, Don? Holding up?"

"Mm," he mutters, a shade uncertainly. "That's about it: holding up." Don pauses, dragging on and then examining his new cigarette as if it is some magic wand. "What're you doing down

275

here? Dressed a bit smart for hanging around with us lot, if you don't mind my saying?"

"Don't mind at all. I was passing. Thought I might stop by for a cup of tea. What's the SCT grub like? Up to scratch? Tuesdays, isn't it?"

Don nods, enthusiastically. "Yes. Bloody good! Hot and tasty, and enough to keep body and soul together." He considers what he has just said and adds, "Not that your body and soul looks like it lacks for any glue."

"No, Don, it doesn't. Say, did you know old Tom?"

"'Course..." He hesitates.

"Simon."

"'Course, Simon, everyone knew old Tom Williams. Part of the furniture, if you like. Most of us have not been around as long as Tom, well, was. One of the old stagers, if you know what I mean?"

"Mm, I do. Did he ever come up this way?"

"No. Used to go over Russel Square on Tuesdays. Said he liked the vegetarian they serve." He chuckles and coughs. "We all knew he had eyes for a girl there. Thought she was sweet on him, did Tom." The notion that a rough sleeper might have designs on those who put themselves out to supply food to rough sleepers embarrasses Don and his grey features assume a little colour.

"Is that how it is? Everyone knows everyone, knows where everyone goes, where they eat, where they sleep?"

"'Suppose so. Most of us know who's about. We look out for each other: helps us tell the wrong-uns from the rest. Shame about Tom, though."

Don quiets, thinking, and when he has made up his mind about his thoughts, he says, "Some people are saying he fell over and hurt himself and others that it was one of us that mugged him. It wasn't, you know. Tom never had anything worth mugging him for. He might have got a bit leery, a bit boozed up now and again, a bit difficult-like. Thing is, the man wasn't a fool. Been at it long enough had Tom. And as for someone doing him in like that, well, it's easier for people to think it might have been one of us; blame someone easy, someone they're frightened of. We aren't like that. We may look a bit grim but it's as I said, we look after each other."

"Yes, Don, I know you do and I'm sure neither you nor any of your mates would begin to think of doing anything like that to anybody. It's just that I heard Tom had taken up with a newbie; you know, new bloke on the skids. Think his name might be Ric or Richard. I wondered if perhaps you'd seen him here at SCT, only it's as I said, I'm looking out for someone, for a friend, and wondered if you might have noticed someone new about town?"

Don examines the end of his cigarette, as if it is relevant to some complex mathematical equation he is mulling over. "See, it's like this," he begins, inclining his head away from the gaggle of others, encouraging Simon to take a step back. "Some of us don't want to be found. That's why we don't use our real names. Don't tell them I said this, but what you know about someone else is power. If you know a bloke's an ex-felon, you've got something you can use on him or against him. Just like it is down in the City in all those tall, shiny buildings with all those high flying young executives, so it is with us. And what you learn about living on the streets helps you just as much as learning how to predict the price of oil. It's all the same." He squeezes one last drag from the cigarette.

"That's very philosophical, Don."

"Oh, believe me, Simon; we get plenty of time to think. Some people say being homeless is as much a state of mind as a physical existence. Well, I think that's one of those nice cosy precepts that keeps academics warm at night." He pauses, kicking at the flagstones.

"Here, Don, another fag?"

"Thanks, mate." He grins, perhaps a touch sardonically. "You sure know how to keep a fellow's attention on a cold day."

"I can see it being a mindset," Simon says. "As for it being a state of mind?"

"Sure," he decides, calming now that the nicotine is working its customary magic. "Some get used to it; some don't. It's a little bit like the five stages of grief."

"How so?"

"Well, you see, you suddenly find yourself out on the street. God knows how it happens or why; you're just suddenly there. You tell yourself it's only for a day, a couple of days maybe, and you let yourself believe it. It's like a kind of denial. Then, when you realise it is for real and you can't see any way back or any route off the streets, you get really angry about your situation. It's the hopelessness of it. Next, you try to keep afloat in a pool of wondering where you went wrong, how you lost control, and why has God done this to you when you weren't such a bad person to start with. And when you can't find any answers to why you've ended up where you've ended up, you find yourself drowning out in the two oceans of guilt and recrimination. And that's where the depression sets in. That's the most important time, because from there all that's left is to accept your fate and learn to survive. 'Course, everyone has their own story and no two of us are ever the same."

"Is that what happened to you, Don?"

He glances nervously. "Something like that."

"I know this is a rude question, Don," Simon hesitates, "and I hope I'm young enough for you to forgive me the... the naivety, no the impudence, yes that's the right phrase, the impudence of my youth, but what did you do before you ended up a rough sleeper?"

"Oh, I..." he glances, again, though this time there is a withering pain inscribed in his expression suggesting Simon has asked him to rip the scab off a wound that has never truly healed.

"I... I was a university lecturer." His pause is deliberate, timed to lend his situation the requisite irony. "So much for education, eh?"

Don coughs, the cigarette smoke catching in his throat. His raw, hacking convulsion tells a tale of cold air, hard pavements and the lack of any regular diet.

"Sorry," he mumbles, his eyes watering. "You got me on one of my favourite subjects. People tell me I can overdo the psychobabble. Guess old habits die hard, eh?"

"Don?"

"Yes, mate."

"Is there anything I can do for you? Anyone you would like me to call for you?"

The rough sleeper's eyes properly well up. But before he has time to object, Simon reaches his arm round the man's shoulder.

The rough sleeper's limbs are awkward, angular and frozen fast, like those of a mannequin.

Simon though, doesn't remove his arm. He holds on for a second, waiting, holding his breath. For some reason he can't fathom, he cannot seem to let go.

Eventually though, Simon has to breathe. Don's odour is overpowering: first the heady perfume of stale tobacco, then stale sweat and very fleet on the heels of the sweat, the unmistakably sweet and yet acid smell of stale urine.

Stale. The word beats at his senses.

Simon lets go of him, slowly, so that the man won't think he has found his odour too repulsive.

One of the gaggle on the steps along from them makes a coarse remark.

"Sorry, Don," he says, "I guess that was more about me than it was about you. Very selfish of me."

"That's okay, mate. Can't say your attention is unwelcome. Long time since anyone's wanted to hug me like that." He stands back, studying. "You wanted to know about a friend of Tom's;

some guy called Ric or Richard. Well," he exhales heavily, as though what he is about to tell implies he is abusing another man's trust, "there was a guy who hooked up with him. Some people are saying he's the guy who beat up Tom. His name's Bootneck or something like that. Don't know much else about him. Might be ex-forces; more of them on the streets now than there used to be. Might be why he took up with Tom, you know, old comrades in arms."

"Is this the man?" Simon shows the rough sleeper the photograph of Ross.

Don studies it, wrinkling his nose as he squints. "Could be. Don't look much like that if it is him."

"What about this mark, here, above his eye?"

"It's like I said, it could be him. That mark's familiar. Thought he might be here today; he comes to watch the movies, sometimes." Don looks past Simon towards the road and his eyes widen. "Talk of the devil and he will... Don't look now, he's coming in the gate."

And like anyone when told not to look, Simon does exactly that.

The man, brown scraggy hair, his chin thrust deep in his black parka, sees Simon standing on the steps. He stops abruptly, turns smartly about and walks back out into Shoreditch High Street. Once through the gate he turns right, picks up his pace and, moving with an easy grace, crosses the Hackney Road, a blur in amongst the traffic.

Simon makes to go after him.

Don reaches for his arm, "If he'd wanted to see you, mate, he wouldn't have run. Best leave him be."

Excerpt 8 from Transcript of Conversation with Joseph Naarda

SP: You said Soraya absorbed information: what sort of information? Do you mean standard subjects like science, geography and history? What were her favourite subjects?

JN: Writing and mathematics, she was good at; geography, too. And history always enchanted her; particularly histories written in English, which I managed to persuade a friend to bring through from Kuwait. And her capacity was not limited by academics; Soraya had a naturally inquiring mind. She always wanted to know everything about everyone. Whether Basrawi, Christian, Mandaean, Shi'a or Sunni, she wanted to understand the differences.

SP: How did you explain that to her?

JN: With great difficulty, Simon. With great difficulty.

That spring, Soraya was in the habit of coming to me at dawn. She would whisper in my ear that the sun was rising and that we should celebrate its arrival by walking in its warmth. At that time, her body was beginning to display the coming of her womanhood and she was even more beautiful than she had been as a child.

Saddam, however, had recently reduced the sentence for the crime of rape from ten years to nothing more than a few months which, as you can imagine, did little to deter those of an unhealthy disposition. And I knew that if I did not walk with her, Soraya would in all likelihood simply go out all on her own.

So, I would rise and we would walk to the Hannah Sheikh and watch the stallholders set up.

One time, as we were walking, she asked me why the Moslems fight with the Christians and the Jews, and why the Ba'athists fight with the Shi'a and the Sunni.

The only way I could think of to explain this was by asking her what she thought was the meaning of hope.

"Hope," she replied, "is a meeting of desire and expectation."

I agreed and asked her to tell me what she thought was the greatest gift one could give a man who was without hope.

She thought about this for a while. "Surely," she answered, "if a man has no food, the greatest gift one can give him is food. So it follows, that the greatest gift one can give a man without hope is hope itself."

Next, I asked her what she thought was the meaning of the word belief.

"Belief," she stated, "is the acceptance of an idea which cannot always be proved."

This is a good definition of the word and I went on to say that if a man believed that *his* God is the *only* God capable of delivering a better life even through death, then it is only natural that this man will die for his God.

Soraya countered this with the thought that her mother's kind are a peace-loving people. "They are interested only in life," she said, "not life that is made better at the cost of death."

The Subba, I replied, are different from many others, as are the Buddhists. They value life above all else. They believe that how they live their lives determines their path after death. They do not believe that in death they will automatically be forgiven for the wrong they have committed in life. As your mother has taught you, most men see the world for what it can provide them, whether this is the shade beneath a tree or water to satisfy their thirst. The Subba, however, believe that the tree and the water are as much a part of life as they are, that life and death are the same and that life above all else must be valued.

Again, she thought for a while.

Finally, I asked her what she thought was the definition of the word power.

"Power," she replied, "provides one man with the right to tell another man what to do and how to think."

Yes, I agreed, power provides a man with the right to proclaim *his* God higher than the next man's God and, in so doing, it helps him to believe that *his* God is better placed to deliver a better life than the God of another man.

And that, I declared, is why people fight each other. Because hope, even if false, is always chosen over despair; belief, even if misplaced, is always chosen over doubt; and power, even if used improperly, is always chosen over weakness.

Soraya nodded and stayed silent. We continued walking.

After a while, she tugged at my sleeve. "Papa, you are Christian, what then do you believe?"

"My daughter," I replied, wondering how I could explain myself simply, "I have come to understand that there are good people and there are bad people, and that this is how our world has always been and how it will always be."

SP: If you will forgive me for pointing out, Joseph, that sounds more fatalist than Christian.

JN: Fatalist? Possibly. Perhaps *Providence* is a better way of

283

describing it. Perhaps Kismet. That at least permits me to keep hold of my belief in a greater, more spiritual power.

SP: Kismet, if I'm right in saying, is an Arab word.

JN: It is. Kismet encourages us to accept God's will, to accept what is written in the stars, if you like. Though it does not encourage us to interpret that text to suit a violent end. Providence, on the other hand, encourages us to find comfort in God's will, to find strength. However, *Providence* has another, second meaning. *Providence* encourages us to provide.

So that morning, as we walked among the traders in the Hannah Sheikh, traders like my grandfather and his fathers before him, traders who because of the sanctions had little to trade, I began not only to question my faith once more, but also to understand that my duty was not to God, it was to provide for my family. And in answering Soraya's question, I began to realise that our time in Basra was coming to an end."

31

A fleeting glimpse of the ghost, there one second; vanished, dematerialised, gone the next. That was as much and as little as he'd been granted. And once into the maze of streets around the Columbia Road Flower Market, Ross would've lost him, so there had been no point in chasing him.

And if it hadn't been Ross?

Bootneck, Don had called him. Bootneck.

He rings Soraya. His call is diverted to her voicemail and he listens to her message, savouring its warmth. When it is time for him to speak, he is caught dreaming of her: "Hi, Soraya, it's me, Simon. Look, I'm sorry about the other day: timing was off. I was wondering, would you let me buy you dinner? Nothing flash, just... Well, call me when you have time... if you... that is, please."

His place in Haberdasher Street is a short stroll from St Leonard's Church and the strip of grey cloud above the alley through to Bowling Green Walk does little to brighten his mood.

In the afternoon, he gets a call from Henry Loveridge asking him if he has any news of Ross. Simon considers telling him that he may have seen the former Marine. He also considers, following on from Elen Phillips' call, asking him if he knows anything about Ross's predilection for seeing the faces of not necessarily the dead, but those whose time is soon to come. And finally, he considers telling him that Ross *may* have been involved in Grant's murder. However, *may* is only a theory and until he proves it there seems little point in saddling the farmer with further concerns, so he doesn't.

The coincidence of Loveridge calling him the same day as Elen Phillips is, though, not lost on him.

Simon sits back in his chair and rests his feet up on the table. The day seems inordinately long which, he realises, it has been when taking into account that his night was shortened by DI Carver's interruption. And as dusk creeps up the street, Simon surrenders.

His phone wakes him. A text message. Soraya. A café. Brick Lane. At 5.

Simon checks his watch.

————————

"I was beginning to think you might stand me up."

Simon pulls back the wooden chair opposite her. "Now why would I want to do that?"

Soraya smiles. "Oh, I don't know. Last time we met you seemed to have more important things to do."

"Important? Yes. Sorry. My editor." He contemplates telling her why his editor had called him back to the office, but quickly dismisses the idea. Any mention of the paper is only likely to remind her of the Nib in which she had been named as the witness to Tom William's murder; the News-in-brief he'd suggested had been written by someone else.

"And when the master whistles, you go running?"

It's true, of course. "Well, it's not exactly like that, it's more—"

"Simon?"

He avoids her gaze, pretending to study the grain of the table. "What?"

"I'm pulling your leg, Simon."

"Sorry, just a bit-"

Soraya is frowning: "Simon?"

"What?"

She reaches across the table and rests her hand over his. "Simon?"

He raises his head.

"That's better. Now, stop apologising, you're making the place sound untidy. Anybody'd think you were suffering some sort of sugar low. You're not diabetic, are you?" Soraya has a generous slice of strawberry cake on her plate. "Go get yourself a cup of tea, eh?"

He watches her while he waits at the counter. She isn't wearing her headscarf, which is odd when he considers how precious she'd suggested it is. Her long black hair is tied back, freeing her face, flaunting the curve of her cheeks and the fullness of her lips. Every time he sees her, she looks a different person. One day vaguely Middle-Eastern or perhaps Persian, the next just *so* London.

"Sweet tooth?" she asks, smiling.

"There are some temptations a man should not resist. No scarf tonight? Pretty cold out."

"No, I must have left it somewhere. Simon, now you've got your brownies, how about eating them? I'm not about to start without you."

"Is that some kind of Mandaean tradition, a politeness?"

"No, just good manners. But seeing as you mentioned my mother..." she arches an eyebrow, mocking him. "She likes good manners just as she likes us to observe traditional celebrations like everyone else: meals for consecrating priests, marriages, wakes. You

287

know, breaking bread, fresh fruit picked within the hour, water from the river."

"Water from the Thames? Fresh fruit plucked from the lamp posts of Brick Lane?"

"Not literally, Simon. I'm sure you must have noticed water flows from the tap and strawberries one can buy fresh from the supermarket."

"And consecrating priests?"

She chuckles. "Wouldn't recommend it. Not much of a party, consecration."

Simon tries hard to match the elegance of her eating. "And your father? He's Christian?"

"I guess you could say he's Christian in principle. Before we left Basra, we would go to church, a Chaldean Church. Mass at Christmas and Easter, most Sundays. My mother would come too, though she did not take communion. These days, my father is not devoted to any particular church. He lost his faith." She sits back for a moment, thinking, frowning. "No, that's wrong of me to accuse him of losing it. What I should say is that his faith deserted him." She pauses, still thinking. "You know, I think faith is like a cat."

"How so?"

"Well, a dog is loyal; he knows where his next meal is coming from. Cupboard love, yes, but love all the same. Whereas one never really owns a cat; a cat owns you. And one day, when it has had enough of you, it gets up and leaves. Faith is like that, don't you think?"

"That's pretty profound, Soraya, though I'm not convinced Garfield built St Paul's."

She smiles, a resigned perhaps slightly patronising smile, but not one intended to offend. "It's true though. Don't all religions deal in moving mountains, metaphorical or otherwise? No, what I meant was those last few years in Basra were difficult for everyone.

Not only for Christians. For Jews, Mandaeans. Even for Assyrians," she adds as an afterthought.

"You're suggesting," he searches for her conclusion, "that all faiths get along fine until one of them decides it can no longer accommodate the others. And because a man has no control over such a happening, a man has no control over his faith, so it just gets up and leaves, like a cat."

She brightens at his understanding. "Exactly. Like a cat, I don't think anyone ever owns a faith."

"So, what do Mandaeans believe?"

"Oh, as I told you, in everything being a natural part of life: the water, the earth, the people, the animals, the nature. In the world of light and dark, in good and evil, and in how everyone deserves comfort irrespective of their character."

Simon is minded to suggest their beliefs are a shade simplistic, a little naïve or maybe even outdated and unacceptably impractical. But he doesn't. And as she speaks, he notices an aura about her, an unpretentious, uncluttered, unambiguous purity.

"Is that what you believe?" he asks.

Soraya sips from her tea, puts down her cup and smiles. "Yes. I believe there is good in everyone, in the same way I believe that in some people the darkness of their soul overwhelms their light. It's up to us to search for it and, once we have found it, bring it out into the light."

The café is busy. Conversation bubbles from the other tables. Office workers and shop staff abandon the rigors of their week and relax in the promise of their weekend.

"Bring it out into the light," he repeats, uncertain of how he should react to such a noble conviction.

If anyone other than Soraya had told him a soul could be restored by bringing its darkness out into the light, he would have made fun of them. He would have leapt to tell them they were being overly simplistic, if not charmingly ridiculous. With Soraya, though, he cannot. And he cannot, because her conviction glows so openly and so honestly that he can't help but appreciate the intense purity of her faith. She doesn't try to hide her faith and yet neither does she permit it to glow too fiercely. No one notices it. No one turns to shield their eyes or shouts for her to turn it down. They have no need to, because her faith is neither blinding nor consuming: it does not glare. And not for the first time, he finds her captivating and charming and, above all, disarming.

Even though the café is busy, Simon feels alone with her and he stares deep into her eyes.

"Bring it out into the light," he repeats again. "A second chance. Is that what you mean?"

"Yes, Simon. We all deserve a second chance. Just like the second chance our family has been given here in London. To live safe, you might say."

"Is that how you feel now, safe?" he asks.

"Now? Yes? Isn't that what everyone wants, to feel safe? It's simple enough when you are; when you are comfortable or when the water comes from the tap or the light from the switch. In Basra, we had few of those things. And at the end, all we had was thirst, hunger and violence. Of those three, violence was the worst because you never knew when or from which direction it was going to come."

"What about what happened to you on New Year's Eve? I'd hardly call that living safe."

Soraya tenses and pushes her seat back from the table. For a second, she looks like she is about to get up and walk.

She doesn't though. Her arms press firmly against the table and her expression suggests she is confused. "You have something you want to ask me, Simon? Is that why you wanted to see me? To bleed some more story out of me, like you did at the coffee house after the inquest?"

"No, absolutely not." Simon tries to resist his urge to smile:

a self-conscious smile born not out of her knowing he wants to know what happened, more a smile born out of his fascination that she seems to be one jump ahead of his thinking. "No, not for a story. For you. For your safety. Look, Soraya, let me get you another tea, something? Maybe we should find a pub, get some dinner? You're right, I do need to ask you a question, although that isn't all of why I wanted to see you. I wanted to see you to know you're okay and..."

"And?"

Half of him wants to confess that he simply wanted to see her, whereas the other half wants, equally simply, to preserve his fragile ego.

"And you wanted to see me because?" she asks again, a little impatiently.

Simon breathes deeply, dredging his confidence for the right words, the adequate words, the clever words. And when nothing either right, adequate or clever comes to him, he says, "Because I wanted to. Because I want you."

He waits, hoping Soraya isn't going to tell him his aim is way off the mark or, worse, collapse in a fit of giggles and leave him sitting red-faced, foolish and alone at the table.

"Oh, Simon," she whispers, softening, "you've no idea how much I've wanted to hear you say that." Soraya leans across the table and kisses him, lingering long enough for others about them to notice.

He lies awake, asking the ceiling where their evening disappeared to; where that priceless, delicious twilight of anticipation so quickly dissolved to.

They had left the café and strolled arm in arm to a tapas bar, where they had ordered little and eaten less.

It had been nearly midnight before they'd got back to his flat and, once through the door, they'd stumbled and fumbled their way into his bedroom. And just when Simon had expected her to yield to the urgency of their common desires, Soraya had surprised him by breaking from his embrace, excusing herself and taking a shower.

He'd waited, patiently, reigning in his want for her and resisting the temptation to join her in the bathroom.

So far, Soraya had shown no reluctance or lack of enthusiasm in enjoying their intimacy and he had not needed to ask her to come back to his flat. She had simply accepted, very naturally, that that was where they were going. Perhaps her showering had been a prelude; some kind of ritual she needed to attend to before they immersed themselves in each other.

And when she'd come back from the bathroom, Soraya had been wrapped in his towel; her hair long, dark and glistening; her smile leaving him in no doubt that she wanted him as much as he wanted her.

Now, they drift in the shallow tide of their breathing and bathe in the languor of their lips and the lethargy of their limbs.

"I can hear you thinking," she says.

"Yes, I am. I didn't mean to wake you."

"You didn't. I was doing the same." She pauses. "Tell me, Simon. Tell me what are you thinking?"

"Only if you will tell me."

"Of course," she whispers.

"When you showered, before we made love, was that all part of it? Being Mandaean? Some kind of custom? An observance?"

She is silent for a few seconds before answering, "Yes, I suppose so. I didn't really think about it until I was in the shower; it seemed like the right thing to do. We wash away sin and impurity from our soul. We observe, as you put it, the need to be pure and I wanted to be pure for you."

"Pure? I thought you said you weren't a true Mandaean."

"I'm not. It's as I said, just now, it seemed like the right thing to do. I'm not sure I can explain it any better than that. I wanted to be pure for you and pure with you."

Simon smiles. "Are there any other traditions I ought to be aware of?"

"A few. Most people don't like Mondays. You remember the song? Well, we don't like Fridays."

"How so?"

"For us, Friday afternoons and evenings are unlucky. The King of Darkness presides over *Yuma d Rahatia,* our Friday."

"New Year's Eve was a Friday, wasn't it?"

"Yes, it was." Her tone is wistful. "At the time, I knew it was unlucky. I think it was one of the reasons why I behaved so... so poorly. Silly, isn't it. After all, today is a Friday and I don't recall anything bad about today." Soraya kisses him. "So, so much for superstition."

"Which are your good days?"

"Oh, Sundays. On the day of *Habshaba* purified souls are taken to the World of Light. Sunday is a good day, except for the sixth hour."

"Because?"

"Because the sixth hour is the hour in which travellers fall prey to thieves."

"Does every day have its own bad spell?"

"No, not every day. We have celebration days, too. We call them White Days: the days in which our world was created. This year they will come in July." Soraya chuckles. "Life is full of contradiction, isn't it? Even on White Days we cook food and store water because we believe something bad may happen while *Ruha* walks the earth."

"*Ruha?*"

"Yes, *Ruha,* one of our divine beings. She represents the senses: the lure, the enticement of the flesh."

"Remind me to thank her sometime." He feels her smile against him. "You have other divine beings?"

"We honour the King of Light, our Supreme Being, and the King of Radiance. There are many others: one who formed our world of light, one who created our world and another who did all the hard work. We have angels, the *Melki*; they do the bidding of the King of Light, much as the Christian God has angels."

"And the dark?"

"The King of Darkness; he has the *Shiviahi* to do his evil bidding; they are the bad angels."

"Angels and demons and purification?" he asks, careful not let any mocking creep into his tone.

"Yes. Angels and demons: good and evil. Mars, too. Mars is the Lord of Clouds and Thunder."

"Mars as in the planet?"

"Yes, we believe in the twelve signs of the Zodiac, the twelve cycles of the moon through the year, and the five planets one can see with the eye. To the five planets we add the sun and the moon, which makes seven."

"Lucky number seven?" Simon mutters.

In the dark, Soraya raises her head to look at him. "What makes you say that?"

"Seven? It's the most common lucky number: seven days of the week, seven colours of the rainbow, seven notes on a musical scale, seven candles on a Jewish Menorah, seven dwarves."

"What's your lucky number, Simon?"

"Oh, three, I suppose."

"Why?"

"Something I once read about Confucius. He said, the wisdom of three people exceeds that of the individual. Not much of a reason; it just kind of stuck with me. What about you?"

Soraya takes her time before saying, "I have three lucky numbers, not necessarily only one."

"Is one allowed three?" he asks, playfully.

"You can have as many as you like, as long as you can remember them."

"How did you come by them?"

"It's as I said, twelve for the cycles of the moon, seven for the planets and…"

"And the last number?" he asks.

She frees her arm from beneath his shoulder and taps him lightly on his nose. "That, Simon, is for me to know."

"I think that's an over-indulgence, having three."

"No, that's called having a good memory and hedging your bets. Tell me, Simon, there is so much I need to know: what do you like?"

"Oh, I think my likes and dislikes are relatively unsophisticated; rather dull, rather straightforward."

"Try me. What do you hate? What do you love?"

"What do I hate?"

Lying so close to him she will be bound, like a living lie detector, to feel the slightest quickening of his pulse and, given her curious ability to read his mind, there's a better than even chance she'll know if he isn't being truthful.

"I hate being late, I hate being doubted and I hate being lied to. Sounds a little dull, I know."

"That's all a little first world, isn't it? I mean, we can't always be on time; some events, some happenings, place time outside our control. Being doubted, too, is beyond our control; that is for others to decide. And," she adds, "as for being lied to; sometimes people lie to protect the truth. It is an injustice, even if sometimes it is unavoidable."

"Injustice," he says, his tone laced with generous helpings of scorn and irony. "I hate injustice, too, which is why, I guess, I've always wanted to be a journalist."

Soraya leans up on her elbow and kisses him. "And what about love, Simon? What do you love?"

He wants to tell her that he loves her... but the words don't or won't come naturally to his lips. For somewhere between his thought and his articulation there lies a barrier, a ravine over which a bridge is only partially constructed. He could, if he forced himself, tell her, but Simon knows that if he cannot tell her with the requisite conviction, then she will see through him and doubt his feelings and, perhaps, think he is telling her he loves her simply because he believes that is what she wants to hear. And that, would make his telling her a lie.

"Soraya?"

"Yes, Simon."

"I need to ask you a couple of questions."

"Oh, why don't I like the sound of that? That sounds a little too much like the journalist you just mentioned." Soraya moves to lie on top of him, her breasts against his chest, her mouth so close to his that he can taste her sweet breath. "Okay, go on. What do you want to ask me?"

"Thursday night?"

"Last night?"

"Yes. Were you working at your father's soup kitchen?"

"Yes. Every Thursday. You know it."

"What was your evening like? How did it go? Was it a fairly standard session?"

"Yes. Unremarkable. Though they're never easy. It takes a lot out of you, helping the rough sleepers. Breaks my heart, if you must know. And it doesn't matter how many evenings I spend amongst them; every Thursday evening they break my heart and I spend the rest of the week trying to put it back together. Why?"

"Did anyone you don't know, someone who isn't a regular, come to see you?"

"There are too many. You can never get to know all of them. And it doesn't pay to get too familiar. You have to distance yourself, protect yourself. Not all of them are fallen angels."

"No, I don't mean a rough sleeper," he says, "I mean another man, a man you may have recognised from New Year's Eve. Did someone come by and threaten you or put pressure on you not to talk to the police about Tom Williams' assault?"

"I'm not sure where you're going with this, Simon. Why should someone want to threaten me?"

"Because the police are treating Tom's assault as murder and you are the only witness. And because one of the men who may have been involved in your assault was murdered last night, in Worship Street, not far from where you and your father have the soup kitchen. I wondered whether the man had been to see you, to threaten you."

And with her heart only separated from his by the flesh that swathes them, he now waits and listens and feels.

"No, Simon, no one came and no one threatened me. So stop asking foolish questions and kiss me. I like you better when you're kissing me."

32

When he wakes, Soraya is gone.

After they'd made love the second time, Simon had fallen into a deep, enveloping sleep and now the only mark of her presence lies in the residue of her perfume and the folds of his bedding.

She had lied to him. Her heart had missed a beat just as she'd denied being threatened.

Why? Had Ross been there at the soup kitchen? Had he been present to see Grant threaten her? Had he followed Grant away from Old Street and murdered him? Is she protecting Ross? And if so, why? What is it that binds her to the former Marine?

He lies back and breathes, taking in the fragrance of her, recalling the movement of her, remembering how she made him feel.

His phone rings. He hopes it is her.

"Peckham," he croaks, clearing his throat.

"Simon?" A man's voice. "Brian. DI Carver."

"Morning. Christ! What time is it?"

"Ten o'clock. Thought you'd be up catching worms."

Simon baulks. "Thank you for that, Brian. Even early birds need to sleep now and again. What can I do for you?"

"Need a chat."

"When? Where?"

"I'll be with you in five minutes, traffic permitting."

"You'll want my address then."

"Got that, thanks. Your editor. Thought it a fair exchange for your barging in unannounced the other day. Tit-for-tat, quid-pro-quo?"

"Why didn't you just turn up?"

"Oh, wasn't sure you'd be in and thought I'd give you some time to get the place straight. You know, see to the housecleaning."

"If you want some breakfast, you'd better bring it with you."

"Done breakfast hours ago. Put the kettle on, there's a good lad. Mine's a coffee, white no sugar."

Simon is watching out the window when Carver arrives.

"What can I do for you?"

The detective casts a keen eye about the flat. "Nice place."

"It belongs to a friend, I'm the paying guest." Simon hands him the mug. "Your coffee."

"Simon?"

"Yes, Brian."

Carver pauses, waiting until he has his full attention, and then he pauses again, lending Simon the microorganism under the microscope treatment. "We've been making some headway on the Williams case. I thought you might like to be brought up to speed."

"Thank you, though you'll forgive me for pointing out that I'm sure this will come at a cost."

Carver grins. "Yes, it will. Let's price it up later."

"Go on, I'm all ears."

"New Year's Eve. You were in the club, Slick, with a friend. Same blonde friend you were in the club with a few days after. You might have told me that—"

Simon makes to interrupt.

Carver raises his hand. "No, forget what you haven't told me. We'll concentrate on what we know. Or, leastways, what I know.

"The rough sleeper, Tom Williams, is assaulted out the back of the club. He gets taken to the Royal London, where he dies. We've found out that the old boy was knocking about with a second rough sleeper. Don't know his name. Don't know where he's from. What we think is, he was there with Williams that night."

"How do you know?"

"We've reviewed a lot of CCTV footage. Not from the club, that's gone missing." Carver raises an eyebrow. "We've tracked a rough sleeper in Bishopsgate from earlier in the evening. He makes off in the direction of Bethnal Green. We can't track him all the way because the coverage isn't that complete, but we pick him up later at a pharmacy in the Bethnal Green Road. Fortunately for us, it's near the nick, so we've got him on our outside camera. He goes in; he comes out. The pharmacist thinks he remembers a man who might have come in and who might have asked for antibiotics. The pharmacist can't, or won't, tell us any more than that, so we are left only to assume that the man did what he *might have* done. We then pick him up later back in Bishopsgate. It may not be of importance: there was no trace of antibiotics in Williams' system."

Simon remembers seeing the box of pills just before he'd found the notebook. "Can't you identify him from the footage?"

"No," Carver sips from his coffee, "we can't. Curious fella, this rough sleeper. He keeps his head down."

"That's not unusual. Lots of them don't want to be identified and, if I remember right, New Year's Eve was a touch chilly."

"Mm, it was cold, I'll grant you. But this one seems pretty handy at avoiding the cameras. He's almost that good at it one might think he keeps his face hidden so that he can't be identified."

"Go on."

"We pick him up later, just after midnight, again in Bishopsgate.

He's walking, not running mind you, he's walking north into Shoreditch which is where we lose him.

"Now, the ambulance was called from the club a couple of minutes before the last sighting of this man, which suggests to us he may have been involved in Williams' and the girl's assault. If he'd been running, we'd take it as more than a suggestion. However, the fact that he's walking with what you might call purpose, makes us think that he wanted to get out of the area and that he didn't want to draw attention to himself by running. Strange, I know. Run? Probably you're guilty. Walk? Possibly. If you see what I mean."

"Yes," Simon agrees. "Damned if you walk; damned if you run. Makes perfect sense." He remembers Candy shivering, rubbing her bare arms. "As I said, it was bloody cold. What about the door of the club? Do they remember who told them to call the paramedics?"

Carver stares at him. "Paramedics? Didn't I just say they called an ambulance?"

"Same thing."

The detective shakes his head, as if to clear a thought. "Anyway, yes, we asked at the club. You'll remember me telling you that the CCTV door footage and the entry list for that night were recorded on discs, and that said discs have mysteriously disappeared? Well, remind me to come back to that later."

"Whatever you want." Simon meets the detective's stare. "Who asked them to dial 999?"

"Not much they remember, really. A couple of the doormen thought they remembered a rough sleeper coming in and asking them to make the call, said the fellow didn't hang around long enough for anyone to get a proper look at him. I gather the queue outside can be a bit of a gold mine for rough sleepers."

"And?"

"And what?" Carver asks back.

"And is that as far as you've got?"

"Pretty much, that *is* as far as we've got: except for some information that has come our way from the bouncers on the door of the club about who might have been in the club that night. Having carelessly mislaid their CCTV recording of the entry list for New Year's Eve," he glares at Simon again, "which, I might add, they were under no legal obligation to supply in the first place, we persuaded them—yes, I think that's the right way of putting it—that it might be good for them, as far as their licence was concerned, to grant us a peek at their till receipts. And nice people that they are, they have recently done so."

Simon's bank card warms against his thigh. "And that's how you know I was in the club on New Year's Eve?"

"Yes, Simon. You know it and the CCTV recording will show it," he glares once more. "And you haven't reported your debit card as lost or stolen, either at that time or since, so don't try to sell me the old story about lending it to a friend. And what's more, I don't have to ask whether you were at the club either in the company of or close by Miss Naarda, because she's already told us she was in the club.

"Now whether you were in the club *with* her or not doesn't bother me. What does bother me, though, is that both of you *were* there and that you conveniently forgot to mention it when you pitched up with Miss Naarda when she gave her statement." Carver doesn't care to soften his dismay.

"It would appear to me that the concept of scratching someone else's back when they scratch yours, doesn't sit so easily with you. So far in our burgeoning relationship, you're *virgo intacta* and all I've got out of it is a sore head and nail marks all over my love-handles. Am I adequately explaining why I feel a little aggrieved or would you like me to be more explicit?"

Simon, though, is neither the school-boy in detention nor the raw recruit on the parade ground, and as angry and physically intimidating as Carver very obviously is, Simon is deaf to his attempted intimidation. His story about Ross is *his*, no one else's, and he's not about to risk blowing it up by lending Carver a sneak preview.

"You've made your point, Brian. What do you want, a refill?" Simon nods at the detective's empty mug.

Carver glances down, his lips curled in disgust. "No, I do not want a second cup. And for your information, your coffee is crap."

"Sorry. I'm a tea man myself."

Carver's shoulders slump. "I'll give you this, Simon. You're a cool one. And let me give you a small piece of advice as well: courage is a commodity which, when you meet someone who boxes for a living, won't get you past the first round. It's admirable, I'll give you that. But on its own, it isn't enough."

Simon scoffs, "Not enough, eh? What are you trying to say? Are you saying you're the professional and I'm the pigeon? That you do this for a living and that I shouldn't be mixing it with you."

Carver grins, a resigned, careworn, almost self-effacing grin. "No, my young friend, you can mix it with me any time you like. Although, I must warn you, I have been round the block a few times and you are, as yet, a little wet behind the ears. No, what I mean is there are people who even I don't mix it with. That is, not unless I've got some serious back-up. And I think one of them was in the club with you on New Year's Eve."

———

"With me?" Simon knows what Carver means, but for now it suits him to play the right measure of pigeon. He has the CCTV recording from New Year's Eve and the information about Ross: letting Carver believe he is a bit of a pushover or in some small way a dupe, won't do his cause any harm. "Are you suggesting I keep the wrong company?"

Carver almost snorts in amusement. "No, not *with* you, Simon. I mean in the club on New Year's Eve along with you, your girlfriend, Miss Naarda and all the other hundreds of drunken, doped-up, dead-heads kidding themselves they're having a good time."

"Not much of a nightclub fan, then?" Simon recalls what a low point in his list of lousy New Year celebrations the night had proved. Perhaps Brian Carver isn't such a bad lot after all. "Me neither, as it happens. So, Brian, who do you think was there? And wouldn't Miss Naarda be a better witness for you?"

"Doubt it. She's already given her statement and by her own admission, she was either drunk, stoned or both."

"I didn't witness any assault, so I don't see how I can be of much help."

"Help?" Carver repeats, pursing his lips as though sampling a foreign dish. "Simon, if I'd thought you could help me or I thought you were withholding information that might help, I'd have you down the nick before you could say Jack Robinson."

"On what grounds? Certainly not any legal grounds I know. You can't force me to hand over evidence. If I had it, that is."

"No, you're right, I can't. However, and if you did, it is within my power to make your life bloody difficult and it would be in your better interest not to provoke me."

"You sure you don't want another cup?" Simon offers. He needs to gift Carver something to make him go away. He can't tell him about Ross and he wants to keep Soraya as far removed from the police as possible. And if he owns up to having the CCTV footage?

"Tell me, Brian: you obviously have an idea about the identity of this person, or these people, who you think may have been in the club on New Year's night; perhaps you've got some photos to show me."

Carver frowns. "Wasn't everyone wearing masks? Isn't that why the CCTV footage is so crucial? That's what places this person, or these people, at the club?"

"Yes, I see that. But don't people take their masks off when they go to the toilet? Make an embarrassing mess if you didn't. And imagine trying to snort the Peruvian marching powder or sip your Margarita through a nose curved like a winkle-picker's beak. There were plenty of masks being lifted at the bar when people were counting their change, too. My guess is you've got some nice holiday shots to show me." Simon's smile is coquettish, suggestive, vaguely camp. "Come on, don't be shy. The day's not getting any younger."

Carver shakes his head. "If only this was all that amusing. All right," he draws an envelope from his jacket pocket, "have a look through these. No ifs, buts and maybes please. Only if you're certain."

Of course, because he has the CCTV recording and the entry records being certain won't be a problem. And Carver probably knows it too. So he takes his time and feigns a deliberate, second look at a few.

Grant's photograph does appear. Simon puts it aside. The next one is familiar from the CCTV footage and may be the second of the three. Immediately after that comes the third: the man he'd had the run in with and who, had it not been for the bouncer's timely intervention, would very probably have spread his face all over the red-carpet runner.

Simon looks long and hard at the image. The heinous individual is staring back, stony-faced, daring whoever is looking at his face to challenge him. The image breathes sheer and unadulterated malevolence: the viper ready to strike, the scorpion ready to sting. Simon's blood chills and he is too late to intercept his shiver before it takes hold.

He shuffles briefly through the rest and slips the two other photos on top of Grant's. He hands them to Carver. "Two definitely. One probable.

"Yes," Carver sighs, "I had a feeling you might say that."

He picks one out and holds it up for Simon to look. "One: Grant. You've done your homework, so you know all there is to know about him and besides, he's out the picture, if you'll pardon the pun."

Carver holds up a second; the one Simon half-recognises from the CCTV. "Two: Eyles, Derek, 29, Broadwater Farm boy, still lives with his mum. Fairly standard low-level type, theft, stolen goods, drugs-possession and distribution, actual bodily harm. In and out of young offenders' institutions, that is until he hooked up with one Jack Sewell. Like Grant, Eyles talks the talk more than he walks the walk, but he is also a bit tasty and needs to be approached with caution. And like most criminals, he's not the sharpest tool in the box. Wouldn't be would he, otherwise he wouldn't need to be a criminal? We'll get around to him the next time he slips up which, as sure as God made little apples, he will." He slides the two photographs back on top of the deck.

"Now this one," his tone hardens. "Sewell. He's the one I'm far more interested in and, judging by your reaction, he's no stranger to you either. Care to tell me?"

Sewell. The face he recognises; the name, though, doesn't correspond to the details listed on the entry log. Simon is as sure as he can be without checking, which he can't do with Carver leaning over his shoulder, that the man went by a different name.

Soraya obviously wasn't the only one using false ID. In her case it was because she isn't yet twenty-one. In this man Sewell's case it is because he wants to fly under the radar, even though he couldn't resist the temptation to throw his weight about.

Simon casts his mind back to New Year's Eve. "He was in the club. Got a little fresh with the girl I was with."

"You're blonde lady-friend?"

"Yes. He touched her up. Upset her. I had no choice other than to pull him up for it.

"He was wearing this sort of plague doctor mask; one of those full-face numbers, deathly white with a hooked red beak. I thought he was just another member of the 40-watt club until he took his Venetian off. It was then I realised he wasn't average. Had this look about him that told me all I wanted to know. It's what you said about boxing: I didn't fancy myself to last a minute with him let alone three. Fortunately for me, this enormous bouncer stepped in and cooled things down. Funny thing was though, I reckon this fellow would have taken me, the bouncer and the rest of security if he'd felt like it. I think he let it go simply because he could, not because he felt threatened. Ugly smile, kind of spiteful. Haven't seen him since: haven't forgotten him either."

"Mm," Carver mumbles, "probably the smartest move you made all evening." He studies the photograph, thinking, weighing something in his mind. "Jack Sewell. Not to be confused with either Grant or Eyles. If they are tasty, Sewell is what you might call *proper tasty* and very definitely not for beginners. Comes from an old Crouch End family. Crouch End, know it? It's where villains retire to, except Jack Sewell's not retired. The story goes that his father was so randomly violent that the gang he used to run around with got fed up with him and buried him beneath a tall building in Canary Wharf. It seems young Jack has been trying to live up to the legend ever since.

"Works solo, apart from with Grant and Eyles. Specialises in mugging people stupid enough to go out wearing mum's pearls. We reckon he was behind a spate of pavement robberies in Belgravia a couple of years back. We picked him up. Thought we had him. Sadly, one of the victims buggered off back to Russia and the other he got to."

"Think I saw something about that when I was digging around on Grant," Simon adds.

"Yes, it did get a fair bit of press. Egg all over our faces. Never been able to stomach them since. So, as you can imagine, I've been waiting for the opportunity."

"You think he had something to do with Tom Williams' murder?" Simon asks. "I mean, a dingy alley out the back of some city dive is a far cry from the swanky avenues of Belgravia. Or do you think the lone man you've got on CCTV is Sewell."

"No, I don't. Security saw Sewell, Grant and Eyles leave the club just before midnight. We think they might be the three men we've got on local CCTV; one of them was hobbling, the other two walking."

They stand across from each other, each waiting for the other to speak, each waiting for the other to reach some conclusion.

"Then, you think the other man you've got on CCTV is not Sewell, but is something to do with Sewell?"

"Not certain," Carver says. "You heard what Miss Naarda said: someone assaulted her, the rough sleeper came to her aid and her assailant assaulted the rough sleeper. She can't recall what her assailant looked like, so at the moment this mystery man we've seen on the CCTV is the most likely suspect. However, I can't shake the feeling that Sewell is connected somehow. It's too coincidental that Williams was murdered when Sewell was close by. You see, the thing about Sewell is that he's well known for picking on rough sleepers. God knows why or what he gets out of it, but he treats them like punch bags. I suppose it's the sociopath in him."

Simon lets the information hang in the air before saying, "And you thought you'd drop by to ask me if I knew anything about what might have happened, because I was there at the same time as Sewell." He pauses, a little theatrically. He wants Carver to know he is lending the coincidence some thought. Then he shakes his head. "Wish I could be of more help. Would love to. Outside of Sewell threatening to tear my head from my shoulders and relieve himself down the hole, I don't know him from Adam. And as far as not owning up to being in the club that night, I apologise, it was wrong of me. Though as you are aware I wasn't under any legal obligation to tell you and I don't know that it's made that much difference to your case anyway."

At the mention of legal obligation, Carver twitches and chews his lip briefly. "No, you weren't, but it might have. It might have helped me get onto Sewell and Grant earlier and it would have been proper of you to have done so. I thought you ought to know who you were dealing with, that's all. Sewell might take exception to what you put in your paper about his mate Grant, so check your front door is locked before you go to bed."

"Thank you, Brian, I will. May I keep the photographs?"

"No." Carver slips the envelope back in his jacket pocket, throws his coffee cup a parting frown and heads for the door. With his hand resting on the lever of the deadbolt, he turns back and smiles. His smile is similar to the resigned, almost self-effacing expression he'd worn when suggesting Simon could mix it with him any time he liked.

"Couple of things you can do for me. One, hand over the CCTV recording and the entry log."

Simon is unmoved. "And two?"

"Work on your coffee."

33

Simon perches on a stool in the kitchen and fires up his laptop.

Carver had not merely sought confirmation of Sewell's presence in the club on New Year's Eve, had he? He had also delivered an invitation: a fait accompli of sorts.

And yet, the invitation had been delivered with a serious and curiously touching caveat: Sewell is not, absolutely not, to be approached and his lieutenant only with caution.

A second cup of tea later he's located Eyles's address, or rather his mother's, and trawled his Facebook page, which is littered with snapshots of corpulent, bare-chested football hooligans taunting foreign riot police.

Simon walks round to Bevendon Street and picks up the 141 to Turnpike Lane. He could get a taxi, it would be quicker. However, his anonymity among the other bus travellers provides him with an empathic calm in which to examine his feelings for Soraya.

In truth, she confuses and enchants him in equal measure. For Soraya would appear to have attained a form of manifold or fourfold vision, as he'd once read William Blake define it. She sees herself and her hopes, her dreams and the nature of the world around her all as one living entity: a supreme collective existence or, perhaps even, an opulent continuum of coexistence. She is naïve yet at the same time knowing and her convictions are strong and attractive, particularly her belief in second chances.

Yet do Grant, Eyles and perhaps most of all Sewel really deserve second, third and possibly fourth chances? Are they simply bad angels, or *Shiviahi* as she called them?

The bus crawls up Green Lanes. The sky promises only rain and he wishes he'd bought a warmer jacket.

Half an hour later, Simon strolls along the side of Duckett's Common and picks up the W4.

"Broadwater Farm," he mutters, as he exits the bus and looks up at the 1960s ziggurat of Old Labour's dream. And he recalls reading that during the estate riots of twenty-five years before, a policeman had been murdered and many others seriously injured. Anarchy had provided many of the Farm residents with a valve through which to vent the frustrations of their pressure-cooker existence, and for the murder of PC Keith Blakelock, three men had been convicted, imprisoned and subsequently released. The police, the press discovered, had tampered with interview reports. However, crime rates had fallen in recent years and the police had seen fit to disband their dedicated Broadwater Farm Unit. So maybe things can only get better, as New Labour's silver tongue had not long ago so dishonestly promised. Utopia. Dystopia. The pendulum swing. The rhythm of life unto death.

Simon is granted access to the hall by a youth coming out just as he gets to the door. The lift is out of order and the Eyles flat is up on the eighth floor. By the time he makes it, his knees are shouting for a break and despite the cold he is overheating.

He starts by knocking on the door of the nearest apartment. Bags of untidily tied rubbish flank a door that bears scratch and kick marks. Greying net curtains conceal the interior and no sound comes from within.

The next door yields a small woman wearing a saree, a dribbling child at her hip.

"Good morning," he says, bright and confident, "I'm a journalist. My name's Peckham and I write for the London Evening Star. Could you spare me a minute to give me your thoughts on how safe you think the Farm Estate is these days?"

With her free hand, she draws her veil over her henna-tattooed face.

Simon takes out his UK Press Card and makes a play of holding it up so that she can compare the photograph with the real article.

Silence.

The woman mumbles what he thinks must be some form of apology and shuts the door.

The next apartment is empty. The third is, judging by the heavy metal howling from within, occupied; those within unlikely to hear his knocking above the racket.

No one is home in the fifth.

Two more and he will arrive at the Eyles address.

He knocks on the door of the next and waits, patiently.

A dog yaps. A woman scolds, "Quiet, Tippy. Who is it?"

Simon clears his throat and runs through his introduction, enunciating and raising his voice as though trying to communicate like a Briton abroad.

"A reporter, yes?" The woman is thin to the point of emaciation and way past pensionable age. A half-smoked cigarette extends from her thin lips. "We don't get many reporters here." Her accent is German or Eastern European: Marlene Dietrich bleached and less sensual.

During the riots three journalists had been shot and wounded. "You've not forgotten that then?" he suggests.

"No, nor should we. What do you want?"

"I'm talking to residents about how safe they feel on the estate. Care to give me your thoughts on it?"

The old lady is not a fan of the estate even though she has lived in her apartment for over forty years. "Do you know they wanted to tear this place down ten years after they built it. They should have, if you ask me."

She bangs on for a few minutes: the unfairness of it all, the crime, the litter, the whole place falling apart, how she hasn't seen a policeman in God knows how long. And Simon is happy to put up with the diatribe if it will lead to her dishing some dirt on her neighbour.

"We don't see many white faces no more. Too many foreigners."

He interrupts to stem the flow of vitriol. "What about your neighbours? Do you get along well? Have much to do with them?"

"No," she scoffs. "I don't see them much. They take drugs down there," she nods in the direction he has come, "and the others, they are always cooking something spicy. Smell it all the time. Like living next door to a takeaway."

"What about the other side?" It is his turn to nod in the direction of the Eyles residence.

She scoffs again and raises her eyes to the leaden sky, "Him? Low-life. Pond-life. A grown man and he lives with his mother. It cannot be healthy. He wouldn't work on an iron lung, this one."

Simon is none the wiser.

"Before your time, young man. Iron Lungs. They were like a big tank. They used to put children with Polio in them. It breathed for them. Like the respirators they use in the hospital."

The ash falls from her cigarette and she flicks the stub artfully over the balcony.

"Not your cup of tea, your neighbour?"

313

"I should not think so. Out all hours of the night. Up to no good. It's people like him make no contribution. His kind, they just take all the time. Take, take, take. Would you like a cup of tea?"

To get over the threshold would normally represent something of a small triumph in the panoply of door-stepping, but... "No. No, thank you, I should say. Kind of you though. I must get on." He looks up the gallery and makes a pretence of considering the other residents on the same floor. "More people to talk to. Mustn't leave anyone out. They'll think we don't care."

"You must suit yourself."

"Look, Mrs..."

"Beránek. That is with an acute accent in the middle."

"Czechoslovakian?"

"Yes. We came here to escape the Soviets in '68. My husband hated them. He's dead now, of course. And who did you say you were?" She squints at him, memorising his face in case she has to describe him later.

"Peckham. Simon Peckham from the London Evening Star. Here's my card."

"Thank you, young man. Now you must remember what I said. They think that it gets better here. It doesn't. This place, too many gangsters. It is they who don't want the police here and it won't be long before there will be another riot. As God is my witness, it won't be long."

The door shudders back and she is gone. Her dog yaps. "Quiet, Tippy."

Simon looks up and down the gallery, turns about and takes in the view of the northern suburbs. If Derek Eyles should pitch up now, there is nowhere for him to hide.

———

If all you had to look forward to when you came home from a hard day's grind was concrete and despair, how easy must it be to sink into a life of crime?

"Don't be so patronising, Peckham," he mutters, as he pays careful attention to the steps in the slippery stairway.

At the start of the second-to-last flight, he glimpses a bald head below him.

Someone is walking up and, as he turns the final corner in the stairwell, he recognises the man who had been adjusting his Tony Blair mask in the queue at New Year.

Simon hesitates. He has nowhere to turn other than back up which will look odd, so he keeps on going.

As he passes Eyles, he tries not to make any eye contact.

The man is broad-shouldered, too broad-shouldered in the narrow confines of the stairs for Simon not to have to step round him.

He glances over at Eyles.

Eyles glances back.

For a split second, the slaphead ignores him and takes a step. Then he reconsiders, obviously placing Simon. "'Ere, you. What's your game? I know you, don't I?"

"Game? I'm not sure what you mean. I don't think we've met." He doesn't offer his hand.

"I'm sure I know you from somewhere. You're not from round here, are you?"

Simon drums up his most disarming smile. "No, I'm sure we haven't met before. Certain of it." He turns to carry on down the stairs.

"Well, I think we have and I don't think it was good."

"No. Really. We haven't."

"What's your name, then?" Eyles asks, belligerently.

"Williams." Simon carries on.

"Oh no it bloody isn't."

Eyles thumps him hard on the back of his head and he tumbles forward. And as he falls, he wishes he'd worn his masquerade mask in the queue to the club on New Year's Eve, just like Candy had told him he sh—

34

Someone or something is blowing on his face. The irregular breath stings him and he tries to swat it away. His hand, though, won't move. A broken arm? Panic swoops like a flock of racing pigeons.

He can wriggle his fingers: his arm can't be broken, surely?

It isn't. His hand is trapped beneath his body.

Simon opens his eyes and tries to focus. He looks up, expecting to see the sky.

His vision, though, is filled with the snout of a dog.

"Get out of it," he mumbles.

"You alright, son?" asks a hoary voice he does not recognise.

"I don't know. Feel a bit..." He remembers. A thin-lipped woman who had nothing good to say. A stairwell. A bald-headed man. Concrete hard, solid and merciless and coming up to meet him. "Yes, alright I suppose. Bit groggy."

"Fallen down the stairs?" asks a hunched senior citizen. "I've been telling them for years they need to put some anti-slip on these steps. Steady as you go. Take your time."

Simon clambers to his feet.

He takes a handkerchief from his pocket and dabs, gingerly at his forehead and cheek. When he stops and examines the cloth, he notices blood and small specs of... concrete?

Walking is awkward: a stilted dislocation of discomfort: Paddy Jennings' slow-motion in his leather suit. Simon doesn't pause until he has made it halfway up the rise of Gloucester Road, where he sits down on the low wall fronting a terrace of pebble-dashed houses.

After a few minutes, a white-bearded man wearing an Afghan round hat and long shirt comes out of the house behind him. The man is kindly-eyed, inquisitive and the keeper of the grey minicab parked immediately before Simon.

He wrings his hands and implores Simon to let him take him to the North Middlesex Hospital: "It is not far."

But the North-Mid lies in the wrong direction and all Simon wants is to go back to his flat so that he can lie down and recalibrate his rattled bearings.

The A10 is longer than it has a right to be and once outside Simon's flat, the cabbie opens the car door and indulges in one last tilt at persuading him to go to hospital.

Simon shakes his head and immediately regrets doing so.

"You should go," the cabbie insists.

"No. Thank you. I'm all right." His knuckles ache as he fumbles in his pocket for a couple of notes.

The Afghan cabbie frowns. "No," he states, raising his hands and averting his eyes. "It is not for me to profit from your misfortune."

And the minicab is gone, bumping and thumping off down Haberdasher Street.

Simon bathes his face in tepid water. Carver had told him to approach Eyles with caution and he hadn't. Not that the narrow confines of the stairwell had allowed him room to do otherwise. His biggest mistake had been the eye contact and he'd known it even as he'd looked.

By the time he's cleaned his face and hands, iced his shoulder and very carefully picked the strands of trouser fabric from his grazed knees, Simon is exhausted. The sofa looks too good to be true.

He dozes and the ringing of his phone wakes him.

He reaches for it too quickly and his body howls in disapproval.

"Peckham," he grunts.

"Simon Peckham?"

"What's left of him."

"Come again?"

"Yes, this is Simon Peckham. Who's that?"

"Martin, Billy Martin. Sorry I haven't been in touch sooner, mate, I've been out the country. My sister gave me your card."

"Yes, she said you were away. I'm grateful to you for getting in touch, Mr Martin." Simon inches upright. "I've got a few questions for you. Wondered if we might meet up?"

"Sure thing. I'm only in London until next Friday, so let's meet sooner rather than later." His accent is less Liverpudlian than his sister's. "What's going on? Loretta said you spoke to her about Ricardo. She got the impression he's in some kind of trouble. If he is, you'd better let me know how I can help."

Ricardo? Help? The man who made a play for Ross's wife? Is he really the one to help? Simon has already made up his mind to dislike the man. "Well, Mr Martin—"

"Billy."

"Sorry. Billy. If I knew what was going on, I wouldn't need to be asking you questions." Simon realises he's sounding a little terse. "Sorry, again, Billy. Having one of those days."

"No problem, Mr Peckham. We all have 'em."

Simon recalls the concrete rearing up at him.

"So, what's up?" Billy Martin asks.

"It's a long story I'll try to keep short. In essence, Richard Ross has gone on the missing list and I think he's sleeping rough somewhere in London. The police want to talk to him, too."

Martin is quiet for a second before saying, "Ricardo? Sleeping rough, you say? Well if he is, you'll never find him. As you know, he's a Royal Marine, so if anyone was ever suited to living rough, the boss would be right up there. It's what we're trained for, living on our wits. What are the police after him for? Not like the boss to go breaking the law. A few heads maybe, but... What's he supposed to have done?"

"Oh, not much. Actual bodily harm at least; double homicide at most."

"Ricardo? Murder? Tell me more."

"The police think he may have beaten up some other rough sleeper and a while after that cut someone's else's throat. The first died in hospital, the second died on the spot and Ross is the number one and only suspect. Do you think that's possible or likely?"

"No, fat chance. No way. One hundred per cent, no."

"Paddy Jennings was of the same opinion."

"You spoke to Paddy?"

"Yes, Billy. Jennings said he would send me a photograph of Ross. Never received it, of course."

"Of course?"

"I guess you haven't heard about Paddy."

"What about him?"

"I'm afraid Paddy died in a motoring accident a couple of days ago. I'm sorry for your loss, Billy. Paddy seemed like a nice guy."

Billy Martin is silent for a moment, no doubt remembering the lanky lance corporal. "Damn shame. On that bike of his, was he?"

"So I'm told."

"God, Paddy did love that bike. Knew no fear, Paddy."

"As I said, he seemed like a nice guy. Very level, too. A professional."

"A brave man. Always the first on your shoulder. Loved the fella, didn't I. In fact, we all loved him. Take a man out at over a mile, could Paddy. Genius with a Javelin, too." There is no emotion evident in Martin's appraisal; no wistful regret. "Still, what's done is..."

"Yes, done. I'm getting to understand that might be what some of this is about. So, on to Richard Ross."

"Mr Peckham?"

"Yes, Billy."

"I've got a free evening, why don't we meet up for a bev. I'm staying at the Radisson, Tottenham Court Road. It's not too far from you, if I've got your address right. Seven o'clock do, will it?"

"Nice idea, Billy. I, er... Look, would you mind hopping in a cab and coming here? With my face as it is..."

"Not sure I get where you're coming from, Mr Peckham. What's up with your face?"

"Forget it, Billy. I'll tell you later."

———

Billy Martin arrives on the dot of seven. He is the very same young man in the silver-framed photograph on Loretta Martin's mantelpiece, only now he is wearing a leather bomber jacket and jeans, and his smile is easy rather than constipated.

"Good to meet you, Mr Peckham."

"Likewise, Billy. And it's Simon, not Mister. You've a couple or ten years on me, so if anyone's going to be calling anyone Mister, it'll be me addressing you. Fair enough?"

"Like you say, Simon."

"Sorry to have to tell you about Paddy."

"Nice place."

"Belongs to a friend. Excuse me if I don't shake hands. Knuckles are a touch sore. Haven't got beer Billy, will tea do?"

"Don't mind if I do, thanks. What happened to your face? Get hit by a truck?"

"No, fell down the stairs. Literally."

"Par for the course when resisting arrest." Martin's compact, muscular build suggests that if someone threw him down the stairs, he'd most likely bounce right back up.

"No, it wasn't like that. I think the bloke who shoved me is involved with what's going on with your man Ross. Tell me, why do you call him Ricardo?"

"Why do I call him Ricardo? Because he talks in his sleep. Talks this weird mumbo-jumbo. Like Latin or Italian or French, only all muddled up. Can get pretty feisty can Ricardo when he's stressed. One time in Afghan, we were overnight in a compound and he walked right out the door. Fast asleep, he was. Pitchers, too. And I mean black dark, and there's Ricardo all casual as though he's off to Jollies for a few beers."

"Jollies?"

Billy frowns as though he is about to have to explain something that should be plainly obvious. "Jollies. It's a bar near CTC, Commando Training Camp, Lympstone, Devon. Weird, the boss's behaviour sometimes. Small price to pay, though."

Simon is reminded of what Elen Phillips told him about Ross's nocturnal aberrations. "What do you mean by small price to pay?"

"Small price to pay for having the best boss in the business."

"Captain Ross that good, was he?"

"That good and more." He nods. "Not to be confused with similar products. Plenty of those about, I know, though not in the Royal Marines of course. Could've been a Major by now, probably a Lieutenant Colonel, but the boss was always happier with the lads." Martin sips his tea. "So, what's he been up to?"

Simon suggests they sit down.

He begins by telling Martin about what happened at the club on New Year's Eve: how the old rough sleeper, Tom Williams, was assaulted and later died; how he met Soraya the next morning at the Royal London and then found the moleskin notebook out the back of the club. He hands it to Martin.

"Yes, that's the boss's bible," he confirms, thumbing through it, smiling, frowning; a man reading someone's private thoughts about himself and others he's known. "Go on."

Simon recalls his difficult meeting with Derek Roarke, the CCTV recording he'd received from the giant Tamati, and his meeting Soraya again at the opening of the inquest into Tom Williams' death.

When Simon tells him about his visit to Abergavenny to meet Ross's mother, Martin moans, "That witch." He shakes his head in disbelief. "Mind you," he adds, "the Major, his father, he wasn't any better. Bloody throwback, he was. Thank God for the housekeeper, Mrs Phillips. She was more a mother to Ricardo."

Next, and Simon steals himself to mention it, he recalls his visit to the farm in Devon and what he learned from Ross's father-in-law, Henry Loveridge.

Billy's face darkens. Pain and regret infect his expression like a necrotising disease. He lowers his head and holds up his hand, urging Simon to stop. "Yes, you can leave that out, if you don't mind. You know it. I live with it. Not my finest hour and if I could take it all back, believe me I'd do it in an instant. There's no excuse, except that I suppose I must have been under some kind of mid-tour strain, stress or anxiety or something."

Billy, though, lays his maudlin self-reproach to one side at the news of Grant's murder. "His throat was cut?"

"From here to here." Simon mimes, drawing his index finger from one side of his neck to the other.

"From the outside? You know exactly how it was done?"

"Yes. I spoke to the bloke who discovered the body. He told me Grant's windpipe was opened up like a section of... Ah, got it. Like a piece of PVC flexi-hose someone had run a Stanley knife over. And to cap it all he was then stabbed in the chest. Why do you ask?"

"Because, Simon, a Marine isn't taught to slit someone's throat like that. Stand up for a moment."

Simon stands. It takes him a couple of seconds, during which time his guest has picked up a knife from the kitchen worktop.

He holds the knife in his right hand, balancing it between his thumb and forefinger, the haft resting gently against his palm. "You see, Simon, everyone thinks you hold a knife tight in your fist with your fingers gripped about the haft and with the blade pointing down away from your hand." He flicks the knife round to grasp it, raising his hand as though it is a dagger with which he is about to stab Caesar in the back.

"We don't." Billy flicks it back to balance it in his hand once more. "We hold the knife the other way. We point it forward with the thumb and the crook of our forefinger at the guard. Holding it this way, we have more control and accuracy." He steps behind Simon.

"We use the other man's weight to help us, like this." Martin carefully drapes his left hand over Simon's shoulder and pulls him backwards onto the knife.

Simon tenses and groans as he is lifted off balance, the tip of the blade pressing against his ribs.

"If, on the other hand, you want to cut your enemy's throat, you bury the knife in his neck, here," he taps the blade against the fold of Simon's neck and shoulder, "and rip his throat from the inside out, *not* across his throat from one side to the other. Besides that, why would you bother to stab someone in the chest if you'd just slashed their throat? It doesn't make sense."

"So, what you're saying is," Simon sits gingerly back down, "Ross didn't do it."

Billy shakes his head. "Definitely not. If the boss had wanted to do for this bloke, his training would have kicked in and he'd have planted the knife in his neck and pushed the blade forward. He wouldn't have been able to help himself. He certainly wouldn't have bothered to give him one in the chest for afters."

"What about if he wanted to make it look like someone else had done it?"

He shakes his head again. "No way. I've just shown you how it's done." He pauses. "Listen to me, Simon If you ever have to kill a man, and I sincerely hope you never have to, it's like I said: with a knife there's a right way and a wrong way. The reason for this is that there can only be one of two outcomes. Either you kill him or he kills you. Simple as that. There is no in between. No grey area. End of." He pauses again, looming over Simon, the knife glinting in his hand. "Now, you were telling me a story."

"I've been looking for Ross, talking to other rough sleepers, showing them a photograph Henry Loveridge gave me. It's not a great photo, Ross looks a bit smart, a bit-"

"I've brought you one," Martin interrupts, pulling the photo out of his jacket pocket and handing it over. "It's only a mugshot, mind."

Simon holds it up to the light and studies it: a clean-shaven, good-looking young man; a strong-boned, even, uncomplicated face apart from a slight dimple to his chin and the only really striking feature a mark above his right eyebrow.

"Wouldn't forget that ugly bastard in a hurry, would you?" says Billy.

"No, not in a hurry. What is that?" Simon points to Ross's forehead. "A birthmark?"

"Correct. Had it since Day One. One of the blokes out in Afghan reckoned it made the boss a bit special; maintained it was some sort of protection against a curse. Daft, really. Work of a clumsy midwife or doctor, more like. Mind you, what with his Mum being a witch, his father stubborn as a mule and him talking all that mumbo-jumbo in his sleep; who knows, maybe he is different," Martin loads his tone with irony. "You've been out looking for him then?"

"Yes... Look, let me finish what I need to tell you, then we'll talk about how we locate Ross. 'Nother tea? Mind helping yourself, I'm a bit seized up."

"Sure." Billy helps himself. "You?"

"No, thank you."

"Know what you need, Simon?"

"No."

Billy grins as he sits back down. "An ice bath. Sort you right out."

"Might as well jump in the Thames. Same result, I'd freeze to death," Simon mutters. "Thanks all the same. So, this detective pops up and asks me for the CCTV recording from the club. It seems they're interested in one of the guys who, I think, beat up the old rough sleeper. Ross wouldn't have done it. A, he had no motive and B, from what I've learned it's not in his behaviour locker.

"The detective showed me some mugshots and I identified these three blokes from the club, one of whom was Grant. A second bloke, name of Eyles, lives with his mum on the Broadwater Farm Estate. I interviewed one of his neighbours and as bad luck would have it bumped into Eyles on my way out, which is why I look like I've been playing Blind Man's Bluff with a dump truck."

"And the third man?"

"A bloke who goes by the name of Sewell. Evidently, he's a known criminal with a habit of picking on rough sleepers. They've been close to putting him away before, but have never been able to make the charges stick."

A wild look flashes large in Billy's eyes when he hears Sewell is the kind to pick on rough sleepers.

"And that is about where we're at. The problem we've got is that I think Ross was present, watching from the shadows if you like, when Grant tried to bully the girl into keeping quiet. I think it's entirely possible that he followed Grant and did for him in a side street. You don't believe that and I understand why, but the police may draw a different conclusion. They also think Ross may have been involved in the death of the rough sleeper, Tom Williams, and unless we can find Ross, they may be inclined to pin it on him for the want of anyone else to blame." Simon pauses to draw breath which, again, pains his bruised ribs.

"Finally, the witness, the girl Soraya, told me that there was another guy present when Tom Williams was beaten up. She's since denied saying so. No, that's not true. She told me she was referring to the guy who beat her up, but I'm not convinced she's being straight with me. I think she's protecting someone. Why? I don't know and I can't prove it; I just get the feeling she is.

"Now, if Sewell did assault Tom Williams and Ross was present, then both Ross and the girl saw him do it. And if Sewell is as rotten as the police suggest, then both Ross and the girl are in danger."

Billy studies the carpet for a moment. "This girl, the witness, Soraya you say her name is, she won't admit to having seen Ross?"

"No, every time I mention his name, she clams up. Does her name mean anything to you?"

Martin purses his lips, trawling his memory, putting names to faces, discarding them, moving on to others. "No, sorry. Where's she from?"

"Soraya lives with her mum and dad, down the Mile End Road. Her father owns a corner shop; she's studying for a degree at the University of East London."

"What you're saying, Simon, is that we've got to find Ricardo before the police or this bloke Sewell. The simple solution would be to deal with this bloke Sewell, but we can't touch him because we haven't any real proof he was involved. Is that it?"

"Pretty much."

Billy chuckles. "Well I could be wrong, but hearing you say this girl's name, Soraya or whatever it is, makes me think you might have a bit of a thing going with her."

Simon blushes.

"Bullseye. Thought so. Okay, let's forget about her for a minute. So how do we go about finding Ricardo? You said you'd been out looking for him. Where've you been? Who've you asked?"

Simon winces. "Mostly, I've been out asking other rough sleepers if they know him, if they've seen him or if they'd seen him hanging about with Tom Williams."

"No luck?"

"They're not the easiest people to talk to. They have this kind of code. They don't like to talk about each other; keep themselves to themselves. One I spoke to seemed to think Williams had been hanging around with a new guy; someone who old Tom had referred to as *Bootneck*."

At this, Billy Martin sits up and takes notice. "Bootneck. It's a nickname for us Royal Marines. Comes from a time when the boys used to carve a strip of leather from their boots and tie it round their necks to keep from having them cut." He chuckles. "Funny that, when you think we've just been talking about the very thing. Where did this old boy hang out?"

"Between the City and the West End. Quite territorial, they are."

"Have you covered that patch?"

"Yes," Simon sighs.

"And nothing? Not a sniff?"

"No. Nothing."

"Then you're looking in the wrong place, Simon."

"You'll forgive me for pointing out that if I haven't found him, that's a bit bloody obvious."

Rather than be offended, Billy smiles. "No, that isn't what I mean. What I mean is, he isn't where you've been looking; he's moved on or cleared off to another patch. You're not looking far enough afield."

"Billy, they reckon there's five hundred rough sleepers in London and I must have seen twice that number over the last few weeks. And if you add all twenty-nine boroughs together, that gives us seventy-five thousand acres of parks, doorways back alleys and basements to cover. It's like looking for a needle in haystack and we haven't got the manpower."

Billy Martin is still smiling. "Yes, I kind of thought it would be that way." His smile broadens into a grin. "What you're not doing is thinking like him. You can't because you don't know the animal. I can because I do. What we both could do with, though, is a few more boots on the ground."

35

Martin promises to give some thought to where the elusive Richard Ross might be dossing, hands Simon the photograph and leaves.

Simon makes a couple of copies and then phones Soraya; something he has been wanting to do ever since Martin had arrived.

"I was so hoping you'd call," she says.

He is pleased to hear her say so, unsure as to whether she might be harbouring second thoughts about sleeping with him. After the satisfying immersion in the pleasures of their desire for each other it had seemed unlikely, but he had steeled himself all the same. To learn that she harbours no such regret, releases the prisoner from the dungeon of his doubt.

"It's late, I'd like to have seen you tonight—"

"Yes," her response is coated with longing, "you're right, it is late. Another time?"

"Yes."

"Simon?"

"Yes, Soraya?"

"Are you alright? You sound tired. I meant to leave you a note.

You were sleeping so soundly I didn't want to risk disturbing you."

If he'd seen her this evening he would have had to explain the abrasions on his face, the soreness of his knees and elbows, and the aching in his shoulders; so perhaps it is just as well. "No, I'm fine, really. I wanted to know you were okay, that's all. I was concerned when I realised you'd gone home on your own."

"I'm a big girl, you know. And they're called Night Buses for a reason. You mustn't worry."

"I don't worry, Soraya. I don't." He pauses. "Only I do and, in a way, I want to. Is that wrong?"

"No. No, Simon. It's not wrong. It's beautiful. Really and absolutely quite beautiful, and I'm so pleased to hear you say it."

A silence falls between them; a rich, luxurious, almost post-coital hiatus.

"How are you fixed for tomorrow?"

"No, not tomorrow. I have duties, at home."

"Duties?"

"Yes. Sunday is a difficult day. How about Monday? I have course studies at the campus. Afterwards would be good. No, I don't mean good. To see you would be better than good. What I mean is," Soraya whispers, "I'd love to."

Excerpt 9 from transcript of conversation with Joseph Naarda

SP: *Having realised that your time in Basra was coming to an end, did you start to make plans to leave? Did you have any idea of where you would take your family?*

JN: In all honesty, no, I could not see a way out. My income existed in working in the oil field and selling the alcohol and the general goods in my small shop. However much I saved, I was never going to save enough to be able to pay our way out of Iraq. My grandmother had left us some jewellery, which I had kept buried in our garden, but at that time I had no way of converting this into cash. Even in the markets, one had to be careful who one spoke to. Many Christians had left, many of the Mandaeans had been relocated, and choosing between Ba'athist and Shi'a would only have brought death into our home.

SP: *What did you do?*

JN: There was an engineer. A South African. A hard man. You

could say uncompromising. He oversaw some of the machinery, pipe-workings, flows and pressures, that sort of thing. At first, I did not take to him. He had this unfortunate manner of addressing us as though we were beneath his consideration; as though we were somehow beneath his contempt.

One day, when we were driving out to the metering station, he called me Abdullah. It was a nickname some foreigners used for Arabs. I had been called this before and was used to it. I told him that I was not Abdullah and that I was Christian. He was surprised. He didn't know that an Arab could be Christian. He thought all Arabs were Moslem. It is a common misconception among the ignorant.

Anyway, this broke the ice between us and we got talking. We became friends; well, not great friends perhaps, but better than mere acquaintances. And after that he always asked for me to be among his working party. Some weeks passed and I felt we had formed a bond. Perhaps I could trust this man, so I told him I had some jewellery and that my family would one day be leaving Iraq. I asked him if he would take the jewellery with him on his next vacation and sell it for me, perhaps keep the money until I got in contact with him. As I said, he was a tough man, maybe even a little racist, but I made him aware of what it would mean to us as a family.

He took the jewellery reluctantly, making me equally aware of what might happen to him if he was arrested carrying this form of contraband. I assured him that if he paid a small bribe, the border guards would not search his belongings.

SP: You took a hell of a chance, Joseph.

JN: Sometimes, Simon, a man has no choice other than to trust another man.

36

Going to sleep is easy, even though it takes him a while to find a comfortable berth for his face against his pillow. He dreams of Soraya, of listening to her voice, of looking into her eyes and of anticipating her touch. And when his phone rings, he assumes it must be nothing more than the soundtrack to his chimerical imaginings.

Sadly, it isn't.

"Peckham," he mumbles.

"Is that Mr Peckham?" says a woman.

There's something about the way she pronounces *mister*. The woman is foreign, only not to him. "Yes, this is Simon Peckham."

"This is Renata."

"Renata?" He glances at the clock: 3:00 AM? "Yes. Sorry. Renata who?"

"Renata Beránek. You came to my flat this lunchtime. You were asking me how I am feeling about the security in Broadwater Farm."

He rubs his eyes awake. "Yes. Yes, of course. Mrs Beránek. To what do I owe the pleasure at this hour?" Perhaps he has handed his card to an insomniac.

"You remember how I was telling you that the man who lives next door was a no-good?"

"Yes, I remember." She said *was*: he is sure of it. "You said *was*, Mrs Beránek. *Was*. Has something happened to him?"

"For sure something has happened to him. Tippy heard it. He was barking. He woke me up and I heard it. There were men arguing, outside. You remember I am living on the eighth floor and the lift is not working. Eight floors, my God! Eight floors! Well, now that no-good man is on the ground floor and he did not take the stairs."

EXCERPT 10 FROM TRANSCRIPT OF CONVERSATION WITH JOSEPH NAARDA

SP: You believed the Second Gulf War was coming, that it was inevitable?

JN: Yes. Late in 2002, the gossip in the market was that the Americans were already in the north, fighting with the Peshmerga, the Kurds. And besides, if one could not smell war on the wind, the fishermen would tell us of the coming and going of the military on Bubiyan Island, only eighty kilometres away. This left us in no doubt.

People began to leave, which was all very well if you had somewhere to go. Others stayed, believing this would be the same as the first time, when the coalition left almost as soon as they arrived. And the secret police, thinking their days were numbered, began to arrest and torture any person who came to their notice or against whom they held a grudge.

Having nowhere to go, we stayed. Many of us thought the war would begin when the moon was at its brightest. The only real debate was whether they would come across the water, from the Shatt al-Arab, or the Khawr Abd Allah from Kuwait, or from the air, directly from Bubiyan.

Now the fishermen told us that the Shatt al-Arab, the Khawr Abd Allah and the beaches were all mined. And the farmers of Abu Al-Khasib said that many tanks were hidden behind great walls of sand in the fields and the date groves. From whichever direction war was to come, we believed it would cost many lives.

SP: Did Salwa see blood on the moon again?

JN: No. This time the weather had been bad. One could not see much of the moon because of the low clouds and the sandstorms. We were afraid, of course, and yet the promise of deliverance from Saddam meant we were a little happy, too. This is a strange feeling, being at the same time optimistic and yet apprehensive. No, apprehensive is to understate how we felt about our future. Anxious or perhaps fearful would be more accurate.

SP: So, when did the war begin?

JN: I remember it was late in the evening of the third day, Al ar Ba a', the 19th of March. Suddenly, there was the thunder of artillery from the south-east and throughout the night the sound of gunfire from the peninsula. This we knew from experience was only a prelude to what was to come. The devil was being allowed out of his cage and he was merely stretching his back. Early the next morning, we could hear the same; but this time it was from the south, from around Um Qasr.

That night the weather was clearer and we would watch the missiles fly towards Kuwait. I thought they looked like shooting stars, quite beautiful. Salwa, though, thought this was *Sin*, her Moon God, and *Melka d Hshukha*, her King of Darkness, sailing in the Moon-ship in search of corrupt souls. She told us that from then on, we should stay indoors.

37

Simon is up early, his face still raw, his muscles still bruised.

He pieces together an article about how the residents of Broadwater Farm believe security has declined since the police removed their onsite unit. And rather than lead the reader in any particular direction, he poses and argues a number of questions. Was Eyles the causal nexus of a system which stifles ambition and kettles frustration? Or was he the master and commander of his own destiny? And what of Renata Beránek, the old refugee now threatened by the new? Is she the real victim in Broadwater Farm's concrete jungle?

Keeping the article concise, he checks it through, makes a couple of minor alterations and emails the final version to his editor, adding the proviso that Barnes should hold off printing the piece until the police have made a formal identification.

Simon then returns to the more pressing issue of finding Ross. 'Boots on the ground' was what Martin had said they needed and he toys with the idea of summoning Henry Loveridge. Putting the two of them together might not be such a good idea, given what had happened between Martin and Loveridge's daughter, but Simon knows he cannot hope to cover such a vast area on his own.

The buzz of the entry phone fractures his shell of contemplation. A registered letter? A parcel too large to fit in the letter box? Perhaps some cleaner accidentally pressing the wrong flat number? He presses the access button without bothering to find out which.

A few seconds later, there is a thump so violent it threatens to break the door off its hinges.

DI Carver had suggested he kept his door locked in case Jack Sewell came looking for him.

"Who is it?" Simon shouts.

"It's Carver, Brian Carver. I need a word with you, Peckham. Let me in, please."

Simon unlocks and pulls back the door.

The detective doesn't wait for pleasantries, he strides right in. "Time for you to stop pulling my chain, Simon, I– Grief, what the hell have you been up to?"

"I don't suppose I can interest you in another cup of my lousy coffee," he says, buying time.

"No, thanks all the same." Carver reigns in his wrath and studies Simon's face. "Why do I get the feeling you were expecting me?"

"I wasn't."

"Then do you want to explain how you got in that," he points towards Simon's face, "shape?"

"Which one of a hundred explanations would you like, Brian? Wasn't looking where I was going. Tripped on the stairs. Walked into a door. Fell down an open manhole. What about cut myself shaving? That's a shade more urbane. Take your pick."

"Mm, like that is it? You may as well know, I've just come from the Broadwater Farm Estate. Curiously and coincidentally, the same estate where Eyles lived."

339

"Lived?"

"Yes, lived. Past tense," Carver eyes him, thinking. "I suppose you're going to tell me you didn't know Derek Eyles has been found dead at the foot of his block."

"No, I'm not. I knew it. Have known it since three o'clock, if I remember right."

"How do you know?"

"Got a call from Elyes's neighbour, a Mrs Renata Beránek."

"And how come she just happens to have your number?"

"Because I went to see her yesterday afternoon. Or, to put it more accurately, I took the bus up to see her not long after you left here. Quite chatty once she got going."

"And you went to see her because?"

"Because, Brian, you told me where Eyles lived and you knew I would pop up the estate to see what dirt I could dig. Don't tell me you didn't expect me to. You knew full well I wouldn't be able to resist it."

From playing the aggrieved copper one minute, Carver now softens his attitude. "Perhaps I did. Or perhaps I thought you might. Doesn't make much difference, really; you obviously put your face where it wasn't wanted."

"I appreciate your concern."

Carver grins. "And what did the kindly old lady tell you about her neighbour?"

"Pretty much the same as you: Eyles was no-good."

"So how did you end up with the facelift?"

"Bumped into Eyles as I was leaving, literally. I'll say this for the guy, he wasn't one to forget a face in a hurry. Cracked me on the back of the head. Knocked me out for a moment and that was all it took for me to lose my feet on the stairs. So, you see, it's like I said, I fell down the stairs."

"And yesterday evening? Mind telling me where you were?"

"Here, licking my wounds."

"All evening?"

"Sure. A friend came by. He arrived at seven and left a fair bit later."

"Name of?"

"Martin. William Martin."

"Good friend?"

Simon smiles. "You mean good enough to lie for me? No, don't know him well enough to ask him to bend the truth on my account. He's staying at the Radisson, Tottenham Court Road."

"After he left?"

"In a nutshell: made a call, went to sleep, got woken up by the charming Mrs Beránek, went back to sleep, woke up and wrote a piece about the perils of living in an inner-city estate. All in an average Saturday night for a disciple of Charles Foster Kane. What about you, Brian? You must be a bit short of sleep what with all this recent excitement."

"True enough." Carver nods. "I sometimes think it would be easier on my marriage if people could refrain from killing each other after five in the evening and before eight in the morning. As Mrs Carver keeps reminding me, the lot of a policeman's wife is not a happy one. So, you didn't return to the Broadwater Farm?"

"I guess if one was to stretch the imagination, I could have got back out of bed, popped in a cab up to the estate and chucked Eyles off his balcony. Which, I also guess, would explain my altered state—"

"You're certainly physically capable of it," the detective points out.

Smiling, however weak the smile, hurts. "I wish I shared your confidence, Brian, but didn't you say that when it came to boxing I wouldn't make it past the first round? Well, as it turned out you were right, I didn't even make it past the first punch. Although in my defence I must point out that it was a rabbit punch and I wasn't looking."

Carver crosses his arms and leans his chin on his chest, considering for a moment. "Okay, I'll agree you're not the sort. Possible, not probable. However, the hair starts to tickle the back of my neck when I consider how fast you appeared at the scene of Grant's murder."

"Text from the office. One of your boys must have tipped the paper off. I was closest. Nothing odd about that."

"Mm, got an answer for everything, haven't you, Simon? All a bit off pat. Although, as you say, not unreasonable."

"So, if I didn't throw Eyles off his balcony or slit Grant's throat, who did? Perhaps Sewell did for both. Didn't you say his dad was prone to acts of random violence and that the son was trying to live up to the name of the father?"

"Yes." Again, Carver thinks for a couple of seconds. "Yes, I did. I can't see why he would do that, though. Eyles and Grant were his foot-soldiers; without them, Sewell has no gang."

"Maybe they spoke out of turn," Simon offers. "Maybe they have something on Sewell and he needed to shut them up. Maybe he's getting together a new gang and wanted his new recruits to know who's boss. Pretty brutal business as I understand it." He is leading Carver away from Ross: the hunt saboteur laying a false trail to draw the hounds from the fox. "Let's imagine for argument's sake that it was Sewell who assaulted Miss Naarda and Tom Williams on New Year's Eve, and that Grant and Eyles were involved either as participants or witnesses. The moment Miss Naarda speaks out at the inquest, you launch a murder investigation, and Grant and Eyles get cold feet. Isn't that enough motive for Sewell to want them out of the way?"

"It would be, Simon, or it might be if it gelled with what I know about Sewell. He might be indiscriminately violent, but murdering Grant and Eyles would be like Sewell burning his only pair of socks simply because the smell offended him. It's not smart."

"Didn't you tell me criminals aren't smart, otherwise they wouldn't be criminals in the first place?"

Carver looks up. "I said that about Eyles, if I remember correctly. Sewel is different: he's sharp as a razor and twice as deadly; a criminal because it's in him. It's not his choice; it's congenital. Which reminds me, I cannot stress strongly enough how important it is for you to stay away from Sewell. If you think Eyles skinning your face was bad; Sewell wouldn't stop there. Any notions you have about popping up to Crouch End to dig some dirt on him will likely as not get you killed." He lowers his head and stares intently at Simon. "Leave him alone. I mean it. Do both of us a favour and stay the hell away from him."

Simon inadvertently fingers the scab that has formed on his cheek. "Sure. I get the picture. Thank you, Brian. And I do very genuinely appreciate your concern and your advice. I'll try not to get in your way or his."

"And I," Carver breathes deep, readying himself for one more charge, "have just come from a meeting with one of the bouncers from the club: big bloke by the name of Tamati. No, maybe big quite doesn't do it. I must say I'm impressed you took him on, though. Now, be good enough to hand over the CCTV recording and the entry log for the club on New Year's Eve. Hand them over right now. And don't think I'm stupid enough to believe you haven't made a copy, so be good enough to make sure you give me the originals."

After Carver has left, Simon sits down and considers the detective's warning. Psychopath, sociopath or savage narcissist: it doesn't matter which label he sticks on Sewell, the time is coming when he will have to leave others more professional to deal with him.

What he needs right now is boots on the ground. Billy Martin's advice haunts him.

He picks up Ross's moleskin notebook and thumbs through

it. Billy Martin's name appears early on and his reference is more detailed than the rest. The warrant officer is coldly calculating, quick and efficient in his use of force, ferocious when drunk, compassionate when sober and the best non-commissioned officer a young lieutenant could hope to have at his side. Simon hopes Martin will prove the same for him.

38

Simon wakes several times during the night, his face itching as the skin heals.

Billy Martin's parting shot still haunts him: *Boots on the ground.* And whilst Simon cannot cast a spell and magic up a brigade of commandos, he can at least call on those who, now it has come to it, have offered to help.

Martin, although asleep when Simon rings, cottons on pretty quickly: "Can't guarantee it. Short notice. I'll make a couple of calls. Paddy would have come, if only..."

Henry Loveridge, being a farmer and therefore up with the lark, doesn't resent his intrusion: "We are right in the middle of lambing," he says and then, "I'll get someone to cover for me. Be on the train up from Tiverton. Be with you this afternoon."

And Elen Phillips needs no second invitation. "Yes, I'll be there right away," she says, as though she lives a short walk around the corner.

There is, of course, the question of whether he should tell Soraya what he knows about Ross and try to enlist her help too;

she might even recognise him from their encounter on New Year's Eve. There is no doubt she knows more about her guardian than she is letting on and that for some reason she is protecting him. Surely, she would want to help in finding him? The logic is obvious, if not compelling. So why? Why does pulling her in seem wrong and keeping her out seem right? There is something about Soraya and Ross; something about the way she seems to want to keep him removed that doesn't sit right.

Martin arrives early afternoon. He is far from happy that Henry Loveridge and Elen Phillips are joining them and is momentarily cowed by the prospect.

Simon dismisses his anxiety. "You'll have to put your differences aside. We're here to find Ross before the police do. For the moment, nothing else matters. Did you manage to drum up any other support?"

"Del Boy, who I gather you've spoken to, and Frankie Watts, who you haven't. They should be here about three. What's the plan?"

"I've been working on it. Now that there are six of us, we have three teams of two. If we put Loveridge with Elen Phillips and Roarke with Watts, they can get out and about: do the hostels, the day centres; get in amongst the rough sleepers where they tend to congregate during the day, St Leonard's Church in Shoreditch, St Martins-in-the-Field. I've pulled some addresses together for them. It's what you and I do that I haven't yet worked out."

The ex-Marine-turned-mercenary rises to the bait and stands a little straighter. "It's like I said, we've got to think like him. He won't be shy of physical effort and he's used to fending for himself. If he doesn't want to be found, finding him won't be easy."

"Yes," Simon interrupts, "that's exactly what Elen Phillips said."

"Not much point in thinking like that, is there?" Billy is

vaguely disgusted. "We've got to believe we will. It's just a matter of working out how."

When Loveridge and Elen Phillips pitch up, they both falter on seeing Simon's grazed face and his new ally.

Simon leaves them to face off in silence while he makes tea.

He hands them their mugs, stands back and waits while their tempers boil.

Loveridge is first to blow. His face swells and the wind-weathered purple veins of his cheeks turn black. "I hoped I'd never—"

Simon intercepts his fury. "Henry?"

Sarah Ross's father, though, is way beyond listening and Simon has to step between them.

"Henry?" he shouts, staring right into his face.

After what seems an eon of twilight war, the bluff farmer yields. "Yes, Simon. I'm sorry, you have to understand—"

"I do and I don't. And I'm not sure I can. To say I do understand would be patronising in the extreme and we're too intelligent for that, all of us. As I said to Billy, we're here for Ross not for ourselves. Afterwards, if that's how you want it, you can have it out with him. But afterwards, not now."

Billy Martin, irritated by being side-lined, makes to quarrel.

The diminutive Elen Phillips cuts him off. "That'll do, Billy. Think of all the times Captain Ross has hauled your inebriated hide out of the Friday night slammer and do us all a favour: nail it shut for once."

Her candour punctures the tension and stuns the men.

"You were saying, Simon?"

The entry-phone buzzes. It is Roarke and another. They take a while to negotiate the stairs.

"Billy," Roarke nods.

The second man says the same. He is a tall man, lean and rangy like Jennings had been.

"Mr Peckham," Roarke acknowledges. "Got off on the wrong foot last time. If you'll excuse the pun."

"It takes two," Simon points out. "If you'll excuse mine."

Roarke shakes hands and grins. "You've not met Frankie Watts?"

Simon introduces the new pair to Henry Loveridge and Elen Phillips.

The housekeeper is gracious. "Yes, we've met... at Sarah's funeral. You were both good enough to come."

"Last time we saw the boss," Watts states, a leftover sadness in his tone. "Gone missing or so Del tells me."

"Yes, missing in every sense." There seems little to be gained by repeating the litany of disasters that have led to Ross's disappearance, so... "Is everyone up to speed on why we're here?"

They all nod, thoughtfully.

"If you don't mind, I've put together something approaching a plan. I've given each pair of you sectors to cover." Simon hands out sheaves of paper on which he has noted specific areas where rough sleepers tend to congregate and the addresses of hostels and soup kitchens; a lengthy list he has trawled from various charity internet sites. To these he adds the photograph he has made copies of. "I hope this meets with everyone's approval. If you can think of a better way to start, don't be backward in coming forward, it's not as though we're on manoeuvres."

Their faces remain straight. To them, Ross is their flesh, their blood. Simon's casual play on words is, therefore, not inappropriate.

"Okay, so if it feels right doing it your own way, just do it and tell us about it later. Most of the rough sleepers will be registered with Streetlink or Outreach, and most of the charities provide Drop-in services. The hostels and day centres need to be covered, though the people working them won't necessarily be forthcoming. Quite naturally, they're protective of their flock and they're not strictly allowed to give out information about the rough sleepers who make use of their facilities. You'll just have to rely on your charm." Simon glances at Elen.

Watts asks, "How's the boss been paying for food? How's he been getting by?"

"Henry?" Simon asks.

"He hasn't touched his bank account or made use of his credit card since before Christmas."

"Three months?" Watts is amazed. "How then?"

The other four know what Simon is going to say and their expectation of the answer only serves to increase the impact of it. "Begging."

"The boss?" Watts, again; this time shocked and appalled. "Begging? Captain Ross? Jesus, who'd have thought?"

Simon, in an effort to soften the blow of Watts' appreciation of the depths to which a man can sink, a man who until now he has looked up to, offers, "It's possible he's been getting day work. Some of the rough sleepers hang around builders' merchants hoping for the odd day's wages." He slides a cardboard box onto the kitchen sideboard. "I've been out and bought you mobile phones and SIM cards."

Candy had been reluctant to approve the considerable cost. But after a little cooing and verbal caressing, not to mention the promise of another evening out, she had consented, remarking only that Barnes would have her 'guts for garters' if Simon's request turned out to be unjustifiable.

"I've labelled them so you'll know your own number and I've input the numbers of the other phones. Reception's good 'most everywhere. But if you're in the underground or in a basement, don't count on it."

"Do we know when and where the boss was last seen?" Roarke asks.

"New Year, we're certain he was dossing in the City around Bishopsgate. He was hanging out with an older guy, name of Tom

Williams, aka Tommy Atkins. I guess Billy here will have told you all about him. Since then the rough sleepers I've spoken to haven't seen him about, though that doesn't mean to say he isn't. Like the people who manage the hostels and the soup kitchens, the other rough sleepers can get a bit protective of their own. They'll very possibly resent your intrusion."

Billy pipes up, "We all know the boss. We know how he always finds a way. This is no different. He may be off his rocker, but he'll have found some means of getting by and somewhere to hang his hat. If this is a case of Post-Traumatic Stress Disorder, then—"

"And the rest," Loveridge scoffs.

"As I was saying," Billy continues, "if this is a case of PTSD, he'll have found somewhere to hide his slug."

"Slug?" Elen asks, mystified.

"Slug: sleeping bag, Mrs Phillips. Now, you two." He turns to Roarke and Watts. "Remember Johnnie Bell?"

They nod, shooting each other knowing grimaces before Watts says, "Yeah, we remember Dinger. After that bomb in Afghan, Dinger couldn't walk near a green car or look a child in the face for fear of bursting into tears. I'm sure that's why he wasn't concentrating when—"

"Yes, Frankie, you're right." Billy is respectfully silent for a couple of seconds. "Well, remember what happened to the boss in Afghan: it could be a touch of the same. Try to think like he might be thinking. Feel what he might be feeling. And remember, he's a Royal Marine and won't be shy of covering ground, which means we've an awful lot to cover. That's why Simon has allocated you your AOs."

"Our AOs?" Elen Phillips' patience with slang and acronyms is wearing thin.

"Area of Operations, Mrs Phillips. The area in which we'd like you to concentrate. Simon and I will look a bit further afield." The stocky ex-warrant officer surveys his curious collection of collaborators. "Right, there's still a couple of hours left, so let's not waste any time. Stay out as late as you like and keep in contact. We've got a head start on the police. As far as we know they don't know what or who they're looking for."

It is clear to Simon that Billy Martin has wrested command from him. In as much as he has a structured and systemized approach, that is perhaps no bad thing. Simon folds his arms and waits for him to finish.

"That's all."

"Where are you staying?" Simon asks Elen.

"Oh, Henry and me, we'll find a Travelodge. You've no need to worry."

He turns to Roarke. Surely his prosthetic will slow him down? "You gentlemen?"

Roarke reads his mind. "Me and Frankie, we won't need a hotel. We'll push on through. You never know where the boss might turn up."

Billy Martin frowns. "Just a thought, boys: if you don't get the information you're looking for, don't resort to any rough stuff. No game faces with this one. And keep out of the way of the police. If they know we're out looking for the boss, it'll only stir them up. Clear? I mean," he glances at Elen Phillips. "are we all singing from the same hymn sheet?"

"Sure," agrees Watts. The others nod.

"You never were much of a one for singing," Roarke decides. "What about this girl? The one who witnessed the assault. Isn't she in danger? What if this fella Sewell decides to go for her?"

"It's a good point," Simon concedes. "With any luck, the police will be keeping an eye on her."

"With any luck?" Roarke growls. "If I believed in luck, Mr Peckham, my right leg wouldn't be made of nuts, bolts and carbon fibre."

"Okay, you're right. I spoke to the copper in charge yesterday:

his name's Carver. Doesn't strike me as an idiot. I'll have another word with him just the same."

However, if he rattles Carver's cage with Soraya, he will only make the policeman's route to Ross shorter. And putting together the Nib in which he'd named Soraya and informed the world she was a student at the UEL was his fault, no two ways about it, though now there now no avenue open through which he can correct that profound error. Grant had found out about the soup kitchen where she works with her father and, fortunately for them both, Grant like Eyles is now permanently out of the picture. However, if both Grant and Eyles knew that much or little about Soraya, it would be reasonable to assume Sewell knows the same.

"I've got to see the girl later. I'll warn her in if the police haven't already."

Soraya. She wrests his attention as though she is a dazzling light he cannot look away from. This time, though, the shadowy figure of Ross comes between them.

"Elen," he says. "You once said to me that if Ross doesn't want to be found, we've no chance of finding him. I'm beginning to see what we're up against. The bad news is that Ross is lost in his own mind; a mind he no longer recognises and a mind far larger and more complex than the city in which he is physically lost." Simon pauses, allowing the others a moment in which to absorb the enormity of the task ahead. Their dour expressions suggest they could do with a crumb of comfort; some morsel of encouragement which will sustain them through the less forgiving hours of their search.

"The good news is that we, all of us, right now, probably know Ross's mind as well, if not better, than he does. That, I hope, gives us a chance."

Excerpt 11 from Transcript of Conversation with Joseph Naarda

SP: And after what your wife told you, did you stay indoors?

JN: Yes, for as much of the time as we could. It was not until later, towards the end of the month, that the war came into the city.

For two days, we listened to the fighting in the farmlands of Abu Al-Khasib. The British destroyed many tanks and many of Saddam's soldiers were either killed or taken prisoner. Some, even before they had to fight, threw their uniforms on the ground and walked away. On the 5th of the new month, a Saturday, the Americans dropped two big bombs on the Al-Tuwaisa quarter and the following day the British arrived. We were very happy.

A day or so after that, I went with Soraya to the shop where I used to sell the alcohol I made. There was still some fighting in the city, but I wanted to see if my shop was in one piece. The looting was terrible: people were stripping anything of value that was not bolted to the ground and as a result we had no water and no electricity.

A British officer of the Royal Marines came. He told me, "*Ma'feesh Saddam, Saddam khallas!*"

I was confused, not sure how to reply: one word I understood, the other two…

"Yes," Soraya interrupted, "Saddam has gone and we hope this time you are right: this time we hope he is finished. You must be careful, there are still *fedayeen* nearby."

"You speak English?" he said to her, surprised.

"Yes. And you speak Egyptian," she replied, "which is why my father was not sure how to respond."

"Sorry. My Arabic is not perfect," the officer said. He was wearing his desert camouflage and beneath his helmet the dust had dried to the sweat on his face. Also, he carried one of those old Nokia mobile telephones, the one they used to call the *brick*, and with him was an Arab.

"My English is not perfect also," Soraya admitted.

"Well, it would appear to be better than that of my interpreter," he said, pointing with his thumb over his shoulder.

We looked at the man behind him and there was something about this man that made us both take an instant dislike to him. It was the way he looked at us, as though we were not worthy of eye contact, as though we were no better than the dirt beneath his boots.

The officer asked, "We are looking for this man." He showed us a photograph. "Do you know him? Apparently, he lives near here."

Of course we knew him: it was the son of our neighbour, the young man who had returned after the first war; the young man to whom Soraya fed Salwa's dates.

"You know this man?" he asked again.

"Yes, but what does this man," I pointed to the interpreter, "want with him? This man in the photograph is certainly not one of Saddam's men."

"My man says he is."

Soraya and I looked at each other, both of us trying to work out why the interpreter should say such a thing. Then, Soraya grinned and frowned all in one muddled expression. "This man who interprets for you is Sunni, yes?"

"I believe so," replied the officer.

"From Kuwait?"

"Yes."

"And this man you seek," she said, her voice filled with conviction, "I know he is Shi'a. His father and our family have been friends for many years. This man was in hospital in Kuwait after he deserted from the Republican Guard. Perhaps, something happened between these two men in Kuwait."

"That's possible. However, what he was is irrelevant. I've got orders to pick him up and take him in for debriefing."

"Interrogation, you mean." Soraya seemed to grow taller each time she spoke.

"No," he replied, his tone more insistent, "I mean debriefing."

"This will not be simple," she replied. "He will not want to come with you. When he came back to Basra, after the war, his father would not tell the police where he was and his father was tortured in the *White Lion*. People here are very suspicious of police and police stations. Are you sure this is not a case of your interpreter trying to settle a grudge?"

By now, you understand, I was little more than a spectator to this battle of wills between an officer wearing body armour and a twelve-year-old girl wearing little more than an expression of resentment.

"Look," the officer said, turning to me, "everyone round here seems to be either Shi'a, Sunni, or the only people in Iraq who've never heard of Saddam Hussein. What are you?"

"I am Christian. We do exist. And you must believe me that this young man you seek, he is not *fedayeen*."

We took them to our street, not far away. The corporal told his officer he was being taken for a fool and that we were leading them into a trap.

Soraya could sense their nervousness, so she suggested that they surround the house while she went in to see the old man and his son. She said she would talk to the man's son and persuade him to give himself up, but only as long as the officer gave her his word that he would not place a hood over the son's head and that no harm would come to him.

"It is important to understand," she said, "that this is about you trusting me and me trusting you. You will be here with my father; I will be the one who is in danger."

The corporal objected. However, the officer, after searching her soul with his eyes, agreed.

Soraya went inside and spoke to the old man and his son. It took her a long time, but because of her friendship with them, they knew they could trust her.

When they came out, the interpreter was rough in his handling of the son, insulting him and trying to hood him. The officer ordered him to desist and, when he did not, the officer glanced at the corporal and the corporal slapped the interpreter so hard I thought his head would roll from his shoulders.

The officer thanked Soraya. I remember he said, "If only we could see through the eyes of children," and then they left.

Two days later, the officer returned with our neighbour's son and without his interpreter, and from then on I worked for the British Royal Marines.

39

Her phone, as always seems to be the case, goes straight to voice mail and not being able to talk to her when he wants to, irritates him, although this time she calls him back almost as soon as he has rung off.

"How was your weekend?" he asks.

"So-so. You know."

He doesn't. *Duties,* she had said, though he has no idea as to what form her duties might take. "Can I see you?"

"Sure." Her economy with words tells him she is in company. "I have to meet someone, early. I'll come to you, later, about nine-thirty."

Someone? What someone? One of the course-mates he had seen her with at the inquest? The young man, Sohail, her partner from New Year's Eve?

He sees her in a café, in a bar, laughing, smiling, familiar; shoulders, hands, touching. They are sharing; he is not. He is outside, looking in, neither a part of her life nor a part of her group. Yet Soraya says she will come to him and her words and the weight of their promise weigh pleasantly in his core.

Her hair sparkles with diamond drops of rain and her coat is damp from the evening drizzle. Beneath it, though, Soraya is warm and supple and she yields to his embrace.

"Still not found your scarf?" he asks.

"No— Simon, your face."

"Fell down the stairs. Stupid. Wasn't watching my step, must have been thinking of you."

He's brought in from a deli around the corner. Vegetarian: filo pastry canapés of aubergine, courgette and tomato, though not mushrooms. When he was queuing at the counter he'd remembered her telling him she didn't eat mushrooms: 'they don't come from seeds'.

But the food proves far too light in temptation and this time Simon showers with her; a shared intimacy which heightens their desire so much that by the time they make the bedroom their lovemaking is thrillingly carnal, if all too brief.

They lie in the dark, fulfilled yet drained, both perhaps self-conscious of their ferocity and the blissful oblivion aroused from their need of each other.

Simon recovers, slowly, his sentience creeping like a thief from beneath a halo of pleasures and fatigues.

"Soraya." He reaches across her to switch on the bedside lamp.

"Simon, I hope you're not going to tell me you've got a girlfriend and she's hiding under the bed." She surveys his body, caresses his chest.

"No, I haven't. It's just that—"

She is grinning mischievously as she interrupts. "It's just that... you sounded very formal, like you were about to admit some dark secret to me."

Simon searches her face for a few seconds and decides there is no reason why she should know his thoughts. "No, it's not like that it's just that—"

"You know, you don't have to tell me you love me just because we made love. And then again, you don't have to apologise to me if you don't." She is smiling, confidently; clearly neither waiting for, nor expecting any affirmation he might feel compelled to offer. "If you want to speak of love, let's leave it for a while. Perhaps we are different in too many ways." She strokes his face so very gently. "Yet we seem to want the same from each other. We seem to want each other. Isn't that enough for now?"

"Yes, it is. More than enough."

Soraya sits up and looks down at him. "Simon, would you hate me if I told you that you were the first—"

"Oh, Soraya. I had no idea. I didn't think—"

"Wait. It's not that. I'm not, or wasn't, a virgin." She hesitates, reconsidering. "And yet, in a way I suppose I was. What I'm trying to tell you is that I've never felt comfortable making love before. I've never been with anyone who has made making love seem so right. Not just physically, I mean. Hey, don't get me wrong I mean physically, too, yes. Making love with you is right." She bends to his face, lays her hand to the side of his cheek and kisses him. "And I mean, *so* very right."

He can feel the warmth of her breath against his face.

"But it's about more than that. The boy I was with before made the process seem... well, exactly like that, like a process." Soraya sits back up. "Something he wanted. Something I suppose I wanted, otherwise I don't suppose I would have gone along with him. But I've only just realised that when I'm with you, I want it for us, together, and that makes it seem right."

Her openness, her honesty, both surprises and intimidates. Simon wants her to carry on talking and at the same time wants her to stop before he is drowned beneath the waves of her expectation.

"That guy you were with at the club? The club on New Year's Eve? Is he your..."

"Him?" she dismisses. Then Soraya softens her tone as if she regrets being so callous. "Sohail? My boyfriend? If by boyfriend you mean he is a guy I hang around with, then yes. If you want to know whether I sleep with him, then the answer is no. He would like to think he is both; he isn't. He carries too much baggage for me."

"Baggage? What sort of baggage?"

"The worst kind of baggage. The kind that makes you jealous of what everyone else has while all the time believing you have less. Sohail's primary emotion is resentment, not love. He sees himself as a permanent second, always one step behind and with little chance of ever coming first. He believes his life will only be worth living if he can have it all his own way."

"Why do you hang around with him then?"

"Oh, I don't know." Soraya frowns, thinking for a moment. "He's not so bad and he helps out at my father's soup kitchen. Though I'm not sure his heart's in it or whether he does it just so that he can be around me. There was a time when I hoped that if I could persuade the gloom of his spirit out into the light, perhaps help him understand that which is most important..."

"Which is?"

"That life is the greatest gift: the gift we should all cherish and not abuse."

"Does he know about me?"

"No, of course not, although I think he knows there is someone."

Simon squirms, playfully. "Let me know if he finds out, will you? I'll do my best to stay out of his way."

"Oh, Sohail is nothing more than an angry puppy."

"Mm, and a very big, very jealous puppy judging by his reaction whenever anyone so much as looks your way."

Soraya smiles. "So you *were* watching me that night in the club. I thought you were. Why were you watching me when that girl you were with was so... so..."

"Good-looking?"

"Yes. Who was she, your girlfriend?"

Now it is Simon's turn to smile. "Candy? No, not with me in that sense. Yes, she is good-looking. She's pretty, an eyeful, a babe, whatever you want to call her. Likes a party, too."

"Where did you meet her?"

"She works at the newspaper. In the accounts. Candy pays my wages and signs off on my expenses."

"You were showing her a good time, huh?" Soraya giggles and feigns to dig him in his ribs. "You bad boy. Tell me, what services do you provide in return for her signature?"

"Mm, I think my editor sees it that way too. Candy is... fun, she's not for me though."

"In what way, not for you?"

He allows her question to hang before asking, "What does this guy Sohail do. Looked pretty sharp to me. Is he a City boy?"

"Sohail? The City?" She chuckles. "No way. He likes his clothes. Likes to look snappy. Which is why he bought me that outfit for the New Year's Eve Ball. Yes, that's what he called it, a Masked Ball. Very grand, only it wasn't, was it?"

"He's not short of a few quid, then."

"His parents have the money, not Sohail. He works for a butcher near Brick Lane. He cuts and packs meat. The man he works for lets him have some for free and he brings it to my father's soup kitchen. Everyone who helps brings something, that's what makes it work."

"Where did you meet him?"

"Oh, around. Friend of a friend. Or at least I think she's a friend."

"You think?"

"Yeah, I think." Soraya contemplates for a moment, clearly puzzled by some misdemeanour her friend has committed. "It was strange. I thought I knew Sabina really well, then she goes and gives my number to a complete stranger hanging about outside the campus gate in Water Lane. Told him about my dad's soup kitchen, too."

"Some friend," Simon scoffs, lightly. Sabina. Sabina wearing the hijab. She was the girl baiting Soraya in the hall before the inquest. "Soraya?"

"Yes, Simon. There's that dark secret tone again. What is it? What have you got to tell me?" She waits for him to reply and when he doesn't, she searches his face for why. Then it comes to her. "No, this isn't about you; this is about me. About something you want to know from me. Okay, go on."

"Last Friday evening, do you remember I asked you if anything unusual had happened at your dad's soup kitchen? If anyone you didn't know had turned up; anyone who wasn't a regular? Perhaps a rough sleeper you didn't recognise? Not one of the regulars? I need to ask you the same question again and I need you to think very carefully before you answer."

Simon feels her tense and begin to withdraw. He slips his arm around her shoulders. "Soraya, this is important. I wouldn't ask you if it wasn't. Tell me, please? Think back to last Thursday."

She turns her face away. "No," she mutters, "no one, no one at all."

"Soraya," he says, more softly this time, "if I have to tell you my dark secret in order for you to understand where I'm coming from, I will. But you must be straight with me. Look at me, please."

At first, she is reluctant and remains facing away from him, her eyes lowered as if in shame.

Simon tries to coax her round.

Soraya resists again, but her resistance is short-lived and though unwilling, she folds and turns to look at him. Her eyes melt. Her will dissolves. "Why do you want to know, Simon?"

"Because I know about the rough sleeper who came to your rescue when you were assaulted outside the club on New Year's

Eve. And I know this rough sleeper is the same man who tried to save the old man from the guys who killed him." He waits.

"Soraya, I know this is the wrong time for me to mention it, though I'm not sure there is an appropriate or right time. But, Soraya, you are in danger and so is the man who rescued you and I don't want any harm to come to either of you."

She is looking down at the ruffled sheets, searching for some form of solace or, perhaps, escape.

Simon raises his hand to her chin and encourages her to face him.

When she lifts her gaze, her eyes are slow to focus.

"I know," he says, trying his level-best to offer her the comfort he believes she so desperately needs. "I know this is hard and I know you've already had to relive it at the inquest and again when you gave your statement. However, I need you to understand how serious this is. Not only for you, for Richard Ross as well."

Soraya flinches and comes to. She stares at Simon. "Ross? Yes, of course, Ross. From Basra. From a long time ago. From long before New Year's Eve. I was so drunk, or drugged," she adds defensively, "that I have been trying to piece together the images of what happened." She pauses, remembering, recalling in her mind all that happened that night. "Parts of the evening make sense. Parts, not all of it and not in any kind of order. I don't know where he came from: he was not there one minute and then the next, there he was. Just when I needed him most, he was there, very suddenly there. He fought with the other men. I was afraid for him, but I shouldn't have been, for it was as though the others were children and he was a man. And when they had gone, he held me and called me *Ghysayib*."

"*Ghysayib?*"

"Yes, it means pigtails. It was a nickname he gave me in Basra; because of the plaits of my hair. That was when I realised I should know him, when he called me *Ghysayib*."

"Wait here for a moment," Simon tells her, "I'll be right back."

When he does return with the photograph, Soraya is sitting up, her legs bent, her head resting on her knees, the sheets pulled tight around her.

Simon sits beside her. "This man," he states as much as asks.

She studies the photograph, remembering. "Yes. I know him now. A kind man. A brave man, too." She looks up at Simon, her expression layered with sadness. "And now this man is living rough on the streets of London."

"Yes."

"What hope is there, Simon? What hope is there that we cannot care for people who risk their future to save us from monsters like Saddam?"

He puts his arm round her once more and pulls her to him. They lie silently, wrapped warm against each other in shared thought, troubled yet content.

"Simon?"

"Yes."

"How did you find him? Ross?"

He tells her about the notebook; about how he tracked down Derek Roarke, Paddy Jennings, Ross's mother and Henry Loveridge; about all he has learned of the Royal Marine Captain, including the death of his wife. And when he tells her about the murder of Grant and Eyles and DI Carver's damning assessment of Sewell, Soraya tenses and clings to him.

"That's why I need to know if Grant came to see you at your father's soup kitchen last Thursday. We think he was one of the men who assaulted you and Tom Williams. The police, however, think Ross may have been responsible for Grant's murder. There's no doubt in my mind he wasn't..."

"Someone did come to see me at the soup kitchen. A man I did not recognise. He was wearing a lumberjack jacket with a hat that had flaps. His hat was all pulled down and I couldn't see much of his face. He said something not very nice to me. Something like 'It's good soup. You'll make some fella a good wife one day; that's if he don't mind living with a sand-nigger'. That's what he called me, a sand-nigger.

"I remember he called me a slut, too, and said something about my father finding out how I put it about for all the boys." Soraya glances at Simon, an apologetic almost appeasing look.

"At first, I thought it might be one of the rough sleepers out of his mind on Spice or one of those dreadful drugs some of them smoke. Only he wasn't. His black eyes looked right into me and I felt afraid. That was when I realised he wasn't one of the regulars. Some of the men can be rough, but they're never rude. They're always grateful for the food we serve."

"What did you do? How did you respond?"

"I must have been in a bit of a daze—you know, like a robot—because I remember I just handed him a cup of leek and potato soup and said 'Mind how you go'. Stupid, really."

"What did he do then?"

"I thought he was going to throw the cup at me. The soup was hot; it would have scalded. I jumped back and bumped into Sohail. He turned around, saw the man and told him to get lost. The man snarled at Sohail. I didn't catch what he said. Then he threw the soup on the ground and walked off."

"Soraya?"

"Yes, Simon."

"Why didn't you tell me this when I asked you on Friday?"

"I don't know. I guess I must have put it out of my mind. The ugliness; the violence in the man's voice. I didn't want to recall it when I was with you. I didn't want it to get in our way."

"You didn't do it to protect Ross?"

"In a way, perhaps. Not consciously though. I think I saw him not far from my house when leaving for the Stratford Campus one morning. I felt his presence more than saw him. Someone was there, following me. Whoever it was, was not a bad person. I knew that inside: knew it and felt it absolutely."

"If Ross has been following you, it's all too possible that he murdered Grant and Eyles to protect you. The police will think so, which is all the more reason why we have to find him before they do. If he runs, they will take it as an admission of guilt. They'll chase him and, given his mental state, I'd hate to think what might happen if they catch up with him."

"You said *we*, Simon: are there others out looking for him?"

"Yes. Others. People who care about him."

Roarke and Watts rousting slumbering rough sleepers from shop doorways. Loveridge and Elen Phillips lying awake, wondering where they made the mistakes and how they could or would or should have done it all so differently. And Billy Martin searching the map of his soul for a route to his redemption.

"But," he adds, "Sewell might be on his trail too, and if he thinks Ross has done for his two mates, he won't rest until he's evened the score. As I've said before, Soraya, apart from Ross you are the only other witness to New Year's Eve, which means Sewell might come after you. He doesn't know that you can't remember much about the assault and the police tell me he's a dangerous man. So, I'm going to call for a taxi to take you home. I'll come with you and get the same taxi back. Please don't argue: I couldn't forgive myself if anything happened to you."

40

"Thank you," she whispers.

"For what?"

"For this evening. For... everything."

The gate swings shut and Simon turns back to the taxi. He pulls the door open and hesitates, staring up the road, expecting to see the Royal Marine standing sentry in the shadows. Soraya's guard. Her angel. Her guardian angel.

On the journey home, the balance of whether he has placed her in jeopardy in order to preserve his story plays havoc with his conscience. Should he have told the police about Ross's notebook? Probably. Should he have handed over the CCTV and entry log from the club sooner? Possibly. Should he have named Soraya in the Nib he wrote following the inquest? Definitely not. Like the others, should he have done it all so differently?

Billy Martin arrives early, too early.

"There's breakfast in the fridge. Coffee on the side. Mine's a tea, black, weak, no sugar."

Simon showers, shaves and dresses.

"You call this coffee?" Billy winces and doubts the contents of his mug.

"You call this tea? I said no milk. Any news from Roarke and Watts?"

"Nothing of any value. Couple of people recognised the boss from the photo; said they'd seen him about at Christmas. What about you?"

During the night, Simon had examined and re-examined the argument for telling Billy about the curious connection between Soraya and Ross; that Ross had called her *Ghysayib*, Pigtails, and that she had known Ross from Basra. Finally, Ross's use of such a term of endearment had persuaded Simon that he should keep Soraya as far removed from Billy as possible. An endearment, he'd reasoned, is an expression of love or if not of love, of affection, and Billy Martin had been already proved instrumental in the fracturing of Ross's mental and emotional state, and his subsequent descent into purgatory.

"No, nothing. I hope you've got a plan for today?"

Billy chews as he thinks. "Yes, I have. We'll work on the assumption that he's not around the centre of town and try our luck elsewhere. Mr Loveridge and Mrs Phillips are covering the Strand, Embankment, Temple and Waterloo; the boys, South London and the City. That leaves us all points north. Do you have that list of day centres within a mile or two's radius?"

Simon sorts through his desk and fishes out a sheet of paper. He checks his list of day centres open on a Tuesday: "Malden Road and Caversham Road, Kentish Town; Vernon Square, King's Cross. Further out, there's St Paul's and Cazenove Road in Stoke Newington, and further still Blackhorse Road in Walthamstow, a Baptist Church in Muswell Hill and a meeting hall in Highgate.

We'll make Muswell Hill the last stop; they don't open until the evening. Where do you want to start?"

Martin inspects another canapé and wolfs it down. "Work our way out from here, shall we?"

"Taxi or slum it on the tube?"

"Tube when we can," he decides. "Plenty of times I've stopped for a kip in a cubbyhole."

———————

Five hours later, Simon's feet are blistered and his legs cry out for mercy.

The former Marine, though, has neither missed a step nor allowed his pace to drop.

According to Simon's tally, they have spoken to thirty-four rough sleepers, nearly all of them happy to look at the photograph of Ross. Ten have recalled seeing him, if not for a good while, and a couple miraculously regained the powers of speech the moment a picture of the Queen was waved under their noses. A couple had stared so madly when questioned, they probably couldn't have told Ross from the Pope if he'd been standing next to them.

The staff in the day centres have proved naturally wary of their motives and mumbled the odd *not sure, maybe, perhaps* and *might have,* but nothing of any consequence.

"Fancy taking five?" Simon puffs. The picnic benches of a pub in the High Street sing like sirens from a green shore sweet with clover.

"You buying?"

"If I've got any cash left."

"I'm sure they'll take a card."

Leaving the perpetual Lothario in him aside, it is difficult not to like Billy Martin. He is urbane even if he seems peculiarly adept at summoning his charm only when it suits.

They sit on reclaimed church pews, a square table and two pints separating them.

"Tell me about Ross."

"What do you want to know?" Billy gazes into his dimpled glass.

"His last tour in Afghanistan. I know you came back on your mid-tour leave. What happened afterwards? What happened when you got back just prior to Ross coming back to Selly Oak? I gather there was a patrol which went wrong. Paddy Jennings mentioned it; didn't want to talk about it. He said you'd know."

"Paddy wouldn't talk about it, eh? Not surprising. Best not revisited some of that stuff."

Simon sits back. "Sure, I get that. And if you don't want to go there, I understand."

Billy looks up, his features now seemingly hewn out of granite, his expression dark and foreboding. "Understand? You? I don't think so, Simon."

"Try me. Indulge me. Imagine I know nothing. Imagine you're talking to a child which, I guess you could say, you are. Try me all the same, please."

"It isn't just what happened in Afghan that's scrambled his mind, you know?"

Simon nods. "I know, Loveridge told me."

Martin shuts tight his eyes and turns his head away to avoid the storm clouds gathering above his soul.

"I'm not interested in that, Billy. What happened between you and him, happened. Maybe it tipped him over an edge. Maybe it snapped the last tie tethering his mind to reason. But," Simon lies, "what went on between you and him, that's between you and him. It doesn't concern me.

"What I'm more interested in is what happened out there, in Afghanistan. People ought to know what makes a man like Ross consign himself to the streets. A man who was once right-thinking and physically strong; a man who other men looked up to; a leader. And he's not the only ex-serviceman living out on the streets. In the same way that the number of rough sleepers is increasing, so is the number of ex-servicemen sleeping rough." Simon pauses.

"Now, I understand every rough sleeper has his or her own story of why or how they've ended up on the street. And if I've learned anything, it's that most ordinary folk are happier believing sleeping rough is down to bad luck and poor judgement. It isn't. Nearly all of it is down to mental health. It's Catch 22: you'd have to be nuts to sleep rough, but if you were nuts, you wouldn't be sleeping rough, you'd be in care. Billy, I've heard some of their stories and none of what I've heard makes easy listening. Believe me, no one deserves to end up on the street, least of all ex-servicemen, guys like Ross who've put it all on the line for us folks back home. That can't be right."

Martin slowly draws the curtain back from the stage of his eyes, drains his glass and makes to the bar.

When he returns, he has regained his poise and brought second pints.

"It all starts with CTC at Lympstone."

Simon throws Martin a puzzled look.

"Sorry, Commando Training Camp at Lympstone, in Devon. Listen, if a nod can survive all the shit they throw at him…

"Look, let me paint you a picture. For one, late-night locker inspections. They turn your locker out, scuff your boots and tie your rig up in knots; and when they've finished, you have only four hours to get it cleaned, ironed and squared away. Four hours when by rights any man flat out on his feet would be sleeping. For two, the physical training. If your body can take the sheer weight of the kit, let alone carry it over rough terrain; if you can hang like a fruit bat from the barrack room rafters for ten minutes, because you're so knackered you've forgotten the word *breechblock* when asked to recite the parts of your rifle; if you can withstand the cold and the battle swim test, make it through Bottom Field, the mud in your eyes, the dirt in your mouth; and Woodbury Common, the exhaustion, the stinging, the itching, the rashes. If you can take the verbal abuse, the physical punishment... Well, if you can do all that and more without losing your marbles, then, Simon, when they hand you your green beret, you believe that whatever life's going to throw at you, you'll be able to handle it."

"A nod?"

"Yes, Simon, a nod. Lots of reasons why they call recruits nods; one is that they are so sleep-deprived they nod off all the time, even when they're standing up."

"And that prepares you for every eventuality?"

Martin takes a swig of his beer and decides, "Clearly not every eventuality." He pauses, looking for a way to explain further. "You suggested I should imagine you know nothing. Well, you write stuff for a living, you report statistics and facts and, when it suits, play a little fast and loose with the truth. Well, try to imagine this:

"You haven't showered or shaved for so long you can't stand your own smell. It's freezing cold and because you've got all your rig on, you're sweating like a pig. You're wearing body armour and webbing and carrying a full Camel-Bak and Bergen, as well as your rifle. Your pockets are filled with kit that keeps you alive; kit like field dressings, tourniquets, headache pills and morphine, glow sticks, extra batteries for your personal radio and night-vision goggles and food. All you can taste is smoking brass, expended link, cordite and the thin metal of your own blood from where you've bitten your lip in concentration. You can't see a thing because even though you've got your NVGs for the dark, you've got sweat and cam cream, camouflage cream, dribbling in your eyes. A bloody great helicopter is hovering over you, ready to evacuate one of your wounded mates, and the wash from the blades is churning the dust up into a blinding, pebble-dashing shit storm. On top of that, you can't hear because of the constant thump of mortars,

RPGs, bombs, cannon and hand grenades. And then, in all the excitement, some bright spark hands you a General-Purpose Machine Gun and a thousand rounds of ammo-that's about half your bodyweight-and orders you to get the hell across to the other side of a swampy canal, which you have reason to believe is mined.

"Imagine that, Simon, if you can. And imagine that if you don't get that beautiful chunk of metal across the canal right away, your best mates won't be your best mates for much longer and you'll spend the rest of your life wondering *what if* you had made it sooner."

"I can't, it's not the kind of experience anyone can imagine." He waits for the temperature to drop before carrying on. "It's what happens to others, isn't it? It's like cancer or having nowhere to go or losing a loved one, only not so." He pauses in case Billy wants to add more colour to his vision of hell.

He doesn't. He stares dreamily out the window: the pavements of Stoke Newington suddenly coated with sand; the grey buildings bleached beneath an unforgiving sun; a mean and callous landscape offering a weary Marine no shade and less hope.

Billy Martin is back in Afghanistan, remembering. "Come on you lightweight," he says. "Drink up, we've got work to do."

For the rest of the afternoon conversation proves difficult at best and although their pace is no less relentless, the boulder of their task weighs heavily in their hands.

They chat with more rough sleepers, both Simon and Billy amazed at how many more wander the back streets rather than beg on the open stage of the West End.

One of them, his limp Harris Tweed jacket decorated with a colourful assortment of pin badges, his hair and beard ginger and wild, tells them he is certain he has seen Ross recently over near Archway. Not only seen him, but that Ross was, as sure as night follows bloody day, in the company of a young woman. He remembers it clearly, so bloody clearly, and do they want to know why? Well, he'll bloody-well tell them anyway: it's because the girl he was with reminded him of the daughter of a friend who had a… He rambles on; his broad, staccato Glaswegian so highly-seasoned with expletives it is hard to separate the likely from the ridiculous.

By five-thirty, the light is fading.

Loveridge and Phillips call in. Elen Phillips seems lightly buoyed that some of the rough sleepers recall Ross and she is convinced they'll find him tomorrow. The farmer on the other hand doesn't share her optimism: the city is a godforsaken tip, worse than Plymouth, and the sooner he ferrets out his son-in-law and gets back to the country the better.

Roarke and Watts are not answering their phone. "They'll be in a pub somewhere down near Waterloo, God help them."

"If they need help, we can be there in half an hour."

"Not them, Simon. The others."

"Sorry?"

"It's the other people in the pub I'm worried about. Del Boy and Wattie haven't slept since last evening and obviously they haven't found Ricardo: some poor soul's going to have to pay for that."

"Shouldn't we…"

Martin bridles his lips, considering. "No, shouldn't bother. A one-legged man in a brawl? It's like cyclists and cars, isn't it? When was the last time you heard of a cyclist getting the blame for an accident?"

Simon says he has one more centre to check out before knocking off, so they part company in Camden. An evening drowning their failure in beer doesn't appeal and he suggests the ex-Marine does the rounds of the pubs near the market on the off chance he can stir up some fresh information.

Once home, he calls Soraya and is leaving her a message on her voicemail when she calls him back.

"How was your day?" she asks.

"Not great. Bit depressing if you must know. You okay?"

"Yes, fine, thank you."

"Busy?"

"Coursework. Rather dull. Exams coming up. Too much revision and I don't know where to start. Who'd be a forensic psychologist, eh?"

He waits, wanting to ask her if anything out of the ordinary has happened to her during the day or if she has felt any unusual presence near her. Instead he asks, "Are you at home?"

"Yes, Simon. I'm here, all safe. Mustn't worry."

"I'm sorry if I cut our evening short. I felt I may have hustled you out the door; bundling you into the cab and taking you home like that. That wasn't my intention. I didn't mean to—"

"You didn't. I understood. Perfectly. There'll be time. There will be. Now, though, I must go. My night for cooking dinner. Let's talk tomorrow, perhaps we can meet up."

"Yes, I'd like that."

"Me too. Tomorrow, then."

He stares at the phone as if he can see her walking away down a street. Simon waits, hoping she will turn and wave before she crosses the road and disappears beyond the traffic.

Before he has time to put the phone down, it rings again.

His heart leaps.

"Peckham, is that you?"

"It's my number, Brian; why would anyone else answer?" His heart bumps back down and lands hard. "I mean, what's up?"

"I was going to ask you the same. You've been a busy lad."

"How so?"

Carver chuckles. "I happened to be standing in the wrong place at the right time and overheard one of our lot saying they'd got a call from a day centre: said some bloke had been in showing photographs, asking if anyone had seen a certain rough sleeper. Wouldn't know anything about that, would you?"

There seems little point in denying it. "Might do."

He chuckles again. "I was wondering whether this rough sleeper might be our mystery man from the CCTV on New Year's Eve. Thought you might be thinking the same. Tell me, Simon, are we both after the same man?"

Simon is resigned. "What's there to say."

"I'll take that as a yes, then. What's the matter, my young friend? Streets of London longer and steeper than you bargained for?"

"Something like that."

"Oh, and another thing I managed to overhear."

"Yes, Brian."

"Bit of a dust up down the Borough Arms, Borough Market. Wouldn't happen to know anything about that either, I suppose?"

"Wasn't me. Wasn't there."

"Interesting thing is, one of the blokes involved had a prosthetic leg. Didn't seem to be much of a hindrance, though. Put a couple of the market boys in hospital. Ex-Royal Marine from down the coast. Said he was in town looking for a friend who'd gone missing. Didn't want to surrender quietly. Bit of a nutter by all accounts. Handy fellow to have about though."

"Did you nick him?"

"What? With a prosthetic leg? Fat chance. Anyway," he chuckles again, "why would you be interested in some ex-Marine banging a few heads down in Borough Market?"

"Must be the journo in me, I suppose. Well, Brian, did you ring me up to pick my brains or did you just want to do the *day-in-the-life-of-a-London-Bobby* thing with me?"

"Well, Simon, my real reason for calling is that I thought you might like to know the SOCOs turned up a knife. From the drains just around the corner from Worship Street. Dunno how they stand all that smell, all that vile, putrid, squalid muck. Lucky for me they do though and lucky for me they're diligent."

"A knife. The one used on Grant?"

"Think so."

"Prints?"

"Yes."

"Any identification?"

"Doing that now. Only certainty is they're not Sewell's. He's one of the first we checked and they're definitely not his."

"Not much I can do with that information, is there, Brian? I can't exactly ask my editor to run a story telling Londoners they can come back out on the streets, it's alright Jack the Ripper's taken the night off."

"Just thought you'd like to know."

"What kind of knife is it?" Simon asks, hoping upon hope the detective isn't going to tell him it's a Fairbairn-Sykes fighting knife.

"Japanese, 'bout six-and-a-half inches long, steel, hollow blade, hollow handle filled with sand."

Simon exhales, his hand over the phone so Carver cannot gauge his relief. "Right, well, thanks for the info. Anything I can do for you? You know, anything I should be doing in return?"

"No. Just thought you might like to know, that's all. Happy hunting. Stay safe, my young friend."

My young friend! Either Carver's condescension is beginning to grate or Simon's fatigue is starting to weigh on his overstretched patience?

41

Billy Martin arrives early, again.

"Don't you ever sleep?" Simon asks, opening the door.

"Do you? You look shocking. Been up all night?"

"Most of it." He pauses, rubbing his eyes. "You know where the tea and coffee are. And do me a favour: just tea and hot water this time, nothing else."

"Doesn't seem right, tea without milk."

The hot shower lifts his spirits and washes some of the soreness from his legs.

"That's better," Simon mutters, sipping. "Get anything out of Camden?"

"Yes and no. Lousy beer, shit company and a bird who was older than Cher. I now understand why they've removed all the mirrors from the toilets? What about you?"

"Got a call from the DI in charge of the murder investigation. They found a knife in the drains near where Grant was killed."

"The murder weapon?" Martin asks, chomping his way through a curled canapé.

"That's what they're telling me. Apparently, the prints aren't Sewell's."

"What type of knife?"

"Japanese, short, metal, hollow blade and handle. Not a Fairbairn-Sykes."

"Don't really use those anymore, but thank God," Martin glances at the ceiling, "anyway."

"My thoughts exactly. Now, I've been doing some thinking and some research. If Ross has gone to ground, it'll probably be somewhere where he won't be bothered by others and somewhere where we wouldn't necessarily think. As I said, I've been up half the night trawling the paper's archives, trying to think a little off the wall."

"Come up with anything?" Martin is holding up the last of the canapés, questioning.

"Go ahead, just don't blame me later.

"I found a story about a guy who's been living up on Hampstead Heath for the past five years. Seems a lot of people know about him and he's sort of part of the furniture. Gets some of his meals at the Baptist Church in Muswell. I dropped by there last thing, got the funny feeling a couple of the guys I spoke to recognised Ross from the photograph. Nothing definite, just a hesitation."

"How much area are we talking? The heath, I mean."

"Including Highgate, knocking on the doors of 900 acres: 360 acres is common land, some ponds for swimming, lots of woods, couple of grand houses, has its own constabulary, wardens, etcetera. Not a bad spot to disappear into. Fancy a trip up there this morning."

"That's a lot of terrain to cover."

"Yes," Simon agrees, "it is, and if anyone would know where to look, it would be you. Think about it: you and Ross, you're both from the same school of survival. How hard can it be?"

The Northern Line tube rattles and lurches. People sway, hanging from straps, eyes dulled and glazed.

Simon studies Billy Martin. He is a good-looking joint of meat, a dense compaction of sinew and muscle fronted by smooth, almost boyish, features.

The red stock brick portal of Belsize Park tube station delivers them out onto Haverstock Hill. A cool and fresh wind blows from the south. Spring is on its way.

There is no alternative other than to go around the concrete and glass superstructure that is the Royal Free Hospital, and as they march down Pond Street, Billy is distracted by a pretty paramedic leaning against a lamppost, eyes down to her phone.

"So, where do we start?" Simon asks. "You want to split up or stay together?"

"We'll stay together."

The paramedic ignores him.

Billy's attention returns. "You keep to the paths and I'll scout. Don't lose contact. We'll try and keep to a grid system, work our way across rather than up and down; less climbing that way. Remember though, if he's there, he's not likely to have his name in lights above the door."

South End Road rises and the Heath opens out on their right.

Simon has to quicken his pace to keep up and as the road sweeps left up the hill, they cut off along a metalled path that runs beside the first of Hampstead's ponds.

Not only will Ross not be advertising his presence, he is also unlikely to be camped on the lower slopes, or so Billy decides. "Too many people about down here and he'd want to be able to see people coming."

They work their way systematically back and forth, down the dip and up the rise to Parliament Hill, and along the straighter path to the café. The going is easier on the lower slopes, the grass is finer and the oak and sycamore not so abundant.

At their approach, the odd rough sleeper grabs his meagre belongings close, and the park wardens, though polite and keen to help, have seen far too many faces to recall any one individual. Occasionally, Martin darts off into the undergrowth only to reappear minutes later, a perplexed, defeated bloodhound.

By midday, they are no better off. They have covered all the ground south of a line running from the Vale of Health Pond in the west to the Men's Bathing pond in the east. The steeper and less open terrain to the north will have to wait until the afternoon.

"This is taking longer than I thought," Billy moans.

"My thoughts exactly." Simon swings the backpack off his shoulder and heads for a bench. "Take a breather? Don't know about you, but I could do with some food."

In the distance, the crystal Shard dwarfs the dome of St Paul's and, behind it, the defensive parapet of the North Downs rings the southern approaches.

"One forgets," Martin observes.

"Forgets what?" Simon passes over a plastic-wrapped sandwich.

"How big it is. Eight million people. No wonder we're struggling to find one."

Simon eats, gazing at the sprawl of the capital laid out before them. "*Where I lie down in storms, in thunder rise*," he quotes, chewing.

"What was that?"

"Not what, who. Oldham, John Oldham. A poet, seventeenth century, died young, tuberculosis. Wrote a satire of London life. Seemed to hit the nail right on the head even back then. "*Here, want of rest a-nights more people kills than all the College and the weekly bills.*

"Not much different from how it is now, eh?" Billy quips.

Simon, though, isn't finished. "*The restless bells such din in steeples keep, that scarce the dead can in their churchyards sleep.*"

"Churchyards, cemeteries," Billy moans. "The place is so full of 'em the God-botherers must own half the city. Imagine if the church gave half of its land over for housing? Wouldn't be a shortage, would there? A man wouldn't need to be homeless."

"Wouldn't catch you dead in a cemetery, eh Billy?"

"No, Simon, not me. Too much bloody noise in a bone orchard. Take me out in the channel and roll me over the side. Fish food. Might as well be of service in death as in life."

"Is that the way you Bootnecks prefer to go? Six fathoms of blue, straight down?"

"Not all of us," Martin says. "My great-granduncle came from London."

"Your what? I thought you were from Liverpool?"

"I am, sort of. My mother was Liverpool-Irish; my father's family are from here." He looks around. "See that steeple over to the north-east. That's St Michael's Highgate Village and below it is Highgate Cemetery where my great-granduncle is buried. Karl Marx in the East Cemetery; my great-granduncle Wilfred in the west. His name's there on the war memorial: Wilfred Carruthers Martin, Private, R.M. Royal Marine Light Infantry," he recites, proudly.

"First World war?"

"Correct, Simon."

"Gallipoli?"

"Correct again. As it says, he was a Red Marine, Light Infantry, before they were put with the blues to form one single Corps."

"Billy, if he was killed in the Dardanelles, surely they didn't bring his body all the back to Highgate. I thought they buried them where they fell."

"They did." Martin grins. "Wilf didn't cop for it in Gallipoli, he got run over by an omnibus as he was walking down Highgate High Street the day after he was demobbed. Drunk as a lord by all accounts." He laughs.

"That's not that funny, Billy."

"Yes, it is. Poor bastard. Anyway, Wilf's my relation, not yours."

Simon waits until Martin's laughter has subsided. "Billy?"

"Yes."

"What you told me yesterday, about having to hump a machine gun through a swampy canal to relieve your mates. Is that what happened to Captain Ross? Did he get stuck somewhere you couldn't get to him?"

Caught off guard, Billy studies Simon's face for a few seconds. "Pretty much," he says. "I'd only just come back from mid-tour leave. Straight off the flight and right up to my neck in it." He stares out across the green fields.

"We were near Garmsir: it's a village on the east bank of the Helmand River, next to what people call the Desert of Death. One of our CPs, our Check Points, was drawing occasional fire from a compound. Not much and not accurate; just enough to be a bother. We could see the bad guys come and go on their motorcycles and, now and then, young children playing outside. Orders came through to get it levelled.

"Our Troop Commander was laid up, so Captain Ross headed up our two sections. I remember we had to get across this canal. It wasn't a really deep one; it was more a large irrigation ditch and the only way across was to wade. The water came pretty much up to our chests, so humping the c4, bar mines and detonator cord made life difficult. The moon was gone, which helped, and it was dark except for the stars. Simon?"

"Yes, Billy."

"You have to see the stars in Afghanistan. They are just... incredible. And I mean incredible. It's like, you're looking up at them and they're looking down at you. And no matter how hard or for how long you look up, they look even longer and harder back down at you. You're familiar with the word awesome?"

"Yes. These days probably over-familiar."

383

"Well, Simon, in Afghan there are two types of awesome. The first is the 2,000-pound bomb and the second is the night sky. On its way, the 2,000-pounder sounds like an express train and if you are too close to it when it hits, it sucks the air out of your lungs, punches you in the face, and bursts your eardrums." WO Billy Martin falters, re-running a film in his head. "The stars in the Afghan night, now they're like the bomb in as much as they take your breath away too. Of course, it's not the noise that is breathtaking; it's that there are so many of them and that they're so silent. Millions and millions of 'em, and their silence is thunderous. Both of them, both the bomb and the stars, are awesome and somehow they both make you feel very close to God. Bonkers when you come to think about it."

"I thought you didn't do the God Thing. What did you call them? God-botherers?"

"I don't do God, Simon. I've seen far too much suffering to believe in that crock anymore."

Aware of the intended deflection, Simon pulls him up. "Go on, Billy, about Ross."

"Alright," Martin frowns, "if that's how it's got to be.

"We moved in at night and cleared and secured the compound. Small detail: there was no sign of the children we'd seen playing. The place was deserted, nothing. Anyway, the assault engineers did their stuff and made the place disappear. One minute it was there; the next it wasn't. Magic. Like Tommy Cooper, only louder.

"Usually after a bang like that, the Taliban would be chattering away to each other about what-the-fuck just happened and our intel guys would be telling us what they were jabbering on about. This time, though, they weren't; they were silent, no chatter, not a word.

"In fact, it was scarily quiet, uncannily so. We thought we'd got off with an easy night's work and we were just looking forward to getting our heads down when all hell broke loose: tracers, RPGs, Chinese rockets, mortars, everything they had. We couldn't make it back along the path we'd come up, too much shit coming down, so we struck off through the brush.

"There was a line of small trees on our side of the canal and we reckoned they'd provide good cover. Most of us were across the canal, Paddy Jennings was about halfway, and there was only Captain Ross, Del Boy and Wattie left on the far bank. One moment we were all thinking life could've been a whole lot worse and the next moment it was. Del Boy stepped on something that blew his leg off."

"Del Boy. Roarke?" Simon asks.

"Yes, Del Boy. Derek Roarke. We all call him Del Boy because he used to do these terrible impersonations of Del Boy Trotter from Only Fools and Horses. Idiot should have been on stage, never mind traipsing around Helmand stumbling on explosive devices."

"Taliban IED or leftover Russian mine?"

"Improvised device or so the clear-up boys decided. Doesn't really matter either way. The important part of it was the Taliban knew it was there and that's why they drove us towards the area. We might as well have put up a flare and said 'Now you know where we are, lay it on us'. They chucked everything our way; knew precisely where we were. Fortunately for Del, the Boss was with him. Paddy had made it back across by that time and Wattie was down at the water's edge on the far bank. Paddy wanted to go back and help the Boss, but I couldn't let him, what with being under a barrage like that and the possibility that there might have been a second device set near the first."

"So, what did you do? Don't tell me you left Ross there, with Roarke?"

Billy Martin grimaces. "What the fuck else could I do?" His tone is sarcastic and dismissive; his eyes wide with incomprehension. "But thank you, Simon. I appreciate your understanding of the situation."

He breathes deep, shakes his head and sighs. "I've got the rest of the guys, twenty-plus if you count the four engineers, safe on the south bank and three guys sitting in what might be a minefield. Don't think for one minute I didn't want to go right back over for them. And don't think for one minute it was easy stopping any of the guys from going back either. Paddy went berserk. I had to slap him. Believe me, if I could've changed places with Ricardo, I would have.

"There was a shedload of crap landing all around the boss and Del, and anyone going back for them would've only added to the casualty list and made it more difficult for us to recover them when the firing ceased. All we could do was wait it out." We had a JTAC, a joint tactical air controller, calling in air cover and a FOO, a forward observation officer, calling in artillery. It was only a matter of time before the Taliban were either erased or fled. Until that time, there wasn't much we could do for them."

"How long were they on their own for?"

"An hour, tops. The firefight ended when an F-16 dumped in the right spot, but it took us far too long to get back and make the area safe."

"I know Roarke lost his leg; was Ross wounded?"

"Ricardo got a tourniquet round Del's stump, gave him a shot of morphine and patched him up as best he could. There wasn't a whole lot more he could do. He just lay on top of Del, made them as small as possible and copped whatever came their way. Shrapnel. In his arms and legs mostly. Some from the IED and some from the barrage. His body armour saved him, no doubt about that."

Simon sits back and tries to imagine what it must have been like: an hour of being shelled while lying on top of a seriously wounded man. He shivers. "Ross was lucky to get off so lightly."

Billy Martin drains his bottle of water. "Yes and no."

"What makes you say that?"

"Well, when we finally got to them, Del was in a bad way. He needed to go pretty quick. However, Ricardo was, in a different way, no better off. You could see what was wrong with Del, it was perfectly obvious. With the boss, it was weird. Sure he was concussed and bleeding from his arms and legs, but it was his eyes. It was like the lights were full-on and yet there was no one home. I've never seen anything like it before. It was as though the barrage had knocked all the stuffing out of him and he was empty, hollow even, like a vacuum standing."

"What did you do, Billy? Where did Ross go?"

"We called in a Casevac for the pair of them. Chinook, the medical helicopter, took them back to Bastion." Martin picks at the quick of his fingernails, then sits back and sighs once more. "That was the last time I saw Ricardo. Ramp on the helo went up, brown-out and there he was, gone."

Simon picks up the last piece of the jigsaw. "And when he gets back to Bastion, he finds out Sarah has died in a car accident."

Billy Martin's agitation gets the better of him. Anger, hate, remorse, regret, something more profound, something far worse, all etched deep in the lines of his scowl. "Yes, Simon. Call it a strike, a double-whammy, a knockout, the straw that breaks the camel's back. In fact, call it whatever you're comfortable with calling it: it all amounts to the same thing. She was dead and he was alive and ever since he's probably wished he could change places with her."

There is a vicious edge to the ex-warrant officer's tone that pricks a memory in Simon: a man he'd interviewed, a man who had described being stabbed as the most intense pain imaginable.

"He's not the only one, is he Billy?"

"No." His head drops. "He isn't. If I was given the chance, I'd do the same, but for completely different reasons."

Simon expects him to head for the hill, but Billy Martin doesn't move. He stands, staring down at the ground between them, an enemy far more terrible than the Taliban waging war in the desert of death that is his soul.

It takes Simon a while to cotton on.

"Oh Christ, Billy. You knew. You knew when you turned up in Garmsir after your leave. You knew Sarah was already dead because you'd phoned the Loveridge house to apologise, the day after you'd seen her. You couldn't face telling Ross because of your part in what happened to her, so you had to swallow that knowledge until someone else told him." The ripples of his comprehension fan out and slap against the inside of his skull. "And worse, Ross would have found out later that you knew. You, the one man he thought he could depend on, the one man he needed to depend on when the going got tough. You knew all the time. Oh, Billy, no wonder Ross has lost his mind."

As with the previous afternoon, conversation shrivels. And it is no longer the enormity of their task which weighs like the boulder of Sisyphus's deceit, it is the mass of Martin's guilt and the fact that Simon now knows all the rotten detail.

He tries hard not to hate the ex-Marine for it, but cannot haul his prejudice from the fact that if Martin had not behaved as he did with Ross's wife, they probably wouldn't be searching for a needle in London's giant concrete haystack.

Billy Martin, on the other hand, beasts himself by running almost everywhere, including straight up the steep slopes of long grass as if they are nothing more than irritants to be squashed beneath his boots.

Here and there, hidden in a coppice or tucked beneath a bush, they come across a sleeping bag, a blanket, old newspapers and discarded bottles and food-wrappers. None of the detritus, Billy tells Simon, speaks of Ross. "He'd never leave his slug on the ground; he'd hide it somewhere dry, off the ground; somewhere most people wouldn't expect to see it. He'd be careful to clean up afterwards, too."

By the time the day gives up on them, they have covered nearly all of Hampstead Heath except for the busy Kenwood House Estate. And when they call the other search parties, it turns out they too have met with no success. Simon persuades them to meet at a café near Old Street.

———————

Elen looks out on her feet and Henry as though he may have only a few miles left in the tank. Roarke and Watts, however, appear ready to deal with every eventuality, be they market boy or pretty waitress. And Billy, at Simon's asking, has stayed away. The group seem a little more relaxed without him and Simon is reminded that according to Elen Phillips it is the four others seated around the table who were present at Sarah Loveridge's funeral.

He decides to tell them of the curious link which chains Ross to Soraya. Loveridge and Elen Phillips have not heard the name and neither Roarke nor Watts were serving with the Royal Marines in 2003, so there's no reason why they should know Soraya. The notion that Ross may now have someone to care for, that he may now hold some motivation that would encourage or entice him in from the streets, boosts their morale.

"The way I see it," Loveridge says, "is if we continue to ask the other rough sleepers if they've seen Ric, they'll warn him and he will go to ground. That'll only make it harder for us."

The café is cosy; the crowd young and smart.

Roarke stirs his tea. "Can't sit on our hands, sir. Like we can't expect the boss to walk out of the woods with his hands up. And if he met this kid in Basra... Well, you know how he was with kids."

Simon is not inclined to agree with Roarke's definition of Soraya as a *kid*, however... "No, I don't, Del. Tell me, how was Captain Ross with kids?"

"Well, brilliant is the only way to describe it. Treated every kid like you'd treat your own. God knows how he managed it with all that kit we had to carry, but he always kept a bag of boiled sweets handy."

Elen Phillips shrugs off her lethargy, blinks and sips her tea. "Why wouldn't he be good with children? With a mother as cold as the Beacons in snow and a father who based his parenting on the precepts of emotional austerity, that's no surprise."

Roarke and Watts trade looks.

"Yes," Elen Phillips continues, "you both know it, don't you?"

"Didn't have it easy, the boss," Roarke offers. "Plenty of people don't. But that's what makes him the person he is and I'd choose him over his father any day. The Major didn't believe you were worthy of your rank until you'd sent a few men over the top. Small wonder the boss thought he had so much to make up for. No small wonder, either, that the stress used to get to him."

Simon recalls Martin mentioning the same. "It was that obvious, the stress?"

"Sure it was," Watts says. He looks at Roarke. "Remember that time we caught him sleepwalking?"

Roarke nods, his eyes wide. "Yes, sure do. The boss walked clean out into the bush." He pauses, respectfully suggesting he has monopolised the floor for long enough and that perhaps someone else might like to speak.

They don't though; they are waiting.

"We stopped overnight in this compound: Wattie and I were on watch, up on the roof. The boss walked by below and asked us if all was quiet, which it was. Then to our surprise he starts off out the pound. By the time we realised he didn't know what he was doing, he was gone. Good thing we had our night-vision goggles or we would have lost him. Billy had to go and find him and bring him back. Strangest thing I ever saw, him buggering off into the dark like that. Eyes open yet fast asleep. Billy told us to forget about it, told us not to mention it; said the boss just got a bit confused, lack of sleep and so on. His rig, sorry, his clothing, was all bloody and untidy, like he'd tried to undress and someone else had stopped him. Scared the living shit out of me, begging your pardon, Mrs Phillips."

Elen smiles, easily. "That's alright, Derek. Curiously, I don't think that was the first time. I told you, Simon, about the time he came in from the woods that night, hypothermic and all covered in blood. Doctor said it was some kind of trance, an ecstatic state or fit of some nature."

Roarke and Watts trade another knowing look and Loveridge adds, "Sarah had the same. Called the doctor out one night when Ric had one of those nightmares. Ghastly, she said it was."

"Derek, you said he was covered in blood?" Simon asks. "At the compound, the night Billy brought him back."

"Yes. We thought he'd hurt himself, but the blood turned out not to be his; there wasn't a mark on him. Next morning, when we left, we came across the carcass of a wild boar. We reckoned the boss must have tripped over it and got all bloody picking himself up."

"Sleepwalking and dreaming of the dead: not exactly classic symptoms of stress."

"Maybe not, Simon," Elen points out, her schoolmarm tone heavy with contempt. "Though I venture to suggest that erratic sleep patterns are nothing unusual in adolescents, particularly in adolescents who've wanted for the affection of loving parents. Furthermore, I also venture to suggest that when a young man is surrounded by death, as you boys were in Afghanistan, then to dream of the dead is not so out of the ordinary. To have to cope with both…" She turns her face away, her lips tight, her eyes tearing.

A maudlin silence descends on the group, as each in their own way pictures Richard Ross the last time they saw him. Simon will have to drag them from their reminiscing. He has no right to, especially as he is the only one amongst them who does not know or has not met Ross, but he has to.

"May I make a suggestion?"

"Of course, Simon," Elen says. "After all, we wouldn't be here searching for young Richard if it wasn't for you." She sits up straighter to show she is paying attention.

"Go back to wherever it is you're staying and get your heads down. Don't spend half the night searching the ceiling for where Captain Ross might or might not be. And you two," Simon glances at Roarke and Watts, "try to resist banging any more heads tonight. Last night I got a call from the detective who's covering the investigation. Seems he got wind of a couple of guys picking arguments with the Borough Boys. Couldn't pinch them up for it; said he would've looked stupid dragging them up before the beak when one of them had a prosthetic leg."

Roarke sniggers. Watts the same.

"Do me a favour, gentleman. Go to the movies, the London Eye, the London Dungeon, anywhere, just for my sake try to stay out of trouble."

"The London Dungeon?" Roarke chuckles.

"I guess I'm going to have to get used to it," Simon says, when she calls him back.

"Used to what?"

"You never answering your phone when it rings."

Soraya laughs. "Hold on a moment, please."

Simon leans back in his chair. He hears her close a door. "You're at home?"

"Yes."

"Revising?"

"No, Simon, waiting for you to call. Yes, of course I'm revising. How was your day?"

"Long, trying, tiring, frustrating and ultimately not very

392

rewarding. Other than that, a barrel full of laughs." The pros and cons of explaining to her why he thinks Ross, her guardian angel, has abandoned his soul to the streets are delicate to balance. "How was yours?"

"Oh, interesting, if you want to know what makes the perfect psychopath."

"And what does make the perfect psychopath? An in-depth knowledge of which chianti provides the perfect accompaniment to liver and fava beans?"

Soraya chuckles. "No, Simon. Not all psychopaths are super-intellectual cannibals. It may surprise you to learn that we all have a little psychopath lurking somewhere inside of us."

"A little psychopath? Inside me?"

"Sure. The psychopath in us controls our empathy. He-"

"Or she."

"Yes, Simon, the psychopath in us dials down our empathy when we need to do something that might have a bad effect on someone else. Dialling out our empathy shields us from the guilt we cannot avoid: it enables us to lay our guilt to one side while we deal with the situation we are faced with."

"Shields us from our guilt?" The rule certainly applies to thugs like Jack Sewell. Does it, though, apply to men like Ross, Martin, Roarke and Watts? Did they, in the short term, dial out their empathy simply because of what they had to do in order to protect people more ordinary? Paddy Jennings had suggested as much.

"Simon, don't tell me you lack for self-confidence, that you're not ruthless or fearless. When you see a story, when you believe that your story has merit, you have to pursue it at all costs. You can't afford to let people stand in your way or you'd never get your story. It's inevitable that people will get hurt and, over time, you will become inured to that?"

The psychopath lurking deep inside him cringes. "I hope I

393

never become so inured to the suffering of others that I don't realise when I'm hurting them."

Simon remembers the first time he saw Soraya, standing in the queue to the club. He remembers the rough sleeper who worked the queue begging for money so that he could buy anti-biotics for his sick friend. And he remembers ignoring the same rough sleeper, because it was easier to ignore him than to address his own attitude towards the man.

"I hope you don't, Simon. I really, truly hope you don't."

And he remembers denying he had written the News-in-brief about the inquest; the News-in-brief which he very definitely *did* write and in which he told the world who she was and where she studied.

"Soraya?"

"Yes, Simon."

He wants, no, desperately needs to tell her. The breakwater which has been holding back the sea of his guilt is ready to collapse. "Soraya, I–"

"Yes, Simon."

If he doesn't tell her now, if any harm should come to her, he will know no peace; he will know only regret.

"Soraya, I'm sorry I phoned so late. I was hoping to see you this evening. The day... it just seemed to evaporate. And tomorrow evening you'll be at the soup kitchen. Your friend, Sohail, will be there?"

"I expect so."

"Then Friday? I know it's not your lucky day. Are you free on Friday?"

"Yes, Simon, Friday. Simon?"

"Yes, Soraya."

"Don't be too hard on yourself. For me. Please don't be too hard on yourself."

Excerpt 12 from transcript of conversation with Joseph Naarda

SP: That must have been a pretty risky business. Working as an interpreter for the occupying forces must have made you a marked man.

JN: Yes, it did. I was careful, though. No one, apart from my family and the old man and his son, knew what I was doing. I wore a headscarf and sunglasses at all times when I was working. Uncomfortable and hot it was, but it was very necessary for me to conceal my identity.

SP: Were most of the interpreters supplied out of Kuwait?

JN: Yes, mostly they were supplied by American companies and mostly they were Sunni. One could not trust them. Some perhaps, though not many. They knew their position afforded them the facility to settle old scores.

SP: And this British officer, the one who arrested and later returned the son of your neighbour, you worked with him?

JN: Often. Yes. The British had marked out certain...

what were they called? Oh, yes, they were called Tactical Areas of Interest. It was strange. Funny, even. They codenamed these places after beers they drank at home. British humour, I suppose. I remember the Presidential Palace was codenamed Spitfire, a bridge over the Ashar Creek was London Pride, and the most curious was a place they called Skull Splitter. Why, I ask you, would you drink a beer if it promised to give you such a bad headache? Other areas were named after cities: London, Birmingham, Leeds and so on. These were all south of the creek. These I could understand. But Skull Splitter?

SP: Did you get to know this officer well? There must have been a bond of trust between you otherwise you wouldn't have put yourself and your family in harm's way.

JN: Yes. Once, after dark, he came to our home to eat with us. He brought food. Fish! The kind of fish we were not used to eating. He said the fish came from Norway. I could not believe it. I asked him how this could be, that fish could be brought all the way from Norway when we were so close to starving? How, amongst all this chaos, how was it possible for him to bring us fish from Norway?

And he said, "I got it from the Australians. They have two seals; two working seals. They help them locate mines in the waterway and they are not used to a diet of warm water fish, so they fly fresh fish in for them. From Norway. Every day."

Yes, Simon, seals. Seals like the ones one would see on the television when they show programs about the Antarctic. And we could not get drinking water!

SP: Madness?

JN: Yes, madness. You know, packs of wild dogs roamed the streets attacking people, killing them and feasting on their bodies? The streets were not safe in daylight, never mind after dark. This officer, he was very brave. He was a good man, a thoughtful man. He had this curious birthmark above his right eye. Sometimes it looked like he had a scar from an old bullet wound, just here, just above his eyebrow.

He made a big fuss of Soraya: he took a shine to her, you might say. He asked me what we called the plaits in her hair. "*Ghysayib*," I told him. "In English, it translates as pigtails." And this was the name he called her by, *Ghysayib*.

He told me that if we ever needed help, we should get in touch with him through the British Embassy in Kuwait. He said they would know where to find him.

42

This time, Simon has the coffee ready. "Good morning Billy."

"Is it? What makes you all chirpy like a bird?"

"Aren't you ever pleased just to wake up?"

"No thanks, Simon. If I woke up all happy like you, I'd worry the day was only going to get worse."

"Plenty of time for that later. How's that coffee?"

Billy ignores him. "I hope you've got some ideas as to what we're going to get up to today; I'm fresh out of them."

"Today? Yes. I thought a little sightseeing."

Again, he ignores Simon. "How'd the meeting go last night?"

"Bit grim. Del told us the story of Ross sleepwalking his way out of the compound when you were on patrol."

"Mm, thought I'd told him to forget about that particular misdemeanour."

"He said so, too. But seeing as that was all in another life, the dim and distant past if you like, I don't see how it can affect what's going on now."

Billy checks the fridge in case a canapé has dodged his watch.

"There's breakfast in the paper bag," Simon offers. "Got it with the coffee this morning. Expensive, that coffee: hope it's worth it."

"It is, and thanks for the pastry."

"Croissant."

"Whatever."

"That got me thinking."

"What? The croissant?"

"No, Billy, that time when Ross went walk-about. Seems he did something similar when he was a lad and again when he was married. Elen Phillips also told me that Ross was convinced he could see the faces of those who were about to die. She said he knew it about their postman and later about some woman he met down his local pub."

Martin stops chewing and throws Simon a similar look to the one Roarke and Watts shared the evening before. "The faces of those who were about to die?"

"That's what she said. Why?"

"Because that's what he thought he'd seen the day before Jo Crudup stepped on an IED."

"Yes, I—" Simon double takes. "He what?"

"The morning Jo was killed by the IED, Ricardo told me he'd had a dream during the night. You see, Simon, you don't really sleep when you're out there; leastways not when you're out on patrol. It's a kind of half-sleep, like you're asleep only not really. Your mind sprints through all these weird scenarios: what if this happens, what if that, who will look after the dog, your mum, your little sister. It's only natural. It's only the fear talking. No bad thing fear, in the right measure; it helps keep you sharp. Too much of it and you get tired, you get lazy.

"When Ricardo mentioned his dream, I thought maybe he was overdue some mid-tour leave. Should have been about the same time as mine. Then our platoon commander, the lieutenant, took ill and Ricardo never got his leave.

"For the patrol that day, Captain Ross ordered Jo down the back, tried to make it so he wasn't first up the path. Didn't do no good though, and neither did the ECM we were carrying."

"ECM?"

"Electronic Counter Measure. A jamming device. It jams the phone signals so the Taliban can't detonate IEDs remotely. Guess the one Jo stood on was detonated by a pressure plate. Bad luck, seeing as five or six other blokes had just walked past it." Billy loses himself in his thoughts for a moment.

"And Captain Ross knew this was going to happen?" Simon presses. "He predicted it?"

"Seemed that way. I told him he was just being stupid. Gives me the shivers thinking about it."

"I'm sorry to bring it to mind, Billy. Really sorry. Now listen, let me ask you a question: did you ever tell Captain Ross about your great-granduncle Wilfred, the one who's buried in Highgate West Cemetery?"

Martin smiles to himself. "Yes, I certainly did. Don't know what was funnier: what happened to Wilf or watching Ricardo die laughing. Thought that was the definition of irony, he did: surviving Gallipoli only to get run down by an omnibus. Christ, he did laugh."

"Right, Billy. Then today we're going to start where your great-granduncle finished, in the West Cemetery at Highgate."

————

In contrast to the previous morning, when the ornate red-stock brick of Belsize Park Station had eased them out into the tree-lined avenue of Haverstock Hill; now the raw, colloidal concrete of London Underground spews them out into the eddying populace of Archway.

Simon starts the long march up Highgate Hill. Billy Martin,

though, drops into McDonalds to collect a more substantial breakfast and has devoured it by the time he catches up outside the Whittington Hospital.

"What's the drill?" he asks.

"I've managed to get us on the tour at eleven. I guess you've visited your great-granduncle's memorial before?"

"Long time ago. Can't we just turn up and wander?"

"No, not these days. I had to book. East Cemetery you can turn up; something to do with the proletariat being entitled to worship at Marx's tomb, I suppose."

"As if," Billy grumbles. "As if that isn't just communist enough for a man who kept servants, played the stock market and rarely settled his bills?"

The hill is steep, the wind sharp and Simon wishes he'd flagged down a taxi.

"There's a pub up at the lights," Billy says. "The Old Crown. Meet me there."

"Why? Where're you going?"

"Same place. Thought I'd drop by and flash them the photo. You take your time."

And with that the ex-Marine is off, running up the steep incline.

Half a mile later, Simon leans to catch his breath in the shadow of St Joseph's rounded chancel. "Any luck" he gasps, as Billy nips between the traffic, towards him.

"No. The cleaner's in; staff haven't turned up yet."

Waterlow Park is neat and tidy. Au-pairs push prams while bemused men stare, and dog walkers stoop, plastic bags in hand. And in the steep Swain's Lane, a half-dozen tourists are checking their watches.

A guide appears and ushers them in through the wrought-iron gates of the Gothic portal.

"My great-granduncle Wilf," Billy whispers, pointing over at the quarter-circle of Portland stone. "His name is inscribed over there, on the wall."

After a brief introduction, the guide herds his flock up through the grave-lined avenues. Obelisks and broken columns rise proud among the sycamore, ash, hawthorn and mulberry trees; and ledger slabs, chest tombs, headstones and family vaults are crawled over with ivy or hedged in fern. Now and again the guide pauses to point out a mausoleum belonging to one of the West Cemetery's more celebrated, or perhaps better-heeled, occupants.

Simon and Billy plod along at the back of the group, their eyes drawn this way and that to narrow paths that lead off between the trees.

The group gathers, nervous at the gloom that lies beyond the lotus columns framing the narrow entrance to the aptly-named *Death Palace*. The Egyptian Avenue, the guide is explaining, is lined with private vaults, each one secured by cast-iron doors, each door embellished with an inverted torch, the symbol of a life extinguished.

"Now's your chance," Simon mutters.

As the group edges its way into the avenue, Billy hangs back and then slips away.

Simon alternates between the front and the back of the group, hoping that in doing so the guide will not notice that though he began the tour accompanied, he is now alone.

A Cedar of Lebanon dwarfs the columbarium of vaults, and later, the pyramid-roofed mausoleum of the newspaper proprietor Julius Beer reminds Simon that he is only present in the cemetery because he is in search of a story.

On one tomb, he notices the decoration of a serpent devouring its tail. An ouroboros: the symbol of life out of death, the nature of the universe, the cycle of life and the fusion of opposites. The image jolts his memory and he has to stand for a moment, separate from the group, waiting patiently for the reason to come to mind.

The wind cannot breach the wooded cemetery; the air is thick and moist and undisturbed beneath the apron of trees.

"Soraya," he whispers. The serpent. He knows it. Or if not knows it, he remembers Soraya talking about it. Gradually, it comes to him. "The charm. The *skandola*. The serpent eating its own tail. The lion, the scorpion and the hornet inside the circle of the serpent." When she'd turned up unexpectedly that first night, Soraya had told him of the charm her attacker had stolen. She'd said the serpent represents life and that the other three gather the souls of the unclean and throw them into the mouth of the serpent. At the end of the world and when the unclean have suffered for their sins, the lion, the scorpion and the hornet ask the serpent to return them. The image is haunting, like the Terrace of Catacombs before him.

"Excuse me?"

Soraya is close by and yet not so. He cannot see her, yet he can feel her.

"I said, excuse me?" the guide interrupts.

"What? Yes. Sorry."

"Your friend? The one you arrived with. Where is he?"

"Oh, he went back. A relation of his. I mean, the name of his relation is inscribed on the Screen Wall of the memorial. Rather got to him, I think."

They stroll, lazily, back down the slope, stopping only to admire the chested tomb of Thomas Sayers, the last of the Victorian bare-knuckle prize fighters.

"When Sayers died in 1856, his dog," the guide is saying, "a mastiff, a stone likeness of which you see lying faithfully in front of the tomb, followed the horse-drawn hearse all the way from Camden High Street to the cemetery. Thousands lined the route."

"Billy? Where are you?" Simon mutters below his breath. He is pretending to pay attention whilst scanning the woods.

"In fact," the guide continues, "one might also say Sayers was the father of the modern sports personality."

"C'mon Billy. Where are you?" Simon mutters again.

He can hang on no longer. The guide insists on looking round to ensure Simon keeps up.

When they eventually arrive back down at the war memorial, Billy is sitting legs crossed, leaning back against the Cross of Sacrifice.

"There he is," Simon says, pointing. "Told you he was there."

The guide is enchanted by the idea that the great-grandnephew is visiting his great-granduncle's memorial stone. He leads the group over and makes to address Martin.

But just as the guide opens his mouth, Billy stands up.

"Silly sod," he proclaims and marches off.

"How'd you get on?" Simon asks, once they are through the iron gate.

Billy grins. Whether at his rudeness to the guide or at his relative success, Simon isn't sure.

"Alright, Warrant Officer 2nd class Martin, don't keep me in suspense. Let's have it."

"D'you know, Simon, you're not as stupid as you look."

"Well, Billy, we all have to be thankful for small mercies. Go on."

"I reckon it's him, Ricardo. Found a slug, a sleeping bag, rolled up in a groundsheet, wedged up in the elbow of a branch and camouflaged with leaves. It was near the big iron gate out onto the top of Swain's Lane. New scuff marks on the gate, too, like someone has recently climbed up over it. Also, some food: tin of beans, packet of biscuits, jam and a couple of bottles of water concealed behind a dogwood. They've been covered up as you would expect. It was the way it was done that rang my bell, like whoever had done it knew what they were doing. It was precise, not sloppy and if that isn't the work of an old Bootneck…"

"You sure about that, Billy."

"Sure as I can be. Any old dosser could've left it there, but this slug was used recently; it was still warm to touch in the centre, no mould, no mildew, no damp. Takes a man who knows how to keep his kit that way."

Simon shakes his head. "Nothing else? Nothing that might identify Ross?"

Martin is still grinning.

"Come on, Billy. Enough of the charade."

"And this." Like a magician drawing the handkerchief from his cuff, Martin pulls a piece of material out from his jacket pocket. "Ta da!"

"A scarf," Simon notes, flatly.

"Yes, Simon. Not just any old scarf, though. Look at it, it's a shemagh, a headscarf." He holds the material up, extending it "See, its longer and lighter than your average muffler. Check out the pattern."

The scarf is blue; lapis or cobalt, he isn't sure; the pattern exotic fruits, flowers and, he peers closer, creatures: angels and birds, peacocks perhaps. The shemagh is fringed with tassels at both of the longer ends.

"I've seen this scarf before, Billy."

"So, have I."

"Where though, Billy. Where?"

"Plenty of them in the middle east, mostly Jordanian or Saudi: they're popular with the kids. Typical colour. Typical design; angels and birds. Where've you seen it before?"

Simon studies the scarf and taking it, he runs the cotton through his hands in the hope that the texture will communicate the identity of its owner to him. He closes his eyes, lifts it up to his face and breathes in the perfume fused within its fibres.

At first, there is no scent and neither does the scarf speak to him, so he presses the shemagh to his face and breathes in, deeper this time.

He turns to Billy: "It's the headscarf Soraya wears. She wasn't wearing it on Friday night and when I asked her why, she said she'd mislaid it."

"Which means what?"

"Which means Soraya has seen Ross. She's known it was him all along."

43

She knew.

Simon is trying to list all their conversations: outside the hospital, after the inquest, when she turned up in the rain, when...

"Don't tell me that's the first time a woman has put one over on you?" Billy is saying.

...when he went with her to the police station to give her statement, when they made love that first time and, again, the second time, not three days before. He reruns and rewinds the recordings. And like a Stalinist inquisitor poring over his reel to reel, he listens out for an evasion, a side-step, a subtlety, a nuance, a sly denial, a moment when she may have implied that she hadn't recognised the rough sleeper who came to her rescue.

"You'll get over it. Don't worry about it."

Soraya had seen Ross. They'd had some kind of contact. The scarf told him that. And Simon had identified Ross for her, on Monday evening. "He called me *Ghysayib*..." she had said.

Then later, she had remarked, 'And now this man is living rough on the streets of London'. Soraya, though, had not been expressing her surprise, as he had assumed. She had not been startled to learn Ross was sleeping rough, because she had already seen him. Soraya had merely been expressing her sadness and frustration at his straightened circumstances.

"Simon?"

"Sorry, yes, what?"

"Listen Simon, women lie from the start. They can't help it. Your mother tells you she loves you, when what she really means is she loves your dad or your uncle, or the next Johnny-cum-lately she's going to let slide between her sheets. They're all the same. Move on."

"Yes, of course." But Soraya hadn't lied; she'd simply manipulated his understanding in order to protect her guardian angel. Simon snaps. "Is that why you can't keep your hands off anything in a skirt, Billy? Some Freudian compulsion? Or do I need to remind you that if you hadn't tried so hard to get your leg over Sarah Ross, we probably wouldn't be here traipsing around London looking for your supposed best mate. What was it your sister said, best of friends, best of enemies?"

A silence, similar to the torpid stillness of the cemetery, descends.

Billy Martin's face darkens. He squares up. "I've flattened men for saying less."

"And I…" Simon's voice falters as his anger boils over. He lowers his head, like a bull readying for one final, inglorious charge. "And I've fronted up to meaner bastards than you, Billy: Jack Sewell being one of them. So if it helps you to exorcise your frustrations by having a pop at me, then go ahead, be my guest. It's as you said first thing this morning, I must've woken up in too good a mood, because the rest of my day isn't turning out the way I'd like."

A hawkish, spectacled lady is watching them from the entrance to the East Cemetery.

They square off and stare each other down. Both ready. Both willing.

Billy's game face eventually cracks. "You know, I like you, Simon. You've got balls and I've met plenty of your sort who've had to pull their heads out of their shoulders every time a mouse farts. But don't forget, I'm the professional and you're strictly the amateur. The two don't mix."

Carver had said much the same about mixing it with professionals. It's as though Martin and Carver are members of a club Simon cannot gain entry to. A club for grown-ups. A club of the real world.

Gradually, like a slow-punctured tyre, the anger between them contracts and they stroll, slightly further apart from each other than on the way in, back through Waterlow Park.

"What are you thinking?" Billy asks.

"I was just thinking Highgate Cemetery is a bit of a hike from where Soraya lives."

"Which is where?"

"Tower Hamlets. Mile End. It's got to be more than an hour's walk. Ross can't be keeping an eye on Soraya and coming back here every night."

"I told you, Simon, distance wouldn't be a problem for him, whatever state he's in. As soon as he knows she's tucked up safe indoors, he's got no reason to hang about down her neck of the woods. Probably doesn't bother to shadow her in the mornings: too many people about for Sewell to try any funny stuff."

They cut across the steps outside St Joseph's monastery and wait for the lights to change.

The Old Crown is open and the woman behind the bar thinks a man similar to the one in the photograph may have been in a couple of nights before.

"Don't need any further confirmation, do we?"

"No, Billy. It's enough."

"What are we going to do?"

"Not much we can do. At least we know for certain that Ross

and Soraya are in contact, all of which means she must know he is watching over her."

"What difference does that make?"

"It means, Billy, that if we want to find Ross, we'll do it by watching her, and tonight Soraya will be working at her father's soup kitchen. My guess is Ross will be not too far away. Let's give the others a call."

———————

They meet at the same café as the previous evening.

Elen Phillips looks less weary; not radiant, just less tired. And Henry Loveridge has cast off his downbeat mood, realising that as they have been called together, something must be up. Roarke and Watts, Simon is relieved to see, bear no fresh scars.

He briefs them, explaining that now they know Soraya has met up with Ross, they must follow her to get to him.

Roarke leans forward to interrupt and the table judders as Billy kicks him.

"Wrong leg," Roarke states. "So, what you're saying is she's been pulling the wool over your eyes from the start?"

"Yes, Del," Billy seethes. "She's been trying to keep the boss out of it. Go on, Simon."

"Billy and I have come up with a plan. It's pretty much sentry duty. Boring and necessary, but probably our best chance of finding Captain Ross."

They are pleased and relieved, or so their body language betrays.

"Might be an idea to take the rest of the afternoon as it comes, this evening is likely to be a late finish. If you want to keep searching, by all means do. What's more important though is that we're all up for it this evening. I've got maps with your posts marked, so you'll see where I'd like you to be. Try to blend in, and by that I don't mean pretend you belong in a Banksy mural which, come to think of it," he nods at Roarke and Watts, "you both do. Just try to look like you're not on the look-out. If Captain Ross is focussed on the girl, then he may not be paying sufficient attention to notice us. On the other hand, if the police are out for him, bearing in mind Grant met his maker only a couple of streets away, then... then try to avoid catching their attention. Here is a mug shot of Jack Sewell." He lays on the table a half-dozen passport-sized copies of the photograph he has downloaded from the CCTV of New Year's Eve.

"So, this is our man?" Roarke asks.

"Yes. Take one each and if you see this guy tomorrow evening, tell me immediately. If for some reason you can't get hold of me, tell the nearest copper and tell him to call DI Carver at the Bishopsgate nick. Don't under any circumstances tackle him yourself."

Roarke looks up from the photo. "This is the guy who assaulted the girl and did for the rough sleeper, Tom Williams?"

"Yes."

"Don't worry, Simon. We'll do our best."

Simon cocks an eyebrow at the two ex-Marines. "Mm, that's what I'm afraid of. Remember, we're after Captain Ross not Sewell and we want to have Ross out of the way so that we can work out what happened to Grant and Eyles before the police decide otherwise."

"What if?"

"What if what, Del?" Billy asks.

"What if the Boss did do for the pair of them? What then?"

Elen Phillips tut-tuts. "And there I was thinking you were halfway sensible, Derek. You should be ashamed of yourself."

"I am both, Mrs Phillips. However, we can't ignore the fact that the boss may have lost some of his marbles, and if he thought these hooligans were a threat to the girl, then he may not have been thinking straight in the first place."

"Del is right," Simon adds, keen to snuff out any argument the moment it ignites. "We can't know for certain what's been going on. We hope," he pauses, glancing at each of them in turn, "that someone else has an agenda with these guys. We can, though, only hope. Billy doesn't believe Captain Ross is responsible. He says the way in which Grant was murdered is not how a Royal Marine would have done it. And neither am I inclined, knowing what I've learnt about Captain Ross, to believe that his style is to go throwing people off high rise balconies."

"There's a *but* coming."

"Yes, Henry, there is and it's this: But we can't be certain. Therefore, we have to find him in order to establish what happened before. If we don't, there'll be no after." He glances again at Henry, "It's horse and cart." And at Roarke and Watts, "It's truck and trailer. It's that simple. Have we all got that?"

They nod, their expressions serious. Even Elen Phillips has adopted something of a game face.

"Good," Simon adds. "The soup kitchen sets up between seven-thirty and eight, so try to be in place by then. Don't forget the phones I've given you and please make sure the batteries are charged. If you have trouble making it or if you are delayed, give one of the others a call. One last thing, and I've said it before and I'll say it again, if Sewell does appear, don't confront him. And that means you two." He looks very directly at Roarke and Watts. "Very specifically, you two. There's precious little point in recovering Captain Ross at the expense of losing either or both of you."

The thought occurs that they might take to what's coming better from their old warrant officer; after all, in the absence of Ross, he is now their boss.

Martin pre-empts his request. "Boys, what Simon's saying is bang on the money. We don't know whether Sewell will show. He might: he might not. The worst part of it would be that if he does and one of us harms him, it might help him get off in court later on. And that would be the worst of all worlds. So, with that in mind, Wattie, you will partner Mrs Phillips, Del will be on his own and Mr Loveridge the same."

Roarke raises his hand in objection.

"Yes, Del?" Billy asks.

"Does Wattie really need all that protection?"

44

So far, they have seen neither hide nor hair of Ross. People on their way home hurry by; people on their way out sport umbrellas.

"Thanks for sorting the lads out." Simon turns up the collar of his jacket and tucks Soraya's shemagh tighter around his neck.

"Easy." Martin stretches his back. "They're good lads. Always were. Del Boy particularly. How he's so level with losing that leg is one of life's greater mysteries."

"Wasn't that level when I first met him."

"No?"

"No," Simon repeats. "Told me to sling my hook in no uncertain terms."

"Can't really blame him, what with you being a journalist."

"That bad, eh?"

"Thing is..." Martin takes his time to choose his words, "you press like it both ways. If it's bad news, it's news. If it's good news, it's only worth printing if the good has come out of something bad."

Simon shrugs in resignation. "Hard news, soft news, local

news, features, editorial, columns. They're all news. And contrary to what people think, we're not allowed to make stuff up."

"No, Simon, I think you're missing my point. What I mean is, you report the news in a way that makes people desperate to devour it. It's like a meal that looks so good people simply have to eat it. You dress it up to be whatever you like, and as long as it looks good enough to eat, you lot don't give a toss whether the ingredients are good for the diner."

"People don't eat ugly food, Billy."

"Not sure about that. A man has no alternative other than to eat ugly food if it's the only food on offer." He pauses. Whatever it is that weighs on Billy's chest requires unloading. "You see, we don't have the time to sit down with a bloke and debate whether he wants to kill us. And there's no such thing as killing a bit, shooting to wound or not hitting someone too hard. Those choices exist only in the minds of your genteel readers, whose biggest bugbear is the aeroplane noise or the inconvenience of not having their rubbish cleared or their internet connected. We don't get to make those choices. We have to stop a man before he kills us, and most of the time we only have a split second to decide what his intentions are. Then, the moment you guys get a sniff of being able to interpret something we do as excessive: Bang! You're all over us like a cheap suit, we're all over your front page and the civil libertarians are calling us murderers."

"Good news doesn't sell newspapers, Billy, not unless it's a Royal getting married."

They are loitering in Bunhill Row, a hundred yards down from the junction with Featherstone Street. A compressed Jenga of flats provides them with some shelter from the driving rain and sufficient shadow from which to keep an eye on anyone walking by. Opposite, a boarded building site lies dark and dormant.

"Mrs Phillips shouldn't be out in this muck," Billy decides. "Remind me, which street is it she and Wattie are in?"

"On the left, Banner Street. Mr Loveridge on the right, Featherstone, and Del Boy straight ahead, where this road runs up to Old Street."

"Can't really pop up to the soup kitchen for a cuppa, can we?"

"You could, Billy. They might ask you to pay, though, you're too neat and tidy to pass for a rough sleeper."

"How long do they stay open?"

"About ten."

"They've been going for an hour already. Plenty of people stopping for something to eat. Poor bastards. Makes you wonder how the government can send all that foreign aid abroad when there's people sleeping on the streets."

"If that isn't a simple truth," Simon sighs. "It seems as though all our worlds are perfect, eh? Look I'm going to take a fly by the soup kitchen and check on the others. If I walk by smartly enough, Soraya won't see me in this rain."

Simon skirts the rough sleepers huddled in groups of three or four beneath the awning of the van. Ross, though, is not among them and... neither is Soraya anywhere to be seen. Her absence stalls his progress. Soraya is always at her father's soup kitchen on a Thursday evening. Always. Only this evening, she isn't. The stern-looking lad, the one Soraya said was Sohail, the one she was with at the club on New Year's Eve, is serving at the counter. Behind him, an older woman is chopping vegetables.

He checks round the back of the van and in the dark nearly bumps into a man bending low over a generator.

"Can I help you?" the man asks, as he stands up. His eyes are dark, his goatee white and his head protected against the rain by a sock turned up on itself.

Caught, Simon isn't sure how to react. "Er, no. Well, yes, actually. I was wondering if Soraya was here."

"No, not just now."

"Oh, I," and Simon's phone rings, rescuing him from the

awkward moment. "Excuse me." He turns around and steps out from behind the van. He fumbles for his phone. "Yes?"

"Coming your way," Billy Martin says, his voice muffled and serious, "a plain clothes copper and two uniforms. I'll follow them up."

Another call. Loveridge: "Two policemen walking towards you."

"Got that, Henry. Stay there, please."

Watts: "Police."

"Roger that. Stand by."

And a third, Roarke: "Coppers. Just walked past me. Coming your way."

"Up the four streets," Simon mutters. "All coming to the same spot. Stay where you are, Del."

Simon walks round the front of the van and waits half-in and half-out of the light thrown by the street lamp and the counter of the caravan. Rain drips inside his collar.

"Mr Peckham. Now there's a surprise." It is Carver.

"Evening, Brian. You looking for me?"

The two uniformed policemen with him loom over the detective. "Matter of fact I'm not, no. But seeing as you're here, you might want to get your pencil out and take some notes. Can't have you reporting I'm not doing my job properly."

"Your job being?"

"Watch and learn, my young friend."

Carver glances at his two assistants. They step over, either side of the caravan. He eases through the crowd.

Rough sleepers stare nervously over their steaming cups. One slips away into the shadows, another steps back from the counter to make way.

The detective looks up at Sohail and speaks. Simon cannot properly hear all of what Carver is saying because his face is turned away and the rain is doing its best to drown out the sound. "Come

down to the station..." he makes out, "ask you a few questions...
now would be best."

Sohail looks confused but, after a little more persuasion, he
capitulates. He takes off his apron, wipes his hands and moves to
the back door of the caravan.

The uniformed policemen stand a shade taller, a shade more
alert.

Carver turns and winks at Simon.

Sohail appears from round the back. He is almost as tall as the
constable beside him.

Then, the decision he has made to come quietly, he reverses.

He glares wide-eyed at the constable, tenses, punches him
in the side of his head and jabs him in his ribs. The policeman
doubles up and Sohail sprints off into the darkness of Bunhill
Row up towards Old Street.

The second constable helps the first up off the floor and
speaks into his personal radio.

"It's all right." Carver wanders over, casually, lest anyone be in
doubt who's in complete control. "He won't get far. There are two
more officers up that road."

They wait. They hear shouting. Silence. More shouting. Then
another prolonged silence, before a shocking scream punctuates
the soundtrack.

Carver glances over at the two constables. One is still nursing
his face and his ribs: the second nods and jogs off up Bunhill Row.

Simon's phone rings. "Yes?"

"Del here."

"Hold on a second." Simon fiddles briefly with his phone.
"You're on the speaker, Del. FYI Detective Inspector Carver is
standing beside me."

"Understood. Well, I've got a fella here. Came running up
from down your way. Couple of uniforms tried to stop him."

Simon smiles. "And?"

"There was a scuffle. The uniforms found it all a bit tiring, so they're lying down having a rest."

"Go on, Del."

"Well, next thing I know, this bloke's tripped over my leg and gone down hard. And I mean hard. I helped him up, but he got all grumpy on me."

"Where is he now?"

"Right now, he's having a chat with the pavement and he's not too happy about it neither. Some kind of excited delirium, I suppose. Should I hang on until someone gets here?"

"There's a couple more coppers on the way. Thank you, Del."

Carver grins. "Don't tell me. Prosthetic leg. Where do you find these people?"

———

The six of them are bunched beneath the awning of the caravan, clutching polystyrene cups of soup. The rain has eased, though the breeze has strengthened.

A police car pulls up, Carver gets out and trudges over. His shoulders sag with disappointment. "Thank you, Mr. . ."

"Roarke," chirps Derek. "That's with an *e*. And it's a rare pleasure, detective."

"Yes, I should think it is."

"Do you want to bring us up to speed, Brian?"

"Not at liberty to say much, Simon. Might queer the pitch if you print too much detail. You know, influence the judgement of the twelve good and true."

Simon laughs, openly. "Okay, if that's the way it's got to be, I'll fill the assembled company in for you."

Carver looks up, sharply. "Okay, this I'm interested to hear. Go on, surprise me some more."

Simon waits until the rest are paying attention. "It was just now, when I was watching that fellow Sohail. Soraya told me he works for a butcher over near Brick Lane; said he cuts and packs meat for a living. And then there's that knife you told me your SOCOs had recovered from the drain near Worship Street. You said it was Japanese, hollow blade, about six inches long, and that it had a hollow handle which is filled with sand. I did a little research: it seems a knife like that is not much use to anyone except a butcher. And I remembered Soraya saying a stranger was rude to her last Thursday, here at the soup kitchen. He may have threatened her; she only half-heard what he said. Her young man, Sohail, intervened and saw the bloke off."

"You remembered this when, exactly?" Carver asks, heavy on the sarcasm.

"Like I said, Brian: just now, when I saw the lad working at the counter. And the last part of the jigsaw? Grant meeting his end only a stone's throw down the road. That's where it all makes sense. This Sohail must have followed Grant and done for him. If I remember right, Grant had been cut from here to here." Simon imitates the gesture the night owl had made, running his thumb from left to right across his own throat. "The person who did that would be right-handed which, judging by the jab Sohail delivered your constable, he is."

"Isn't your jigsaw a little larger than that?" Carver asks. "What about Eyles? How did you manage to fit him into your puzzle?"

"I didn't need to, Brian. You did that for me when you asked me to hand over the CCTV recording from the club. You knew I'd been up to see Eyles: the neighbour told you and I didn't deny it. Sohail must have followed me and you've checked him on the CCTV of the route and the recording from the bus I took up to Chalk Farm. How am I doing?"

"Why would this Sohail be following you around?"

Simon doesn't want to bring Ross into the equation, so… "I guess he found out I was seeing his girl and wanted to know what

I was about. For all I know, he probably knocked on the same door as I did. That neighbour lady, Mrs Beránek, she would have told him the same as she told me, only he must have been bright enough to confront Eyles later in the dark."

"Excuse me," Elen Phillips pipes up. "So, what you're saying is that this young man murdered these other two men?"

Simon defers to the detective.

Carver shrugs. "At this time, it looks very much that way. Unless of course there's another reason why he ran off like that. We need to check his prints against those on the knife. I'll hazard a guess they'll match." He surveys Simon's motley crew and chuckles. "I don't know what you good people are up to and don't take this the wrong way, but I really do hope our paths don't cross again. Now, I must be going. Have a good evening and do," he shoots Derek Roarke a stiff look, "try to stay out of any further trouble."

Simon follows him to the car. "That seems to be that then, Brian."

"I wish it was, my young friend. I wish it was. Somehow, I don't share your confidence. Cheerio."

The door slams shut. The car sweeps off up Bunhill Row.

"What about Ric?" Loveridge asks.

"Yes, Simon," Elen Phillips footnotes. "This Sohail may have gotten young Richard off the hook, but we're nowhere nearer to finding him, are we?"

"Time for a beer, eh?" Roarke suggests.

The rain has returned in force and combined with the wind, sharp pellets of water fly horizontally in pursuit of Carver's ride.

"Yes, sure," Simon concedes. "I don't think the odds on finding Captain Ross have been improved by this charade. Why don't you two call it a day. You too, Billy, if you fancy it?"

"No, I'll let the boys go. Might stick around for a bit."

"Elen? Henry?"

"Thank you, Simon, I think we've had quite enough excitement for one night and as for the weather..." Elen shields her face. "Come on, Henry, let's go and find a quiet corner to curl up in."

When they've gone, Simon is left to wonder where Soraya might be and Billy Martin is chatting to a few of the rough sleepers across the way.

Now reduced to two where they would normally be four, the couple running the soup kitchen are labouring to clear up.

"Can I help?" Simon asks.

The man stops in his lifting, turns and stands upright. "That is kind of you, thank you. We will manage." His English is stilted as though it is not his native language, yet his pronunciation is precise as if he knows it well.

"Rough evening for you, the police turning up like that?"

"It was not ideal." His dark eyes study Simon, taking in his detail. "Then again, life is not always ideal. We normally stay until ten. However, after what has happened perhaps it is probably better that we close up now. Tell me, please, you asked after Soraya. Do you know her?"

"Yes, I do. We met a couple of weeks ago. Soraya was attending an inquest with a study group from her university. I was covering the inquest for my paper."

This information stands the man up even straighter. "I see. Are you the man who put her name in the paper?"

When Soraya had asked him the same question, he had lied. If he hadn't, would Grant have come to threaten Soraya? Would Sohail have murdered him and then, later, Eyles?

"Yes, I'm afraid so. Are you Mr Naarda, her father?"

"I am. I am Joseph."

"I'm Simon and I'm sorry, I shouldn't have put her name in the paper. Bad judgement on my behalf. I can only hope you'll forgive me."

"Forgiveness is not ours to grant. Perhaps, it is wisdom you need to acquire."

"May I ask, Joseph, where Soraya is?"

"Of course." Soraya's father simply stands and watches, his dark eyes boring holes in Simon. "You must come and see me, at our home. I would like to talk to you; there are things you should know."

"I look forward to that, Joseph. Right now though, what I need to know is why she's not here? Would you mind telling me?"

He smiles. "No, Simon. I will happily tell you. Soraya has gone to meet someone who has found her *skandola*. It is very important to her. You know what this is, her *skandola*?"

The *skandola*. The pendant with the ouroboros. The serpent circling the lion, the hornet and the scorpion. The seal the midwife had given her at birth. The charm Jack Sewell had snatched from around her neck when he assaulted her on New Year's Eve.

"Yes, I do." A chill claw steals up his back and he feels helpless, as if Soraya is travelling in a foreign land far away. And without trying to frighten or trouble her father, he asks, "Do you know exactly where she has gone to meet this person?"

Joseph Naarda shakes his head, slowly, his expression sad and apologetic. "No, I'm sorry, Simon. She told me she had received a message and that she must go."

45

"Those guys over there," Billy Martin is at his shoulder, "they say they've seen Ricardo about. Told me he's been here. Said he never goes up to the counter; always asks one of the others to get his food for him. Guess he didn't want the girl or her father to recognise him." He reseats his cap. "Bloody rain! Simon, what's the matter? Mate, you look like you've seen a ghost."

"Not seen one, heard from one."

"Tell me."

"Soraya has gone off to meet Sewell. That's why she's not here. He's got something of hers, something very precious to her, a charm she wants back. He's called her and arranged a meet. Oh Soraya, you stupid..."

"Where's she meeting him?" Even Billy Martin, the man who doesn't understand the meaning of the word panic, cannot keep the alarm from his tone. "When's she meeting him?"

"Don't know and don't know. She got a message. Christ, she's always getting messages. I've never known her answer her phone when it rings."

"Hang on a second," Billy asks, "how the hell would Sewell have gotten hold of her number?"

"One of her bitchy mates from uni. Apparently, Sewell or Grant or Eyles, one of them, came looking for her at her university after I wrote the News-in-brief after the inquest." Simon winces. He knows what's coming. "One of her bitchy mates gave out her number—"

"Whoa, you put her name in the paper? You?" Billy asks, mystified. "Why the fuck would you have done that?"

Simon stares back at him.

"Oh, don't tell me... You're a journalist; it's what you do. Christ, you lot make me sick. You're all fucking hypocrites. You moan about injunctions muzzling the press until you need to apply for one to protect yourself." He puts his hands on his hips and fixes Simon with an uncompromising stare. "And there you were all pious and mighty giving me a bucket load of grief about hitting on my mate's wife, when all the time this can of worms is only open because you couldn't resist getting your... Oh, for Christ's sake."

"This started when Sewell assaulted Soraya. I didn't start it."

Billy's anger overwhelms him. He grabs Simon by the collar, pulls him back and whispers in his ear. "Maybe not, you miserable bastard. But you're sure as hell going to finish it. And if any harm comes to that girl or my mate, or if you can't find a way of working out where she's meeting this bloke Sewell, then I'll—"

"Is there a problem?" It is Joseph Naarda.

The rain now slants across the arc of the street lights. Yet however hard and relentless its fall, the rain will not fall hard or fast enough to douse the heat of Billy's glare. Slowly, he releases Simon.

"Yes, Joseph, there is." He steps away, tugs his jacket and eases his neck from the confines of his collar. Simon pulls his phone from his pocket and speed dials a number.

The tall man frowns, unaware that the young man he has met not five minutes before is now dialling his daughter's phone.

They wait: Billy staring at Simon and Simon staring at the pavement. Joseph Naarda stares at them both.

The call goes directly to voicemail. "Soraya, call me, please. As soon as you get this message, call me, please."

"Soraya?" her father asks.

"Yes."

"Did it ring?"

"No, her phone is switched off."

"It is never switched off."

Simon turns his attention back to his phone and dials her number once more. As soon as his call is directed to the voicemail, he presses the star button and four zeros.

Nothing happens.

He rings off and tries again, this time pressing star, followed by the numbers one, two, three and four.

Again, nothing.

He tries once more, tapping four threes after the star.

This time too, the numbers produce no result. Soraya's voicemail access is not pre-set to her phone-providers standard security PIN; her phone is set to enhanced security.

"Look, Joseph," Simon is unsure how familiar he can be with a man he has only just met and whose daughter he has placed in danger. "I know this is going to sound strange, would you mind telling me Soraya's birthdate? It's important. I wouldn't ask if it wasn't. You'll have to trust me on this."

Billy Martin scoffs.

"You're not helping," Simon mutters.

"Can you tell me why you need this?"

"I could, Joseph, but it would take too long and I'm concerned Soraya may be in danger. Please, her birthdate?"

Joseph Naarda studies Simon for a moment before making up

his mind. "Soraya has told me that even though you put her name in your paper, she trusts you. And like the wind that cannot lie and the stars that always see, Soraya is a good judge of character. She was born on 25th June 1990."

"Thank you, Joseph. I appreciate your faith. I will not let you down." Simon dials her number a fifth time, presses star and follows it with two, five, six and zero. However, this combination doesn't provide him access to her voicemail either.

"What the hell are you doing, Simon?" Billy Martin asks.

"Never you mind." He turns away from the two men and screws up his face in concentration. Soraya has set her own Personal Identification Number to allow her to access her voicemails remotely, a combination of four numbers only she knows.

"What," he mutters, "what would they be?" He thinks back, rerunning once more the tapes of their conversations, searching for a clue as to what numbers were closest to her heart and why. The *skandola* comes to mind, but he cannot recall any numbers associated with it. Her birthdate. Her name. Simon raises his face to the sky. "Oh Soraya, you must tell me. You must. I know you're there, somewhere."

The rain spatters his face. If only he could see her. If only he could see the stars.

He still has her shemagh around his neck. He takes it off and again runs his fingers through the cotton scarf.

As he does so, he hears her voice and sees her lying next to him. He'd told her his lucky number was three. He didn't really know why he'd said three; no one had ever asked him if he had a lucky number.

Soraya had said her lucky numbers were… The twelve signs of the zodiac, the five planets visible to the naked eye plus the sun and the moon, making seven. Twelve and seven: one, two and seven, and… The last, the fourth number, she'd said the number was for her to know.

"Soraya was born on the 25th of June," Simon says, to no one in particular.

"Yes," Joseph confirms.

"The date," Simon muses. "The sign of the Zodiac for that date is?"

"In her mother's world, *Sartana*. To most people, Cancer, the sign of the crab."

"I remember Soraya telling me all names relate to numerical values. Joseph, does *Sartana* have a numerical value?"

"Naturally." He thinks for a moment. "For most people, the New Year begins in January with Capricorn. But for the Mandaeans, the New Year begins with *Umbara* or Aries which, therefore, has a numerical value of one. Taura the Bull is two, *Silmia* or Gemini is three and *Sartana* is four."

"So, Soraya was born in the fourth month?"

"Yes, Simon. The fourth cycle."

"Thank you, Joseph. Thank you." He dials her number, hoping, knowing that if this combination doesn't grant him access to her voicemails, then he is lost and Soraya along with him. His call is diverted directly to her voicemail. He presses slowly and methodically: star, one, two, seven and four.

Simon waits.

46

"So that's how you hack someone's phone," Billy says.

The taxi pulls left off Great Eastern Street into Holywell Lane. It feels like the wrong direction, but the cabby knows he has to hit the bottom of Shoreditch High Street before he can get into Bishopsgate. Traffic is light, the streets varnished with rain, the denizens of the City long gone home.

"Yes, it's that simple and that's why they're all at it."

"All?"

"Those who can't resist it." He means Bobby Smith, the man he must prove wrong, the man who doubts him.

"Look, Billy, it's like dreaming of that pot of gold at the end of the rainbow. You know how it works, you run after it and every time you think it's within your grasp, the rainbow disappears. Then one day, you wake up to find the rainbow has been right in front of you all the time and all you have to do to grasp the pot of gold is to tap a few numbers into a magic box. Unfortunately, there's a down side: a distinct possibility that if you grab it, the rainbow will disappear for good. If, on the other hand, you leave it, there's every chance someone else will grab the pot of gold and the rainbow will disappear anyway. Result: no more rainbow to chase, no more pot of gold. What do you do?"

"Simple," Billy says, "you take the money."

"And destroy the rainbow?"

"Sure. You said if you don't, someone else will, so you might as well. The rainbow's finished either way."

"Is it really that simple?"

"Absolutely."

"Why, Billy? How come you're so sure?"

"It's human nature, isn't it? It's the money, the power, the prestige. It's how people are. It's the nature of the beast."

"Saddam Hussein," Simon mutters to himself.

"What was that?"

"Nothing."

The cab motors noisily past the club, Slick in the City, where it all began.

Only it didn't begin in London, did it? It began with Saddam, three thousand miles away, in a city of canals lined with palms and mulberry orchards, in a country where people farmed dates and traded them for coffee and silk and sugar. It began in a city where people were once safe, whatever their creed, whatever their faith.

Thursday evening, Ladies' Night, and a train of scantily-clad young women huddle together in the rain, waiting for the club to open.

They stop at a red light.

"Cabby?" Billy calls.

The taxi driver slides the glass partition back and cocks his head.

"Twenty quid for every light you have to run."

"More than my life's worth," he grumbles.

"Be more than someone else's life is worth if you don't."

The cabby slides the partition shut and the offer of a few notes has the desired effect.

They swing hard left into Monument Street, the gilded urn of the Fire of London shining high above them. Then sharp right into Fish Street and immediately right again.

The driver guns his black cab along Upper Thames Street, passing Thames Wharf where Soraya had come forward at the inquest into the death of the brave old soldier, Tom Williams.

"Millennium Bridge," Martin says. "Why would he choose the Millennium Bridge?"

Simon had listened to the voicemail on Soraya's phone: Jack Sewell, smooth, uncompromising, like a knotted scarf twisting tighter against her throat. "I've found this pendant," he'd said. "Doesn't look much, but a little birdie told me it might be valuable. We should meet up. I'm sure you'd like it back."

He could hear the intent, the promise, the subtle malice. He could hear Sewell, just as he'd heard him in the club three months before.

How Soraya could have fallen for the man's patter, he has no idea. Perhaps she didn't. Perhaps she has her guardian angel in tow and believes she is immune to any harm Sewell has in mind for her. Perhaps Sewell believes Ross will be with her, too.

"Why the Millennium Bridge, Billy? Because it's a footbridge and at this hour it'll be relatively deserted. Because it's ten or eleven metres straight down into the water and the water is cold and flows faster than a man can swim. And because it's dark and it'll be child's play for him to bundle her over the side without being seen. Do you want me to go on?"

The partition slides back. "Where exactly do you want, guv?"

"Closest you can get us to the bridge," Simon says. "Quickest we can get onto it."

"Right, I'll turn off down to Broken Wharf, you can follow Paul's walk from there. You'll have to cut back up the stairs to the bridge. Hope you blokes are fitter than me."

Simon fishes in his pocket. "I haven't got enough."

"You journos! I give up." Martin snatches the notes, adds a couple of his own and hands them forward.

"Right," the cabby says again.

They swerve left off the dual lane, narrowly missing a garbage lorry, then slew right before screeching to a halt. The door locks click open

"Thank you," Simon shouts as they both fly out of the taxi.

They run, fast. The pavement is slippery and they bounce off a wall before turning parallel with the river. The Millennium Bridge is fifty metres away, the neon footlights glowing blue against the night.

Simon can see a couple near where the bridge first crowns.

Billy Martin is ahead scrambling up the steps three, four at time. He halts, suddenly.

Simon head down, cannons into the back of him and grabs hold to keep from falling. "What is it?"

"There, by the first pier. A couple. Doesn't look right. Body language is all wrong. They're looking the other way, leaning against the rail. Is that her?"

Simon wipes the sweat from his eyes. His heart thumps in his chest, he gasps for breath and his eyes refuse to focus.

"Come on, boy. Shape up," Martin urges.

Simon stares. Across the river and through the rain, the lights of the Tate Modern and the Globe Theatre muddle his view. "Yes, I think so."

"Okay, you stay behind me," Martin says, his tone imperative. "Whatever happens, stay behind me. Is that clear? And let me do the talking. If I can get her away from him, you grab hold of her and leave the rest to me."

"Understood."

"Good."

"Billy?"

"Yes, Simon."

"You won't be having to pull my head out of my shoulders, so stop worrying."

"Good man. Tread carefully. Don't let him know you're nervous, eh? Come on, let's go."

They jog, casually, along the approach to the bridge: a couple of Fleet Street late-stayers on their way to catch the bus home.

Simon glances down: the Thames is full and just past the turn of the tide; the water black, the waves slapping against the bank. The bridge rises to the first pier, then drops away to the longer, central section. What or whoever lies beyond the crown, they cannot yet see.

The couple are still facing away and one of them seems to be struggling against the other.

A shout carries on the wind.

Billy, leading, is now only thirty or so metres from them.

One of the couple, the man, is arguing with someone standing down on the central span of the bridge. He glances nervously their way.

"Right, he's clocked us. Here we go." Billy slows to a smart march.

"Sewell? Jack Sewell?" he shouts, the drill sergeant addressing his nod.

Sewell turns; his partner, too. It is Soraya. Sewell has his arm tight round her. "What the fuck do you want? Go on, piss off. Can't you see me and the little lady are out for an evening stroll?"

Soraya, her long black hair blowing around her, looks vulnerable and anxious, and yet not as frightened as she has a right to or perhaps should be.

Billy keeps walking, Simon in his shadow. "I want a word with you, Sewell."

"God, not another one?" Sewell moans. "Which rock do you lot keep crawling out from under?"

His response stops them in their tracks. They are fifteen metres from Sewell and now, because they can see over the high-point of the walkway, they notice another man standing the same distance the other side.

In the dull blue of the footlights, Simon has trouble making him out. He wipes his eyes. The man is medium height and medium build, and wears a black parka over a tracksuit, the hood of which is pulled up over his head.

"Ross?" Simon whispers, in awe. "It's Ross."

"Yes," Billy agrees, quietly. "Ricardo Ross, Captain, one-time Royal Marine and recent rough sleeper."

Sewell doesn't understand the silence. He looks this way and that, unsure of who is going to deliver the greatest threat.

"Ricardo?" Billy shouts.

"Billy," comes a response ironed flat of emotion.

"I've got this, Ricardo. Stand away."

"No thanks, Billy. This man murdered my friend. My only friend. A brave man. One of us, Billy. He's going to pay."

While Sewell has his head turned towards Ross, Billy and Simon step forwards.

"I used to be your friend," Billy says, close enough now that he no longer has to shout.

Sewell turns towards them and they notice Ross move forward.

"Used to be," Ross says.

"Still am, Ricardo."

A curious game of *What's the time Mr Wolf* ensues, with Jack Sewell cast in the role of wolf.

"With friends like you, Billy, I don't need any more enemies."

"Come on, Ricardo, we all need friends. After all, where would we be without them?"

Simon whispers, "Strange question considering your part in this."

"Shut up, you idiot," Billy growls.

By now, Sewell's head is swivelling from left to right like a spectator at Wimbledon. His expression, though, stays unflinching. "Mob-handed, eh. Reckon two of you is enough, do you?"

"You comedian, Sewell," Ross shouts. "There were three of you on New Year's Eve and you couldn't handle me then. What makes you think you can do it on your own when there's two of us. And let me tell you," Ross points at Billy, "compared to him, I'm kindergarten."

They are now only three or so metres away.

With his right hand, Sewell lets go of Soraya's waist and grabs her by her hair, dragging her upper body up over the rail of the bridge. He raises his left arm, in his fist, a gun.

"Now who's going to play brave little soldiers, eh?" he sneers, pointing his weapon first up then down the bridge.

Billy pushes Simon further back and somehow seems to make himself larger. "That's Royal Marines to you, Jack. Now," he pauses, making certain he has Sewell's attention, "I've been told you're not as stupid as you look. I've heard you know how to play the odds. Smart man that Jack Sewell, or so they say. Well, be smart now, Jack. Play the odds. You might get one of us; you won't get both. Now, let the girl go, chuck the firearm over the side and we'll have a little chat about letting you walk."

Sewell pushes Soraya hard up onto the rail. The top half of her torso is clean over the side, her legs about to follow.

She struggles, then stills when she realises if she struggles too hard, Sewell will merely let go of her and she will fall. One more push, one shove and the Thames will claim her.

"Simon?" she shouts as she turns her head against Sewell's grip. "Let him go. Leave him. The water doesn't scare me. You know that. I told you. The water is where we are from and it is where we all go back to. Leave me. I'll be all right."

"You'll be what?" Sewell screams in frustration. "You'll be all right? You stupid bloody cow!" For the first time, he looks away from Martin and Ross and stares incredulous at Soraya as he realises his hostage is not afraid of the dark waters below. "You're off your bloody rocker, you—"

It is all the distraction the two Marines need. They rush him, hitting him from both sides at once.

Sewell pushes Soraya, lifts his gun and fires at Billy Martin.

Soraya falls, but Ross jumps up onto the rail and dives after her.

Billy and Sewell struggle. The gun fires a second time. One of them screams and they wrestle each other upright and onto the rail, where they balance, teetering on the edge. Each has their hands on the gun as they scrap for it high above their heads. Then, almost as if a strong gust of wind catches them, they too overbalance and are gone, over the side and down into the black.

Simon rushes to the side.

All he can see is the conjoined forms of Billy Martin and Jack Sewell, arms and legs flailing, as they slap flat and hard, like a third gunshot, against the marbled surface of the river.

Immediately, they are gone, swallowed by the Thames, swept away by its current.

And Simon is alone.

Excerpt 13 from transcript of conversation with Joseph Naarda

SP: Please correct me if I am wrong, Joseph, but I understand you came to the UK in 2003. Was that shortly after the invasion of Iraq or later in the year?

JN: We left later in the year, a few months later.

SP: Were you still working as an interpreter?

JN: No. I trusted this officer. Soraya did, too. And after he was gone, we were not so comfortable, not so friendly, with the new soldiers. The worst part of it was that once Saddam's army had been defeated, a different war began.

SP: Another war?

JN: Yes, another war, the fourth war in my lifetime. The Shi'a returned in great numbers and with their returning we learned there was no longer room for Christians in Basra. If I am honest with myself, I knew it was inevitable that morning Soraya and I strolled in the Hannah Sheikh; that morning she asked me to explain the difference between Shia and Sunni, and between Christian and Subba. That was when I knew.

When the fighting had finished, when things settled down, I went back to work in the Rumaila Field. But only briefly. In August, the workers went on strike. There was much arguing, much disagreement and you must remember that I was not Shi'a. If one was not Ba'athist under Saddam, death was easier to find than work. With the Shi'a and not being Shi'a, why would one expect one's prospects to be any different?

SP: *So how did you make ends meet?*

JN: I continued to make the Arak, I brought in beer from outside and I sold pretty much anything that I could get my hands on. Like now, with my shop here in the Mile End Road, I fill it with everything and I sell everything.

SP: *If things were going so well, why did you leave?*

JN: Everything went well until the religious police came to my shop. They told me I should no longer sell alcohol. I told them they did not have the authority to demand this, that I had a licence granted by the council. We argued. They said only Christians were selling alcohol and therefore to be a Christian was bad. We argued some more and, eventually, they went away.

That night, when I went home, Soraya said she had seen some men going into the home of our neighbour. She said she had seen the old man's son leave with them and that he had not yet come back.

I went to see the old man; he was very upset. He was worried that the men who had taken his son might beat him for information in exactly the same way the *mukhabarat* had once beaten the old man. He said they had asked him and his son questions about me, my family and my shop; about how I was selling alcohol and how this was soon to be banned because good Moslems should not drink alcohol.

Now one did not need wisdom to see how this was going to end. The son of our neighbour was a good man also and though recovered, he had been injured quite badly in the war. Given that he already knew pain, he was unlikely to resist their methods of questioning for too long.

SP: He was Shi'a, too, wasn't he?

JN: Yes, that's true. However, he had information they wanted. He had information they could set to their purpose. Why would they care if he was one of theirs?

So it was with much sadness I realised, taking into account the old scores the Sunni had settled, that as soon as the Shi'a found out I had worked as an interpreter, they would come for me and no one would ever see me again. These people are the people you meant when you referred to the demons of my past, yes?

SP: Yes, Joseph. And they left you with no alternative but to leave this city in which you were born and in which you had spent most of your life?

JN: Yes, that night I moved our family to the compound of a friend in Al Qadimah, the old part of the city, and when they were settled, I hurried to my shop to remove as much of value as I could carry.

But, I was too late. Two streets away, I could smell the smoke. A crowd was standing watching the fire. Watching to see who would come to put out this inferno of my future.

I went back to our home but there, too, people were watching for my return.

It was over. Our life in Basra was finished. Do you know, Simon, there were Christians in Basra before there were Moslems? Now there are only a handful. It is the same with the Subba.

A friend of ours drove us to Safwan, to the border with Kuwait, but the immigration authorities refused to let us in. They said too many were seeking to come across the border and that they had no cause to allow us into their country. Our friend then took us to Az Zubayr; there, we stayed for a few days. We could not go out and we had very little money.

SP: So, how did you get out of the country and make it here, to Britain?

439

JN: The kindness of people. The kindness of many people. A friend who was a fisherman; he took us in his boat to Kuwait. Another friend, the one I used to get the books from for Soraya, she took us in. The British Embassy in Kuwait, the United Nations High Commission for Refugees, the people working within the Gateway Protection Programme and, once I had located him, the Captain from the Royal Marines: they all helped us. Without all these people, who knows?

SP: You must have felt as though you'd been through rather too many hands by the time you got here.

JN: Yes, one does feel like just one more page in a book of infinite length. Yet these people were kind, kind and necessary; without them I would be dead and probably my family also. I have nothing but praise and admiration for them. Oh, I nearly forgot, and the South African man.

SP: Don't tell me you caught up with him and he still had the jewels?

JN: Yes and no. I traced him through the South African Embassy in London. It was not easy and one had to be very patient. At first, they didn't want to help and I had to be determined, to be persistent. Eventually, I made contact with him and he told me he had sold the jewels for a decent sum and deposited the funds in a bank account managed by his solicitor. He, too, was a man of his word. It is rewarding, is it not, to know that there are people like him; especially when one has lived much of one's life in a city where... where so many men are not worthy of their word and where so many words are not worthy of the men who speak them.

With that money, I set up the shop here and with that money, we began our new life. Our new, our safe life. Providence, perhaps, but now at least I am able to provide. There are many who were not as lucky as me: many people left with nothing more than a pocketful of hope.

Simon, I have a few questions for you.

SP: Yes, Joseph, ask away.

JN: What happened to the rough sleeper who tried to help Soraya? The old man. Tom, I think you said his name was.

SP: That's good of you to ask. Yes, Tom Williams. Well, the most likely outcome for poor old Tom was a pauper's grave and, considering how he had surrendered his life in order to try to save Soraya's, we didn't think that was just. So, we got in touch with his old regiment and they put us in touch with the Commonwealth War Graves Commission. They thought old Tom ought to be buried in either his home town or at the Parachute Regiment plot in the Aldershot Military Cemetery. But, seeing as he didn't have any living relatives left down in Wales and as he hadn't given his life in service of his country, we at the paper suggested he should be buried here.

JN: In London?

SP: Yes. Better than that though, Joseph. We thought it might be a nice idea if old Tom was able to look down on the city he'd spent much of his later life living in. We launched an online appeal and within two weeks the public had donated sufficient funds to pay for a plot in Highgate Cemetery. Old Tom Williams is now buried close by Billy Martin's great-granduncle Wilfred. The War Graves Commission are considering adding his name to the Roll of Honour in due course.

JN: What about Mrs Phillips and Mr Loveridge?

SP: Well, now that she's back in Abergavenny, Mrs Phillips has told me she is going to arrange for Mrs Ross to move to the British Legion Care Home near Taunton, where she can receive the continuing care she needs. Mrs Phillips is hoping to return to work at the school where she used to teach. I think after what has happened she's realised how very finite life can be.

JN: Yes, I know what you mean by this. One can never know how long one will be permitted to walk one's path. And Henry Loveridge?

SP: Henry Loveridge, as I came to learn, wasn't much of a fan of the city; the concrete jungle is not his natural habitat. However, he admitted to me that walking the streets and meeting and talking to so many rough sleepers had opened his eyes. As you may imagine from what I have told you of Henry, he also admitted that he regretted having had his eyes shut for so long. Ashamed was how he described feeling. Henry has gone back to the farm: gone back to the land he told me he could see and feel and understand.

JN: And the two Marines, Mr Roarke and Mr Watts. When did they learn about what happened on the bridge? What was their reaction?

SP: I called them as soon as I'd finished dealing with the police and the emergency services. They were more than a little upset. . . no, sorry, upset isn't the right word. Perhaps I should say they were angry beyond reason that they'd missed out on both confronting Jack Sewell and saving Soraya, Richard Ross and Billy from the river. But once I'd made them aware of exactly how they couldn't have got to the Millennium Bridge in time to have made any real contribution, they calmed down and understood. Though I'm not sure they'll ever forgive me for, as they saw it, denying them their part in the action.

I met up with them the next day. With them and Elen and Henry. We talked the whole thing through and discussed whether, if we'd done anything different, the outcome might have been other than how it was.

You might like to know that both Roarke and Watts were very interested in what Soraya had said about the psychopath in us; about how he dials down our empathy when we're faced with a situation in which we cannot avoid doing harm to others. They both recognised that in themselves in terms of the emotions they'd had to suppress in order to carry out their duty. They realise that now, of course. At the time, though, neither of them had given it a moment's thought.

Derek Roarke very graciously pointed out that history has taught us how to treat physical traumas; whereas, only now are we beginning to learn how to treat the traumas one cannot see.

JN: And what of your prospects, Simon? Your story, has it been well received?

SP: Yes, thank you, it has gone down well. So well in fact that I've been approached by a national.

JN: Oh, that is good news indeed. To be taken on by a national newspaper at such a young age; that would be considerable reward, would it not?

SP: Yes, of course, it is the prize, the prize we all hope for.

47

Sunday March 21ˢᵗ 2011

From outside, laughter seeps in and dissolves their melancholy.

"They have been to the hospital to see Billy Martin." Joseph stands and leaves the room to answer the door.

Simon turns off his voice recorder, pockets it and gets to his feet.

The hall is narrow.

Soraya's father pulls back the door and the delight of high-spirits flood into the flat. Joseph has to stand on the raised step at the foot of the stairs to allow room for the newcomers to ease the wheelchair into the flat.

"Simon," Joseph says, beaming, "I believe you have not met Maia."

Soraya's little sister is also beautiful and her smile would shame a thousand candles. "You must be Simon," she giggles, hiding her face behind bent wrists and crooked fingers.

"I am. Pleased to meet you Maia. Soraya has told me all about you. She tells me you can be a bit tricky."

Maia looks up, her eyes shine and she laughs out loud. "I'm not as much trouble as she is. In the living room, please," she orders.

"Yes mam," says the man behind her chariot.

Simon stands back. "How are you, Ric? How are you getting along? I must say you look a different person from the shadow I met on the Millennium Bridge."

Richard Ross is clean-shaven and casually dressed in jeans and a sweater, and now, but for a few new lines etched in his face, more resembles the man from the photograph Henry Loveridge had given Simon.

He eases the brake-handles of the wheelchair down and locks them into place. His smile is slow and uncertain, like that of a man who has stirred from a long sleep and who is only now reacquainting himself with the light of day.

"I'm doing okay. Getting some help: doctors, psychotherapists, a lot of good people at Combat Stress. I know I should have got in touch with them sooner. If I'm honest, I knew that at the time. Just couldn't face it, I guess. Easier to run away. It seems I can be my own worst enemy at times."

"Talking of enemies, how was Billy?" Simon asks.

"He'll do. Takes more than a bullet and a dunking to keep our Billy quiet. Don't envy the nurses, though."

"Must be some swimmer."

"It's how they train us. Although I think in Billy's case, having his foot on someone's head probably helped keep him afloat. Didn't do Jack Sewell much good."

"Probably just as well," Simon states.

"Mm, that copper, Carver, said much the same."

Simon watches Salwa and Soraya through the open hatch into the kitchen. They are preparing tea for the family of four; four plus Simon and Richard Ross. Joseph, Salwa, Soraya and Maia. The family of four. Four, Soraya's last lucky number.

She smiles at him. "So, have you and my father been talking?"

"Yes," Joseph answers, "and our talk has been very mutually beneficial." An amused, knowing smile creeps across his face.

She glares at Simon. "You were supposed to be asking for my—"

"Yes," Joseph interrupts, "we didn't get around to that."

"We've been gone a couple of hours," Soraya says. "What on earth have you been talking about?"

Simon chuckles, "Good question, Soraya, what have we been talking about? Well, I guess the answer is Ric. Ric and you."

"Me?"

"Yes, Soraya, you. The heavens, the earth and you: the wind between two worlds."

Mazzeri

Love and Death in Light and Shadow

A novel of Corsica

Published by Matador June 2013
ISBN 9781780885384 (pb)
ISBN 9781780885814 (eBook)

It is the last summer of the twentieth century in Calvi, Northern Corsica, and an old man sits watching the kites fly. The festival of the wind is a lively and colourful celebration, but the old man's heart is heavy, he has heard the Mazzeri whisper his name. He accepts that people prefer to believe the dream hunters belong to the past and yet he knows only too well that at night they still roam the maquis in search of the faces of those whose time has come.

Ten years later in the high citadel of Bonifacio, in the southern tip of the island, Richard Ross, armed with only the faded photograph of a Legionnaire standing beneath a stone gateway, finds the locals curiously unwilling to help him uncover his family's roots. He rents a villa on the coast and meets the singularly beautiful Manou Pietri, who enchants him with tales of the megalithic isle, its folklore and the Mazzeri — the dream hunters.

For a while Ric's life beneath the Corsican sun is as close to perfect as he could wish. Then a chance encounter with a feral boy turns Ric's life upside down, and he is drawn deep into a tangled web of lies and deceit. On an island where truth and legend meet, where murder is commonplace and most crimes go unsolved, only the Mazzeri know who will live...

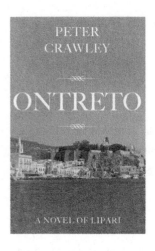

Ontreto

Love and Death in Light and Shadow

Published by Matador May 2015
ISBN 9781784622213 (pb)
ISBN 9781784629298 (eBook)

Arriving on the unspoiled island of Lipari, off the coast of Sicily, Ric Ross carries with him a letter of introduction to Valeria Vaccariello, an aging star of Italian cinema who lives alone in the La Casa dei Sconosciuti, *the House of Strangers; a woman known locally as* La Strega — *the witch.*

Ric is also befriended by Il Velaccino — *the sailmaker, who seems to know everyone and everything that goes on in the island. But when a politician is shot dead, Ric's search for his family's history soon grows into a quest to prove his innocence.*

Told through the eyes of a young man who comes to Lipari in search of his forebears, Ontreto *is the standalone follow-up to Peter Crawley's first novel,* Mazzeri.

Boarding House Reach

Published by Matador May 2014
ISBN 9781783063390 (pb)
ISBN 9781783065646 (eBook)

Five strangers come to spend the weekend in a guest house on the Norfolk coast. The Reach offers sanctuary for guests Hacker, Phoebe, Audrey, Philip and the landlady, Stella — all of them drawn together by the secrets of their past.

As the strands of their individual stories are woven together, each guest will confront the painful truths of their personal lives and, as the hours tick away, confess their sins. In a story which encompasses blackmail, rejection, infidelity, redemption and love, the characters of Boarding House Reach know they can run, but will they ever escape the stark reality of their tangled lives?

The Truth in Fiction

Published by Matador July 2018

ISBN 9781784625368 (pb)

ISBN 9781785894107 (ebook)

Padraig O'Rahilly has just walked the Camino de Santiago, but why? What burden has he shouldered over the last 500 miles that he now feels ready to lay down?

High above the Rio Douro, in Porto, the guardian of the Dom Luis Bridge watches her next challenge approach and wonders.

In Geneva airport, a young UNHCR lawyer is approached by a timid Iranian refugee, who asks the lawyer to record in a journal the strange tale of how he has come to be abandoned to the city.

And, two women meet at a wake in London only to discover they both knew the recently departed rather better than many of their fellow mourners.

The Truth In Fiction is a collection of eighteen short stories set in the towns and cities of Europe, and as far afield as the mountains of New Zealand. Through love and sorrow, intrigue and humour, the characters of each story learn how it is that the harsher lessons of life are often those most valuable.

Finally, in the Appendix Peter Crawley, author of Mazzeri, Boarding House Reach and Ontreto, provides a glimpse of how much truth exists in fiction.